THE SITE

BY

CARLOS VALRAND

First edition published 2013

Second edition published 2021

Third edition published 2024

This is a work of fiction. Names, characters, places, and incidents are products of the author's imagination or are used fictitiously. Resemblance to actual persons, businesses, or locales is entirely coincidental.

ISBN: 9781736757369 (paperback)

Library of Congress Control Number: 2021900717
LCCN Imprint Name: Dramtes Enterprises, Pasadena, TX

To my family and friends, who showed me what I know about life,
and to the teachers, mentors, and supervisors who instructed
me and guided me.

CONTRACT

CHAPTER 1
MANIFESTATION

1

Cicely Denfeld placed the thin book she had been reading on the night-stand by her bed and turned the clock radio on. She listened for a moment to the BBC's weather forecast for England and Wales, then set the alarm. She pulled out the tortoiseshell pin holding her coiled up hair and placed the ornament on top of the book. Her blond hair fell to her shoulders, framing a pleasant face that seemed to waver between plainness and beauty.

Cicely switched off the bedside lamp, pulled up the bed cover and laid her head back against her pillow. A gas fire cast its dim glow into the room. Drowsily, she recalled a fragment of the poem she had been reading: *You are today what yesterday you were—tomorrow you shall not be less.* It brought a smile to her lips as she fell asleep.

She opened her eyes and surveyed a room she had never seen before. It was quiet, but periodically she heard a rushing sound. Waves. She rose from the bed. Beyond the tall open windows was a beach. A warm breeze brought in the sharp scent of the sea. An uneasy, disorienting feeling crept over her. In the pale light of sunset she could see the foamy outline of the ocean. Not far away there was a small pier, and moored to it, gently rocked by the waves, was a trim blue and white cabin cruiser.

The phone rang with the compelling vividness of reality, but in a detached way Cicely knew this couldn't really be happening. She walked across the bedroom and sat on the small hard chair. An airline ticket holder and a man's wristwatch and wallet lay beside the American style telephone on the coffee table. She picked up the receiver.

"Mr. Ryder?" said the pleasantly mellow female voice at the other end. Then Cicely heard herself say "Yes, who is this?" in a baritone voice. A man's voice.

"I'm Vivian Venables, Mr. Robinson's associate," the caller replied. "I hope you're over your jet lag. Do you need anything?"

"I am fine," the man said.

"Do you have a cell phone with you?"

"No," he answered. "I was instructed not to bring it with me."

"Good. Mr. Robinson does not allow us to carry cell phones or satellite phones. They can easily be tracked or monitored."

Cicely thought she must be dreaming, and she had a vague remembrance of recent dreams, as oddly disturbing as this one. Reflexively, she tried to withdraw, as if, mistakenly, she had walked into someone else's room.

"Mr. Robinson is free to see you now," said Vivian. "He is in the library. Downstairs to the right. The last room. Just walk in, he'll be expecting you."

A gust of wind blew in through the window, carrying the sound of birds angrily twittering and fluttering their wings. Against the darkening sky, Cicely saw darting seagulls made pink by the gleam of dusk.

"I'll be down in about ten minutes," Cicely heard herself say in the man's outwardly calm voice. She shared his feeling about the upcoming meeting—a mixture of excitement and apprehension. There was risk in what Robinson wanted him to do.

Cicely woke in a cold sweat. Her breathing was rapid, irregular. *What was happening to her?* She dug her fingers into the bed sheets. She lay on her own bed. In the semidarkness across the room she saw the outlines of her little dresser and of a Matterhorn poster, both familiar features of her bedroom. The rushing sound of waves was gone, replaced by the well-known hiss of the gas fire. She touched her face. She was herself again.

A dream! How strange. What a vivid clarity for a dream!

2

Cicely Denfeld drove over the hill, away from the town of Chesham. Aylesbend Manor could be seen a mile ahead, lying peacefully in the bright autumn sunlight, amid the varying green of oak, beech, and elm. So close to London, Cicely thought, and yet so remote and untouched.

Cicely found the wrought iron gate easily and drove her MG down the twisting road through the grounds until she came to the large, sober Queen Anne house. She wore a brown blazer over a white silk shirt and a beige wool skirt. As she walked past a precisely pruned laurel hedge to the door she made a concerted effort to collect her thoughts. She would tell Angie her troubles and maybe in the telling they would lose their oppressiveness and go away.

She rang the doorbell, her legs feeling the chill of a sudden blast of wind. A moment later, the door opened and she was greeted by the butler, a man neat but forbidding in appearance. Cicely stepped into the big square hall. As the butler closed the door behind her, Cicely saw Angie, just coming out of the drawing room.

"Well, look who's here!" said Angie, rushing toward Cicely with a look of delight.

Soon they were alone in the large bookcase-lined chamber Angie's uncle called his music room. Each girl held a cocktail in her hand. They were both in their mid-twenties. Cicely had a long, pale, delicate face, with straw-blond hair softly framing it. Her friend's face was angular, a study in planes, alert, with ironic black brows.

They listened quietly to the Stones' *Sympathy for the Devil* and then Angie pressed a button recessed in the arm of her chair and the music stopped.

They talked of their friends from Cambridge. It was Angie who had the most to say. Since the death of her parents, Cicely had gradually lost touch with most of her schoolmates. Not because they snubbed her—Cicely was too well-liked for that—but because Cicely's reduced financial condition prevented her from frequenting most of the clubs and social functions that brought the rest of them together. Only Angie, among her best friends, had remained close.

"How's school?" Angie crossed long, nicely molded legs. She wore gray pants and a blue and pink striped shirt.

"Fine." Cicely would rather not talk about work. She looked about the room, at the polished paneling and the heavy Victorian furniture. "This place is sumptuous."

"We are not quite certain how Uncle Harold is able to afford it. He's away for the weekend, at Antibes."

"Lucky he." Cicely looked into her friend's eyes. "Angie..."

"Unhuh."

"The oddest things have been happening to me. I found a key in my purse the other day. It's not one of mine. I have no idea of how I got it."

Angie looked into her glass. She dipped a finger in her Rum Collins and made the ice spin. "Someone played a trick on you."

Cicely took a sip from her drink and then put it down. She brought her hands together on her lap. "I'm beginning to think I'm going out of my mind."

Angie cocked a dark eyebrow.

"I've been having these dreams..."

"Are they nasty? Do you get ravished?"

"Don't be silly. These are not ordinary dreams." Cicely spoke softly, almost in a whisper. "There is something *bizarre* about them. Often they are about a woman. And then, last night..." She looked pleadingly at her friend. "Angie, I'm worried. It's all so odd. I need to tell someone."

"Then tell me."

"The woman's name is Vivian. It's been going on for a week. Always foreign places. And I'm someone else. In the dreams I'm someone else. I can't make it stop." Cicely bowed her head, her eyes brimming with tears.

"Easy, girl." Angie moved to the couch and sat next to her.

"Last night I saw myself. I was in a strange room, a bedroom. Upstairs, with windows facing a beach. I opened a pale blue door and walked into an adjoining private bath—plush, with gold fittings. I started to comb my hair. There was a gold-framed mirror and I looked up at myself—I had wary gray eyes and a thin straight nose and dark hair..."

"So?"

"I was a man!"

"A man? Well, at least you were dark and handsome."

"Angie!"

"Everybody has spooky dreams sometimes, Cicely," Angie said, taking a sip from her drink.

Cicely bit her lip. How could she make Angie understand? She made one more attempt.

"My dreams are usually fuzzy, and I forget them right away. These are so clear—so lifelike. No one I know appears in these dreams. And I never used to dream of being other people. My dreams usually centered on me."

"How selfish of you, dear."

"Oh, Angie, *listen*. I'm nowhere in these dreams. At least not as I know myself."

Cicely picked up her glass and then nervously placed it back on the inlaid leather cocktail table without drinking from it. She looked across the room and absently fixed her gaze upon a portrait of a young Edwardian couple. "The dreams about this girl...sometimes I think I might be turning a bit peculiar."

Angie glanced at Cicely and put down her glass. "I'm not going to let you ruin a perfectly beautiful weekend with talk about weird dreams."

Cicely felt let down. She wished her friend took her problem more seriously.

Angie stood up. "I'm going to get dressed and go riding. And you," she said, pointing at Cicely, "are coming with me."

"But, Angie, I just got here and—"

"No but's, Cicely." Angie's tone was imperious, and she talked rapidly. "If you keep having the weirdies, call me next week or whenever, and I'll give you the name of Aunt Jane's Harley Street witch doctor. Charges a hundred quid an hour. But right now, get your rear moving, girl. I'll help you unpack; the maid has gone to Chesham already. The weather is perfect and we're going *riding!*"

3

It was a vague, unsettling dream.

Uneasiness. A motion like unsteady tumbling. A slight nausea. Moving, definitely moving. Rhythmic bumps. Spinning, and from far away, noises. Closer then, soft sounds. Voices.

"...up, Charles. Wake up..."

A woman's soft voice, very faint, but urgent.

"Charles, please!" It was a familiar voice, but Cicely could not place it. It was all very confusing. She felt groggy, at the edge of consciousness.

"Maybe," someone said, "you should let him rest longer. He may be in shock."

Strange. It sounded like a man's voice now. Cicely felt a cold panic enter her numbed mind. This was not her.

A hand touched her forehead lightly. "Please wake up, Charles."

This can't really be happening, thought Cicely. *Oh God, not really. Surely all she had to do was open her eyes and see...*

Dark hair framing a good-looking, resolute face. Cobalt blue eyes. Cicely's head rested on Vivian's lap. She tried to sit up, but the dark-haired girl stopped her. The effort to rise made Cicely dizzier.

"Can you hear me? Are you all right?"

"I think so," Cicely murmured.

"Just rest now. Don't move." Vivian's voice was light and gentle.

Cicely realized she was lying on the back seat of a car. It seemed to be afternoon. She could see quite well now that her mind was clearing. They were moving. It was warm and humid, a place in the tropics.

"You have the lives of a cat, Ryder," the driver said, taking his eyes briefly from the road. He was a balding, round-faced man with a walrus mustache.

"Where are we going?" Cicely heard herself ask weakly in a man's voice.

"We are driving to Matanzas," the driver answered. Somehow Cicely knew that the man's name was Guisa. They were in Cuba. Cicely shook her head, bumping lightly against Vivian's thighs. She had to clear her mind of this. If she only could figure out a way to snap out of it. Maybe she could will the dream away.

The sound of Vivian's voice drifted over the noise from the road. "...thought at first you were dead, Charles. The place was such a mess..."

She felt very lightheaded again and everything spun about her. She blinked hard and rubbed her eyes, then tried to sit up. But Vivian still wouldn't let her.

Cicely saw a blur of green as the car sped under a canopy of lush vegetation. The fragrance of jasmine wafted in through the open windows.

"And Arteaga, how is he?" The words just formed in her mouth. Charles' words.

"He was dying when we arrived," said Vivian. "We had to leave right away, the police were near."

In her mind Cicely repeated, go away, go away. The voices receded for a while, and she became drowsy.

A thought rushed to her mind. "Did I kill him?" she said with Charles' voice.

"Arteaga?" Vivian asked.

"No, the other, the big man. I think I shot him. I must have hit him. He fired at Arteaga. Then everything went blank."

Her hand went to her side. The pistol was gone, but she could feel the film canister still there, in her pocket. Part of the document was recorded on the film. *Oh, God!*

Someone shook her shoulder. Cicely woke, breathless, within the reassuring confines of an Aylesbend guest bedroom. Angie, in a white silk nightgown, leaned over her.

"You screamed, Cicely."

4

Dr. McClellan's office was located in St. Marylebone. Cicely drove carefully along Oxford Street. Her heart was beating uncommonly fast and she felt tense and awkward. She concentrated on her driving, her fingers gripping tightly the steering wheel of the MGB. Soon she drove by a small dark brick church with a square turret, which she recognized as St. Peter's Chapel, and parked her car.

She walked at a brisk pace to Cavendish Square, and oriented herself by the pair of stone-faced eighteenth century houses at the center of the north side. She crossed Henrietta Place and proceeded north on Harley Street, which made the west side of the square. Except for a few modern blocks of flats, the solid buildings she passed looked like they had been in place for a century or two.

Cicely searched diligently for the physician's address. Practically every doorway carried a consultant's brass plate. The exercise helped her to pull herself together. She walked on, looking briefly at the overcast sky.

Someone bumped into her side. Cicely glanced around and saw a young couple. A boy with lusterless brown hair muttered "Sorry" while his girl rolled her green eyes and shook her head. They both walked on, unconcerned, ignoring Cicely's weak "Pardon me." As she turned from them, Cicely finally spotted the brass plate announcing the practice of Dr. Burton T. McClellan. She climbed the five steps to the heavy door and pushed it open.

A West Indian male secretary greeted Cicely from behind a cluttered desk across the reception room. He had her sign a register and gave her forms to fill out. Cicely applied herself to the tedious task and barely noticed when a plump gray-haired woman entered the room through an inner door and passed by on the way out. A moment later the secretary informed Cicely that the doctor was ready to see her and led her to his office.

Dr. McClellan greeted Cicely at the door. He asked her to take a seat in a large and deep easy chair. Cicely took the seat, and he walked around a heavy wooden desk and sat behind it.

The desk was bare except for a gilt pen set, a note pad, and a gray intercom set. He wore a double-breasted dark brown suit. Cicely adjusted her position in her chair. She sat facing slightly to his left. The room was spacious, its walls displaying diplomas and certificates except for the area directly behind the desk. This held four large paintings, all landscapes.

"What is troubling you, Miss Denfeld?" Dr. McClellan asked. He was a man in his mid-forties, thickset, with dark eyes and wavy brown hair.

"I have been very nervous..."

"For how long, Miss Denfeld?"

"About two weeks."

"No problems of this kind before this?"

"No."

Dr. McClellan questioned her at length about her medical history and wrote down the name of her physician. Cicely reported that, as far as she knew, she was in excellent health.

Dr. McClellan looked at Cicely closely. She avoided his eyes and studied the pattern of her tweed suit. He glanced at the questionnaire she had filled out earlier.

"You are a schoolteacher. Any particular problems at work? Trouble children, that sort of thing?"

"No, Doctor," Cicely said. "I can handle the kids well enough." She turned slightly and looked over Dr. McClellan's shoulder at one of the paintings on the wall. The foreground showed rocks and bushes at the edge of a calm blue lake. Behind the lake a dim shore rose to pine covered hills. And behind them a pale gray sky covered sharp icy mountains.

"Do you feel threatened?" Dr. McClellan's voice was neutral, unemotional. "By someone you have had a dispute with, for instance."

"I've had no personal problems lately." She forced a smile. "Other than this. I wouldn't say I feel threatened as much as terribly confused. Sometimes I wake up trembling and then find it hard to go back to sleep. I don't understand what's happening to me."

Dr. McClellan brought the fingertips of his two hands together, a pair at a time, forming a steeple. He looked at his fingers, and then back up at Cicely. The pupils of her eyes were dilated—a sign of anxiety. "This nervousness—what form does it take? Did a specific event bring it about?"

Cicely brushed a strand of blond hair back from her face. She took a deep breath. "I have been having very strange dreams. They are vivid, unsettling, like no dreams I've had before." She looked at Dr. McClellan, who had returned to looking at the steeple he had formed with his fingers.

"Unsettling," he said, not looking up. "Not frightening?"

"They frighten me by implication. I do not appear in these dreams as myself. I'm someone else—a man." She looked at Dr. McClellan closely. "There's a strange quality about the dreams. Something abnormal..."

"Would you say you have a good recollection of the dreams, Miss Denfeld?"

"Yes, Doctor."

He turned to face Cicely. "Are the dreams recurring?"

"They have never repeated. But some of them appear related, some-what...continuous. Several have involved a woman—the same woman. Both the man and the woman speak with an American accent."

"Tell me about one of your dreams. Not only the dream, but how you felt about it."

Haltingly, Cicely recounted the dream she had experienced while visiting Angie, and her growing concern. Dr. McClellan listened attentively.

A buzzer in Dr. McClellan's watch went on and he turned it off quickly. He pulled a small paper pad toward himself and wrote on it rapidly, occasionally looking up to meet Cicely's green eyes. "I believe I can help you," he told her. "Dreams like yours are a message from the subconscious. We will interpret the dreams and decipher the message. Then we will focus on the underlying problem and we will make it go away." He paused, and for the first time smiled. "Or it may go away by itself. In either case I shall take full credit."

He stood up and walked around his desk.

"I want you to make sure you can recall all that you dream about. You may want to jot down some notes when you awake." He handed Cicely a slip of paper. "I'm prescribing a mild sedative. Take one tablet a day if your nervousness persists."

They walked together to the door. "I think it is best to see you twice a week for now. Can you come on Friday?"

"Yes, Doctor," Cicely said. "I'm sure I can arrange it."

"Good. My secretary will schedule a visit for you." Dr. McClellan opened the door. "He will also discuss financial arrangements with you." He smiled at her for a second time. "I understand you are acquainted with Lady Torrington."

"Yes. Her niece, Angie, is a close friend of mine."

He nodded approvingly. "Good evening."

Dr. McClellan closed the door after Cicely and returned to his desk. He sat thoughtfully for a moment, tore off a sheet from his prescription pad and wrote on its plain back side: *Neurotic anxiety. Dreams symbolize repressed or forgotten experiences.* He was left with a puzzled feeling. There was something else in the wind.

5

"Jeremy."

"Yes, Miss Denfeld," the ten year-old responded.

Jeremy sat with twenty-two other students in a room with pale green walls. To the right and the back there were windows. The left wall was covered with maps and a huge illustrated chart titled *The History of Civilisation*.

Cicely stood by her desk, holding a red notebook loosely in her hand. She smiled at the boy. "We talked earlier about clouds, and we said they could be divided into three major groups. Now tell the class, Jeremy, the names of these three groups."

"Oh." Jeremy glanced furtively at the map of South America, as if hoping to find an answer there. Then he turned his glance to Cicely. "Low, medium and large, Miss Denfeld."

The class started to break into laughter, but a stern look from their teacher averted the small disaster. Only a few giggles were heard.

"Thank you, Jeremy. Low and medium are correct." She addressed them all: "Which is the third group?"

The answer came in a chorus. "High!"

"That is very good. Now, who can tell me the name of one type of low cloud?"

Half a dozen small hands waved in the air.

"You tell us, Karen."

"Cumulus, Miss."

"That's right, Karen. Thank you. Cumulus is the familiar white cauliflower-like cloud. Another type of low cloud is cumulonimbus, a large, vertically developed, threatening cloud."

After the science period, Cicely told the class that she would show the slides from their last excursion. "Laura, please pull down the shades," she said. A long-haired girl rose to briskly take care of this chore.

"Should I lower the screen, Miss Denfeld?"

"Yes, please, Stewart."

The boy rose from his seat and walked toward the screen rolled in a cylinder above the blackboard. He was the tallest in the class and was usually selected for this duty, which required jumping up to grab the handle that lowered the screen.

"May I help too, Miss Denfeld?"

"Not now, Jeremy. Take your place, we're about to begin."

Finally the screen was set up.

"Will your picture show up, Miss?" a freckled boy asked.

"Yes, remember, that nice gentleman took a picture of us all."

"When we were by the river?"

Cicely adjusted the position of the slide projector to line it up with the screen. "That was later, Kevin, by the river Wylye," she said. "Our driver took that one. Now all sit down and be quiet when I dim the lights."

There was a chorus of "Yes, Miss." The lights were dimmed with only a minimum of "boos" and giggles. The first slide showed the class standing in a row alongside a red bus. A man in uniform stood with them, holding a cap in his hands. "This was taken here in Bromley, just before we started out," said Cicely.

The next slide showed Cicely in a yellow dress with several smiling boys and girls, tightly grouped before a great block of sandstone.

"Remember, children? This one was taken at the ruins in Stonehenge."

When her classes were over, Cicely planned her lessons for the next day, as was her custom, then stayed an additional half-hour, grading homework. She was glad with the way her school day had gone.

On the way out of the school building she met a stooping elderly man, the caretaker. He smelled of recently mowed grass. "How are you, Mr. Prescott?" Cicely said.

The man smiled at her, brushing back a wisp of gray hair from his wrinkled brow. "I'm fair, Miss Denfeld. Have a nice evening."

Cicely walked to her car, got in, and started the drive across London. She tuned the radio to her favorite station and let the coaxing words of Rod Stewart blot out the sounds of the traffic that soon surrounded her. The weather was good, blue skies with some clouds to the south. There remained two hours of daylight.

On impulse, Cicely decided to do some shopping on the way home. She visited several stores, shopping carefully, with a keen eye for price tags. Black shoes with thin straps, a simple white blouse and a pink and blue striped one, a rather long navy skirt, things she could wear equally well to work or to a casual meeting. When her expenses totaled fifty pounds she stopped and took her prizes gaily back to her car.

She stopped once more on the way to her flat in Highgate, for tea and a beef sandwich at a small restaurant near Paddington Station. It was eight-thirty when she arrived back at her flat.

Cicely was undressing when the telephone rang.

"Hello," she said.

It was the young man she had been seeing lately. "Would you like to go to a play the evening after tomorrow? Spence recommended the one that just started at the *Almeida*. It's really avant-garde, with lasers and all kinds of weird goings on."

"I'd love to, Greg." She was wearing only her pantyhose and felt an irrational embarrassment at talking to her friend while practically nude. "What time will you be coming by?"

"Sevenish."

As she put the receiver down she experienced a nagging feeling, like a memory not quite recalled. It had something to do with Stonehenge.

6

Cicely opened the door to her flat and they entered quickly, hurrying away from the lashing rain.

"Let me take your coat, Greg," Cicely said, taking off her own and carefully folding it over the back of one of her tall chairs.

Greg handed her his coat and she hung it inside the small closet by the doorway. The stretching of her arms pressed her breasts hard against her blouse, and she sensed Greg's scrutiny.

When Cicely went into the kitchen for wine he stood by the single window, at first regarding the reflection of his own suavely handsome features, then peering into the darkness outside and listening to raindrops splatter against the glass. A moment later she returned, a warm glow in her eyes. As she handed him his wine glass, he bussed her cheek.

They drank Beaujolais and discussed the play, sitting on Cicely's softly padded sofa. After a while he bent toward her, cupped her face in his hands, and kissed her on the lips. She kissed him back.

They talked of visiting Brighton, but mostly exchanged kisses with increasing frequency. Greg was eager, and for once Cicely seemed disposed to yield to his impatience. They drew closer.

He unbuttoned her blouse and at once started to touch her, his hands gliding up and down her side, to the small of her back, and then cupping her breasts. She felt the remaining tenseness within her melt away. The top of his shirt was open, a few dark blond hairs showing above the tan vee of his shirt. Her fingers caressed the back of his neck.

He was direct and purposeful; his hands softly assaulting her breasts and then searching lower on her body. Cicely circled his chest firmly with her arms and planted soft kisses on the top of his head. She smiled at a brief wild thought of her class seeing her like this, felt a grasping hand on her right buttock, and let herself slip slowly, contentedly, into the enjoyment of his body.

Later Cicely set the clock radio's alarm for half an hour before daybreak, since Greg would have to leave before nosy neighbors took interest in the new day. She turned out the lights and joined him again in bed, naked, her body softly molding to his already sleeping form.

Warm rain lashed at her. She walked along the sloping bank of a shallow creek, over mud and rocks, carrying a rifle in her hands. Just ahead, a tall dark-haired young woman in rain-soaked clothes carefully stepped over an exposed, gnarled tree root. For a while, the two trudged on downstream, past round mossy boulders and green bushes.

Suddenly, the rain stopped. Soon a soft breeze brought with it the salty smell of the sea. Clouds raced overhead to reveal an immaculate blue sky and a yellow afternoon sun.

There was something odd about the way she felt, the way her body responded.

Cicely slipped on a slick rock and came to her knees abruptly, balancing herself on the rifle. As she stood up, her gaze traveled in an arc and she saw, at most a half-mile upstream, a group of men on horseback.

"Vivian!" Cicely heard herself shout in a man's voice.

The girl ahead turned around, sliding to a halt on the slippery surface. In spite of her soiled clothes and disheveled hair she presented a striking figure. Long-limbed, athletic. Her wet blouse adhered to full, rounded breasts. A pistol butt showed darkly against the white fabric of her blouse, pressed against her flat belly by the waistband of her skirt. The blue of her eyes matched the color of the tropical sky. "What is it, Charles?"

Cicely pointed to the approaching riders. Some of them held rifles in their outstretched arms.

"I say we try for the boat," Vivian said.

"All right. The shore can't be far," Cicely heard herself say.

I need to wake up, she thought.

They moved off rapidly, in short dashes, their bodies bent at the waist, making the most of the cover provided by tall grass and mangrove trees bordering the stream. The sea smell grew stronger until, finally, they heard the welcome crash of waves.

Directly ahead, the gravelly streambed widened and the vegetation stopped abruptly. They came to a wide beach. A white lifeboat bobbed on the blue-green sea in front of them.

The roar of the ocean did not quite mask the sound of distant shouts. Cicely glanced back warily through Charles' eyes and saw the glint of sunlight on the lead horseman's raised rifle.

A gunshot rang out loudly, then another. The group of uniformed men approached as fast as their horses could take them. With dull thuds, bullets sank into the sand, inches away from where the two stood.

Cicely woke with a start, her heart racing. She touched her face, her hair. She was herself again, back at her flat in Highgate. She heard the rain outside. Greg lay beside her. Cicely stumbled out of bed and felt her way to the bathroom in the dark. In the medicine cabinet she found the small plastic bottle with the pills Dr. McClellan had prescribed and took two of them. Shivering, she returned to bed.

She thought of waking Greg, but what could she tell him? That she dreamt of being a stranger? He'd think she was daft, or worse. Why was this happening to her? She laid still, her eyes open, her body covered with a cold sweat. Trembling. Until the drug took effect and she slept again.

CHAPTER 2
ENCOUNTER

1

Vivian threw herself down on the sand, and Charles did the same. She wheeled to sit with her back to the sea, her knees drawn up and close together. Gripping her pistol with both hands, she began firing at the group of approaching horsemen.

"Shoot everything you've got at them, Charles, then let's run for it."

Charles knelt and fired the Kalashnikov. The acrid smell of gunpowder filled the air. His first burst, unaimed, kicked up a hail of sand in front of the riders. The men, there were seven of them, shot from their mounts with handguns and rifles. Charles held his breath and pulled back gradually on the trigger, keeping a horseman aligned in his sights, until the rifle kicked sharply at his shoulder. The Cuban militiaman fell backwards off his horse.

Two of the soldiers dismounted and took cover behind a brambly bush. The others rode on toward Charles and Vivian. A burst from Charles' rifle hit one of the riders and he toppled as Vivian continued to methodically fire her pistol, bringing down another man. He was close enough that Charles and Vivian could hear his cry. Charles fired a last burst and a horse and rider fell heavily amidst a spray of sand. The remaining horseman fired back, his mount bucking and rearing, and rode back to where the others had taken cover.

"Let's go," Vivian said.

She put down her pistol and stood, quickly shook loose her shoes, threw aside her skirt, and dashed off. Charles pried off his shoes and followed her, rifle in hand.

She ran diagonally across the splendid beach, following a zigzag course in the general direction of the lifeboat, her body graceful in flight, her mahogany hair streaming behind her, the muscles of her glistening legs rippling with each stride. Charles ran as hard as he could, but slowly lost ground to her. The sand was wet and smooth as a china plate. The single white figure at the boat, seeing them approach, started up the outboard engine and cruised closer to shore.

The firing behind them grew heavier. The water's edge came closer, forty yards, thirty. Bullets thudded into the sand around them, sent plumes of water into the air when they breached the sea a few feet ahead of Vivian. She took four strides into the water, then dived headfirst. Charles dropped the rifle and ran into the ocean, water spraying all about, until the water came to his knees. He dived after her and swam as fast as he could, the salt water biting maddeningly into the scratches on his body.

Deafening sounds surrounded them: waves crashing against the beach, hands and feet cutting into the water, the sharp loud bursts of gunfire, the angry shouts of the soldiers ashore.

"Oooh…"

Charles heard Vivian's cry, turned just in time to catch a strong wave in the face and swallow a mouthful of salt water. She had a wound on her head.

Charles swam toward Vivian, found and held her arm. "I'm all right," she said.

A hail of bullets whizzed close by. They swam together, desperately, toward the beckoning dull rumble of the boat's engine.

"Stay clear of the prop," the sailor warned.

The white wooden boat loomed ahead. The gray-haired sailor threw them a rope. Vivian went up first. Climbing aboard was difficult. The sides of the boat seemed impossibly high. Charles helped Vivian up and she disappeared over the side. The sailor reached down to help him. Charles gripped his hand.

There was a dull popping sound followed by a short gasp and, abruptly, the sailor plummeted overboard. An instant before his body hit him, Charles saw a neat black hole on the man's forehead over his left eye, just beginning to secrete blood.

The blow pushed Charles deep under water. He struggled for the surface, the white ridged bottom of the boat above, his head aching, his lungs aflame. The man's bloodied body, driven by the waves, continued to push him down.

Charles broke free and thrust his head to the surface. His lungs filled with air and he struggled blindly, hearing bullets slam against the hull. He groped overhead, then hoisted himself in and rolled astern. A quick bruising movement took him to the motor. He turned the throttle to full power. The engine roared and the craft tilted up as it gathered speed.

Charles slumped in the back of the boat holding the tiller in the crook of his arm and steered away from the island. He stared ahead numbly, giving a reprieve to his aching body.

Vivian laid up front on her back, resting or asleep, her body rocked by the motions of the boat. A threadbare smile was on her lips. Blood from the grazing wound on her scalp had trickled onto her wet, torn blouse. Charles' eyes traveled over the long well-formed legs that, caressed by the mellow light of the setting sun, took on the color of gold.

2

Charles yawned. He lay on a narrow bed in a snug wood paneled bedroom, half asleep. The wind carried the sound of voices through the partially open slats of the window.

"Soon after they gained consciousness," a man said, "they asked me to contact Mr. Robinson in Miami. Is he their employer?" The British voice belonged to Gary Smith, the man who had found him and Vivian when their safety boat drifted ashore.

"Mr. Robinson heads a private investigations bureau," another voice said. "I am the firm's attorney and Vivian is a minor partner. Charles has been assisting temporarily in what I think is an embezzlement case. It was very fortunate that you were able to help them as soon as you did." Charles recognized the new voice. It was Benjamin Lawrence's.

He heard a clinking sound, like ice on a glass.

"It's been little trouble for me," Smith said. "Joann has been the one to take care of them, mostly. She and Dr. Lemmon."

There was a tapping above him on the wooden slats of the window. A gull, perhaps. Smith's chalet was near the sea.

"It's been very nice of you. Mr. Robinson will repay you for all expenses, of course."

"It'll be mostly Dr. Lemmon's bills," Smith said. "I'll have to give something to the local police, they've been very understanding."

Charles felt very sleepy, but the tapping bird kept him awake a few moments longer.

"When can I see them?"

"Well, they're asleep now. I'd leave them be for a while. They were up for lunch today and took a short walk just before you arrived. Why don't you stay for dinner? There'll be plenty of opportunity afterward to talk to them."

There was a short scraping noise outside, like a chair being slid on the terrace floor. "Mr. Ryder wanted you to have this. He said it was very important."

"What is it?" Lawrence asked.

"Microfilm. It's all they had with them."

3

Dr. McClellan looked across the wide desk at his patient. He had just finished reviewing his notes. Cicely Denfeld looked tense and ill at ease. She toyed constantly with a lock of her straw-blond hair.

"Have the pills helped any?"

She looked at him directly, a little sullenly. "They help get me over my panics," she said, a faint smile appearing on her pale lips. "But they also slow me down. I can't," her voice caught for a moment, "can't take them while at school. I fear I will go to sleep in front of the form."

"Have you missed any workdays this week?"

"No. It helps me to be with the children," Cicely said. "It takes my mind off…things."

"Good." He watched her closely. "It is important that you continue to function as normally as possible, while we look further into this."

"Doctor, how long will this go on? Before I get better."

"It depends on what we find. Some patients experience a marked improvement within a year."

Cicely let out a long sigh.

"Your condition is treatable," the doctor added. "I expect you will notice a reduction in your nervousness almost immediately. You will be able to cope better."

Dr. McClellan made a brief annotation on his papers, made sure the recorder was on, and then swiveled his chair so that he looked away from Cicely.

"Now tell me about the latest dream."

Dinner was served promptly at seven by the Smiths' cook, an elderly black man. He set six places. Vivian sat to Charles' right, and across from them sat Lawrence and Dr. Lemmon. Gary and Joann Smith sat at opposite ends of the oak table.

The white windows were ajar, framing grass and roses that could be seen dimly outside, and permitting a breeze to blow through the room. The walls were bare, except for a cuckoo clock, an oval mirror, and a picture of a schooner at full sail, cutting a foamy path through a rippling blue sea. A radio, in an antique wood cabinet, lay on a small table set against the wall opposite the windows.

Dr. Lemmon had dropped by for a routine checkup on Charles and Vivian. He was a portly man in his fifties, with pouches under shrewd eyes. The Smiths had asked him to stay for dinner and he had promptly accepted. Now he was the first to dig heartily into the fruit salad they had just been served: diced pineapple, pear, and melon.

He smiled at his two patients. "In two or three days you'll be totally recovered and fit to travel," he said.

Charles looked past the physician at his own reflection in the mirror. His face still looked haggard. He ran a finger under the collar of the borrowed khaki shirt, where it chafed against his neck. Then his attention turned inward. Questions kept running through his mind: What was the significance of what Arteaga had discovered? Who had killed him? He wondered if they would ever find out.

Both Vivian and Charles wore the sunglasses the doctor had prescribed. There were patches of peeling skin on their foreheads—the remnants of severe sunburns.

"Is it all right for us to travel about the island, Dr. Lemmon?" Vivian asked. Her dark brown hair spilled over her shoulder as she reached for a loaf of bread. She wore a white cotton dress that Joann had provided.

"The day after tomorrow, for a couple of hours. But you must wear hats and long-sleeved shirts," Dr. Lemmon answered, tugging at his gray beard.

Charles sipped his iced tea leisurely. A few cracks remained at the corners of his thin lips. "What are those?" he asked, pointing at a stack of cards lying in a small wicker basket at the center of the table.

"They are Tarot cards. Joann uses them to tell fortunes," Gary Smith said with a grin. He was short, somewhat military-looking, with thinning blond hair. "It's an amusing pastime."

Joann looked sharply at her husband. "It's more than a pastime." She addressed the others: "The Tarot is an ancient Celtic method of divination."

The cook returned and started serving the main course. Steamed grouper and conch fritters.

"Perhaps you will treat us to one of your readings tonight," Dr. Lemmon said to Joann.

Joann looked approvingly at the seafood on her plate. Wispy red hair framed her pixieish face. "We may give it a try later," she said.

The cook placed down the last dish, Lawrence's. "All's well, mon?" he asked.

"Yes, Maurice," Gary answered, his precise British accent contrasting with the cook's Bahamian brogue. "The grouper looks particularly good."

"I'll be going to Nicholls Town now, mon," said Maurice, leaving the room.

"How far is Nicholls Town?" Charles asked, neatly slicing his fish.

"We're about six miles out," Gary said.

"Which may be far by Andros' standards," added Lawrence. "The island seemed fairly small when I flew in." The lawyer was about forty, with a slender build and neatly trimmed brown hair.

"North Andros," said Dr. Lemmon, "where we are, is about sixty miles long, and about thirty-five at its widest." He ate the conch fritters greedily. "Conch puts spunk in your back trunk," he said, chuckling. "Invigorating."

After dinner, Vivian helped Joann clear the table, while the men listened to the news broadcast on the ancient radio. Bahamian Customs had captured a gang of drug smugglers aboard a hydrofoil yacht in shoal waters near South Andros. The smugglers had been making a run from Cartagena to the Southern Bahamas when they were intercepted by Bahamian naval units assisted by two United States Marines helicopter gunships.

"That must have been an interesting action," declared Gary. "It reminds me of an encounter we had off the Falklands."

Charles listened halfheartedly to Gary's story about his service aboard the British destroyer *Sheffield*. He drew close to the wall and, hands clasped behind his back, examined the cuckoo clock. Intrigued by the wood-and-metal mechanism, Charles watched closely as small doors opened and a bird, its tiny wooden wings flapping, excitedly announced eight o'clock.

When the women returned, the group moved to an adjacent room, dimly lit by a small kerosene lamp, and took seats around a card table. Joann ceremoniously set down rows of the oversize Tarot cards and read Charles' fortune. Her voice, growing deeper as she spoke of "what is before him," gradually cast a pall of uneasy excitement over the company. She drew a last card and set it down, saying "What will come," then pulled abruptly away from the table. The card showed a man and a woman chained to a pedestal upon which sat the devil.

4

Reynold Robinson opened the heavy mahogany door and motioned Charles, Vivian and Benjamin Lawrence into his library. Robinson's body was heavyset and muscular. A deep tan contrasted nicely with his graying hair.

Once all were in, he closed the door and moved to take a seat behind a neat Danish Modern desk near the far wall of the spacious room. The others sat on straight chairs across his desk. The wall behind Robinson was covered with maps.

Robinson picked up a metal-stemmed pipe and a tobacco pouch and began filling the bowl.

"Any problems on the flight from the Bahamas?" he asked, addressing no one in particular.

Lawrence was the first to answer. "It was fine, sir. All went well at Customs."

Robinson lit his pipe and took a few experimental puffs. "Good show," he said.

"You two are well?" he asked Charles and Vivian.

"We're quite well now, sir," Vivian said.

Charles nodded.

Robinson took a puff from his pipe and cleared his throat. "We were quite concerned about you. Lawrence telephoned me earlier with a summary of your report." He paused, and then indicated slips of yellow paper on his desk. "I also have two radio messages from Guisa in Cuba, so I have been able to form an idea of what happened. But it might help to clear a few points if you give me a brief account of the meeting with Arteaga."

Charles leaned forward. "I contacted Mrs. Lopez at the address you gave me," he said. "She sold me the microfilm of Arteaga's document and set up the meeting with him. It took place at a small house on the outskirts of Havana, near a place called Cantarranas."

Adele Lopez had remained behind in the car. Charles walked slowly on a dirt lane paralleled by a line of royal palms. A light morning breeze gathered particles of the reddish soil into small cloudy balls, then rolled them by the edge of the road and finally scattered them over the sparse grass lining it.

The wind picked up, carrying with it the distant lowing of cattle and the shrill, broken sound of hens. A hundred feet ahead, just beyond the stark trunks of the palms, the house came into view.

The wind died and the crackling of the palm leaves ceased. Charles walked on, suddenly alerted. His steps made the only sound on the deserted lane.

The wood house was very small. Peeling red paint covered the boards. The single visible opening was a narrow gray door. Charles approached it uneasily.

He knocked on the door, the unpolished wood rough on his knuckles. Minutes passed by before he heard the muffled sound of steps inside.

Leo Arteaga was thinner than Charles remembered. The man, about thirty, opened the door only part way and looked searchingly outside.

"Hello, Leo." Charles tried to smile. "It's been a while."

Arteaga's face showed surprise. "Five years. What do you want, Charlie?"

"The document," Charles declared. "I thought Adele Lopez would have told you."

Arteaga regarded him closely. "She did," he said, ushering Charles into the room. "I didn't expect *you*."

A rough wooden table and chairs were set in the center of the room. At the back there was a small white enamel sink and an alcohol-burning stove. A tall narrow cabinet was propped against the bare right wall. The only other piece of furniture was a folding bed set under the single shuttered window on the left.

"I'd like you to go back to the States with me," Charles said.

A wan smile peeled Arteaga's thin lips back from his teeth. "Have a seat," he said, pulling a chair away from the table. He did not appear to be carrying a gun.

Charles hoped the pistol he carried concealed under his *guayabera* remained undetected. "I'd rather stand. I've been riding for some time."

Arteaga shrugged. "Who came with you?"

"I am alone," lied Charles. "Adele Lopez gave me directions."

"Who sent you after me?"

"A man in Miami," Charles said.

Arteaga sat down. "Robinson?"

"Yes."

Arteaga's mouth turned down. "Do you know who it is he works for, Charles?"

"He said for himself. I'd like to ask you some questions, Leo. What is this mess all about? You're suspected of being a spy."

Arteaga put both elbows on the table and brought his hands together, fists closed. He rested his chin on the cradle they formed. "You are hardly in a position to ask impolite questions or to dictate terms." Arteaga paused for a moment, as if considering something.

Charles felt less nervous now than when he had come in, but was still unsure about how best to proceed. He looked into Arteaga's watchful protuberant eyes.

"Adele knows about this fellow Robinson," Arteaga said. "She thinks he's a front for CIA. I take it you have actually seen him."

"Yes."

"Describe the man."

Charles hesitated for only a moment. "Heavyset, of average height, fit. About forty-five. Has a British accent…"

"Not one of them." Arteaga cleared his throat. "You brought the money with you?"

Charles placed a bundle of hundred-dollar bills on the table.

"How did you get involved in this?" Arteaga inquired sharply.

"Robinson had trouble finding information about you. Apparently someone has been going around systematically destroying all records relating to you. Your driver's license, Social Security, school records—they are all gone. The FBI had a file on you. It has vanished. Robinson only knew your place of employment, your last address, the identity of a few acquaintances. He started looking for photographs of you, or someone who could positively identify you. An old loan application, where you had given me as a reference, led him to me. When he found out I could speak Spanish, he asked me to come here, buy back the document, and talk you into returning."

"You must be crazy," Arteaga said. A grin twisted his trembling lip. "You're likely to get killed. How much is he paying you?"

"Enough. Leo, you must come back, explain things, get this behind you," Charles pleaded.

Arteaga leaned back on his chair and cracked his knuckles. "I am not a spy. I'm doing this for my country. For the world we live in." He looked directly at Charles. "It's a long story."

Charles paced the room, careful not to turn his back on Arteaga. "Do you have the document here?"

"There." Arteaga indicated the cabinet.

"Would it be too much to ask how you came about it?"

Arteaga pursed his lips. "No, not too much." He brought his hands down, shrugging his narrow shoulders.

"I must go back a bit." He let out a big breath. "I bought land near Palmdale—a speculation. There has been a lot of construction around the airport there. It's close to Los Angeles. To finance it I took a second job, as a programmer, with Algoronics. They are a think tank working for the government.

"I worked the night shift, supervising the operation of some of their computers. Machine operators and network guys did most of the work; I just kept them honest. Sometimes there were network server problems or screwups with the batch jobs and I figured how to make things work right again.

"Some of the batch jobs ran for hours and terminated abnormally. I would get the computer to list the program and I would go through it and try to spot the bug. If I found it I would rerun the job or leave a note for the programmer indicating what I thought was the source of the problem."

Arteaga paused. He drummed on the table with his fingers, collecting his thoughts.

"There were six servers and two mainframes under my care. The mainframes were linked to three others in another building. The executive programs were designed in such a way that one of the remote machines acted as the master for mine. Whoever operated the other machines could in principle override my instructions and take over my machines, although they seldom did."

Arteaga stood up and walked jerkily to the cabinet.

"One night one of my machines hit an error termination and I asked for a listing of the program it was executing. I left the room to refill my coffee cup without looking at what the printer was starting to display.

"I didn't know it then, but the master computer had just gone down. When I returned I went to the printer and found something different than what I expected. The printout was a mess, a meaningless jumble of letters."

From the cabinet, Arteaga extracted a stack of computer paper. He took it to the table and placed it there.

"Is this it?" Charles asked.

Arteaga nodded. "I made an error in my request, asked for the wrong listing," he said. "Normally a security routine would have prevented me from accessing the material, but with my machine acting as the master my administrator's authority overrode it."

Arteaga paged through the computer listing. "It's from a green door project," he indicated the page he had turned to. There was a slight tremor in his hand.

Charles came close to the table and looked at the sheet of paper.

"It's word processor output," Arteaga said.

At the very top were the words TOP SECRET.

"I was going to destroy this, then I thought of turning it over to Security." Arteaga pointed at the page, shrugging again. "It's a draft document. Look at the title."

Charles leaned closer. RPT. OF THE SPECIAL COMM. OF THE S.A.B. ON E E. AND.

"It seems that they weren't too sure what to call it themselves," went on Arteaga. "Or they deleted part of the title for security reasons."

"This is an index," said Charles, reading the sheet.

Arteaga nodded. "A table of contents for a six-part document." He flipped through a few more pages. "The index page is the only one not in code and even it has information so abbreviated as to make it unintelligible."

Arteaga sat down and Charles read through the computer listing.

"I spent the rest of that night poring over the stuff," Arteaga said slowly. "I locked it up in my desk, intending to turn it over to Security, but I never did. It became a challenge, trying to break the code, to at least find the meaning behind that cryptic index."

Arteaga looked at Charles with a slight turn downwards at the corners of his mouth. "It was a mistake to get involved, Charles," he said, his face darkening. "This is too big."

"Give the document back to them, Leo."

"No. It must not be kept secret." He shook his head slowly.

"I would think the government is better qualified to make that judgment."

"No!" Arteaga snapped. He shuddered. "I don't think I could back out now, anyway."

Charles looked at the man closely. Leo Arteaga appeared to be under considerable stress. It would serve no purpose to enter into an argument with him.

"I take it you continued to work on the decipherment."

Arteaga nodded, making a visible effort to calm himself.

"It took a lot of work, but eventually I figured part of it out. I may never have if I hadn't had that land out in the desert. As it was, once I began asking questions things started moving pretty fast. You see, the place is practically right—"

Arteaga turned his head suddenly. "What was that?"

"What do you mean?" Charles said.

"You heard nothing?" Arteaga stood up.

"There are cattle out there."

They were both silent for a moment, listening. Charles felt increasingly spooked. They heard only the slightest of sounds: leaves rustling in the wind, the song of a distant bird.

"You broke the code?" Charles suggested.

Arteaga sat down. "I found what kind of code they used. There are multiple codes, with prime number keys."

Arteaga pointed to a chair. "Do sit down," he said. "You make me nervous."

Charles pulled the chair back and moved around it.

Arteaga cocked his head and glanced uneasily at the shuttered window. "I was able to make progress early even—"

The door burst open. Charles, in the process of sitting down, fell back startled against the wall. The entire room rocked, became full of an overwhelming din. A tall shape appeared at the entrance, outlined against the brightness outside.

Arteaga rose in panic, upsetting the table and sending the computer papers tumbling to the floor. The trespasser strode quickly into the room. His hand moved. Metal flashed in it, shining like chromium in blinding sunlight.

There was a loud cracking noise and a blaze as bright as lightning filled the room. Leo Arteaga fell, yelling hoarsely, clutching his stomach. Charles reached for his pistol. There was a pungent smell...

The stranger noticed Charles and turned towards him. Charles fired, and the brutal sound of the Colt Commander filled the room. The stranger kept turning, his arm extending toward his new target. Charles continued to fire, the rounds following each other in staccato rhythm. The stranger's weapon pointed straight at him now. There was a bright flash…

Robinson's pipe was dead. He lit up again using a small gold lighter. He puffed several times, filling the room with the rich smell of the aromatic tobacco.

"Would you say you scored a hit on him?" he asked.

Charles nodded. "Several. They didn't faze him."

"Odd. What happened after that?"

"Guisa and I heard the explosion," said Vivian. "We reached the place within minutes. Adele Lopez was in the car, dead. There were severe burn marks on her body."

Robinson frowned, but gestured for Vivian to continue.

"The front of the house was demolished. There was a lot of debris about. Charles was just outside, unconscious."

"And Arteaga?"

"He was incoherent, dying from a deep abdominal wound. There was blood all over him and he was badly burned. We had to leave the bodies behind; the Cuban police were very close."

Robinson took another puff from his pipe. He shook his head. "Messy. And the stranger?"

"Guisa and I never saw him," Vivian said. "We assume he carried an explosive device of some sort, and that it was set off by a bullet fired by Charles. We left immediately, could not stop to search the place."

"It troubles me," said Robinson, "that you didn't find the body. You saw no body parts or clothing?"

"No, nothing like that."

"What did you do next?"

"We took Charles to a safe house in Matanzas. The next day Charles and I traveled to the rendezvous point near Maximo Gomez. We were spotted by *Milicianos*. They killed the sailor in the boat that came to the beach for us. We never found the ship."

"The ship's captain could not become involved once shooting started," Robinson said. "He had to resume his course."

Vivian's blue eyes fixed on Robinson. She lifted her chin slightly. "It was," she said with a hard edge to her voice, "less than we hoped for."

Lawrence spoke, trying to break the sudden tension. "The Cubans instituted a search by patrol boats. The ship was not actually boarded, but it was challenged soon after the incident."

"We had no compass," Charles said. "We tried to steer north, towards Florida. It is only about a hundred miles, but there was a storm…"

"I think we know the rest," said Robinson, putting out his pipe. "All around a good job." His face hardened. "Queer business. We must get a look at the microfilm you brought back. Only way to find out what those people were killed for."

CHAPTER 3
ANXIETY

1

Cicely was early for her appointment and Dr. McClellan's West Indian secretary asked her to wait for a few minutes. She sat on the couch across from the secretary's desk, glanced at the stack of magazines, and looked in her handbag for her compact. While delving through the collection of articles she rediscovered the strange key. It was steel gray, with square cuts on one edge of the thin flat blade. The word *Mosler* was inscribed on one side, and a four digit number was stamped on the other.

"Hello, Cicely." Dr. McClellan said.

Cicely looked up and smiled. She regarded the key and for a moment thought of mentioning it to Dr. McClellan, but an inner voice told her not to and she let it drop back into her purse.

"How have you been feeling?" Dr. McClellan asked.

Cicely stood up and followed him past the secretary's station into his office.

"I'm…bewildered, Doctor," she said.

The secretary closed the door behind them. Cicely took a seat while Dr. McClellan walked around his desk to his chair.

"But, physically?" He regarded her closely from across the heavy desk.

"Oh, all right. I get shaky at night sometimes. After one of the bad dreams."

"Some of your dreams depict violent situations," he told her. "They suggest a subconscious urge that may place you in a dangerous predicament. You want to look out for this."

The psychiatrist consulted the notes on the desk before him. "In a way," he said, "we live more in our minds than we do in physical locations. Everything we encounter, all that happens to us, is filtered through our perceptions, so the realm beyond our bodies is entirely a mental structure. Our memories are the vestiges of such structures."

"Like listening to someone talk over the phone with a bad connection, and then trying to remember what was said," said Cicely.

"Yes, that's part of it, and also, memory is selective even when it is not faulty. Your dreams are a representation, maybe an elaboration, of past experiences."

"But I recall no such experience."

"Not now, but be prepared to accept such recollections should they appear."

"Before I forget, Doctor. I have something for you." Cicely retrieved an audio cassette from her handbag and handed it to Dr. McClellan.

He took the cassette and examined it. Cicely's name and a date was penciled on the label.

"I have been recording recollections of my dreams, while they are fresh on my mind. You can listen to them when you have time."

"I use a digital recorder for our sessions,' said Dr. McClellan.

"I know. I prefer cassettes. When I inherited my MGB it came with a cassette player. I didn't use it for a time, but then Mrs. Dalgetty gave me a cassette recorder and I've become accustomed to mixing my own tapes to listen on the road. Now I found another use."

"I don't have a cassette player," said Dr. McClellan, holding up the cassette.

"Oh, you'll have to get one, Doctor. See, the nice thing is you can continue listening to a cassette right where you left off when you insert it, and I will write dates on the labels so you can keep them sorted."

Dr. McClellan put the cassette on a desk drawer, made a note for his secretary to buy a cassette player, and returned his attention to his patient. "Have you felt a need recently to do something particularly impulsive? Something you might not ordinarily consider?"

"No, Doctor," Cicely said. "That is," she paused, uncertain, "I've become closer to Greg. We've made love."

"Tell me how things stand between the two of you."

Cicely talked for a while about her boyfriend and their somewhat detached relationship. She thought Greg was more detached than she was.

"I see no real issues there, Cicely. Do you?"

Cicely searched for the right words. "It is a bit wild of me. I haven't known Greg for very long, really. We do have a lot in common, and it's been nice with him, but I'm not sure I want to make a permanent attachment. I've been so upset with the dreams and all; I'm concerned that he might notice. I've told him nothing of my problems, you see."

She sighed. "I'm afraid, if I tell him, he'll think I'm batty. Which I am, I guess," she added, ruefully. "Shall I tell you about my last dream? I talked about it in the cassette."

"Just tell me a bit now. I will listen to the recording later."

Cicely closed her eyes. "I was Vivian. It was cold..."

2

They stood next to a buzzing printer, anxiously waiting for the results of the latest computer run. Vivian looked up from the printer and regarded the others. She wore a navy skirt and a white blouse that fit closely to the curves of her body.

Robinson, in beltless charcoal slacks and a blue long-sleeved shirt, tapped nervously on the printer with a pen. "It's taking too long again," he said.

Lawrence frowned and shook his head slowly. Next to him stood a man of fifty-five, wearing a rumpled white suit. He was Cyril Lehnert, Robinson's cipher expert.

Around them was equipment that could have belonged to a bank's data processing department. The gray boxy shapes of computers, disk drives and workstations were arranged in rows about the windowless room.

Vivian shivered. The room, attached to the main structure of Robinson's house, was kept at 68 degrees Fahrenheit. It was Cyril Lehnert's preserve.

The printer's clatter finally stopped, and Lehnert pressed a button on the side of the unit. The machine ejected the last sheets of paper and the older man ripped them off. He took the stack of computer paper to a nearby table and they all crowded about it.

"Not the right key," said Lehnert, shaking his head. He was thin and tall, slightly stooped. When he spoke a gold molar flashed in the bright overhead light. "I'll keep trying, but it's a tough cipher. It could take us several days," he gestured toward the gray forms of the computers.

"I don't have the time, Lehnert," said Robinson, impatiently.

"I can only continue to try," said Lehnert, shrugging his shoulders and paging through the listing.

Robinson started to reach for his pipe, but stopped in midmotion, glancing at the NO SMOKING sign on the wall. He frowned.

"All right, keep trying," Robinson said. He pondered for a moment. "But there is something else we can do."

"And what would that be?" asked Lehnert.

"Have a copy of the input data made," Robinson answered. He turned to face Vivian. "I have an assignment for you. You will be flying to Baltimore the day after tomorrow."

Lehnert looked up from the listing. "What is this all about?"

"I want to make an independent effort to decipher the document," Robinson said. "While you continue your effort here, I want to run the data through the NSA decryption programs. Miss Venables will help us do that."

Robinson turned to Lawrence. "Let's meet in the library in one hour, after I make a call. I need some research done. You may have to work late tonight."

"And just how," asked Lehnert, "will you get the NSA to do this bit of work for us?"

"They won't know how helpful they will have been," Robinson said, grinning.

3

"I don't understand," Dr. McClellan said, "why it is that you are particularly concerned about this dream." He waited a moment for a response from Cicely, but there was none.

"Did you find it particularly frightening?"

Cicely slowly shook her head. "On the contrary, Doctor. It was," she searched for the right word, "more remote."

She felt her pulse quickening. "Oh, why did this keep going on and on?" She thought. There had to be an end to it. The doctor had told her not to hold anything back. "I'm feeling very anxious now, Doctor," she said. "I'm not well."

Dr. McClellan rose and went around his desk to stand by Cicely. He took her arm by the wrist and looked at his watch. Her pulse was 130, her breathing agitated.

"Close your eyes," he said, "and lean your head back against the chair. Just lie back and relax, Cicely."

She did as she was told, a lone tear rolling down her pale cheek.

"Relax," Dr. McClellan repeated. "Take a deep breath and hold it."

Cicely obeyed.

"Now let go of your breath. Let your body go completely loose and limp. Say to yourself, I feel relaxed." Dr. McClellan spoke in a soft, measured voice. Gradually, Cicely's tenseness subsided.

"How are you feeling now?" Dr. McClellan asked.

Cicely opened her eyes.

"I'm all right," she said.

"Splendid." Dr. McClellan consulted his watch. "We still have a few minutes."

Cicely looked at her watch also. The doctor's time was costing her a fortune. She was determined to make use of every minute.

"The dream didn't frighten me particularly," she spoke hesitatingly. "It made me concerned because it was different."

"In which way different?"

"The texture. And I wasn't there."

Dr. McClellan raised his eyebrows.

"That's the feeling I had: Charles wasn't there."

"I see," Dr. McClellan said, starting to feel very concerned about Cicely's deteriorating prognosis.

<h1 style="text-align:center">4</h1>

Vivian rented a gold Chevrolet from Hertz at Baltimore-Washington International Airport and traveled southwest on Highway 295, the Baltimore-Washington Parkway. It was midafternoon, and the light traffic moved swiftly through tree covered rolling hills. She monitored the odometer closely, as Robinson and Lawrence had instructed her to do. To her left was Fort George G. Meade. A few minutes later she exited onto Savage Road.

She drove on for a few hundred yards. The road widened. Before her was a Cyclone fence topped with a V of barbed wire. A few moments later she came to a wide gate. Beyond, in a shallow depression surrounded by pine trees, were the buildings of the National Security Agency. She took a deep breath.

Before leaving Miami, she had spent a whole day training for her mission. Robinson had a mockup of the NSA facility constructed to familiarize her with the approaches and the acres of parking lots. Lawrence had flown a man in to coach her on how to move within the facility without attracting undue attention to herself.

There were two Marine guards at the gate. A sign by the gate said SPEED LIMIT 20. She slowed down to 25, the speed of the car ahead of her. As she came to the gate she held up the fake ID badge she had been provided with and smiled. The Marine waved her on.

She passed another fence, which Robinson had told her was electrified, and then a third. In her mind, she reviewed once again what she was to do. "Behave confidently," Robinson had told her, "never hesitate. Move deliberately and rapidly, as you would if you owned the place."

Driving 5 miles per hour over the speed limit, she navigated a tortuous route through the maze of lanes to the space marked S237. She parked and locked the Chevrolet. The main building was a quarter mile away. It was a three story structure of concrete, glass and steel. Behind it was the nine-story Operations Building Annex. She walked towards it, carrying in her purse a thumb drive with the encrypted data.

Vivian spotted the glass entry doors and headed towards them. A balding black man in a rumpled brown suit walked hurriedly past her. She quickened her steps, trying to keep up with him. There were few people about, and it would be best to appear to be accompanying someone. She followed two paces behind the man.

As she neared the doors she clipped the NSA Contractor's badge to the lapel of her dark blue business suit. "What a nice day," she said to the man ahead of her.

The man half turned towards her, without interrupting his stride. "Ah, yes," he said, as he reached the door and pulled it open. Vivian used the moment to catch up with him. He held the door open for her.

There was a Marine guard just inside the door. He wore a sidearm, like the ones at the gate. Vivian met his glance for an instant and moved on, unchallenged. The black man followed her inside and turned right, as hurried as ever.

She walked on to a bank of elevators. Another Marine paced back and forth there. She pushed the UP button and waited for the elevator to arrive.

The Marine looked at her, appreciating her figure. She gave him a frosty smile. The elevator seemed to take forever. Two other people joined her, a young man holding a thin briefcase and a stout older woman in a green skirt and white blouse.

This was the part of an assignment that Vivian enjoyed the most: the start of the action, when events she had only imagined began to actually unfold, after the tedious briefings and preparations were over, but before the nasty, dangerous twists that often occurred began to happen. She felt a trace of fear and consciously welcomed it, knowing it would help focus her attention. Deeper in her mind, the little fear excited her and set loose eddies of dark pleasure.

The elevator doors opened and three men walked out. Vivian moved in, followed by the other two. "I don't know if the RFP is ready, but we can ask Keith Franklin," said the man, as Vivian pressed the button for the second floor. "Three please," said the woman. Vivian pressed that button and the elevator doors closed in front of her.

"I don't think Mr. Franklin will know, David," said the woman behind her. The elevator accelerated swiftly, and just as swiftly came to a stop, leaving a queasy feeling in Vivian's stomach. The doors opened automatically and she stepped out onto a spacious hallway.

She turned left and walked briskly down the hall. There were a few people about, all walking with the detached single-mindedness of men and women going about customary tasks. Vivian tried to imitate them, while fiercely concentrating on spotting room 2049. The odd-numbered doorways were to her right. She passed 2061, then 2059. It must be close, she thought.

As she walked further down the hallway she noticed something that sent a chill down her spine. The hallway was partially blocked by a desk. A Marine guard sat behind it, looking straight at her. It was a checkpoint. She slowed her pace. Why hadn't they told her about this!

She passed 2055. Ahead, a man in a light blue suit stopped at the desk and handed over his identification badge to the guard. The Marine looked the blue-suited man and then his card over carefully. Vivian suspected her fake badge would not pass such close scrutiny. Her hand tightened on her purse.

About thirty feet from the guard's desk she passed the door to room 2051. She could see 2049 ahead, immediately before the security checkpoint. Although she would not have to enter the secured area, she would have to walk within three feet of the Marine in order to enter room 2049.

Vivian walked on, giving the guard one last glance. She directed her eyes away from him and toward the entrance to room 2049. Her stomach tensed and sweat ran down her back and between her breasts. She felt the man's eyes on her, but ignored the impulse to peep back at him. The entry to the room, unlike most others, had no door. She went inside.

The room was smaller than she expected. It was square, about fifteen feet to the side. A gray metal table was pushed against the wall to the left. It was covered with computer listings in neat stacks and a cardboard tray filled with printed forms. The right wall was bare except for a large electric clock. The far end was a honeycomb of rectangular cells about eighteen inches deep. About a third of them contained diskettes, USB flash drives, optical data disks or computer listings, the rest were empty. A balding man in striped slacks and a white shirt squatted with his back to Vivian, removing a listing from one of the lower receptacles.

She went to the table and looked in the cardboard tray for a blue job submittal form, as she had been told. There were none. "Oh, God," she said.

"What could she do now?" She thought. Leave and try again later? Robinson had been in too much of a hurry and had left too much to chance. If she wasn't careful she could end up in jail over this.

"Excuse me." The voice startled her. It was a short plump woman in a brown suit. Vivian moved away from the table, making room for the woman.

"I can't find the job submittal forms," Vivian said.

The plump woman glanced at the tray and shook her head. She placed a cardboard box she had been carrying on the table and walked angrily to the back of the room. "Julius," she cried out, peering through the honeycomb of pickup boxes at the computer room beyond. "You guys are out of blue forms again, Dodo."

Vivian smiled.

5

Vivian walked hurriedly along the crowded airport hallway, past a fast-food stand. She held a carryon suitcase in one hand and in the other her handbag. Her eyes scanned a row of blue telephone booths lining the gray wall to her right. They were all occupied.

She glanced at a clock on the wall and stopped. Putting her suitcase down, she waited impatiently until a teenage boy wearing a University of Maryland T-shirt left one of the booths.

Moving swiftly, Vivian just beat a burly businessman to the vacant booth. She set down her suitcase, placed her purse on top of it, inserted quarters into the telephone's coin slot, and dialed a long distance number.

"Hello." It was Robinson's voice. There was a barely audible background sound, like from a muffled voice.

"Robinson?" Vivian asked.

"Yes. How did it go?"

"Not well. I'm at a phone booth. I have a flight out of Dulles in twenty minutes. Are you alone?" There was an eddy of anxiety in her voice.

"No." Robinson sounded a bit distressed.

"Is Cyril with you?"

There was a pause. "Yes."

"The results were negative. Your man inside broke cover to tell me the details. Gave me a scare. He said there was nothing meaningful in the thumb drive. Just random data. No pattern at all."

"Are you all right?"

"I'm fine, just worried," Vivian said. "Perhaps there's been a mistake of some sort. I have to go now. See you first thing in the morning."

"Wait." She overheard a question from someone in Robinson's office. "Who is that on the phone?" a faint male voice asked.

"Miss Venables," Robinson said offline. "It seems things didn't work out. She'll be in tomorrow morning. Better plan on meeting with her first thing, Lehnert. At my office."

"Did you hear that?" Robinson's voice became clearer.

"Yes, sir."

"I will ask Mr. Lawrence to sit in as well," Robinson said. He sounded worried. "Goodbye."

"Good night, sir."

Vivian picked up her small suitcase and her purse and set off at a rapid pace toward the gate. While she walked through the fast-moving crowd, her eyes drifted past the hurrying travelers and the airline posters on the walls of the concourse. In her mind, she went over the series of events relating to the data on the thumb drive. She knew Robinson would be doing the same.

There was a short wait at the gate, and then an airport bus took her to the airplane. She had felt an unpleasant suspicion since her conversation with Wickes. Robinson had given the microfilm of the Arteaga document to Cyril Lehnert for decryptment. To facilitate his analysis, Lehnert transcribed the document to electronic form and stored it in his computer's hard drive.

The data on the thumb drive she had taken to Baltimore was copied directly off Lehnert's computer. And it had random data. Or so Wickes had told her. Perhaps it was all some stupid accident and Lehnert had made backup copies; in which case there would only be a delay. But how could Lehnert not have noticed? It could be that Lehnert's original record had been altered by someone in Robinson's organization and his computer now held only random data. If it occurred to Robinson that someone who wanted the document suppressed had penetrated his outfit he would be furious.

Minutes later the airplane took off, roaring into the sky and banking away from the setting sun. Vivian worked the crossword puzzle in the airline magazine, then started to read a story on the growing wine industry of Texas. But she stopped halfway through the article and stuffed the magazine into the pocket at the back of the seat before her. She looked out of her window at the passing darkening clouds. She did that for a long time.

CHAPTER 4
REVELATION

1

Dr. McClellan made an entry on his note pad and returned the gold pen to its holder on his desk. "What has been your experience so far with the relaxation exercises? Have they helped you?"

"I've been doing them at least once a day," Cicely said. "Most days I play the recording twice, as you asked me to. I haven't been as nervous lately."

"That's good," Dr. McClellan said. "Have you had any more of the special dreams?"

"Yes. I still get very upset right after, but it's a bit easier to calm down."

Cicely looked for a moment at the lower of the four landscape paintings behind Dr. McClellan's desk. The other three had lakes and hills in them. This one had a rugged shoreline and a narrow beach facing a blue-green sea.

"Doctor," she said, "I read an article the other day; a column in the Times."

Cicely brushed a strand of hair away from her face.

"Go on, Cicely."

"Well, it seems silly, but this woman heard music every once in a while. In her head. They found out it came from a bridge on her teeth. It was picking up radio broadcasts."

"I'm not sure if I read that particular story, but I've read about similar cases. Bits of metal or ceramics act like a radio receiver and stimulate the auditory system."

"Well," Cicely said, "I wondered if something similar could be happening to me. When I dream, I mean."

Dr. McClellan swiveled in his chair so that he faced Cicely squarely. "Do you have any bridgework on your teeth?"

"No."

"Fillings or capped teeth?"

"No, I never have had cavities."

"It is dental work of some sort, or a metal part used in prosthetic surgery, that sometimes acts as a radio frequency amplifier," Dr. McClellan said.

Cicely sighed. "I'm just trying to make sense of things."

"There is a neurological disorder, musical hallucination, which causes hearing of scraps of music. But your experiences are based on the presentation of well-organized sequences, including both aural and visual elements." Dr. McClellan paused for a moment. "I think it is most likely that what you experience are your own dreams. Don't you think so?"

"I guess so, Doctor," Cicely said, sheepishly.

"Later we will practice the relaxation exercise again," said Dr. McClellan, swiveling his chair to look slightly away from Cicely. "But, first, tell me about your latest dream."

Cicely leaned back in the deep easy chair. "In this one I was Vivian again…"

2

She walked hastily down the hall, taking a last glance at the watch on her left wrist. Its tiny hands told her she was ten minutes late. In her right hand she held the thumb drive she had taken to the NSA. She had forgotten it when she first left her apartment that morning, and going back for it had cost her a few minutes.

Robinson's library was the last room on the left. Vivian knocked twice on the heavy mahogany door. A muffled voice from inside invited her in. She turned the sculptured glass knob and rushed inside.

A blond-haired young man in a seersucker suit stood by the table at the center of the room, thumbing through a stack of envelopes. It was Victor Hardgrave, one of Robinson's assistants. There was no one else in the room.

"You are late, dear," he said, continuing to sort through the mail.

"I know, Victor. Where is Robinson?"

Hardgrave looked up, interrupting his task. "They left a few minutes ago. I passed them on my way here."

"They?" Vivian asked.

Hardgrave went back to sorting the mail. "Mr. Robinson, Ben and Cyril. They probably went to crypto."

Vivian turned around and headed for the door. She felt a wave of a peculiar discomfort, like a vague unsettling presentiment.

"Mr. Robinson looked like he was in a fairly bad mood," volunteered Hardgrave.

"Great!" Shaking her head, Vivian walked out of Robinson's library.

She hurried down the hall and then turned, heading for the north side of the house. In a minute she reached the cryptography section. Still holding the flash memory drive in her hand, she opened the door and entered a room lined with file cabinets.

The only occupant was a girl in a khaki blouse, busily writing on green-lined yellow paper. She didn't wait for Vivian's question but pointed with her pencil at the door to the computer room.

Vivian walked past the girl and down a row of desks and file cabinets to the far end of the room. She opened the heavy door there and strode into the computer room. In an instant she realized there was something wrong.

Robinson and Benjamin Lawrence stood next to each other by a printer near the center of the room, their faces tense and drawn. Cyril Lehnert was backing toward Vivian while pointing an automatic pistol at the other two.

"If you make the slightest move I'll shoot," Lehnert was saying, "I'll shoot you both. The film has been destroyed, Robinson, there is nothing for you to gain. It wasn't yours to begin with."

"You'll never get away, Cyril," Lawrence said.

"Oh, I think I will," Lehnert said, raising his pistol to aim directly at Lawrence's head. "This room is soundproof."

Vivian stood by the door. Lawrence hadn't seen her yet, but Robinson had, and Lehnert would notice her in a moment.

At once, with a motion full of power and swift precision, she threw the thumb drive at Lehnert. The device traversed the room in an instant and scored a direct hit, audibly impacting the back of Lehnert's head. Completely startled, the man slipped, speechless, and as he dropped his skull cracked against the metal edge of the table by his side. A moment later Robinson drew a revolver and put a bullet in him. Lehnert's eyelids pulled macabrely back from his rolling eyes. His pistol skidded over a table and then clattered to the floor.

Vivian, Robinson and Lawrence looked at the lifeless form, their bodies frozen. For a moment, the room was totally silent.

3

Cicely sat on the grass in the shade of a tree, her legs tucked under her. It was midmorning, and she was using the recess period to write a letter to Angie, who was vacationing at Ibiza.

It was that rarity, a perfect English day. The sky was bright and blue, the grass a perfect green, and a soft spring breeze tugged lightly at her hair. She was writing of this to Angie, a fond smile on her face.

"Miss Denfeld."

Cicely looked up from her letter. It was Rosalie.

"Miss Denfeld, where has Charlie gone to?"

Cicely looked past the girl at the other children playing about the schoolyard. She didn't see Charlie Gallagher's red hair among the group.

"Have you seen him, Miss? We need one more for our team." Rosalie pointed at three other children behind her, waiting listlessly for their missing playmate.

Cicely smiled at the girl. "I saw him walking with Jeremy a few minutes ago. They went…"

"Oh, I know where Jeremy is," Rosalie said, turning to run away. "Thank you, Miss Denfeld."

Cicely looked after the running girl for a moment, and then a thought struck her, just as she was resuming writing her letter. Charles Ryder had not appeared in her dreams for several nights—it had been Vivian. She had wondered where he was. And now she knew.

Charles was at his home in the city of Edmonds, near Seattle, in the state of Washington. In America.

All of a sudden Cicely knew that, and more. Charles was not a professional agent, like Vivian. He was an engineer, and he had returned to his job in Seattle. Robinson had only hired Charles for the Arteaga case, because he knew Leo Arteaga and was able to identify him, and because Charles spoke Spanish. He had lived in Cuba as a child when his father, a Marine, was stationed…

She felt a pressure in her brow, and her pulse started to quicken. Slowly, she put down her letter and pen, closed her eyes, and started to do the relaxation exercise Dr. McClellan had taught her.

That evening, at her apartment, Cicely placed a transatlantic telephone call. She asked for directory assistance in the state of Washington in the United States.

"City, please," said the oddly metallic voice.

"Edmonds," Cicely answered.

"Name."

"Charles Ryder."

"Spell the last name."

"R-Y-D-E-R."

There was a long pause.

"I have no listing by that name," the operator said.

4

There were three of them and Robinson. They were in Robinson's office. The three, Charles, Vivian and a wiry short man named Gaspar Miro, sat in stark chairs across Robinson's desk.

"We're very glad you could join us again, Ryder," Robinson said.

Charles shifted uneasily in his chair. Gray pants, a white button-down shirt and a blue blazer draped neatly over his tall frame. Leaning forward, he focused his gray eyes on Vivian, then let his gaze drift to Robinson. "I have been told of the, uh, problem you've had, and your offer is…extremely generous. But you must understand, I cannot keep taking leaves from my job."

Robinson nodded. "I do understand, Mr. Ryder, and I am extremely grateful for your cooperation. This shouldn't take more than a couple of days." He took a long drag from his pipe. "As Miss Venables has told you, we have lost the microfilm you obtained from Mr. Arteaga. We are still looking for copies that may have been made, but, frankly, I do not have much hope along those lines. There may be another way, a different type of search. One that depends on you, Mr. Ryder."

He paused briefly, as if to let his words sink in. "No one looked at the film Mrs. Lopez gave you, except for Mr. Lehnert, and he," Robinson glanced at Miro, "has unfortunately departed for an extended assignment abroad. But you saw the originals, the computer listings."

"I saw them only for a moment," Charles said.

"No, Charles," Vivian said, "you told us, remember. You were with Arteaga and he showed you the computer listings. You read them."

Charles turned to face her. "It was gibberish!"

Vivian shook her head. "Not the index. You said the index was in plaintext. You read it."

"You told us that during the debriefing," asserted Robinson.

Charles nodded slowly. "Yes, it was like a table of contents."

Robinson leaned forward across the desk. "There may be something, some information, in that table of contents that we can follow up on."

Charles shook his head. "But I can't remember. I only read it once."

Robinson smiled briefly. "You probably can remember more than you expect." He looked at the wiry short man sitting next to Charles. "Dr. Miro will help with that. He's a professor at the University of Miami."

"Dr. Miro is a philologist," Vivian added. "He also is a memory expert."

The short man beamed. "What we experience is stored in our minds," he said, tapping the side of his head. "And we can retrieve a good part of what is in there."

"Memory works in stages," said Dr. Miro. "A copy of the external stimulus is held in sensory storage briefly. If one attends to the stimulus, it is entered into short-term memory and encoded. The coded data then passes into long term memory. Once there, a memory is never completely lost."

Dr. Miro had appropriated one of the rooms in the north side of Robinson's house. He had insisted on comfortable chairs for everyone, but particularly for Charles. After some haggling Victor Hardgrave had produced them, as well as an overhead projector and a voice recorder. Now Dr. Miro sat at one end of the table supporting the equipment, a projection screen behind him. Charles and Vivian sat across from him. The voice recorder had been turned on.

"Now let's go back to the point where you first took a close look at the listing," Dr. Miro said. "You are at the table, Mr. Arteaga is next to you. Picture yourself there, Mr. Ryder."

Charles closed his eyes. For an hour, he had been trying to recreate that last meeting with Leo Arteaga.

"The top sheets are flipped back, and now you are looking down on a printed page. What do you see?"

Charles waited for a moment. He spoke slowly, "It's a page of text, all caps. At the very top it says TOP SECRET. That is followed by a warning, something about unauthorized access and U.S. Code provisions."

"Very good," Dr. Miro said, "we'll skip the details about that paragraph for now. What do you see next?"

Charles made an effort to remember, but the details were missing. "There's a title, but it's like a rough draft perhaps, there are a lot of abbreviations. I think a part is missing. Omitted on purpose."

"Tell us the parts that you can remember."

"It says REPORT OF something OF THE SAB or SAC on EE."

"Good. We'll come back to this later. What's next?"

Charles shook his head. "There are some short words. Numbers. Like a document number. I don't remember."

"What is below that, Charles?" Vivian asked.

"Several lines, numbered. A table of contents. There are five or six items in all."

"What does the first item say?"

Charles shook his head. "I can't remember. I can't remember the order of the things. Just scraps."

Dr. Miro had been writing with a grease pencil on a sheet of plastic foil. He now turned on the overhead projector and a sketch of the document Charles was describing appeared on the screen behind him. "Tell us anything that comes to your mind. We'll worry about the order later," he said.

"An extract, T-I-E-C-K, a name I think. Some more acronyms or abbreviations. UCB, IR, MW. Anomaly. Variance anomaly, something like that."

"That's very good, Mr. Ryder," Dr. Miro said, encouragingly.

"There are some words, names or something, they don't make sense. Something representations. B-I-T-H-I-N, a word like that. Something model. That's the second or third entry, near the top…"

They went on for three more hours, Dr. Miro's grease pencil adding details more and more slowly. They met again the next day, after Charles had a chance to sleep and clear his mind. Vivian had someone from the computer section type up what they had, using computer printer fonts like those Charles would have seen in the original. It helped Charles recall a few more details.

They went over the matter again and again. Then, in midafternoon, Dr. Miro pronounced his job done. He asked for Robinson to be called in.

"This is fairly close to what Mr. Ryder saw," Dr. Miro said, pointing to the projection on the screen behind him. "He may remember a few additional details later."

Robinson, Hardgrave and Lawrence sat with Charles and Vivian across from the beaming professor.

"I've put X's or N's where there are known lost elements. X's for letters, N's for numbers. I believe we have achieved about sixty per cent recall."

After Dr. Miro's departure, the others remained, continuing to look at the image projected on the screen. Robinson was the first to speak. "Still cryptic, eh?" he observed.

"It may have been made deliberately so," Lawrence offered. "It was the only part of the document that was not encoded. The rest, it seems, was classified at a higher security level. The abbreviations could be explained as an effort to declassify this page to Top Secret."

"But why didn't they encode this too?" Charles asked.

TOP SECRET

EXAM. BY UNAUTHORIZED PERSONS IS A CRIMINAL
OFFENSE.   WHEN HANDLING REVIEW PROV. U.S.
CODE TITLE 18, SEC. NNN, NNN

RPT. OF THE XXXXXX XXXXXX S.A.B. ON E.E. AND

PART 1
XXNNNN

1   NRO EXTRACT OF XXXXX TIECK (UCB) THESIS ON
    XXXXXXXX IR/MW RAD. VARIANCE ANOMALY S.W.
    SECT.

2   EVXXXXXX BITHIAN REPRESENTATIONS—COSPENC
    MODEL

3   PROJECTS GILGAMESH AND OZMA

4   XXXXXX XXXXXXX AUTOPSY RPT. ON X.X. NESTER,
    COL., USAF (OSI)

5   XXXXXX XXXXXXXX DATA ON E.E. NNN, HR 56
    88NN, LA NN 212NN

6   THE AMES XXXXX XXXX XXXX RPT. ON AUTOMATON
    XXXXXX

PREPARED BY
XXXXXXX XXXXXXX

DO NOT REPRODUCE XXXXXXX XXXXXXX
XXXXXX XXXXXX

"The document may have been too awkward to handle otherwise," Vivian answered. "To navigate from one section to another and so forth. Decryption was probably slow, and they may have consulted this index frequently."

Lawrence shook his head. "This doesn't tell us much," he said. "The real information is in the missing encoded material."

Robinson banged his fist on the table. "Damn!" he said. "We should have paid more attention to what Lehnert was doing. There are all manner of key words here. It should have been possible to break that code."

"If we ever get the rest of the document back we'll be able to do that, Mr. Robinson," Hardgrave said.

"Little chance of that," Robinson muttered.

"Perhaps there is enough information here," Vivian said. She pointed at the screen. "It seems like a collection of data, doesn't it? Various reports. If we can figure out what the reports are, we may be able to obtain them."

"You may be right." Robinson turned in his chair to face Charles directly. "I would like you to stay with this for the rest of the week, Ryder."

Charles sighed. He pointed at the image on the screen. "This is labeled Top Secret." He gestured toward Lawrence. "You are a lawyer, Ben. What does the law say about us dealing with this stuff? What does U.S. Code, Title 18, mean to us?"

Lawrence looked at Robinson briefly, and then turned to Charles.

"Title 18 of the United States Criminal Code defines federal laws related to espionage, sabotage and related matters," he said. "Unauthorized possession of the original of this document could be a crime, depending on our intent. To be found absent of malice we would be required to return it to its rightful owner."

Lawrence paused for a moment, deliberating on his choice of words. "We do not have the original. We have a partial recollection of what may have been an unauthorized copy. Specific ownership is undetermined. I would say that, as long as we do not use this information to the injury of the United States, we will not be in violation of the Code."

"In a way we are acting for the FBI," Robinson said. "It was my intent to turn the document over to them, but there is little to turn over now." Concern showed on his face. "I lost a man over this, before you became involved, Ryder. Then Arteaga and the Lopez woman were killed, and now Lehnert subverted. It's not the way I would expect a U.S. Government agency to proceed."

"But this must have originated within the government," Charles said.

Robinson nodded. He turned to Vivian. "I want you to work this full time. Use anyone you need. Concentrate on the document."

"I'll follow up on Lehnert's records," Hardgrave said.

"Yes," Robinson nodded, "and see what you can dig up on Arteaga. Maybe he left behind notes, or a copy of the document."

# REGRESSION

CHAPTER 5
RED TERROR

1

It was a cloudy day, warm and breezy. The heat and the wind conspired to rapidly erase the remaining evidence of the early morning rain. Vivian drove the red Mustang convertible slowly under the canopy of shade trees. Next to her, Charles looked attentively at the houses they passed. They were mostly single story, stucco, with flat roofs and concrete block or brick walls. Charles didn't find them attractive, but he knew their chunky sturdiness would withstand hurricanes well.

"The next block, I think," Vivian said. She kept some of her attention on the empty street ahead as she leaned toward the central console, repeatedly pressing the radio push buttons until she heard a song to her liking. Suddenly, Lady Gaga was singing *Poker Face*, and Vivian returned her full attention to the road.

"Nice neighborhood." Charles turned his head and faced Vivian as they slowed down for the approaching intersection. Her skirt had slipped well up her thighs, and his eyes swept over her well-formed legs. "Tell me about the man we are supposed to meet," he asked.

"They call him the wise man. He's a researcher."

Vivian paused, stopping the car momentarily to let a pink Lincoln pass. "Mr. Robinson has worked with him before. He might be able to help us."

They drove across the street. There was no other traffic and Vivian steered the Mustang very close to the curb on the leaf-strewn street. Charles turned his attention again to the houses they slowly passed.

"This is it," he said, indicating a single-story white stucco house with a roof of fired clay tiles.

The door was wide and high. It was painted sky blue, like the shuttered windows. There was no door bell, and Charles used the gleaming brass knocker.

Moments later they were greeted by a smiling girl, about thirteen, slim and brown-haired. She wore a plain white dress.

"We'd like to see Mr. Swan," Vivian said. "I called earlier."

"You are Miss Venables?"

"Yes."

"Please come in," said the girl in a clear voice. She held herself very erect and then took a studied bow, letting them into the house. "What is your name, sir?" She spoke with a slight Spanish accent.

"Charles Ryder," he answered. "And yours?"

"I'm Gisela," she said, closing the door behind them. "Please follow me."

The girl took them down a short hall to a small windowless room with walls painted in a yellow-gold shade. The only pieces of furniture were a card table and chairs, and a mahogany and glass cabinet displaying Chinese pottery. A few pictures hung on the walls: black and white photographs of sailboats and girls in their early teens at the beach.

"Alden is expecting you. He will join you soon," said Gisela, smiling.

"I go tell him that you're here," she added, walking away with swift gracefulness.

"Pretty girl," Vivian observed.

"More than pretty," said Charles, looking into the hallway where she had gone.

Gisela returned a moment later. "Alden is delayed," she said apologetically. "He has received an urgent call and will be busy for some time. Can you wait for a few minutes?"

"We can wait," said Vivian.

"Please sit down," said Gisela, indicating the chairs around the card table.

The three of them sat down, but after a moment of silence Gisela rose. "I'll be back in a moment," she said, and walked away.

She soon came back, bearing a tray that she laid down on the table. "We'll play the Jewel Game while we wait," she said, sitting down again.

The tray held several objects, some were semiprecious stones of various kinds, others were a mix of personal ornaments and household utility and decorative items. "Take a look at these things," Gisela said.

Charles and Vivian gazed at the items. There were about a dozen of them. "But not for long," said the girl, and soon proceeded to cover the tray with a tablecloth.

Gisela ripped off two sheets from a small ring-bound notebook and handed one sheet each and a pencil to Vivian and Charles. "You have a couple of minutes to write down a list of the items you just saw. The one that lists the most correctly wins."

Charles and Vivian both found it easy to recall the first few items, but harder to remember what the others had been. Gisela seemed delighted to see them frown and glare in concentration at the covered tray.

Vivian won the first game, and Gisela collected the tray and left to bring it back with changed objects for a second round. While they waited, Charles and Vivian silently turned their attention to the room they were in.

The articles in the cabinet were meticulously arranged. The top two shelves held exquisitely decorated porcelain plates. The third shelf held vases and pots. The lowest shelf displayed delicate porcelain figurines.

Both Charles and Vivian were drawn to the collection. Vivian was examining one of the plates closely when they were joined by their host.

The man facing them wore a white suit. He was of medium height and build, with thinning blond hair, and appeared to be in his early forties.

"Good day," he said. "I'm Alden Swan. Sorry for the wait."

"Hello," Charles said. They introduced themselves.

"This is beautiful," exclaimed Vivian, indicating one of the plates she had been admiring.

"Yes," said Swan, approaching them. "It's a favorite. It was made for the emperor Kien Lung."

"From a Chinese emperor," remarked Vivian, impressed. "It's so perfect. Is it very old?"

"The plates are fairly recent; most were created two or three centuries ago." Swan motioned toward the lower part of the cabinet. "The vases are older. My oldest is Sung dynasty. Tenth century."

"These are wonderful works of art, Mr. Swan," Charles said. "You must know a lot about Chinese porcelain."

"I know a lot about many things, Mr. Ryder," Swan stated. "Chinese ceramics were developed and used throughout Chinese history. They reflect a symbolism useful in understanding their attitudes toward life and death."

For a moment Swan glanced in admiration at his collection. He then turned his attention to his guests. "I am Curator of Oriental Arts at the Museum of Fine Arts," he said. "But I suspect you did not come to see me for that reason."

"We were told," said Vivian, "that you could assist us in obtaining some information."

Swan smiled. "Libraries and newspaper morgues have information. What I offer is wisdom."

2

"There is something else I wanted to tell you, Doctor," said Cicely, glancing at her watch. Her hour was almost up.

Dr. McClellan used a stubby pencil to write down a few notes on Cicely's history form. "Was that all of the dream?"

"No, there was some more."

Cicely shifted her position in the chair. Dr. McClellan looked at her closely. She had appeared fairly relaxed during the session, but now he noted that an uneasiness had crept over her.

"I wanted to make sure I didn't forget to tell you about this other thing. It's happened only a few times." She felt her pulse begin to quicken. "Relax," she thought, taking a deep breath. She knew Dr. McClellan was staring at her, and she turned her eyes away from his, to the landscapes on the wall above him.

"I get a feeling, no, not a feeling, it's a flash, and I know something."

Dr. McClellan put down his pencil. "A flash? Like light?"

Cicely shook her head. She looked directly at the doctor. "No, I mean something quick. Like I was at school one day and all of a sudden I knew, I just knew, where Charles lives. His hometown. Edmonds, near Seattle."

"You had a sudden insight," Dr. McClellan spoke slowly, choosing his words deliberately. "While awake."

"Yes, and a certainty that I am right," Cicely reported.

"This indicates some progress, Cicely."

She smiled, gently tugging at a strand of her hair. "It's progress, Doctor, but for better or worse?"

"I should say for better. As you know, one remembers only part of what one dreams. You should be able to recall daylight musings better than nightmares. It will make it easier for us to identify the cause of your problems."

"They are more than musings," she protested.

"Of course, Cicely. But the daytime insight experience was less taxing than your last dream, no?"

"There was no panic," she conceded.

A buzzer went off momentarily in Dr. McClellan's watch. It indicated the session would soon be over.

"Let's discuss that next time," the doctor said. "And I want to hear the rest of that dream."

Cicely and Dr. McClellan both stood up. She started to walk to the door, then stopped suddenly. "I just had another one," she said, turning toward Dr. McClellan. "Another…insight. The house they were in. The wise man's house. It's in a place called Coral Gables. In Florida, near Miami. That just came to me; it was not in the dream."

3

Swan led Charles and Vivian through a short hallway into a large room, and invited them to sit down on a comfortable couch. He sat across from them in a high-backed stuffed chair.

There was a door at the end of the room opposite to the hallway. In the center of the room, between them and Swan, a low table held a silver tray with an assortment of chocolates. All the walls, from floor to ceiling, held row upon row of books.

Swan picked up a cube of chocolate. "Please have some," he said. "They're Swiss. I only buy the best."

Both Charles and Vivian obliged him.

Swan looked at them with an unsteady gaze. Vivian had brought a copy of Dr. Miro's recreation of the document. She handed it to Alden Swan, telling him only that it was a partial reconstruction of a document that had once been stored in a word processing system, and that they would like to learn as much as possible about it.

Swan studied the sheet of paper silently for several minutes. At last he spoke. "It would help if I knew its provenance."

"The document was obtained from a firm working under government contract by an employee that came by it accidentally. It was encrypted, except for the index which you now see. The person who took it may have deciphered it, but in any case the document has been lost. This is all that remains."

Swan handed the copy back to Vivian. She started to hand it back. "You may keep this," she told him.

Swan held up the palm of his right hand. "It's not necessary," he said.

Vivian put the sheet back into her purse.

"Is the person that took the document also…lost?" Swan asked.

"Yes."

"Killed?"

"Killed," Vivian conceded.

Swan took another chocolate. He bit into it slowly. "How was the reconstruction made?"

"I saw the document briefly," answered Charles, "before it was destroyed."

Swan paused to swallow the last of the chocolate. "I can tell you part of it now," he told them, "but for most you will have to wait a few days."

Charles and Vivian looked at him intently.

"For today's work," added Swan, "my fee will be one thousand dollars."

Vivian nodded. That's how he affords original Chinese art, she told herself.

Swan leaned back into his tall chair. "It is an index," he said. "A Top Secret document, although this may refer only to the index itself. The missing encrypted portion may have a special clearance level. The initials S.A.B. on the title probably stand for Special Advisory Board, so what we have is the Report of the blank blank Special Advisory Board on E.E. Any idea on the meaning of E.E.?"

Charles and Vivian shook their heads.

"We may be able to figure that out later," Swan said. "This is Part One, which means there is another part somewhere. The first part is a compendium of reports. Probably where all the hard data is. There are six sections or chapters. They use abbreviations, which obscures things a bit."

Swan closed his eyes for a moment. "The first chapter is the easiest. NRO Extract of something Tieck UCB Thesis on something Infrared/

Microwave Radiation Variance Anomaly Southwest Sector. NRO stands for the National Reconnaissance Office. They are responsible for satellite surveillance. UCB is the University of California at Berkeley. Tieck probably is or was a student and his research evidently used something like side looking radar measurement data from satellites. He noted an anomaly, probably in the southwestern United States. Infrared would indicate a temperature anomaly."

"We should be able to track that down," Vivian said. "Tieck's report."

"I should be able to get a facsimile within a week," Swan said.

"Now, the second chapter..." Swan shook his head. "Ev something Bithian Representations Cospenc Model. The first word could be evaluation, or evaluation of." He looked at Charles.

"It's possible," Charles said. "In fact, it's likely. But it still doesn't mean anything to me."

Swan nodded. "Bithian and Cospenc remain unknowns. I'll look into that."

Vivian brought the sheet of paper back out of her purse. "The third section is about Projects Gilgamesh and Ozma," she read from the paper. "Do you know what they are?"

Swan tapped on the arm of his chair with the thumb of his right hand. "It's difficult to understand how they could be connected. There may be more than one project using each of those names. Project Gilgamesh is something medical. It's privately funded. I'm fairly sure it's in Houston, at the Baylor College of Medicine. I'll look into it."

Gisela walked in, bringing lemonade. She placed the three tall glasses on the table. "I thought you might get thirsty," she told them.

They all thanked her and drank the ice-cold drink. She left smiling, as swiftly as she had come.

Swan put his glass down. "Ozma was in West Virginia. The project used the Green Bank radio telescope to listen to the stars." He shrugged. "They looked for artificial transmissions, but as I recall only found background clutter and an occasional pulsar. I'll check them anyway."

"Blank blank Autopsy Report on," Vivian read from her sheet.

Swan picked up the words. "Something something Nester, Colonel, United States Air Force OSI. That last is the Air Force Office of Special Investigations." He stood up and walked to the book lined wall. After a while he came back carrying a thick three ring notebook. He paged through it. "The officer corps of the United States Air Force," he said. "Or, I should say, those above the rank of Captain."

"Only three Nesters," Swan announced after a while. "This will be easy." He placed the notebook on the table.

"The next one has a reference to E.E., as in the title of the document, and what may be rural phone numbers."

"Blank blank Data on E.E. blank, HR 56 88 blank, LA blank 212 blank," read Vivian.

"I'll have to look into that," Swan said. "And the last one. You remembered very little," Swan looked at Charles accusingly. "The name Ames. The only other significant word is Automaton."

"Device," cried Charles.

Swan and Vivian looked at him.

"The last word is device," Charles explained. "Automaton device. I just remembered." He smiled sheepishly. "I know that doesn't help much."

Suddenly, Gisela entered the room. She appeared agitated.

"There is an urgent phone call for you, Miss Venables," she said.

Vivian stood up.

"Gisela will take you to the telephone," Swan said.

Gisela and Vivian left the room.

Charles stood up, taking a large drink of lemonade.

"I will get back with you within the next week," Swan said, rising from his chair.

He handed Charles a business card.

Alden Fownes Swan

WISDOM

Coral Gables, Florida

305 336-9473

Vivian hurried back into the room. She picked up her purse from where she had placed it at the table.

"We must go at once," she said to Charles. "That call was from Hardgrave. There's been an attempt on Robinson's life. He's injured."

She turned to Swan. "We'll get back to you as soon as possible. We have to go now."

4

Cicely set the alarm clock and turned the lights out. Under the covers, she stretched languidly. It had been a busy day, and she was tired. She turned on her side, enjoying the smooth feel of the cool bed sheets. With a slow, lazy motion she moved one of her pillows so that it lay lengthwise by her. She hugged it, her lover for the night, closed her eyes, and slept.

The mist was patchy, so thick in places that visibility was limited to ten paces, while at times it parted to fully reveal the boulder-strewn terrain. Charles moved cautiously, his feet making low crunching sounds as he stepped on the gravelly ground. He wore skintight white clothes. In his right hand he carried a thin blue wand, about three feet long.

Ahead, the mist cleared a bit. There was a smooth path between two house sized boulders. He walked toward it, his face hardening. As he neared the closest of the boulders he gained a view of the area beyond. There was a natural path between parallel rows of the rounded boulders. He moved on.

The mist grew thicker again, but Charles could see clearly the area directly ahead. There was the clattering sound of pebbles rolling down the face of a boulder. In an instant, a dark shadow covered the path ahead of him. With a loud crash, an immense shape landed in front of him.

It loomed ten feet in height and stood erect on its hind feet. Its reddish skin was smooth and hairless. An intermediary set of arms was set between its upper and lower limbs. The head was massive, with a gaping mouth that seemed to glisten in the dim light. It was not a being that could have evolved on Earth. The beast uttered a deafening roar, steadying itself. Hideous rage-filled eyes focused on Charles' paralyzed form.

Straightaway, the huge foul-smelling being leapt upon him. Sharp talons sank into his flesh, and the several arms at once held and tore at him. Charles struggled to free himself, the pain on his side and leg excruciating. He drove an elbow hard into a gaping nostril and succeeded in freeing his torso. His attempt to rise and run was arrested by twin arms grabbing and tearing at his waist.

Charles pressed the stud on the hilt of the wand he still held in his hand. It immediately started to emit a high-pitched hissing sound, and the blue of its shaft acquired a silver sheen. Charles swung it rapidly in a short arc toward his horrible attacker. The wand struck an arm and severed it clean. Thick red blood splattered him and the bellowing being.

A huge reddish hand gained a hold on Charles' neck. It closed powerfully, deliberately choking his throat.

Cicely woke up abruptly. She could not breathe. Covered in sweat, gasping for air, she crawled away from her bed. She passed out before reaching the door.

CHAPTER 6
BISCAYNE BAY

1

"The chauffeur will remain in the hospital for two or three days," Hardgrave said. "He's expected to recover fully, but he'll have a broken leg and second degree burns to contend with for a while. Mr. Robinson managed to get out with only cuts and bruises."

Hardgrave walked slightly ahead of Charles and Vivian. He had met them at the door to Robinson's house, now guarded by a uniformed security guard, and was leading them along the main hall.

"When you called," Vivian said, "I thought Mr. Robinson had been badly hurt also."

"We didn't know the details at the time," Hardgrave explained. "His wife had just taken the call from the police."

"Is he all right now?" Charles asked.

They reached the large central dining room. It was dominated by a long table and a chandelier of sparkling crystal above it. Along the far wall, a staircase rose to the upstairs rooms.

"The doctor had to use a couple of stitches to close a cut on his forehead," Hardgrave said. "That must cause him some pain, but he's holding up well. He asked to meet with us as soon as you two arrived."

They walked past the table and turned left, moving swiftly along the back wall of the atrium. A moment later they reached the door to Robinson's office. Hardgrave knocked twice and opened the door, leading the others in.

Robinson was standing by his desk. He looked haggard. The stitches on his forehead were clearly visible, the skin around them puffy. His left sleeve had been rolled back and a bandage covered part of his forearm. He was pouring brandy into a goblet.

Benjamin Lawrence was already in the room, sitting on one of the straight-backed chairs in front of the desk. He greeted the others.

"Please sit down," Robinson said, taking a sip of brandy.

"I'm glad you're well, sir," Vivian said. She and the others sat down.

Robinson gave her a thin smile. He sat down on the corner of his desk and put down his glass. Very slowly, he rolled down his sleeve, gingerly avoiding the bandage on his arm.

"I have a headache," Robinson said, "and both my wife and my doctor want me to get some rest." There was a bit of a tremor in his hand, but his speech was clear.

"I'll be going up for a nap in a moment," he went on, "but I wanted to have this meeting as soon as possible." Robinson studied his hands. Then, abruptly, he said, "I was called to City Hall for a briefing on the mayor's new anti-smuggling campaign. On the way back, Tyrone picked me up in the Daimler. About two minutes later a car moved next to us. It came upon us very rapidly; all I remember is that it was blue. From the car, someone threw something at us. An instant later there was an explosion. I must have blacked out. All of a sudden I found myself sitting on the door of the car, with blood all over my head."

Robinson took a sip of the brandy. "They almost got Tyrone, and the Daimler is a total loss, I'm sure."

"You were very lucky," Charles said.

"You're bloody right," said Robinson. "And I don't want to press my luck. I have decided to terminate the investigation into the Arteaga document." He paused for a moment, letting his words sink in. "I run a business; I have to look at the bottom line. In this case I see on the one hand considerable risk, and on the other..." He raised his shoulders, letting his eyes sweep over his people.

"I want to thank you all for your efforts," Robinson said. "This was quite a caper."

Vivian and Charles exchanged glances.

"The visit to City Hall was not a total loss," commented Robinson. "We have a surveillance assignment in Colombia for you," he gestured toward Vivian.

"I want you to back her up, Victor," he told Hardgrave, "and act as liaison to the mayor and police. I don't want Miss Venables identified: she is X as far as they are concerned. Ben has all the details."

Robinson stood up and faced Charles. He held out his hand. "I want to thank you for your efforts," he said. "I don't want you placed in danger any longer. I would recommend that you return home tonight, but I also want to settle financially with you, and that will have to wait until morning."

Charles shook Robinson's hand. "This has been a remarkable experience," he told the older man.

Robinson smiled. "Take a vacation, Mr. Ryder, rest for a while. That's what my wife and I intend to do."

2

They went to a Cuban restaurant on S.W. 8th Street. Its decor attempted to replicate fifties Havana. The floor was marble, the buff walls were lined with bas-reliefs of pillared arcades. A trio of wrought iron chandeliers illuminated the large room.

Silver threads on Vivian's white strapless dress glittered under the electric candles. She looked the place over approvingly, oblivious to the synchronized turn of male heads.

The restaurant was windowless. Its tables, set in neat rows, were densely populated, mostly with couples and small groups of well-dressed regulars, but also with more casually dressed tourists, and here and there with an advance guard of real Cubans, venturing out to recapture the ambiance of their old country.

A black-haired young woman steered Vivian and Charles swiftly through the mass of tables to one just being cleared and set by two hurried busboys. The restaurant provided little in the way of luxury; it had survived in Miami very nicely for more than two decades on its efficient organization and the devotion of its clients to its fine cuisine.

They slipped into their seats, facing each other, and started to examine the menus the hostess handed them. A single slim red candle adorned their table. Freshly-baked bread loaves and butter were set down before them. Soon a portly waiter appeared and took their order. Vivian ordered *carne asada con arroz* and Charles *boliche con papas*. They decided to share a bottle of a Chilean red wine.

Next to their small table, a large family carried on a boisterous conversation in Spanish.

"I wonder what it would be like to have four brothers and sisters," Charles said. He was an only child.

"Four of each?"

"No, one brother and three sisters. Like he has." Charles pointed at the younger of two plump boys at the next table.

"We do not point at others, dear," said Vivian in a schoolmarmish voice.

The waiter returned and served their meal with nonchalant precision.

Vivian cut a slice of roast beef, piled a few grains of the wild rice on it. Before consuming the mouthful she declared: "I'm thinking of buying a horse while I'm in Colombia."

Charles took a sip of the tangy wine. For the first time he noticed a thin white scar on the second joint of her little finger. "How did you get that?" he asked, touching her finger.

Vivian glanced at the small scar. "Sultan did that—Mr. Cates' bulldog—while I was lancing a boil in his ear." She cut another slice of beef. "My father was a vet. I used to help him in summertime and when his assistant didn't show up."

"I had a summer job repairing lawn mowers when dad was stationed in Georgia," Charles mentioned. "Is the horse you're getting a race horse?"

"Cross country. I should be able to get one with a good bloodline for a third of what he'd cost me here."

"I somehow didn't picture you as a horse fancier."

She gave him a wide-eyed stare. "Well, revise your picture, sweetheart. I've loved horses all my life." Her eyes gleamed violet in the candlelight and she said, smiling, "Which reminds me of something: How's the Lone Ranger's horse Silver like the audience at a Van Cliburn concert?"

Charles grinned. He looked at her from the corner of his eyes. "I don't know."

"They both go clop, clop, clop."

Charles smiled, shaking his head. He poured the last of the wine into her glass. "Clearly we need another bottle."

The dinner was excellent. One of the best Charles could remember. But it was not only the good food and pleasant wine that made him raise his glass and say: "To us!"

Vivian smiled and touched her glass to his. "Salud!"

Over coffee, Charles grew increasingly pensive and their conversation momentarily came to a halt. "I think we should talk about us," he told Vivian, looking into her eyes. She took a sip of the rich espresso and returned his gaze, her eyes full of the soft brightness of melting ice.

"I've been thinking about you a lot, Vivian. There's never been anyone like you." Not pleased with his choice of words, he paused, then went on, his voice catching a bit. "I find myself wanting to be with you all the time. I enjoy your company more than I've told you."

Vivian reached across the table and took his hand. The white dress struggled to contain her breasts. "You're flying home tomorrow, Charles."

"I know," he admitted. "Look, if we want to stay together we can find a way."

Vivian held onto his hand, her thumb gently caressing his wrist. "I like you a lot, sweetheart," she said softly. "We've had some very good times together, and we will again." She leaned closer to him and her hand pressed his more strongly.

"I know how you feel, Charles. But this isn't the time to form a permanent attachment." She let go of his hand and sighed. "Tomorrow afternoon you'll be three thousand miles away, in Seattle, and I'll be in Medellin."

Charles knew better than to press her. "I'm going to miss you."

"I'll miss you too, dear," Vivian said, her uncompromising smile displaying a row of glistening teeth. "I'll come to see you in December," she added.

"It's cold there in winter," he said.

"We'll find ways to keep warm," she said, smiling. Then, leaning fully across the table, she kissed him softly on the lips. "Don't get maudlin on me. The night is still young."

"I've got an idea," Charles said. "Let's go dancing. We can go to the place up the street with the neon palm tree up front."

"We better not stay out too late," Vivian said after a moment. "I need to get you back to Robinson's tonight. Why don't we go to my place instead?"

Charles leaned back in his seat. "Well now."

"I mean, the night is not *that* young."

After dinner they drove over dark, wet streets to a tall white and gray building in Key Biscayne. Vivian's apartment was on the sixth floor. The living room was furnished with elegant but Spartan modern furniture set on a gray marble floor. Opposite the entryway, open sliding glass doors led to a small balcony and let in a soft breeze and the faint sounds of the street traffic below.

Charles sat on a red leather and chromium couch at the center of the room. He glanced idly at a copy of Elle and a biography of Jack London lying on the smoked-glass low table in front of him.

"What are your plans—when you get back home?" Vivian asked.

Charles looked across the table at her, standing near a set of shelves inset on the eggshell-white wall. "I'll be working my butt off for a while. Our group was beginning work on a new inlet design when Robinson got me involved in all this. I shudder to think of the work that has piled up on my desk."

"An inlet design?" Vivian replaced a leather bound book on the top shelf, among a dozen novels and biographies framed by bronze horses.

"A variable-geometry air intake for an advanced jet engine—an air turborocket."

Vivian knelt down by the lower of the inset shelves. They held stereo equipment, a portable television set, and rows of compact disks. "Do you like Adele?" she asked, reaching among the recordings. The hemline of her white dress slid up to reveal a slash of tanned, shapely thigh.

Charles nodded. Vivian inserted a shiny disk into the player and, as the music started, rose and walked around the glass table to stand next to him by the couch. Her half-open lips seemed on the verge of a smile.

"Tomorrow..." he began. But she pressed a finger against his lips. She unzipped her dress and let it fall to the floor. "Quit worrying. We'll find a way to get together. Let's not talk about tomorrow now."

She stood naked before him. Charles' eyes traveled over the tapering contours of her waist and belly, past the outthrust swell of her breasts, following the firmly curved surfaces to reach the smile that teased at the corners of her lips.

Charles drew her to him, his arms circling her slim waist. Vivian sat gently on his lap and kissed him softly. She started to undo the buttons of his shirt.

On the stereo, Adele sang *Set Fire to the Rain*.

While Vivian slowly undressed him, Charles drew the tips of his fingers lightly down her taut stomach. Her smooth skin quivered. "Oh, that feels nice," she said. She planted light kisses on his wrist, then slid the tip of her tongue along the inside of his forearm.

"You're teasing me to death," he whispered, caressing her breasts. "I'm never going to let you go."

She bit his neck lightly. "Is that a promise?"

"In writing, if you like." He kissed her navel.

"You can keep me as long as you go on doing that."

His lips closed on a stiffening nipple. She gave a small groan and guided his hand between her legs. They made love with an intensity that kept at bay thoughts of their coming separation.

3

At eight o'clock on the next morning, Charles and Robinson stood at the door to Robinson's office. The tremor in Robinson's hand had gone, but the area around the stitches on his forehead had taken on a purplish cast. Charles found the bruised flesh slightly repulsive.

Robinson closed the door behind him and handed Charles a thick envelope. "As we agreed," he said.

Charles placed the envelope in an interior pocket of his coat. He thought Robinson looked slightly better than he had the previous afternoon. The muscles on the man's heavyset body sagged uncharacteristically and he moved slowly. Charles had the impression that Robinson was concealing a certain amount of physical pain. But the man's spirits had noticeably improved.

"Is Vivian in yet?" Charles asked.

Robinson brought out a small gold lighter and lit his pipe as they started to walk. "She and Hardgrave left about an hour ago," he remarked. "Lawrence was able to book an early flight for them."

"Oh." Charles' features tightened despite his attempt to conceal his disappointment. His hopes of seeing Vivian before leaving had been dashed.

Robinson took a puff from his pipe, the aromatic smell of the tobacco enveloping them both as they walked down the hall. "It was the only direct flight available today," he added.

They reached the atrium and turned toward the front entrance.

Robinson noted Charles' disappointment. "Anything wrong?" he asked.

Charles shook his head. "Well, I…" He sighed. "I had counted on seeing Vivian before I left."

Robinson nodded understandingly. They were approaching the front of the house.

"I'm sorry you missed her," Robinson said. "I was eager to get them started on their new assignment and insisted that they leave right away. I think it is safer for all of us to make a clean break with the inquiry into Arteaga's document."

As they reached the front door Charles stopped. "I'll need to call a taxi," he said. His eyes located his suitcase.

"That won't be necessary," Robinson said, opening the door. "I'll give you a lift to the airport."

"Thank you," Charles said, picking up his suitcase and following Robinson out the door.

A security guard still stood outside. The man and Robinson exchanged greetings.

"I'll be going for a short spin," Robinson declared, indicating the lustrous black Cadillac parked in the driveway. He put out his pipe.

"Will you be needing an escort, sir?" the guard asked. Charles noticed the man carried a walkie-talkie as well as a revolver.

Robinson put away his pipe in a pocket of his coat. "No, I'll be all right," he told the guard.

Charles took a deep breath of the warm morning air. In the garden, the cicadas were droning. Occasionally, when their monotonous calls subsided, the waves could be heard breaking against the nearby beach.

Robinson motioned toward the waiting car and started to walk toward it. Charles followed him, suitcase in hand.

They put the suitcase in the trunk and took their seats. A moment later the black sedan was in motion, rolling past carefully cropped bougainvillea and a black iron gate. Robinson drove carefully, getting the feel of the car. "It's my wife's car," he told Charles. "Only the second time I've driven it."

They turned left onto Venetian Way and Robinson made the Cadillac pick up some speed, glancing occasionally into the rearview mirror. Traffic was light. There were dark clouds stretching all the way to the horizon, but the threatened rain had not materialized. Charles gazed through the windshield at the green sea glimmering on both sides of the land bridge.

"Not a bad day," Robinson commented. He looked at Charles. There was something curious in his glance. It was aloof, appraising. He glanced again into the rearview mirror.

Gradually but deliberately, Robinson slowed down and veered off into the outside lane. He brought the car to a stop among the palm trees that lined the side of the road. Leaving the motor running and without saying a word, he opened his door and stepped outside the car, gesturing for Charles to follow him.

Robinson walked to the edge of the causeway and looked over Biscayne Bay. Its waters were slightly ruffled by a breeze. Charles joined him, puzzled, his steps making soft crunching noises on the sandy soil.

They stood under a leaning palm tree.

"We only have a few moments," Robinson said. "Lawrence made a sweep of the car this morning. It should be free of listening devices, but this is safer still," he explained. "There's one more thing I want you to do."

Charles started to protest, but Robinson held up his hand. "Let me finish. Yesterday morning I received information about a person who may tell us about Arteaga's activities during the period just prior to his leaving the country. The woman was acquainted with Arteaga. Until recently, she shared an apartment with Arteaga's girlfriend. She saw him frequently."

"Why not talk to Arteaga's girlfriend?"

"Because she's dead," Robinson explained. He handed an envelope to Charles. "There's twenty thousand dollars. She's been offered four thousand to talk to us. If she seems to have anything of value, give her twice that much. The rest is yours."

Charles held the envelope in his hand. He didn't like this. The whole dreary business was far more perilous than he had bargained for. But Robinson provided a link to Vivian, and Charles did not want that link broken.

"You better put that away," Robinson said, indicating the bulging envelope. "Only you and I should know of this," he warned. "If you learn anything useful call me from a pay phone, or a disposable wireless phone, and say that you found Mr. Frost. Only that. I'll then arrange to meet you. Or if you prefer, mail your information to the address inside the envelope. You need do nothing else. If it turns out to be a red herring, just keep the money."

"Tell me something. The other day you said that you had lost a man, before I became involved. How did he die?"

"Swenson was following Arteaga's trail," Robinson said, looking impatiently at the highway. "He was found dead in a motel room in Sarasota. His body had severe burn marks, as if lightning had struck him."

"Like Adele Lopez and Leo," Charles said. "I suppose the murderer hasn't been found."

"At the time I suspected Arteaga. What are you getting at?"

"These odd murders, the disappearance of Arteaga's records, the attempt on your life: all done to preserve a secret?" Charles thought for a moment before he continued. "Arteaga's girlfriend—how did she die?"

"I don't know," Robinson replied hoarsely.

Charles shifted a little on his feet. "Why are you doing this? I thought you were dropping the investigation."

Robinson's face tightened. "There is a secret group of people behind this, powerful and merciless. They are in government, but they are not *the* Government. I want to find out who they are."

"That's scary," Charles said grimly. He let his gaze wander to the shoreline, where a dark-feathered duck waddled in from the water.

"I want to know what their game is."

Charles turned around and looked at Robinson, who had started to walk back to the Cadillac.

"Wait," Charles called out.

Robinson stopped and looked back at Charles. "Will you do it?"

Charles pursed his lips but there was agreement in his eyes.

Robinson grinned. "The young woman's name is Kathryn. She works at a club in Los Angeles called The Red Chalice. It's on Hawthorne Boulevard. Meet her there at eight tonight. You'll find other details in a note inside the envelope."

It started to rain and they hurried back inside the car. It did not escape Charles that in this new assignment he would be like a canary in a coal mine. He thought of backing out of the deal—he didn't really need the money, and people were getting killed in spectacular ways.

Robinson playfully double-tapped the steering wheel with the palms of his hands. "I had forgotten that I actually enjoy driving," he said, a satisfied grin on his face.

The doubts Charles had just entertained vanished as he acknowledged that he was intrigued by the puzzle that lay ahead. Like Robinson, he wanted to know what the game was.

CHAPTER 7
THE RED CHALICE

1

Cicely thought Dr. McClellan looked like an owl, his dark eyes unblinkingly trained on her. Avoiding his gaze, she let her vision drift until it came to rest on one of his diplomas on the wall.

"The dream about the monster has particularly upset you," Dr. McClellan said. He leaned back in his chair.

Cicely turned to face him, the features of her long face set. "I'm more than upset, Doctor," she said angrily, "I can't take this any longer. I just can't handle any more."

"Calm down, Cicely."

"Oh, sure," she said, her voice low and shaky, "calm down. That's easy for you to say. You didn't have to face that horror."

Dr. McClellan said nothing for a moment.

"I want you to make the dreams stop, Doctor," demanded Cicely.

"Let's talk about that a bit," said Dr. McClellan. "About dreams." He rolled his chair closer to his desk.

"It's something we all have in common. When sleep comes, so do dreams. They are often unpleasant and sometimes frightening. Not only for you, Cicely, but for everyone. But dreaming is necessary. When we are awake, our minds receive an enormous amount of information. Much of that information cannot be analyzed and correlated until we are asleep. Dreams are a way of sorting things out; they help us to remember and to integrate newly learned material. Most people have several every night, though few are remembered."

Dr. McClellan took a pen from the holder on his desk and toyed with it, tapping it against a thumbnail. Cicely regarded him quietly.

"Dreams are usually about people with whom we are emotionally involved, but they are often symbolic. People and objects often stand for something else. The monster in your dream stands for something or someone that is threatening to you. That type of dream is common."

Dr. McClellan returned the gilt pen to its holder.

"The unknown people in your dreams: Charles, Vivian, Robinson and the others. They stand for something. They are symbols, and we need to sort them out. Your feelings during these dreams, your fear or anger or delight. The feelings are important. They serve as clues and will help sort out the symbols."

There was a buzz from Dr. McClellan's watch.

"Doctor," said Cicely, "you can't be saying my dreams are normal."

"The fact that you have dreams is normal. Even the fact that most of your dreams are unpleasant is normal." Dr. McClellan paused, ordering his thoughts. "You have lucid dreams—you know that you are dreaming while you are dreaming—which, while not very common, is certainly not abnormal. The fact that you are not the central character is unusual," he stated. "In these dreams you also do not appear as a recognizable secondary figure, or a spectator, and that is quite unusual. It's likely that the central figures represent you, in a form of fantasizing."

Dr. McClellan rose from his chair. He smiled at Cicely. "We'll work it out."

2

The club occupied a squat single story gray building located between a used car lot and a Vietnamese dry cleaning shop. A well-executed mural of a beckoning seminude woman lying on her side decorated the side of the building.

Charles found a parking space on the street only a few feet past the locked doors of Duong Brothers Cleaners. He locked the rented Ford and walked past two feuding dogs back toward the club. A small neon sign in a recessed area by the entrance simply stated: THE RED CHALICE. Above the open metal doors there was a row of pulsating light bulbs. They illuminated a painted sign proclaiming TOPLESS ENTERTAINMENT and FREE PARKING IN REAR.

Double glass doors led to a small foyer and the strains of hard rock music. Charles followed a scantily dressed waitress into a large dimly lit room. There was a long bar to the right, and six men seated on stools. The men, except for two engaged in a conversation with the bartender, faced away from the bar. Their attention was directed towards an elevated stage that ran half the length of the room. The stage was set against a mirrored wall opposite the bar, and was ringed with swiveling chairs.

A dozen customers sat near the stage, some intent on their drinks, but most on the bikini-clad brunette dancing on the stage. The left side of the room and the area between the stage and the bar held twenty tables, irregularly spaced and populated with men and women boisterously enjoying a good time. Waitresses milled about through a haze of cigarette smoke, deftly balancing trays full of drinks.

"Would you like to sit by the stage, sir?" asked Charles' waitress. The pert redhead wore what appeared to be the uniform of the day: braless T-shirt and white short shorts.

"I'd rather have a table."

She led him past the bar to an even more dimly lit area set with about a dozen tables. Only two were occupied.

Charles took a seat and ordered a draft beer. He had a good view of the stage and, through the mirrors behind it, of most of the room.

The song ended amid cheers and applause. On the stage, the dancer removed the abbreviated top of her outfit to reveal generously proportioned breasts. She threw the garment to the right of the stage. There, attached to the wall, enormous glossy red lips, widely parted, framed a dark-curtained entryway.

Almost at once, the staccato beat of drums introduced a new song. From behind a glass cage to the right and above the stage, a disc jockey exhorted the already appreciative audience.

"Lovely Michelle, gentlemen, returning with a little less on. She's going to show us more of what she's got."

The brunette moved swiftly along the stage, swaying hips and breasts to the rising rhythm of the music.

Soon the redheaded waitress returned with Charles' beer.

"Our lovely ladies," called out the disc jockey over the loud music, "work for tips and tips alone. Show Michelle your appreciation, gentlemen."

Charles paid with a ten dollar bill for his $6.75 beer.

"Do you know if Kathryn is in tonight?" he asked the waitress, indicating she could keep the change.

"The new girl? She's in the back," she gestured toward Charles' right, where a doorway stood at the end of the room. "I think she's on after Michelle."

Two men rose, as in response to the entreaties of the disk jockey, and stood by the stage, taking turns slipping dollar bills on the sides of Michelle's G-string. They were rewarded with hugs and kisses.

"That's the way to do it, gentlemen," voiced the disc jockey.

At the end of the number, Michelle collected her top and a bill that had fallen to the stage and sauntered away, exiting through the opening framed by the giant glistening lips.

The disc jockey spun the platter again as he introduced a new dancer. "Beautiful Kathy will be with us in a moment," he chuckled, "as soon as she puts some clothes on." The cadence of a Steve Winwood song filled the room.

In a moment, the dark curtain within the giant mouth was swept aside and the new dancer pranced onto the stage. She snapped her fingers to the beat of the music and moved down the stage swiftly, with the long powerful strides of a natural athlete. The overhead spotlights, blinking on and off in tune with the music, burnished her blond hair in multicolored hues. High heeled shoes finished in blue satin accentuated her long legs.

She wore a white outfit, trimmed in shimmering blue. The V-cut bottom rode high on her hip and plunged dangerously low up front. It left her rounded buttocks exposed. The top consisted of two outrageously small white triangles held together with thin blue straps.

Kathryn moved faster and more deliberately than the previous dancer, and the crowd responded with increasingly enthusiastic yells and cries.

Just then, Charles spotted Michelle, in a T-shirt and short shorts, moving between tables, carrying a tray in her hand. The girls evidently alternated between dancing and waitressing, he thought. He took a sip from his beer and formed a plan for approaching Kathryn.

When the song ended, Kathryn quickly discarded her top, letting it fall to the stage and then kicking it casually toward the mirrored wall with the tip of her high heeled shoes. Then a new tune started to play and she wheeled back to the center of the stage, outthrust breasts bobbing. As she started the dance, the muscles played beneath her skin, and her hair streamed behind her lithe body.

"Our lovely dancers work for tips and tips alone, gentlemen," intoned the disc jockey. "Show Kathy you appreciate her hard work."

Charles had been waiting for this. He took a ten dollar bill from his wallet and walked toward the stage, taking his place behind three other men already waiting there. Kathryn continued to dance for a while, ignoring the men, but then approached the edge of the stage and knelt down, accepting the tips as they were slipped under the sides of her G-string.

Her blond hair fell down her back. Charles slipped the bill under her one remaining garment, twisting it around the blue strap. "It's close to eight o'clock. Please see me when you get a chance," he told her. Her belly showed the doubly-domed curves of perfect muscle tone. A thin film of perspiration covered her body, and he noted on her right wrist a narrow silver bracelet studded with garnets.

"Are you the man from the East?" she asked, a little taken aback.

"From Florida. My name is Charles." He noticed a sprinkle of freckles on her shoulders and on her chest above her pink-tipped breasts.

"I'll join you in a while," she said in a high lilting voice.

She kissed him lightly on the lips, rose to her feet, and continued her dance.

3

Kathryn appeared at the rear of the room, tray in hand, a few minutes after finishing her dance. She approached each of the men that had tipped her on stage and thanked them, giving them each a kiss. Charles was the last one she came to.

She wore a T-shirt and shorts, like the other waitresses. The girl gave Charles a brief kiss and a hug and, placing her tray on the table, sat down next to him.

"Do you have the money?" she asked.

"Yes."

"I can only sit down with you for a couple of minutes now," she told him, "but I'll be back." She fidgeted with a stack of napkins on her tray.

"Can we meet later? I have a room at the Hyatt, we can talk there."

"No way," she said. She cleared her throat. "I'll tell you all you want to know right here."

"I didn't mean…" Charles began to say.

"I know what you didn't mean," she interrupted him. "We still do whatever we do right here."

Charles noticed a small design on her T-shirt. It was a miniature version of the widely parted red lips at the entrance to the stage.

"What can you tell me about Leo Arteaga?" asked Charles.

"I know him fairly well," she said. "I haven't seen him for over two months." She leaned forward toward Charles. "Put your arm around my shoulder," she said. "Look interested."

Charles did as he was told. Her body was firm and warm.

"I'd like to know as much as possible about his actions for a month or so before you last saw him."

"Is he in some sort of trouble?" she asked.

Charles looked over his shoulder. "Leo got involved in a very nasty deal," he told her. "He may be dead."

The girl drew back, astonished. She caught herself and brought her chair closer to Charles. "How," she muttered, "what happened?"

She looked very pale just then.

"I don't really know," he lied. "He's missing. It doesn't look good for him."

"Whew," she sighed, her eyes open wide. "I figured there was something funny going on. But not that bad." She shook her head. "Look," she said, "I need a drink." She leaned closer to Charles and kissed him. He saw wetness in her eyes. "You're paying for it. Ladies' drinks are eight dollars."

She rose from her chair and placed a couple of napkins on the table. "I'll bring you another beer," she announced, departing.

On the stage, a slim dark-haired dancer undulated to the beat of fresh music, bathed in hot lights and her own sweat. Someone in the small crowd milling around the bar laughed boisterously.

Kathryn returned a few minutes later. "Fourteen seventy-five," she said, putting down his beer and picking up his empty mug.

Charles gave her twenty dollars, and Kathryn sat down next to him. She took a sip from her own drink. Half of it was already gone.

Charles touched her bare arm. "You noticed something funny was going on," he prompted her.

"Leo was very uptight the last few weeks," she said. "At first he stayed home a lot. He would spend hours with a little computer he had. Then he started going on trips all the time. I mean *all* the time. He took time off from work, he'd call in sick and get in his car and go away."

"Go away where?"

"Foxy Debbie on the stage now, gentlemen," cried out the disc jockey. Charles noticed the redhead that had originally served him, now wearing a green fringed bikini and a cowboy hat borrowed from someone in the audience.

Kathryn took his hand away from her arm and gently placed it on her thigh. "I said you need to look interested," she explained.

"He would go north of town, into the desert. He had land out there, near Mojave. For a while I thought that's where he went, but then..." She fidgeted in her chair. "Well, I didn't see it myself, but my friend Annette, you know, she's the one that dated him, she went out there with him a couple of times."

Kathryn took a sip from her drink. "I'm going to need another of these, dude," she said, looking at Charles questioningly.

Charles nodded. "And what did she see?" he asked.

She moved closer to him, her breast pressing softly against his arm. "Well, my friend said it looked like he was prospecting for gold or something. They didn't go to his property, they went into the hills, somewhere between Willow Springs and Tehachapi. They took a little road off from the main highway."

"What main highway?"

"I don't know. It runs north, parallel to—I don't know the number—the freeway that goes to Mojave. This highway is maybe fifteen minutes from the freeway."

"And what was he doing out there?"

"Nothing. Looking around. He had a lot of equipment. You know, heavy boots and canteens. Pick axes and ropes. Mountain climbing stuff. He was looking for a ridge that ran north and south and two fingers at a straight angle to it that later joined, like a letter Y."

"They didn't find it?"

"Not the right one. They spent most of the time driving around the hills." The girl leaned very close to Charles, putting her arms around his neck. "Listen," she said into his ear, "I've got to move around a bit or I'm going to get fired. I'll be back in a little while. Have my money ready when I return and I'll tell you whatever else you want to know."

She kissed him and Charles found himself enjoying her soft lips.

"Go to the men's room," she told him, taking an envelope from her tray and placing it carefully on the table, "and put the money inside. Be discreet," she cautioned, "or Vice will bust us both."

It was a good thirty minutes before she returned, and Charles had plenty of time to visit the men's room and surreptitiously place six thousand dollars inside the envelope she had given him. He bought a pack of cigarettes, emptied it, and hid another ten hundred-dollar bills inside.

"Need another beer, lover?" Kathryn asked loudly, setting her tray down upon his table. She looked tense.

"Please," he said, slipping the envelope as casually as possible from his coat pocket and placing it on the table. She put two napkins down on the table and took away the old napkin and placed it on her tray, together with the envelope.

"You must like beer a lot," she said, leaving again.

She was back five minutes later, looking more relaxed. She collected another twenty dollars from Charles, set down his beer and her own drink on the table, and slipped into the chair next to Charles.

"Well, it looked like the real stuff," she commented. "What else do you want to know, Charles?"

"Just tell me anything else that happened those last few weeks," he said.

Kathryn twirled a stirrer in her hand. "That's about it, Leo just disappeared. He wrote a letter to Annette a couple of weeks later, from Florida, saying he was going on a long trip. He asked her to pack up all his things and put them in storage."

"Where are his things now?"

"Nowhere I know. When she got to his apartment his stuff was all gone. He got ripped off."

Charles shifted in his seat. He drew closer to Kathryn. "Everything was gone?"

"The place was totally cleaned out." She placed the stirrer she had being toying with back in her tray.

Charles took the pack of cigarettes from his pocket and placed it on the table.

"Is there anything else you can tell me?" he asked.

Kathryn shook her head.

"Did Leo ever say what it was he was looking for in the desert?"

"No. Just the ridge with the other two ridges butting into it."

With the tip of a finger, Charles lightly tapped the pack of cigarettes.

"There is one thousand dollars inside this," he told her. "It's yours if you can remember anything else."

She looked at the pack of cigarettes. "I can't remember anything."

"Come on, Kathryn," he said, "there is always something."

She looked up to the stage, to a slightly plump brown-haired girl doing a split.

"She has no style," she commented.

"Is there something Leo could have left with his girlfriend?" Asked Charles.

"No," she answered.

"Are you sure? Perhaps some notes. Letters."

"I'm sure," she insisted.

"Tell me, what happened to Leo's girlfriend?"

"I don't want to talk about Annette."

Kathryn crossed her arms across her chest. She looked at the pack of cigarettes again.

"Leo went to downtown L.A., to some government buildings. He stayed home a lot, did a lot of reading. Annette hated it." She paused for a moment, thinking back. "He went to Westwood several times," she said. "It was during the last few weeks. He spent hours there."

"What did he do?"

Kathryn shrugged. "Annette said he wrote down a lot of stuff in a notebook he carried around. He went to the library and read books. It was the library at UCLA."

"Anything else?"

Kathryn thought for a moment. "I remember now. Leo sometimes took along some special equipment."

"Like what?"

"Rented. I remember once she and I took the units back to the store for him. A metal detector and a yellow box with dials and a gizmo connected to it."

"The box. Could it have been a Geiger counter?"

"Maybe. It was after he was at the library that he started prospecting. He got a lot of maps and he'd stay up at night going over them."

"What kind of maps were they?" Charles asked.

"Oh, road maps." She tugged at her ear. "Some were really big. They folded out all over the dining table. Those were not road maps. You know, they showed mountains and things. And he had some photographs."

"Aerial photographs?"

"I think so. Leo said…"

"Kathy, check sound please," called out the disc jockey.

"Look, I've got to go now, I have to choose my music," said Kathryn. "I really don't know anything else."

Charles took the pack of cigarettes and placed it on her tray.

"Nice knowing you, Charles," she gave him a wet kiss and a hearty hug. Smiling, she picked up her tray and walked away, her hips swaying in rhythm with the music.

CHAPTER 8
TEHACHAPI

1

The University of California at Los Angeles is in Westwood Village, a few miles from the Pacific Ocean, between Beverly Hills and Santa Monica. Charles found it a nice campus, spacious and attractively landscaped. A girl on a bicycle directed him to the library building.

Charles rode an elevator to the Math/Science/Engineering Library. It was on the 8th floor of a steel and concrete tower near the center of the campus.

As he entered the library area he saw several rows of study tables directly ahead. The students milling about or poring over books at the tables were mostly dressed in decrepit jeans and T-shirts. Charles stood near the entrance for a moment, hands clasped behind his back. There were tall stacks of books to his right. Row upon row of bookcases stretched as far as he could see. He looked at them in dismay. Then he noticed the librarian's dais to his left and walked toward it.

The head librarian was an elderly man in gray slacks and a starched long-sleeved white shirt. Charles could see him stooping over a computer display in the back of the checkout area. An overweight girl in the inevitable T-shirt was helping two giggling students check out a large-format book. Charles had already started to get in line behind them when a short Oriental youth popped up from behind the counter and addressed him.

"Can I help you?" said the student, adjusting his thick eyeglasses.

Charles extracted a slip of paper from his shirt pocket. On it he had carefully written: "Background IR/MW Radiation Variance Anomaly Southwest Sector,"Tieck, Ph. D. Dissertation, UCB.

Charles placed the slip of paper on the counter. "I'm trying to locate this paper," he said.

The student studied the note for a moment. His long black hair fell down over his glasses and he brushed it away.

"Hey, Bertha," the assistant called over to the girl next to him at the counter, "do we carry any Berkeley thesis stuff?"

"Only UCLA papers," answered the girl, looking up briefly from her dealings with the two students, "unless it made a periodical."

"We may be able to order a copy from Berkeley," said the assistant.

Charles had begun to shake his head when a spectral voice said: "Look in the cross-reference catalog, Chul."

The elderly librarian looked over from where he stooped over his files display. "Bring that here to me," he ordered, his voice a rasping whisper.

Chul took the slip of paper back to the catalog area and the man peered at it for a moment. "Try the subject keyword index," he said. "It won't be listed by author."

"What key words should I use, Mr. Bradley?" Chul asked.

The old man thought for a moment, then scribbled something on the back of an index card. "Try those," he said, handing the card to the student.

Chul led Charles past a row of cabinets to a cluster of computer terminals. Only one was being used.

"Have you used these before?" Chul asked.

"No."

"I'll do it for you," volunteered Chul, sitting down at one of the terminals. He made a number of entries on the keyboard and the screen displayed a panel.

Consulting the index card, Chul entered: EARTH RESOURCES. Instantly, another panel appeared on the screen. Referring to Charles' note, he carefully entered the title. The terminal did not respond for over a minute. Both Charles and the student stared at the screen impassively. Finally, there was a beep, and the screen displayed two lines of information.

"Ah, good," Chul said. Taking a well-chewed pencil from his shirt pocket, he laboriously took down the data.

Charles picked a secluded table and sat down with the book Chul had handed him. Looking at the card inserted in a little paper pouch inside the back cover, he had already noticed something of interest. The book had last been checked out three months earlier, by L. Arteaga. It had been published by the U.S. Government Printing Office: *Photogrammetric and Earth Resources Imagery of Western North America*. Tieck's thesis, apparently unabridged, had been incorporated as one of two dozen chapters.

Tieck's writing, Charles soon discovered, was stilted and his paper crammed with data tables, formulas, graphs, and photographic illustrations. His original purpose had been to evaluate geometric registration techniques used in correlating satellite imagery. He had first noted the feature that he later came to call an anomaly in Landsat Thematic Mapper images. It was distinct and large enough to be picked up by the lowest resolution satellite sensors, and Tieck had decided to use it to validate his registration techniques.

The feature was irregularly shaped, about one mile across. It was located at 35 deg. N, 118 deg. 29 min. W, in Kern County, about 70 miles north of Los Angeles. In the false-color infrared photographs it appeared as a red blob near a winding blue streak which was identified as the Los Angeles Aqueduct. The side-looking radar images showed the feature as a bright spot amid fainter clutter and the bold outline of the rough terrain encircling it.

But several 1:50,000 scale monochrome and color photographs taken during Skylab missions showed nothing of particular interest at the expected location, which fell on the foothills of the Tehachapi Mountains. Captions stated that, in their original form, the monochrome photographs could resolve items as small as four meters across.

TIECK: BACKGROUND IR/MW RADIATION VARIANCE ANOMALY SW SECTOR

Scale 1:50,000

Resolution: 4 meters

N35-108/W28-50   N35-128/W29-20

Datum: WGS   Ref. N35W29/Skylab/96L812

Coordinate Reference System: Geographic

Monochrome Image Map Of Infrared Anomaly Area

Looking carefully at the Skylab photographs, Charles noticed the ridge and two smaller hills perpendicular to it, in the area where the anomaly was expected to lie. The main ridge ran mainly north and south and the two fingers met and joined into a single ridge to the east, forming the Y that Arteaga had earlier noticed. One of the photographs showed a thin line near the place where the two fingers met. It could be a secondary road, thought Charles; freeways appeared distinctly in the photographs.

A caption read: TIECK: BACKGROUND IR/MW RADIATION VARIANCE ANOMALY SW SECTOR, above a monochrome image map of the infrared anomaly area. The image was marked Datum: WGS, Ref. N35W29/Skylab/96L812, Coordinate Reference System: Geographic.

Tieck had been unable to correlate the temperature and microwave radiation anomalies to any surface feature. This presented no particular problem for him, for he felt his registration techniques had been amply demonstrated. Noting the proximity of various fault zones, he concluded that a subsurface geothermal source was involved.

Charles had Chul show him to the copy machine nearby. He copied the entire article, taking particular care to obtain good reproductions of the photographs.

Later, in his room, he located Tieck's anomaly on Southern California road and terrain maps. It was located 18 miles west of State Highway 14, the major freeway Kathryn had mentioned. He drew a circle where the feature ought to be, 12 miles south of the town of Tehachapi.

2

With some difficulty, Charles got Hertz to exchange his Ford sedan for a 4-wheel drive truck. He then bought heavy-soled hiking shoes, a canteen, a knapsack and a compass at an Army/Navy store. Later, at a Sears, he bought a hunting knife, jeans, a work shirt, and binoculars. This consumed most of the morning. It was near noon when, having donned his new apparel and then eaten hurriedly at a McDonald's, he set out to investigate the feature that had so attracted Arteaga.

He didn't know what it was that he would look for, except something out of the ordinary. There was no evidence, he thought, that Arteaga had ever found the presumed location of Tieck's feature. If the temperature and microwave radiation anomaly was caused by some sort of Earth crust hot spot, its appearance in the secret document would be extremely puzzling. It occurred to Charles that a dump for spent nuclear fuel could perhaps account for Tieck's observations. But there could be no such dump in the area; it was too close to the aqueduct.

He drove north on Interstate 5, climbing away from Los Angeles smog, over the San Gabriel Mountains. When he came to Newhall, he shifted to Highway 14. The freeway turned and climbed up through the mountains. Soon he started a descent and the brush-covered hills gave way to arid flat lands bordering the Mojave Desert.

Highway 14 went through Palmdale and then Lancaster. There were no real trees about, except a few planted in the towns, only Joshua trees, cactus and sagebrush. The string-straight road stretched ahead, seemingly endlessly. Charles finally came to the town of Rosamond, which consisted of only a few houses. To his right were the dry lakes and Edwards Air Force Base. He turned left, leaving the freeway. Straight ahead, the Tehachapi Mountains were dimly visible.

The temperature had climbed gradually inside the truck, despite the air conditioner set on maximum cool. He stopped at Willow Springs for a Coca-Cola and topped off the truck's gas and water. The very low humidity kept him from sweating, but he found the heat oppressive. A thermometer at the gas station read 102 degrees.

When the paved road ended he could see the Tehachapis clearly ahead. He had to be within ten miles of the site. The problem was that the dirt road he was on did not appear on the map, and after a mile or two he had lost track of his position. There was absolutely no traffic and no sign of habitation. The gently sloping barren land offered no landmarks.

Charles pulled to the side of the road and stopped the truck. At first he left the engine running, but the temperature gauge soon reached the hot zone and he shut it off. With no air conditioning, he rolled down the windows. Instantly, he was immersed in an ocean of hot air.

He consulted the map and took a bearing with his compass. The road seemed to be leading him generally northwest, which was the right direction. He decided to press on.

Soon he came to rougher terrain, the road climbing and taking various turns. There was little vegetation about. In some places, the road was partially washed out. There were signs of erosion on the hills. More and more often, he had to detour around debris from rock falls.

Then, after carefully negotiating a hairpin turn, he saw something dark moving ahead. There was a dip in the road, and he lost sight of it temporarily. At the next rise he gained sight of the shape again. He slowed down and pulled the binoculars from the glove compartment. Through them he saw a man and a mule, perhaps two hundred yards ahead, moving slowly along the side of the road.

The man was deeply tanned, lanky and bearded, in his sixties. He wore soiled chino pants, a torn long-sleeved shirt in a blue and white square pattern buried under many stains, and a well-worn Western hat. In his hands he held a small harmonica, and he played a forlorn tune well. His mule carried a large tan pack on its back.

The mule and its master stood impassively, watching Charles approach in the truck.

"Howdy," said the old man, putting away the harmonica and watching Charles get out of the truck. The greeting carried clearly in the still air.

"Hello," answered Charles, welcoming the chance to stretch his legs.

The old man wiped his face with a brown handkerchief.

"Hot day," Charles said. He noted the mule carried a shovel and a small barrel.

"It'll get cooler in a bit," predicted the old man. "You rock hunting?"

"No, I'm doing research on a paper," Charles said. "I'm…looking for evidence of early settlement in this area."

The old man regarded Charles steadily. His brown eyes swept over the new clothes and shoes. "No one ever settled in these parts, son." He spat into the dirt. "Not even Indians. Too damned hot."

"Well, in that case I'm on a wild goose chase," Charles said. "Still, I've got to try and look."

"You're wasting your time."

"Maybe you can help me," Charles said. "I'm looking for a particular feature, and I'm having trouble finding it." He gestured vaguely in the direction of the looming mountains.

"It's a ridge running north-south, with two smaller fingers running away from it and then joining." Charles drew the ridges on the dirt with the tip of his shoe. "It should be nearby. I can show you the feature in some aerial photographs of the area," he added hopefully, gesturing toward the truck.

"No," said the old man, "no need to. That's Spur Gulch. It's thataway." He gestured down the road. "You just go on a bit, you'll pass the aqueduct; a mile or so further there'll be a fork on the road. Take the left. It'll be a mile and a half beyond that."

The man took out a small can from a pouch on the pack the mule carried, and extracted a portion of chewing tobacco. He returned the can to the pouch and put the tobacco in the corner of his mouth.

"That an all-wheel drive vehicle?" the man asked, indicating the truck and raising the rim of his hat a bit.

"Yeah," Charles said.

"You should have no problem," stated the man, chewing the tobacco. "It gets steep in places," he added.

"Well, thanks," said Charles, starting to walk back to the truck. "I appreciate your help."

"Glad to oblige," the other replied, waving.

"It's a lonely spot," said Charles, escaping the blinding sun by entering the truck.

"That it is," replied the old man, taking the reins of the mule.

As Charles drove past, the man called out to him: "There's nothing out there."

The driving got fairly hazardous at times, with deep ravines just a few feet from the crumbling edge of the road. It took Charles an hour to cover the few miles to Spur Gulch. Once there, he immediately recognized the area in the Skylab photographs.

The road had been blasted across the two smaller ridges, about a quarter mile from where they joined together to the east. The area between them was fairly flat, about 300 yards across. It extended west past a pile of boulders and ended in the distance at the face of the larger ridge.

Charles parked the truck off the side of the road and walked over to the boulders that blocked direct access to the broad ravine. They rose ten to twenty feet high, and he walked along seeking a way across. About a hundred yards from where he had parked he found a fairly low spot. He climbed over foot-high rocks and then onto larger boulders that were apparently the result of blasting through the ridges.

Slowly, he worked his way up until he could peer over the rocks into the area beyond. He saw a gently sloping area between the two hills, like on the other side of the road. It stretched for what Charles estimated to be three quarters of a mile to the side of the large ridge. Using his binoculars, he panned the area. There were no buildings, nothing but natural features, not even a trail. In places, there were a few brambly bushes, but the ravine and the hills were mostly bare rock and sandy soil.

Charles decided to return to Los Angeles then and tackle the site in the morning. It was going to take him about three hours to drive back, and night was approaching. He didn't want to have to find his way back in the dark.

3

It was a fair mid-spring afternoon with tenuous white clouds dashing across a blue sky. On the way home from school, Cicely stopped at her favorite music shop, in St. James's, and treated herself to a new CD by Pink. She had wanted to buy it for weeks, but it was one of the little luxuries she had found herself forced to postpone. The cost of Dr. McClellan's therapy was straining her finances. Being extremely watchful of her expenses, she saved every pound she could to pay for her next holiday. She and Greg were planning a trip to Brindisi.

She was in rare high spirits, and drove her MG with flair, finding empty spots in the traffic and accelerating into them, advancing ahead of a few cars each time she did so. The day had gone rapidly at school. It was close to the end of the term and she had finally caught up with her Arithmetic schedule.

Cicely parked the car and put up its top. She walked rapidly to her flat, holding her new album tightly. Her new neighbor, a stout man with a beard, greeted her along the way.

"Good evening, Miss Denfeld," the man said.

"Hello, Mr. Dramley." She smiled at him. "Going out to have fun?"

"Just a stroll before dinner."

The telephone was ringing when she arrived at her door. She picked up her mail and hurried to answer it.

It was Greg.

"Hello, dear," she said, putting her purse, the mail and her album down on the table, all the while precariously juggling the telephone handset.

"How was your day?"

"Terribly busy. It's always like this at the end of term."

"No monsters after you today?"

"Oh, no," Cicely said. She had finally sat down with Greg and told him about her dreams. Now she felt better for having done it.

"First thing in the morning, Mr. Fortescue wanted to review attendance records. Then, right in the middle of class, Alice Willers walks in wanting to borrow last year's Grammar exam. It was like that all day. All of a sudden, I lifted my eyes to the clock and it was time to come home."

"Sometimes I think you drive yourself too hard."

"You should tell that to Mr. Fortescue," Cicely said. "I am so glad you called," she added.

"Would you like to come over for a while? I just purchased a new CD; we can listen to it together."

"I…ah…don't think I can manage it tonight," Greg said.

"Oh, come on," said Cicely encouragingly, "I'll throw some things together for us to eat."

"I really can't, Cicely."

"Oh, all right. I'll stay home and play my album without you, spoilsport." She started to look over her mail while she talked. "I had hoped we could get together tonight, we haven't talked in almost a week."

She noticed a manila envelope. "I've called you at home, but you must have been out."

"The office has been very busy lately," she heard him say.

Cicely balanced the handset between her cheek and her shoulder and opened the envelope while Greg described his day. Suddenly, a wide smile lit her face. It was a travel brochure from Cook's.

"Oh, Greg," she cried, "guess what I just received in the post."

"What? A doctor's bill?"

"No, silly. It's a brochure from the travel agency—about Brindisi."

She opened up the folder. It was full of photos of ornate Italian hotel rooms and sunny Adriatic beaches.

"Oh, you have to look at this, Greg. It's going to be beautiful."

"Cicely, I have to tell you," said Greg, clearing his throat. "We're going to have to postpone our trip."

"What?" She felt like she had received a blow.

"I don't think this is the right time for it."

"It's holiday," she said, "how can it not be the right time?"

Cicely pulled a chair over and slowly sat down. The Brindisi catalog slipped from her fingers and fell to the floor.

"Darling," he said, "you're not well. A trip abroad is bound to be stressful."

"Oh, no, I'll be all right, dear." Tears welled in her eyes. "I've looked forward to this holiday so much."

"Perhaps we'll do it some other time," he said. "I must go now, Cicely." Then he hung up.

"Oh, God." Cicely put down the receiver and cried.

She sat at the table for a long time. It was dark by the time she stopped crying. Then she turned on the light and walked slowly to her bedroom.

Later, after a long warm bath, she sat down on her couch and started to play her new album. After a few moments of listening to the music she became nervous. She removed the Pink disc and replaced it with one of selections from Mendelssohn. After a while she opened her best bottle of brandy and called up Angie on the telephone.

She took occasional sips of the warming liquid while she told her friend of her dashed romance.

"Greg is an animal, Cicely," declared her friend. "All men are. Just forget the bastard."

"I don't know if I can, Angie. In a way he's right; I would probably be no fun on a holiday."

"Blast it, Cicely, don't think like that. You are a wonderful person."

"I don't feel very wonderful just now."

"You need to get this out of your system. I tell you what, we'll kidnap lame-brained Greg and I'll hold him while you pour acid down his throat."

"Angie!"

"Oh, you are right. The acid should be poured lower than that. Right between his legs should do, eh?"

"Oh Angie, you're *terrible*."

4

Sleep came very late. When the dream came she welcomed it.

She stepped out of a huge American vehicle and walked along a dirt road. It was very hot.

Charles had bought two additional items that morning: a small pickaxe and a wide-brimmed straw hat. He thought of purchasing a Geiger counter, but couldn't think of where to get one on short notice. It was eleven o'clock when he arrived back at Spur Gulch.

He walked along the piles of rock and found again the low point he had seen the day before. With unpracticed hands and feet, he climbed over the boulders, the knapsack containing his pickaxe, binoculars and other items bouncing on his back.

Once on the other side he took out his binoculars and again surveyed the area. The ridges to his right and left stretched ahead until they merged with the taller hill in the distance. For ten minutes he carefully examined the sides of the hills through his binoculars. He saw only rough bare rock and sandy soil.

He moved along the bottom of the ravine in a zigzag course that took him at intervals near both of the opposite ridges. The searing heat continued to build as the day wore on. By one o'clock he had traversed the length of Spur Gulch. He rested for a while and then walked the entire base of the far ridge. There was a little more sagebrush in that area and, for an instant,

Charles caught sight of an animal; a jackrabbit. It was the first living thing he had seen in the ravine.

This was the area beneath which the anomaly should lie. There was no construction in sight, not even a shed. So far, he hadn't seen any of the detritus of man's activities: nails, beer cans, splinters of wood, discarded clothing.

With great care, Charles started to climb the face of the large ridge. He found the going rough. The hill was steep. He used the pickaxe to gain a purchase in the rock from time to time. When he had climbed about seventy feet he made the mistake of looking down and became giddy. He kept his eyes to the face of the hill from then on.

He was half way up the hill when the tremor struck. Suddenly, a loud rumbling sound swelled from deep inside the earth. The rock under him shook and then vibrated wildly. His hold loosened and Charles found himself slipping down the bucking ridge. The roar beneath grew steadily.

CHAPTER 9
THE RESSEPS

1

Alone in his office, Dr. McClellan had spent the last hour going over Cicely Denfeld's case history. One by one he had considered and abandoned a series of diagnoses. There were elements of depression, but that was not the root cause. In fact, a less sturdy self might not have withstood the inexplicable dream sequences without incurring severe trauma. Early on, he had considered the possibility of a sexual inversion, based not only on some dream elements, but on Cicely's relationship with her friend Angie. As therapy had progressed, however, Dr. McClellan had become convinced that Cicely's sexual development was quite normal. There was nothing to suggest unresolved parental conflicts.

Her experiences of depersonalization baffled him. For some time, he had entertained the idea that he may be facing one of the very rare cases of multiple personality. He had encountered only one such case in his entire career and Cicely's case had prompted him to read widely on the subject. But no second personality had emerged during the sessions and no telltale gaps in Cicely's life or other signposts of the multiple personality syndrome had appeared. And yet there were multiple personalities in the dreams. Charles was a perfectionist, guileless and idealistic; Vivian was assertive and pragmatic.

Feeling at an impasse, he decided to seek advice from his friends and colleagues and to use hypnosis if there was no improvement in Cicely's condition.

2

Charles struggled to regain a grip as his hands and feet skipped over the rocks. A stone hit his head and he winced in pain.

His hand automatically grabbed at a piece of jutting rock and he gained an uncertain purchase on it. Sand and small rocks rained on him as he moved his feet in a frantic search for a foothold. All the while, the earth shook and rumbled under him.

Then, as suddenly as it had started, the tremor stopped.

Charles clung precariously to the side of the hill, his heart racing. He moved carefully to gain a better hold on the rock. Very slowly, he climbed down the hill.

"This is the end of this assignment," he told himself. Reaching the base of the ravine, he dusted himself off and inspected the bruises and scrapes he had acquired during his fall. He glanced up for a moment at the searing sun. If he had broken a leg, he thought, he would very likely have died before reaching help.

Charles took a sip of hot water from his canteen and started the long trek back to the truck. He would get a full night's sleep and fly back to Seattle in the morning. The plane trip would give him time to write a note to Robinson, outlining what he had learned.

The fact that the Tieck thesis was legitimate lent credibility to the Arteaga document. The dancer's description of Arteaga's behavior during the weeks before his disappearance was consistent with Arteaga's own account of his obsession with the document. But the nature of Tieck's anomaly remained a mystery, as did its relationship to the other topics listed in the document's index.

It might be possible to unravel the whole thing, he thought, but Robinson would have to invest significant resources to do it. It would take four men a week to methodically search Spur Gulch. And there was the matter of the people that had ransacked Arteaga's apartment—possibly the same ones that had later tracked him to Cuba and killed him. Their determination and ruthlessness would place formidable obstacles in the way of anyone trying to follow in Arteaga's footsteps.

Charles had lost his hat during the fall. The scorching sun made the top of his head feel unbearably hot. Listlessly, he trudged on. In his mind, he imagined himself back at his engineer's job, working out design tradeoffs and worrying about office politics. Let Robinson worry about the Arteaga document, he told himself.

The day grew progressively hotter. He walked along the bottom of the ravine, wending his way among the few outcroppings. Out of habit, he continued to look for any signs of habitation, but he saw only the bare rocky land and the occasional thorny bush. The one jackrabbit he had seen earlier must have sought refuge from the earthquake in its burrow.

Then he noticed a darkness on the side of the ridge to his left. He had not seen it earlier, on his way in. It was a hundred yards away. Thinking it might be a shadow, he examined it through his binoculars.

There was a crevice there now, several feet across. He decided to take a closer look and turned away from the still-distant far side of the ravine and toward the dark spot on the side of the hill.

As he approached the area, Charles noted a pile of rocks scattered at the base of the ridge. The crevice was about six feet high and roughly triangular in shape. The broad lower portion, near ground level, was about two feet wide. Its sides narrowed gradually and peaked at the top. Evidently a layer of rock on the face of the hill had been loosened by the quake and had crashed down, exposing the fissure.

Charles stepped over small loose boulders and regarded the crevice. As he did so, a lizard skittered past him. This was not just a fault in the surface. He could see that the crevice led to a larger cavity. Bending his head, he first peered inside and then walked sideways through the crack in the rock.

It was a cave, he thought. The floor, covered with rubble, widened ahead. He walked a few feet inside. The back was pitch black. With his hand, he felt the wall to his left. The rock felt cool and roughly textured. When his eyes started to adapt to the darkness he was able to see indistinctly a wall to the right, about fifteen feet away. Except where the wall had collapsed, the sides curved gradually inwards as they rose. As his vision improved, he slowly continued his inward progress. He looked up and judged that the cave was eight or nine feet at its highest. Its cross section further in was a precise semicircle. It must be eighteen feet wide, thought Charles. He had found a manmade tunnel. The entrance had been plugged.

He needed a flashlight if he was going to explore much further. It had not occurred to him to bring one along. He did not even have a match. His wide open eyes began to smart. Slowly, feeling his way along the wall, he pressed on. The floor of the tunnel became smoother. He had gone on about fifty feet, when he heard something ahead. Stopping, he listened intently.

He heard the sound again, from further ahead in the tunnel. It was faint and regular. The echoing sound of steps. Suddenly, he saw a faint light ahead. The field of light moved jerkily and varied in intensity.

Gradually, the sound of footfalls grew louder. Charles looked uneasily at the growing illuminated area. The tunnel veered to the right about fifty feet ahead. Someone was approaching and would soon reach the turn in the tunnel.

Charles turned around and started walking back toward the entrance. He tried to make as little noise as possible. Then there was a voice, calling out something. Charles could not understand it. The illumination grew brighter and he heard the sound of steps behind him quicken their tempo. Charles' heart thumped within his chest. He started to run.

The lighting was very poor. Charles guided himself mostly by the bright vertical slit that he saw ahead—the crevice at the entrance to the tunnel.

All of a sudden, the ground started shaking again. Charles slipped and fell to the floor. Over the growing rumble, he heard the steps behind him draw nearer. He was bathed in light, and he again heard the voice, its sound overwhelmed by the mountain's hollow roar. With great effort, he struggled to his feet, but the ground seemed to jump under him and he made little progress. He clutched wildly at the wall, trying to keep from falling again.

Looking behind, he saw a figure approach in the shadows and then was blinded as the light was trained on him. The roar of the mountain became deafening, the shaking of the earth more intense. Charles fell down again and felt himself lifted up, propelled into the air by the wildly shaking ground. Then the tunnel walls split and the roar became an intolerably loud continuous CRACK.

Fragments of rock fell on and about him and the floor he stood on buckled. He was thrown about like a rag doll. Then something hit him very hard and he lay unconscious in the darkness, as the world about him fell apart.

3

The pain told him that he was alive. He was lying on his side and he could not move. There was darkness and silence all about him. Was he paralyzed? An attempt to move only brought dizziness and a ringing sound to his ears.

Dear God, had the quake crushed him and trapped him under the weight of the mountain? His mind pursued those thoughts, racing in mounting panic. How long would he last? He might live for days blinded, immobile. Charles heard his own heart pounding wildly. He screamed in panic, and found that he could move after all—at least his arms. Something held his legs.

Then he heard a noise from outside himself, a faint cry. The pain lessened and he found that he could move his torso. He managed to raise his upper body, but could not stand. Tentatively, he wriggled his toes. He felt them move inside his shoes. Using one hand as a prop, he reached ahead blindly with the other and felt an object across his legs, holding them down.

The ringing in his ears subsided and he heard a voice. A man's voice. It sounded near, perhaps only a few feet away. Charles stared into the darkness and wondered if he had been permanently blinded. He paid close attention, but could not understand. The other man spoke in a foreign language.

"I cannot understand you," muttered Charles, his voice a weak croak. "Who are you?"

The other's voice stopped. Charles cleared his throat and repeated his question.

Suddenly, a light illuminated him and his surroundings. He was trapped in a section of tunnel about eight feet wide and twelve feet long. There was a metal girder across his legs. He could see the pale form of a slender man half buried in debris a few feet away.

"I had not experienced an earthquake before," said the other in a clear unaccented voice.

Charles surveyed his surroundings more carefully. He found it impossible to orient himself. Jagged rock had thrust through the tunnel's walls. With some effort he undid the straps that secured the rucksack to his back. He extracted the compass. The glass had cracked, but it seemed serviceable. Holding it with both hands, Charles steadied it and took a bearing. He knew the tunnel ran roughly north-south. With the help of the compass he determined the direction in which the tunnel mouth should lie. He was going to have to dig his way out of the place.

His attention returned to his companion. He wore a glossy white outfit, now soiled with dirt. There was something peculiar about him, although Charles could not pinpoint what it was.

"Who are you?" Charles asked again.

After a moment's silence, the other replied: "I am the Resseps."

"What?"

"The Resseps Scahn," the stranger said. "What are you doing here?"

Charles brought the pickax forward and, slipping it under the beam that held down his legs, used it as a lever to lift the beam. It budged a bit, but the pickax did not provide a sufficiently long lever arm. After several attempts, Charles succeeded in pulling his legs partly from under the beam. But he was not able to push the girder high enough to free his feet. Out of breath, he had to stop, exhausted. His whole body was covered with sweat.

"What are you doing?" the stranger asked.

Charles explained his predicament and his intention to dig a way out of the space they were confined in.

"That is not a good plan," stated the other.

"Why not? Do you have a better one?"

"Yes. You must dig in the opposite direction."

"Into the mountain?"

"Towards the main tunnel."

Charles noticed that, although the stranger's speech was normally accented and his pronunciation was correct, there was a remarkable quality to his voice. Its timbre had a characteristic like a very mild reverberation or a slight echo. Perhaps it was the acoustics of their confined space, but Charles had not detected it in his own voice.

"I want to return to the surface," Charles said.

"That may be done in time, but first we must reach the tunnel."

"Are you with the Government?" Charles asked.

He looked more closely at his companion. The man had been trapped beneath the rubble. Rocks and metal beams had fallen on him, pressing down on his legs and one of his arms. There was no blood, but the man was clearly very restricted in his movement. Charles noticed his pale broad face and bald head.

"Yes, I am with the Government," said the stranger. "We must proceed at once."

"Where does the tunnel go?" Charles asked. He again used the pickax to try to lift the beam. He slid his feet an inch or so further out, but could not manage any more and gave up, panting.

"To the processing facility," said the other. "Stop what you're doing. You will not succeed in freeing yourself that way. Listen carefully. I will tell you how to proceed."

"What kind of processing facility?" Charles asked. He started to dig under his foot with the pickax, but made slow progress. The surface was as hard as concrete.

The light suddenly went out. They were enveloped in an ink-black gloom.

The irrational fears Charles had just managed to suppress bolted into his thoughts under the cloak of darkness. Without light he had no hope of escape.

"Hey," cried Charles, "what happened? Turn that light back on!"

There was no response. Charles heard the sound of his own racing heart. His panic grew. Had the man died? His breathing became more labored.

"Hello, are you all right? Resseps, is that your name? What happened to you?"

For a while the only sound Charles heard was that of his own breathing.

"Listen to me," said the other at last.

"What happened to the light? Are you all right?"

"Be silent. If you listen in silence I will restore illumination soon."

"I'm listening," said Charles immediately.

"Good. Pay close attention. There are approximately sixteen cubic meters of air in this space. We have used a lot of the oxygen already. Unless we take action, we will be asphyxiated soon. I cannot free myself without assistance, and neither can you."

"I think I can pry my feet loose," Charles said.

"By the time you free your legs you will be near death. Even if you were free now you would lose consciousness before you reached the surface. It is at least fifteen meters away. You cannot dig through that much rock and debris in time."

The stranger paused for a moment. "Do you accept what I have said so far?" he said.

Charles thought for a moment. He already knew they were running out of oxygen. For quite some time he had felt an oppressive heaviness closing in on him. "I accept it," he answered.

"What are you called?"

"Charles Ryder."

"Very well, Charles Ryder. If you agree to follow my plan, I will assist you in freeing yourself."

"How are you going to do that?" Charles asked.

"I will explain in a moment."

The light was restored. Charles felt as if a weight had been lifted from his shoulders. He eyed his surroundings, delighted to see again.

"Listen. If, once freed, you proceeded in the proper direction, toward the undamaged portion of the tunnel, using your axe, you would still perish. It would take you too long."

"Are you saying we're doomed?"

"Precisely. Unless we act in concert." The stranger placed the light down and brought forth a small dark box. Holding it in the palm of his free hand, he pointed it at the walls of their confined space in a sweeping motion. The box emitted a series of musical sounds.

"The tunnel lies two meters away. After you dig a cavity through the first meter I will provide the means for producing an explosion that will break through the remaining material."

"If you have explosives, why not use them now?"

"In this confined space, a sufficiently powerful explosion would kill us. We need to remove part of the rock wall first. After the explosion occurs, you must go out into the tunnel and reach a blue box. They are set in the tunnel wall at intervals of about a hundred meters. The box will have a large square button on its side. Press it. Help will arrive soon afterwards."

"You said you would help me free myself."

"Yes."

"What happens when we get out?"

"You will have saved my life. I will reward you in many ways, Charles Ryder."

Charles tried to chuckle, but only succeeded in coughing. "Really? And how will you do that?"

The light went out.

"Oh, don't start that again," pleaded Charles.

"If you do as I ask you will experience wealth and power beyond your greatest expectations."

Charles sighed. In the confined space it sounded like a puff of wind that momentarily intruded on the absolute calm.

"I give you my solemn word," stated the other. "Hurry, or we will both surely die."

Charles did not really have a choice. "Very well, I agree," he said.

The cavity was illuminated again.

4

"Wait while I prepare the *imdermi*, Charles Ryder."

"What did you say your name is?" Charles asked warily.

"I'm the Resseps Scahn," answered the other, manipulating the tool he held in his hand. The object did not have the characteristic bulbous head of a flashlight. It was rod-like, about an inch in diameter and eighteen inches long. The Resseps held it down with his body and twisted it with his hand. All of a sudden, the rod doubled in length. He pressed something on the rod and it started to glow all over. The dim green glow added substantially to the available illumination.

"I will throw this in your direction. Be certain to catch it."

The Resseps swung the object awkwardly. It traveled across the tunnel, spinning slowly, and skittered over the rocks. Charles lunged and caught it while it was still in motion.

"Use it like you used your axe," the Resseps said. "It should provide sufficient mechanical advantage."

Charles eyed the glowing rod dubiously. At least, he thought, now that he held the light source his companion would not be pulling any more "lights out" tricks. He pulled the pickax from under the beam and substituted the rod, now three feet in length. Wedging the rod under a rock, he pushed against the beam, half expecting the rod to bend. But the rod remained rigid and the beam lifted slightly. He took a deep breath and pushed again, raising the beam several inches. Hurriedly, Charles extracted his feet.

Free at last, Charles crawled on his knees toward his companion. He dragged his pickax along, and held the illuminating rod in his hand.

"This is a fancy light you have here, Resseps," said Charles, noting etched rings and markings on what he took to be the grip end of the rod.

Charles shined the light on the other, for the first time getting a good look at him. He took a sharp breath of air, shocked by what he saw.

His companion wore a white form-clinging outfit. He appeared to be of average size and proportions, except for his neck, which seemed uncommonly long. Half his body laid buried under girders and debris. His head was as wide as Charles had seen on any man. The high and narrow nose blended directly with the forehead. The irises of his large eyes were a striking orange color. There were no eyebrows. The skin covering the bald skull had a bronze sheen.

This, Charles thought, was either a very peculiar human specimen, or…

The Resseps caught Charles' stare. "You have noticed I look different," he said.

Charles nodded, accepting the understatement.

"I will explain this to you in time." The Resseps pointed at the far side of their confined space. "You must start digging at once in that direction." His words carried the insolent certainty of command.

Charles did not move. The other's ears were uncommonly small and rounded, he noted. They lacked earlobes.

"You must trust me now. The only alternative is death."

Charles did the best he could with the shreds of self-possession that were left to him. "What goes on at this place?"

"I will explain once you start to dig."

Charles felt a growing shortness of breath. He decided to follow the Resseps' suggestion. There seemed little point in throwing away a chance at survival just because he appeared to be sharing a collapsed tunnel with someone that might not be human.

He worked mechanically, ignoring the heaviness of his arms and the growing dizziness. Death was very near and he preferred not to dwell on it. He devoted his entire attention to his task, swinging the pickax repeatedly against the rock and dirt.

"Stop now," shouted the Resseps over the sound of the pickax.

Charles stopped and looked dully back at his companion. Drops of sweat fell from his chin. The Resseps was not doing well either, his chest was heaving and he looked ill.

"Bring the *imdermi* here."

Charles had dug a shallow cavity in the wall. It was now about three feet deep. He crawled away from it and toward the Resseps, dragging the light along. He started to give the glowing rod to the other.

"No," said the Resseps, "hold it tightly."

While Charles held the rod, the Resseps grabbed it and twisted it. The rod sprang back to its original shorter length and the green glow ceased. The Resseps performed other manipulations, and the device started to hum. It emitted a pulsing red glow.

"Drive it at once as deep as you can into the cavity, with the bright end against the rock. Then get as far as possible from it. It will propel a shaped charge against the wall in a few seconds."

Charles hurried across their small prison and rammed the pulsing rod forcefully into the rear of the cavity he had dug. Panting, he rolled away across the pit and lay down on the floor, bracing himself.

The humming increased in pitch and was followed by a whooshing sound that rapidly increased in volume until it assumed the loudness of thunder. A blast of incredibly loud noise pushed Charles against the tunnel wall. There was darkness for an instant and then the clatter stopped. He found himself covered with dirt and pebbles and bathed in a soft red light.

Charles stumbled out of the pit and onto a wide corridor. He peered at his surroundings through a cloud of dust. The red light came from narrow strips high on the curving walls. He must find the blue box, he thought. With uncertain steps, he careened into the side of the tunnel and fell down.

He felt totally exhausted. Slowly, he picked himself up and staggered down the corridor. He could hear a faint whirring sound. A dull pain gnawed at his side. He realized he was bleeding. "What kind of place is this?" he asked himself.

Then he saw the blue box.

TRANSFERENCE

CHAPTER 10
JULY

1

Cicely had come directly from school and wore a gray business suit. With sad eyes, she looked at Dr. McClellan.

"Your holiday starts next week, does it not?" Dr. McClellan asked.

"I shan't be going to Brindisi," she stated. "Greg doesn't want to go any more."

Dr. McClellan's face did not show it, but he was disappointed to hear this. He had counted on the trip abroad to break Cicely's routine and take her mind off her dreams.

"I'll just stay home." She worked a curl of hair around her finger and twisted it into a gold spiral.

Dr. McClellan looked at her closely, but said nothing.

Cicely sighed. "I could go visit my uncle, I suppose."

"Where does he live?"

"In Lurgan, near Belfast. He moved there from Leicester two years ago."

"Do you think you would enjoy a visit?"

Cicely considered this for a moment. "I think so. It's pretty where he lives. There's a lake, and one can see hills in the distance. He has horses—thoroughbreds. They are beautiful animals."

"I was in Belfast last summer for a convention. We had a good time. It was very quiet. I expected barricades and police sirens."

Cicely smiled. "I think it's not as bad as the telly would have us think."

"Do you miss your parents, Cicely?"

"Yes, very much," she said, a bit startled by the question.

"Have you thought of a possible link between your parents and some of the people in your dreams? Robinson, for example."

Cicely considered his question for a moment. "No, I hadn't thought of that." She let go of her hair and brought her hands together on her lap. "Father was not like Mr. Robinson at all. He was thin and tall and very kind. Mr. Robinson is calculating and cold."

Dr. McClellan looked at her, but said nothing. Cicely fidgeted in the deep chair.

"I have been more nervous lately," she said. "I think partly because of the argument with Greg. All of a sudden, I find that I can't stand listening to some of my favorite music; the harder rock. It makes me very nervous. I never have been a great fan of classical music, but it's the only music I can enjoy now. It calms me down."

"Well, perhaps you are faced with a natural development in your music appreciation," said Dr. McClellan. "No point in dwelling on that, Cicely. For the time being it is probably best to avoid unnecessary excitement."

Cicely sighed.

"I purchased a voice recorder," she said. "I talk into it right after I wake up, so that I can recall the dreams better."

"That's a very good idea. We will go over the dreams in a moment." He made a note on the sheet of paper before him.

"I'll be meeting with some colleagues next month, and the opportunity to discuss certain features of your case may present itself. It is possible that such a discussion would provide a useful insight. I would not be using your name. Would you have any objection to my discussing your case?"

Cicely shook her head. "I don't mind, Doctor. I would do anything to free myself of these dreams."

"Very well." He made another note and then turned his chair, so that he faced slightly away from Cicely, and locked his hands behind his neck.

Cicely stretched in her chair and prepared to recount her latest dream.

"It started pleasantly. I felt like I was floating. No weight, no stress on any part of my body. Very comfortable. I enjoyed it. Then, gradually, I developed an awareness of my environment. A diffuse whiteness surrounded me, like a cloud. Later, a very faint sound intruded. A mechanical sound, a whir."

Cicely closed her eyes.

"Very, very slowly, I felt myself fall. Eventually, I felt a gentle pressure on my back. My eyes must have been open before, but I don't recall seeing anything until the curved white surface above me rotated out of the way. The whiteness was replaced by gray. Someone took my arm and assisted me to a sitting position. I realized at once that I was Charles. But where…"

2

His helper's head was bald and his skin was of a peculiar bronze color. Charles thought, at first, that it was the Resseps that was assisting him. But, when the man turned, Charles saw that the expressionless face was that of a very young man.

"Hello," Charles said, testing his voice.

"*Ucilaum mudipe*," said the other. He held a small ovoid object in his hand and pointed it at Charles. The instrument clicked faintly and the young man, satisfied, put it away.

The man wore a pale green skintight shirt and what looked like cutoff slacks, also green. Charles' own clothes had been replaced with some similar to those his attendant wore.

Charles stared at the other. The man had a curiously smooth wide face that was kept from being characterless by oddly watchful eyes. He stood motionless, regarding Charles steadily, as if expecting him to do or say something.

"*Ucilaum mudipe*," repeated the man. When Charles failed to respond, he added: "*Cunu eldi. Oldet birece paem.*" His voice was singularly even.

With mounting apprehension, Charles turned and looked at his surroundings. He sat on the edge of what looked like a modernistic Pullman car bed. It was at the center of a large round room with a domed ceiling. There didn't seem to be any doors or windows and he could not tell where the light came from.

"I don't understand you," said Charles, returning his gaze to the man.

The green-attired man uttered another string of incomprehensible sounds. Then, after making a palms down gesture that Charles interpreted as a request to stay where he was, the other turned and briskly walked away. As he approached the curved wall, a square opening suddenly appeared. When, just as the man crossed the portal and Charles, astounded, started to look closely, the opening disappeared.

Charles slowly shook his head.

He slid carefully from his perch at the odd but comfortable structure and stood up. Feeling a trace of dizziness, he placed his hand on the flat surface to steady himself. It had a smooth yielding texture, like a marshmallow.

The curved walls were a light gray that faded gradually into the eggshell-white ceiling. There was no furniture, other than the odd covered bed and a brown hemispherical mound across the room, opposite the area where the portal had briefly appeared.

It occurred to him that he might be in detention. He paced the circular room. It was about twenty-five feet in diameter. Large for a jail cell. He wondered how the Resseps had fared. The strange man had seemed alive right after the explosion, when Charles had last seen him.

Then, suddenly, the opening in the wall reappeared and a woman entered the room, followed by the young man that Charles had seen earlier. Immediately after the man entered, the opening disappeared behind him. The doorway, Charles noted, worked soundlessly, and whatever mechanism activated it took less than a second to operate.

The woman had the peculiar bronze skin. She held herself very erect and moved with swift determination. Her clothing, consisting of green clinging shirt and short pants, similar to what her male companion wore, revealed a thin but well-formed body.

Turning to the man she said: "*E amldronemdu, Pagres.*"

The other gave her the ovoid object Charles had seen earlier, and she proceeded to point it in Charles' direction. It clicked as before. Charles noted what looked like a very small screen on the top of the device. The woman looked at it attentively. Her broad face was almost handsome, her features very symmetrical, but unusual. Her nose had the same chiseled narrowness and it blended into her forehead in the same manner that Charles had seen earlier in the Resseps and in her companion. Unlike the others, she had hair. It was a lustrous gray.

"Do you speak English?" Charles asked. He stood still, inspecting the others while they unemotionally examined him. The woman looked up from her instrument for a moment. Charles gasped. Her irises were a speckled white, only slightly darker than the whites of her eyes. With some effort, he checked the wave of anxiety that was rising inside him.

"*Drie e limnen,*" the woman told the other curtly.

The man departed immediately. This time, Charles watched the portal more closely. He could detect no mechanism. In a fraction of a second, a square section of the gray wall disappeared. The wall itself had a finite thickness. Charles estimated at least two inches. There was a corridor beyond. Charles caught a glimpse of movement. Once the man had left the room, the wall was returned to its previous state instantly.

Puzzled, Charles began to approach the area of the wall where the opening had appeared, but the woman touched him firmly in the center of his chest. She wanted him to stay in place.

"Where's the Resseps? I want to see him," demanded Charles.

The woman ignored him and continued to point the instrument in his direction, deliberately covering his entire body with a series of slow sweeping motions. Charles noted a blue metal device on her shirt collar, like a cross inside an ellipse. There were three small red circles under it. Then she did something that startled Charles. She drew a few steps back, away from him, and said: "*Ilaemdul*." Instantly, a blue surface emerged from the floor.

Charles jumped back instinctively, at the same time as the woman pointed at the surface with her left hand. She repeated the gesture, and the corners of her lips lifted slightly, in a suggestion of a smile.

At that time the green-clad man walked through the portal again, and it again disappeared behind him. Wordlessly, he handed a small object to the woman. She regarded it for a moment. It was bronze colored, about the size and shape of a bean. She inserted it in her ear.

Then the woman approached Charles, pointed again at the blue object that had just emerged from the floor and, in a clear voice, said: "Sit down." Her tone made it clear it was a command.

Charles looked at the blue object. Higher than a normal chair, it took him a while to discern how to use it. He climbed on the upper part, which was a generous seat, and then hooked his feet behind the lower part, so that it ended in front of his shins. Then the whole contraption tilted slightly and adjusted itself, so that cushioned surfaces supported his shins, the back of his thighs, and his buttocks. His feet touched the floor, but carried little of his weight.

The idea of making a dash for the door crossed his mind, but he felt weak, and it seemed unlikely that he would make it very far. There were bound to be more of the bronze-skinned types around. Charles was very concerned by the level of technology implied by the equipment they so casually used.

Once she saw him settled, the woman resumed her scanning, her movements slick and economical.

"Your physical state is now normal," she stated. "There is nothing to fear. Try to relax."

Charles was trying his best to do just that. "Do you have food?" he asked.

She said a few words to the young man and he departed swiftly. Again Charles watched as he went through the portal. For the first time, he noticed a faint narrow band around the door. It was less than a quarter-inch wide, and a shade of gray just barely lighter than the rest of the wall.

"How does the door work?"

She looked up from her instrument momentarily, her white eyes disconcertingly probing. Charles again thought he saw the barest suggestion of a smile form briefly on her lips.

"It is not what you know as a door," she said. Her voice had the same sonorous quality as the Resseps'. Despite the unusual timbre, Charles found it pleasing. Her pronunciation was unaccented and precise. He wondered why she had been so reluctant to speak English earlier.

"There is a force field generator on the sides of the opening. It seals the room from external air currents and sound. A projector—it may be either at the top or the bottom of the opening—creates a laser image tuned to blend with the adjoining wall."

"You mean there is really nothing there?"

"There is no matter in the...doorway."

Charles decided not to pursue that any further. "Where are we?" he asked.

"We are in the clinic, underground. About half a kilometer from where you and the Resseps were found. You were wounded and were brought here for treatment."

"But where, what clinic? What is this place?"

She looked at him again, then continued her scanning. Charles wondered if it was she who had cleaned his wounds and changed his clothes.

"We are about two hundred meters under the surface, in the Indane-Aliemt compound."

Before he could phrase his next question, she went on. "It is part of a Dramtes manufacturing facility, jointly operated by Indane-Aliemt and Bithian interests, and licensed by the United States government."

She put away the instrument she held and looked directly at Charles.

"What are you called?" she asked.

He thought of giving a false name, but saw nothing to gain. "Charles Ryder."

"The Pagres will bring food soon. I am Kneth Karyprit. You will address me as Mistress."

She went over to the wall and pressed something there. An object about the size and shape of a small book slid out and she took it in her hand. As she walked back her fingers moved swiftly over its surface and it emitted a few beeps and clicks.

"Your name is inconveniently long." She paused for a moment and then added: "I will call you Chasrydel. Once you are able to speak Galamic, you may address the Pagres by his name, Drimtul, or you may call him Pagres, as you wish. He does not communicate in English."

Before Charles could respond, the Pagres returned, followed by a cylindrical chromium object, about two feet high, apparently self-propelled. The Pagres gestured toward Charles, and the object moved silently and came to a stop next to Charles. Its flat top rotated, revealing a dished semicircle filled with glistening purple crystals and a few translucent balls.

Karyprit took one of the crystals from the chrome cylinder and daintily put it in her mouth. Small flawless teeth gleamed behind her pale lips.

"Eat," she commanded.

The crystals had the consistency of jellybeans. They had a sharp, salty taste, something like caviar, that Charles found appealing. The translucent globes, about the size of marbles, were filled with a fresh liquid.

"How did you enter the facility?" Karyprit asked. Evidently finished with her scanning, she returned the ovoid instrument to the Pagres. The two now stood by Charles, watching him attentively.

"There was an earth tremor earlier. It must have cracked the surface covering the entry to one of your tunnels. I went in and was trapped with the Resseps when the second shock hit us."

"How did you know the Resseps would be there?"

"I didn't."

Karyprit frowned. "You will address me as Mistress!"

Charles suppressed an impulse to tell the woman to go and perform an unnatural act.

"I didn't, Mistress. I didn't know the tunnel would be there."

Karyprit gave him a curious look. "Your presence at the tunnel entrance was accidental?"

Charles decided that he would have to reveal part of the truth in order to tell a credible story. But he would not reveal his connection to Robinson. If these people decided to hold him, only Robinson could conceivably expose them and force them to set him free.

"I didn't know about the tunnel, but I suspected that I would find something in the area."

"Why did you suspect that, Chasrydel?"

"I came across a report that identified a background radiation anomaly in this area, Mistress."

"Expand."

"It was a dissertation for a doctorate, by a student called Tieck. In the course of surveying remote sensor data he detected an anomaly in infrared and microwave radiation from this vicinity. I became curious and decided to take a look."

Karyprit looked at him dubiously.

"What are you people? This technology, this place, what are you all about?" Charles saw a frown begin to form on Karyprit's wide brow and quickly added: "Mistress."

"Our expedition originated in a system called Omver."

Charles shuddered. "A system?" he asked in a weak voice, looking into Karyprit's white eyes.

She watched Charles closely. "A star system, about eleven light years away, in the constellation Eridanus."

Charles felt very weak and his vision clouded. He started to slip from his seat, his body suddenly limp. The Pagres moved swiftly and caught him before he could fall.

It had to be some sort of shock-induced hallucination, Charles thought. This couldn't be true. Maybe he was back at the cave. Oxygen deprivation could do dreadful things to one's mind.

He looked at the Pagres and tried to wish him away. But the bronze-skinned man remained. The barest trace of concern showed in his face. Behind him, Karyprit regarded him coldly.

It was true. It was real. As real as the strange chair he sat on. Unless he and the others were insane. Aliens!

The Pagres pressed something cold against his arm and soon Charles felt relief from his anxiety. It was as if he had taken a few steps back from himself and his own problems were no longer of immediate concern.

They helped him to the bed and he went willingly to sleep.

3

They sat in a circle on the odd self-adjusting seats that Charles had come to accept. Charles, Kneth Karyprit, the Resseps Scahn, and another of slightly military bearing that Karyprit had introduced as Kneth Cupahr.

"*Ucilaum mudipe*," Cupahr said. Charles had learned this meant something like "remarkable event". It was a standard greeting. Cupahr, like the Resseps, wore a white outfit. Karyprit and Charles wore green.

"*Ucilaum mudipe*," echoed Charles in response.

"Why has Charles Ryder not been fitted with a *limnen*, Kneth?" asked the Resseps.

"For security reasons, Lord," she answered. "Since his entry to the facility was not authorized, Obiredes Nesadl directed that his access to information be restricted."

"And yet you told him of Bithia and Indane-Aliemt and the Dramtes," the Resseps said. "Why?"

Karyprit shifted her position slightly. "It was done to ascertain Chasrydel's reactions. To determine what he already knew, Lord."

"Chasrydel?" Cupahr asked.

Karyprit turned slightly to face him. "I have registered him under that name, Kneth," she told Cupahr.

"I am bringing an attendant for," there was the merest of hesitations, "Chasrydel," said the Resseps.

"He will not require an attendant here, Lord. The staff sees to his requirements."

"Chasrydel will not remain here. He will reside in the Bithian compound."

"We have not yet completed his examination, Lord," Karyprit objected. "I have planned—"

"Have you not healed him already, Kneth?"

"Why, yes. He is well."

"Then there is no reason for him to stay in Indane-Aliemt quarters. Chasrydel's attendant will soon arrive outside, Kneth. Go meet her and direct her here."

Karyprit stood up and bowed almost imperceptibly in the direction of the Resseps. "Yes, Lord," she said, and left the room.

The Resseps turned to face Charles. "I am glad that you are well," he said.

"Thank you," Charles said. He added, uncertainly, "Lord."

"Our agreement with your government includes a secrecy provision," the Resseps said. "You are in effect neither authorized to be here, nor, given what you already know, to return to the surface. Kneth Karyprit has aggravated the situation by giving you additional information. Did she mention the word Omver?"

"It is the name of the star you come from."

"Its Earth name is Epsilon Eridani."

The Resseps regarded Charles with shrewd coral eyes. "I will study options that may make your return possible. In the interim, we need the assistance of people such as you. Our project is undermanned. It will also be an opportunity for you to learn. What is your occupation, Chasrydel?"

"I'm an engineer."

"Well, you will be amazed with our technology."

"I already am, Lord."

"You will have initially the status of a Pagres," said the Resseps. "You will work under Kneth Cupahr's direction."

The Resseps stood up. With a gesture, he indicated for the others to remain seated.

"I promised you a reward there in the tunnel, Chasrydel. Your involvement in the Bithian enterprise will help us to determine how best to implement it. I must leave now. *Loerde fivuresci.*"

"*Loerde fivuresci,*" echoed Charles and Cupahr. It was, Charles had learned, a form of farewell. It meant "may chance favor you."

The Resseps left the room.

Charles glanced at Cupahr. The man had very short gray hair and was powerfully built. He carried himself very erect and his countenance was stolid.

"We will work together well, Pagres Chasrydel," said Cupahr, offering a terse smile. His teeth were small and even. On his shirt collar, Charles noted a small golden seven-point star, and three red circles under it.

In a few moments, a well-formed, attractive woman walked briskly into the room. There was a pleasing smile on her face. She had long blond hair and her skin displayed a light tan.

An American woman, thought Charles. At last! He left his seat and stood up. Perhaps she would help him get out of the facility.

Almost at once, Charles noted that her ears were remarkably round, and that her nose blended a bit too smoothly with her forehead. He looked at her intently.

Cupahr stood up, a trace of sardonic amusement in his eyes, and touched Charles in the arm. "Your attendant will direct you to your quarters, Chasrydel. I will see you again later. *Loerde fivuresci.*"

The young woman walked slowly toward Charles and stood in front of him. She was nearly as tall as he was. Her skin was flawless, her eyes a clear green. The white outfit she wore reached down to mid-thigh. It showed off her fine legs and clung to the curves of her body.

"You look..." muttered Charles.

"I am your attendant, sir. I hope you were not inconvenienced by my being delayed." Her voice was a pleasant contralto, somewhat monotonous. Her English was perfect.

"I didn't know about you until just now. What is your name?"

"Lealdrelquidrutul."

"That's going to be difficult for me," Charles said.

"It is a temporary name. It is expected that you will choose a name for me."

He thought of Robinson Crusoe. Friday. "What day is today?" he asked.

"The first day of July."

"No, I mean...but that will do just as well. I will call you July."

She smiled. "Thank you, sir. Is my appearance to your liking? I was remodeled to appeal to you better."

"Remodeled?"

"Yes, sir. My physical appearance and my programming were altered to better suit your expected requirements."

Charles' mind reeled. He met her gaze.

"What do you mean? What are you?"

July smiled. "I am an android, sir."

CHAPTER 11
TRINITY

1

Alex Denfeld met Cicely at the airport in Belfast. He covered the twenty miles to Lurgan in half an hour, driving the Jaguar sedan swiftly and doing most of the talking while Cicely admired the green countryside. His talk was of stables and horses and foals. Cicely's few words concerned schoolwork, London traffic and a trip of the Prime Minister that had been on the news.

They passed a last built-up area. Dingy cafes, a greengrocer's, a flower shop, anonymous businesses with windows painted half-way up and weathered bills pasted on the windows. Then they ran down a slope out of town. Beyond lay open country, clean and neat and shining from a recent rain. Lough Neagh spread to the north, flat and blue in the last hours of daylight.

The estate was called Villecassel. When they arrived, Cicely's uncle insisted on carrying her single piece of luggage. He casually ran an arm through Cicely's, the warm friendliness of his clasp sending a rush of emotion through her. She felt wanted and safe, among her own.

———⊛⊛⊛———

Several horses' heads protruded inquisitively from their boxes. The place was notably clean. There was only a suggestion of the dung, mud and sweat which are the unavoidable companions of horses. The stud-groom, Spencer, a wiry blond man of indeterminate age, led the way, guiding Cicely through the stables.

"I hear you haven't been riding much," he said. His accent was Irish.

"It has been a while," Cicely nodded. "I never was very good."

"Well, we must get you up." His clear blue eyes ran over Cicely's spotlessly clean riding clothes.

They walked along, Spencer drawling on in a rambling discussion of the pedigree, character and physical attributes of the various animals. Villecassel was not only a breeding establishment, it was also a school for those who would jump or show horses.

Spencer stopped by a particularly handsome horse, very dark brown, with a rudimentary white star and a ring of white on each foot. "Would you like to ride him, Miss Cicely?" he asked.

The groom led the horse out of its box. "His name is Raymar. He's a new acquisition."

She smiled, undecided. "He's beautiful," she said, admiring the horse's physical conformation. "I guess I might try him," Cicely ventured, in her demure way.

Spencer hailed a stable hand. "Rick, bring a saddle for Raymar."

"A snaffle bit, sir?"

"Right."

A few minutes later, Cicely walked Raymar to the edge of the yard. The horse walked composedly down the track between grassy banks sprinkled with wild flowers. As they came within sight of a gate he danced a little. Cicely touched his neck, and he quieted down. They went through the unlocked gate and came to an open range. Raymar trotted on.

"You are beautiful, Raymar," Cicely said, a smile on her lips. She closed her knees and Raymar broke into a slow canter. They passed clumps of bushes. The air caressed her face, bringing the smell of grass and leather.

They passed groups of beech and juniper trees. The land rose gently until they came to a double row of bushes. They formed a natural avenue, about forty yards wide. Raymar bent his head and started to gallop of his own accord. Cicely let him speed up. The wind buffeted her face. She felt elated, sensing the fine turf slipping under her, as Raymar's hooves drummed below, effortlessly propelling them along.

The lane narrowed at the end and Cicely pulled lightly on the reins. There were rows of bushes ahead. But Raymar had other ideas. His pace didn't slack.

Cicely pulled back harder on the reins and she felt the horse shudder slightly. But it was too late. A hedge was right in front of them, five feet high. The turf rushed by her. She felt alarm and then panic.

Then, all of a sudden, she knew what to do. Her body swung with the horse's rise as he heaved her into the air with a thrust of his quarters, his ears erect and confident. She settled back down as Raymar landed smoothly on the other side of the hedge.

On the way back, Cicely rode Raymar at a slow canter. Her thoughts raced for a while. Raymar had surprised her. She had almost gotten herself thrown. But she had done the right thing, back there at the hedge.

Never before in her life had she jumped with a horse.

The image struck her rapidly. It came and went in a moment: The roar of a crowd. The feel of a horse rising and falling under her, her body moving as if she were part of it. Her horse's head turning toward the next barrier, leaping over a red and white hurdle. Vivian's horse. In South Carolina.

2

July led Charles to a corridor and they walked on for a while. They passed several people, all wearing green. Once, one of the bronze-skinned women emerged into the corridor through one of the automatic doorways. He still found it disconcerting, but was growing increasingly accustomed to people popping in and out, seemingly walking through walls, and became more conscious of the lighter-colored borders that outlined the doorways.

Two Indane-Aliemt men walked by, talking animatedly in their strange language. They glanced curiously at Charles and July. Charles recognized only one word: *Kneth*. He had heard it used in association with both Karyprit's and Cupahr's names. He asked July what it meant.

"It is the rank of certain functionaries, sir, like Master Cupahr. There are eleven ranks, or degrees. The lowest is Pagres." She hesitated, as if deciding whether Charles required further information. He was looking at her attentively.

"The highest degree, that of the leader of the Dramtes, is Exaege," she went on. "The ranks immediately above Pagres are Kliettaes, Kneth, Eberenze, and Berenz. Indane-Aliemt terminology is different in some cases," she explained. "Their equivalent of the Bithian rank Eberenze is Nollecion, and instead of Berenz, they use the title Obiredes."

They came to a wide semicircular area and July indicated Charles should cross one of the many portals dimly outlined in the periphery of the curved wall.

"How do I know I won't bump into somebody on the other side?" Charles asked.

July approached the portal and pointed at the light band outlining it. "This would pulse if a collision were likely, sir. It would turn black if the doorway were closed." Her manner had an air of competent superiority that he found slightly intimidating.

Charles walked through into a small featureless chamber. July joined him. "*Hrobu Bithia, dercer mave,*" she said. Immediately, a feeling of acceleration indicated the chamber was in motion. Characters flashed on a panel by the black edge of the closed doorway. They moved up for a while, then decelerated and traveled horizontally.

"What's going on?" Charles asked.

"We rose to the sixth level of the Indane-Aliemt compound, sir. Just now, we entered the tunnel connecting to the Bithian structure."

"How long is this tunnel?"

"One hundred and ten meters," July replied. As she did so, Charles felt deceleration of their horizontal motion, followed by the unmistakable sinking feeling that indicated they were headed down again.

Anticipating his next question, July said, "We are now descending to the twenty-first level, sir."

"How does it know where we're going? Does it act on voice command?"

The blonde's green eyes locked on his momentarily. "Yes, sir. Most of the automatic equipment responds to voice command."

"In Bithian only, I suppose."

"The equipment responds to standard Galamic, sir. That is the language of Bithia and Indane-Aliemt."

The chamber came to a stop. Instantly, the edge of the doorway turned a light gray. Charles and July stepped out.

The Bithian area was noticeably different. The walls and ceiling were light shades of blue, instead of the gray and white of the Indane-Aliemt compound. There was less of an emphasis on circular motifs. Charles' quarters were a set of interconnecting rooms: A large chamber, taking half of the space, served a multitude of purposes. Charles thought of it as a lounge. Three triangular rooms served as bedroom, bathroom and July's room. The apartment was laid out in the shape of a hexagon.

July explained how various features of the apartment operated. With a few exceptions, the furniture and appliances were normally concealed. On voice command, seats and drawers and cabinets emerged from the floor or the wall. When not needed, they could be banished just as easily.

Charles looked at July closely. Her features were perfectly symmetrical, her body extremely well formed and feminine. The details of her grave face were practically indistinguishable from those of a human being. Her eyebrows were perfect arches, and he could discern individual blond eyelashes. Her eyes glistened tantalizingly in the bright light of the room. On her chest, the skin-tight shirt she wore revealed not only the rounded shape of her breasts, but the subtle outline of her nipples.

He leaned closer to her, so that his face was only inches from hers. She made no attempt to pull back. Only the peach fuzz was missing, the almost microscopic hairs that he should have seen on the surface of her ears.

"Does everyone have an attendant?" Charles asked.

"Most functionaries above the rank of Pagres have attendants, sir."

"The Resseps said my status was to be that of a Pagres."

"An exception was made in your case, sir. It was felt that I would facilitate your orientation."

Charles felt he would indeed require a lot of orientation. Particularly if he was ever to find a way out of the place. The facility must be huge, and he found it utterly complex.

"Would you like to sit, sir?" July asked.

"Yes, but let me do it," Charles replied. "I might as well get used to this."

He looked for the outline of the seats on the floor and took two tentative steps away from the faint markings. "*Ilaemdul,*" he said. Instantly, a pair of the adjustable seats, a light brown in color, emerged from the floor.

"What do you know about my status here?" Charles asked, settling into one of the seats. July stood by, watching as his seat adjusted itself.

"You have been brought to the Bithian compound under the auspices of the Resseps Scahn, sir. You have been registered in the Dramtes as Chasrydel, and at present report directly to Kneth Cupahr." She glanced down at Charles and added: "It is unusual for an earthman to join the project. There are only a few others here."

Charles wondered if she would stand until he told her to sit down. "Just what is an android?"

"A synthetic semi-biological humanoid, sir," July said placidly.

"You are a robot," Charles stated coldly, "a mechanical contraption."

"Yes, sir. Essentially. I am programmed to be your close companion, to assist you in all ways you wish. There are tasks, too complex for machines, that I can perform on your behalf. Functions that, because they are uninteresting or laborious, you would otherwise carry out without really wanting to at all."

Suddenly, Cupahr materialized in the room. His erect, gray haired figure appeared above a pale yellow mound that occupied a corner of the room. Charles, startled, nearly fell out of his seat.

The Bithian turned about slightly, his eyes meticulously inspecting the chamber before focusing on Charles.

"*Ucilaum mudipe*," he said. Glancing momentarily at July, he spoke to her briefly in the language she had called standard Galamic.

"*U gire iguri nalnu, lemur*," she responded.

It was then that Charles first realized the Kneth was not in the room. He was looking at a projection. A flawless three-dimensional projection. But it wasn't full scale. The image was only about five feet high. Cupahr was at least 5-foot-6. Looking more closely, Charles noted that the image's feet didn't quite touch the top of the yellow mound.

"How do you find your quarters, Chasrydel?" Cupahr asked.

"I am...still learning about them," Charles responded, still slightly taken aback. "They seem quite nice, sir."

"Good. Is your attendant satisfactory?" Cupahr's image made the slightest of motions toward July.

Charles smiled. "Quite satisfactory."

"I will meet with you later today," Cupahr said, a hint of displeasure appearing on his face. "*Loerde fivuresci*."

The image vanished.

"That was a projection," Charles stated.

"Yes, sir. Most rooms have such a projection device." She indicated the yellow mound. "They can also be used to replay audiovisual recordings. I will explain its operation later, if you wish."

"I need to talk to it in standard Galamic," Charles said.

"Yes, sir," July agreed pleasantly. Then the tone of her voice changed perceptibly. "You must address the Kneth as Master, sir. It is improper to do otherwise. Formal forms of address are observed except between very close associates."

Charles looked into her emerald eyes. She regarded him steadily. Whatever July was, he thought, she was more than a mechanical device. The fact that she still stood in front of him, seemingly untiring, began to unnerve him.

"Please sit down," he said.

July slipped into the seat next to his. "Thank you, sir." She touched something on the side of the seat and, even as it adjusted to her shape, it turned so that she faced him.

"Would you like something to eat?" she asked.

Charles nodded and July called for a servitor. Moments later a squat chromium cylinder entered the room and positioned itself next to them. The dished semicircle at its top offered a variety of colored crystals and spheres.

Charles drank the liquid from one of the spheres and then took one of the purple crystals. "Tell me about this facility, July."

In an unemotional voice, July described the Dramtes facility. There were five main components. The Bithian and Indane-Aliemt quarters, a port facility, a factory, and a remote site that was something like a mine. All were underground, connected by tunnels twenty-five to thirty meters wide. There were walkways in the tunnels, as well as passageways for a transportation system like elevators, except with an additional capacity for horizontal travel.

The Bithian quarters housed the Bithian contingent: about two hundred and ten, including androids, a small number of earthmen, and seventy-five myrmidons. The latter were synthetic humanoids, but unlike July fully biological in nature. The concept made Charles shudder. Besides living accommodations, the Bithian structure contained working space for many of the Bithians, and what Charles understood to be a form of recreational area. July described the structure as being two hundred meters high, shaped like two squat cylinders set on top of each other, the lower cylinder one hundred meters in diameter, the upper one twice as wide.

The Indane-Aliemt quarters housed similar numbers and connected to the Bithian facility via a tunnel. The Indane-Aliemt edifice was barrel shaped, also about two hundred meters high.

Tunnels led from both Bithian and Indane-Aliemt quarters to the port facility, a huge structure, three hundred meters in diameter, able to receive and launch Bithian spacecraft. Its top was near the surface, the entranceway camouflaged and protected by electromagnetic concealment and defensive devices.

The factory complex was near the port facility. July said it was similar in size to the Bithian quarters. The factory produced crystals used by the Bithian and Indane-Aliemt spaceships. The raw material for the crystals came from the remote underground mine via a tunnel several kilometers long.

Charles heard July's description with mounting apprehension. The facility was immense. It implied an alien presence on Earth that was long established and that exploited the planet's natural resources. And there were people in the United States that knew about it. People in government. There had to be a conspiracy of silence.

Charles wanted to hear more, but July was adamant. He must accompany her, she said. It was time to go.

"Go where?" Charles asked.

July stood up. "You must be fitted with a *limnen*. The Kneth has ordered it."

3

July insisted on having Charles change his clothes before departing. The Pagres Drimtul had always assisted him before, while he was in Karyprit's care. He looked uncertainly at the white garments that were presented on a chromium tray that had just emerged from the wall.

Noticing his vacillation, July ran her fingers along the side of his green Indane-Aliemt shirt. It parted easily and she deftly removed it from him. Before Charles could object, she did the same to his short pants. Then, with efficient, practiced motions, she proceeded to dress him in his new white outfit. Her hands were warm and soft where they brushed against his bare skin, but her touch was impersonal. Throughout it all, Charles remained silent, too surprised to react.

Charles had noted a small golden star on the collar of his new shirt and a smaller red circle under it. He had seen similar ornaments on others. He asked July about it as they left the room.

She explained while they walked along the blue corridor outside. The seven-pointed star was a symbol of Bithia. July herself and all Bithians wore it on their tunics. The small red circle was an indication of rank. In Charles' case it showed him to be a Pagres. Charles looked automatically at July's collar. There was a white figure under her star.

Charles asked her what a *limnen* was, and why was he being fitted with one.

"It is a device that will allow you to communicate better, sir," she told him.

They reached an open area and entered one of the elevator-like chambers. July said something to it in Galamic and they were taken down swiftly. Soon they emerged in another blue bay. They followed a corridor and walked through a portal into a large chamber. It was shaped like three interlocking hexagons.

There were several pieces of equipment in the room. Gray, brown and blue shapes dotted the area. A half-dozen people dressed in white stood or sat near the rounded forms of various machines. July approached one of them.

She greeted the Bithian woman and spoke to her briefly in Galamic. Then she made one of the adjustable seats pop up and asked Charles to sit down. The bronze-skinned woman produced an ovoid instrument similar to the one Karyprit had used and went about scanning Charles' head. While she did this, July walked away a few feet and activated one of the mound-shaped projection machines. In a moment Cupahr's shape appeared in the room. From a distance, Charles could see July communicating with the Kneth.

Soon the woman finished her scanning and walked away, first gesturing for Charles to stay in place. A moment later he could see her a few feet away, bending over the blue shape of a particularly large apparatus.

One of the men in white approached the woman and talked to her briefly. He then moved toward Charles. As he came closer Charles recognized him as an earthman. A white man in his thirties, with black hair and brown eyes. Charles started to stand up, but the other's action stopped him.

"Don't bother, fellow," said the man, holding out his hand. It closed warmly on Charles' right hand. "I'll join you for a moment if you don't mind. I just heard about you from the Kliettaes."

Charles nodded. "Please," he said, looking at the man closely and assuring himself that this was a real human and not another android. "I haven't seen an earthman since I got here."

The other said "*Ilaemdu*" and a seat instantly rose from the floor. The man sat down next to Charles. "My name is Chadwick; I'm with the Directorate of Operations. We didn't know about you. Welcome to Site One."

"Do they have other sites?"

"Just one other, as far as we know. A small installation in the Altai Mountains, near Semipalatinsk, in Russia."

"They call me Chasrydel."

"I was told that," Chadwick said. "What is your real name?"

"Charles Ryder."

"How did you get here, Charles?" Chadwick's eyes darted about the room, but they mostly concentrated on Charles. They missed little.

Charles told him the same story he had told Karyprit. There was no mention of Robinson or Arteaga's document. He had the distinct feeling that Chadwick knew he was leaving something out, and tried to stall any questions with one of his own.

"What is the Directorate of Operations, Chadwick?"

"Uh, CIA. Actually, I'm attached to the National Security Council. My boss at the Agency doesn't know what I do."

"How many people know about this place?"

"In the government? Maybe two dozen. Probably not that many. There's only three in the National Security Council, counting the National Security Advisor; the Director for Operations and a couple of others at CIA; a few at the Pentagon, and so forth. There's a few more here, but, like you, they're not getting out."

"Why do you cooperate with them?"

Chadwick chuckled. "Are you kidding? What choice do we have?"

"We could resist, make them pay us a lot for whatever it is they are mining or doing in our country."

Chadwick shook his head. "You don't understand, pal. These people wield incredible power. They're star travelers, ruling commercial empires. That's what the Dramtes is, a giant commercial empire."

"We could reason with them, bargain with them if necessary. That's what commerce is all about. I don't see any excuse for secrecy, for the U.S. Government to be involved in the greatest deception in the history of mankind."

"You're a babe in the woods," Chadwick said acidly. "These folks are ruthless. They arrived fifty years ago and they laid down the law. They wage commercial wars. Maybe they are at peace now because of the Dramtes, but I—"

"What exactly is the Dramtes?" Charles interrupted.

"The Dramtes," July said, "is our governing body; it is all of us, sir." She had approached them unnoticed. "Literally, it means trio." Both Charles and Chadwick turned to look at her.

"Not quite," Chadwick said, rising. "I'd say it means Trinity, the-three-that-are-one, for the three commercial groups that form it."

The Bithian woman that had been with Charles earlier returned then. She held a small object in her hand.

July spoke to the woman briefly in Galamic and she in turn said something to Chadwick.

The CIA man glanced at July's collar for a moment. "A type sixty-three," he muttered. "Didn't know they went that high."

July turned to face Chadwick directly. "Your presence is not required here," she told him.

"Must go now, Ryder," Chadwick said, "your nursemaid is running me off." He bowed slightly to the Bithian woman and more deeply to July. "*Loerde fivuresci*," he added, and walked off.

Charles pivoted in his chair. "He said——"

"You must hold still now, sir," July interrupted, "while the Kliettaes installs the *limnen*."

Charles sighed, but sat still. The Kliettaes moved around and took the seat that Chadwick had vacated. She was a slight woman, with a mobile face that showed intelligence. She seemed to be about thirty, although her short hair was white.

"*Iguri bumtre eldu em lo uatu*," the Kliettaes said softly. Her yellow eyes looked directly into Charles'. She held his head firmly in one hand and with the other inserted a small tan object into his ear. For a moment, she continued to look into his eyes.

Then she said, "*Daeme uyul hrales*."

Charles understood perfectly. "You have gray eyes," she had said.

He looked up at July. She smiled at him and patted his shoulder.

CHAPTER 12
MENAGERIE

1

Kneth Cupahr's quarters were on the nineteenth level. Charles exercised his newfound mastery of standard Galamic upon entering the transport module, by issuing the command himself.

"Nineteenth level." He looked at July uncertainly as he spoke the command. She smiled approvingly. Instantly, the rim of the doorway darkened and they felt the smooth surge of acceleration. A moment later the chamber came to a stop and they walked out onto the central bay area.

Charles felt a peculiar excitement. Part of it was elation from the continued exposure to a dazzling technology, but the rest was a wariness that grew as he gained familiarity with a strange society that regarded him at best with indifference and possibly with veiled hostility.

The device in his ear, the limnen, had provided him with an instant knowledge of the language the Bithians spoke. The Bithian woman that had fitted him with it, Kliettaes Salfors, had described it as an auxiliary mind with an organic liquid memory. It sensed auditory nerve inputs, extracted Galamic language information, and projected an English language translation electromagnetically directly into the temporal lobes of his brain. When he wanted to speak in Galamic, the device sensed his thought patterns and projected appropriate stimuli into the premotor region of his frontal cortex. In time, Salfors had told him, his brain would develop the proper associations and he would be able to speak Galamic unassisted.

The bay was arranged exactly like those in the other levels. Two banks of transport modules were set on either side of the blue chamber, facing each other. The bay was about fifty feet wide and twice as long. At either end were two wide corridors. Each set off at an angle.

July led the way. They crossed the bay and took the corridor to the left. A small gray machine, about the size and shape of a one gallon paint can, skittered out of their way, emitting a weak droning sound.

"What is that thing?" Charles wondered aloud.

July glanced at the device, now moving slowly along the opposite side of the corridor. "It's a sonic broom, sir," she declared. "It cleans the hallways."

Once they passed by, the machine returned to its original location. Looking back, Charles saw it making short darting moves back and forth on the spotless floor.

"Is it intelligent?" he asked.

"It has very rudimentary programming," July said, looking sideways at Charles. "Like a simple animal. It is not conscious of itself."

A moment later they came to Cupahr's quarters. They were near the end of the corridor. The rim of the doorway was black. On its side was a small panel with the numeral 1911 in Galamic script.

"Pagres Chasrydel and attendant to see Kneth Cupahr," said Charles. He had not been told that this was the proper form for requesting access to the Kneth's residence. He had simply known it. Evidently the limnen was more than a language translator, thought Charles. He found the realization slightly disturbing.

The doorway's rim turned clear and Charles and July entered. The Kneth's reception and living area was a hexagonal room as large as Charles' entire quarters. Kneth Cupahr and another Bithian stood by one of the mound-like projection devices, engaged in conversation with another whose image faced them.

Cupahr turned to Charles and July. "Remarkable event," he said. "Please approach, both of you."

As Charles and July neared them, Cupahr terminated the communication and the projected image disappeared. The man with Cupahr wore four small circles under the star at the collar of his white tunic. Cupahr introduced him as Eberenze Fermilo.

"I understand you have some technical training, Chasrydel," said the Eberenze.

"Yes, Master."

Fermilo looked at Charles appraisingly. The Bithian was short, perhaps 5-foot-4. His slim body was muscular and his gray hair was longer than Charles had seen on any of the Bithians. His demeanor showed dignity and composure.

"You may want to turn this matter over to the Pagres, Kneth," Fermilo suggested.

"Yes, that will save us some time, Master," Cupahr responded. "I will brief him."

"We must coordinate any repairs with Obiredes Dahlgers' people," Fermilo said.

"Yes, Master," Cupahr said.

"Chance favor," Fermilo said, turning to leave.

"Chance favor," the others echoed.

"Sit down," invited Cupahr, once the Eberenze had departed. He commanded seats to appear and took a seat across from Charles. July remained standing.

"How are you doing so far, Chasrydel?" Cupahr asked.

"I am well, Master. It is nice to understand the language."

"Good. I will describe your position here." There was an affectation in Cupahr's patronizing manner that bothered Charles. "You are a

Bithian now. Forget about the world outside. Should there come to be a time when you return to the surface, to your nation of origin, you would not find yourself at home. You would have changed. You have changed already."

The Kneth lifted a finger, in a gesture meant to draw Charles' attention. "It may occur to you at some time to leave here. To find a way out of the facility and return to the surface on your own. Do not pursue that thought. Come and talk to me. Seek the Resseps Scahn and ask for his advice. Such an unauthorized exit is impossible, and it could be dangerous. There are automatic defenses at all entry points. They are there to keep intruders at bay, but could harm someone seeking to effect an unannounced departure."

Charles reflected for a moment on what Kneth Cupahr had just said. It made him feel caged. The moment passed, and Charles, pursing his lips, started to view his situation as a survival exercise—one that called for extreme caution until he found a practicable way out of the site.

Cupahr then said "Liaser", to no one in particular. In a moment, a woman entered the room. She came through a doorway that led to the rest of Cupahr's quarters. Moving swiftly, she walked across the room and stood at Cupahr's side.

To Charles she said: "Remarkable event, sir. I am Liaser." She bowed slightly to Charles and more deeply toward July. The woman was extremely graceful. She had long white hair and bright yellow eyes that contrasted strikingly with her gold-bronze skin. Under the seven-pointed star on the collar of her white tunic was the white numeral 46. It meant she was an android—type four, version six.

Charles nodded at Liaser. "I am Pagres Chasrydel." He turned his head slightly toward July and added: "My attendant, July."

"I was told today, Master," Charles went on to say, "that Bithia and Indane-Aliemt are commercial empires. Is that so?"

"He met the earthman Chadwick, sir," July explained.

"Likely, that is Mr. Chadwick's understanding," Cupahr smiled. "It is true in the sense that this facility is a commercial venture. Also, our relationship with the government of the United States is essentially a commercial one."

"He said you fought commercial wars," stated Charles.

Cupahr's finger rose again, and his smile became thinner. "That is a misunderstanding on Mr. Chadwick's part. There has not been a single battle since Bithia, Indane-Aliemt and Nesdelsen joined and formed the Dramtes more than three of your centuries ago."

"By Earth standards we are a most peaceful people, sir," added Liaser, a smile also tugging at her lips.

Cupahr caused additional seats to emerge and invited the androids to sit. July and Liaser sat down.

"As a Pagres," Cupahr said, "you will receive eight hundred Dramtes shares each major cycle." He glanced at July.

"A major cycle is about three hundred and fifty days," clarified July.

"Your quarters, food, clothing, medical attention, your attendant, are all furnished by Bithia," Cupahr said.

Then the Kneth looked at Charles sharply and added: "There are certain things we expect from you. Loyalty is one. Another is that you carry out such assignments as will be occasionally given to you. I will describe two of these to you now, Chasrydel."

Cupahr made a vague motion toward the brown hemisphere near them. "The official you saw us communicating with earlier indicated that there is a concern some damage may have been caused by the recent earthquake. The Vadycrel is responsible for the operation of the facility's transportation system. He charged the Eberenze with investigating the matter. I want you to look into this. It involves reviewing the status and maintenance records of the transportation modules and identifying any malfunction pattern traceable to the earthquake. My attendant will help you with the details." He indicated Liaser.

"There is another matter. Something you may find entertaining. It is like a game." Cupahr gave Charles a lackluster smile, and then turned toward July. "Take the Pagres to the fourth level. Kliettaes Rathiz has prepared a course of tests and instruction for him."

2

The fourth level was different. Upon reaching it, the transportation module moved horizontally for some time before coming to a stop. Charles and July walked out directly into one of the hexagonal rooms, instead of the wide bay area Charles had come to expect.

Kliettaes Rathiz met them and introduced himself. His eyes, a deep orange, were deeply set under his hairless brow. He regarded Charles astutely for a moment. Then, dismissing July, he led Charles through a doorway to a small triangular room.

A squat white machine filled half the room. It was shaped somewhat like a huge roll top desk, with a slick gray surface like a clouded window at its center. A single seat was deployed in front of it.

"Sit, Pagres Chasrydel," the Kliettaes said.

Charles took the single white seat. It adjusted itself rapidly and swung slowly so that Charles faced the viewing panel.

"The monitor will address you directly," said Rathiz. "It will administer a test. Speak to it in a normal tone of voice." He pointed at Charles' head. "Remove your limnen when I leave."

"Why? I won't be able to understand Galamic without it."

"The limnen furnishes a faculty like total recall. It would interfere with tests of your short term memory. The monitor is fluent in American English."

Charles nodded.

"There will be questions. Pay close attention and respond as rapidly as possible. I will be notified when this series of tests is complete and will return for you."

Rathiz indicated the area at the center of the machine. "Some data will be presented visually," he told Charles. Then he turned around and left the room, the portal closing silently behind him.

"Black is to white," said the monitor in a deep male voice, "as dark is to light."

Charles took a deep breath. Through the window in front of him he saw a black and a white square, then a dark amorphous shape next to a bright textured surface.

"Circle is to sphere," said the monitor, "as..."

A circle and a globe appeared on one side of the window. Then, on the other side, a cube, a cylinder, a square, and a triangle were displayed.

"As square is to cube," Charles said.

The window became clear instantly.

"Heavy is to light," said the monitor, "as..."

The words soft, affirm, disguise, blur, and deny appeared on the window.

"Affirm is to deny," Charles responded.

He remembered what Rathiz had said about the limnen and took it off, laying the tiny capsule on the monitor.

The test went on for a long time. Some of the questions were very complex, and it took Charles a long time to respond. The monitor always waited for Charles' answer before proceeding to the next question. It never commented on his performance.

"This test is complete," announced the monitor in its deep voice. The window at the center of the white apparatus went blank.

Charles reinserted the limnen in his ear and rose from his seat. He had begun to stretch his legs when Kliettaes Rathiz entered the small triangular room.

"Very good, Pagres," said Rathiz, smiling. "Please follow me now."

3

Rathiz led Charles back to the hexagonal room and then through a portal and along a corridor. They walked along until they came to another portal. The dark strip outlining it indicated the doorway was locked. Two men stood by on either side. They were tall and powerfully built. The muscles of their bodies showed through the tight white tunics. Their faces were harsh. They were identical.

The one on the left raised a hand and Rathiz stopped. The Kliettaes turned to Charles. "The myrmidons," he said, "will take you into the training area. They will give you a familiarization session. I will return for you later."

Charles took his eyes from the two large men and looked inquiringly at Rathiz. "Familiarization with what?"

Rathiz took a small thin disk from a pocket in his shirt and gave it to one of the myrmidons. "The games, Pagres," he said to Charles. Turning to go he added: "Chance favor."

"You are Chasrydel," stated the myrmidon on the left. The single red circle on his collar indicated his rank was Pagres.

"I am."

"Follow me." The large man held the disk in front of a panel by the portal and its black outline changed to clear.

Charles glanced at Rathiz' retreating back and followed the myrmidon through the doorway.

"I am Esandos," said the myrmidon. "Since this is your first session, you will be exposed to a minimal hazard." He walked briskly, leading Charles along a corridor. Unlike all other corridors Charles had seen in the Bithian compound, this one was a dun color, and its surface was roughly textured.

"What do you mean by minimal hazard?" Charles asked. Cupahr had said this was to be a game.

Esandos walked on in silence. From a fold in his tunic he extracted a small red object, like a thimble, and slipped it over his thumb. The wall on the right suddenly stopped. Charles came to a halt immediately. They had reached the edge of a large open ground. It lay twenty feet below them and stretched to the left as far as Charles could see. To the right, below, were a series of cubical rooms.

"What are…" Charles' question died on his lips. He heard a loud feral roar, and then a sound like a repeated thumping. A shudder raced through his body.

"Come," Esandos said, taking Charles' arm. "Don't worry; they can't leave their cages at this time."

4

"You are to walk in that direction," the myrmidon said, "for about one hundred and fifty meters. There is a pond there. When you reach it, your test will be complete."

The myrmidon's voice had a monotonously even quality. Charles found the other's calmness disconcerting.

"Is that all?" Charles asked.

"Some of the beasts may attack you along the way," Esandos stated matter-of-factly.

"I'm not going anywhere," Charles said.

Esandos' face darkened. "Move!"

Charles stood his ground.

Swiftly, Esandos raised his hand. His fingers curled loosely, as if making a lax fist. The thumb stuck out, pointing at Charles. There was a slight motion, a flicking of the wrist, and the red device on Esandos' thumb shimmered.

For an instant, Charles felt the most excruciating of pains, like a raspy needle driven through every nerve on his body. He staggered, his breath escaping his lungs.

Very slowly, Charles raised his head and met Esandos' cold gaze. "Don't do that again," he said with a fury almost beyond his ability to control.

Esandos lowered his hand. "Now will you go?"

Charles felt like choking Esandos, but knew he was powerless against him. He would have to bide his time. His throat tightened. He forced out the words. "I will walk to the pond."

The myrmidon gave him a wand, about three feet long, instructed him in its use, and then left him alone.

Charles stood on a ragged plain. There were mountains in the distance, blue-gray shadows seemingly many miles away. Charles walked cautiously on the boulder-strewn terrain. The sky above was a slate gray.

Part of it had to be an illusion, thought Charles. He was underground. From what July had told him, he knew the Bithian structure was about an eighth of a mile at its widest. But his immediate surroundings were real enough. His feet made crunching sounds as he walked on the gravelly earth. He held tightly to the thin blue wand Esandos had given him. It was a weapon.

There were several large boulders to the right, about twenty feet away. Charles kept his distance, circling around them. He still had two thirds of the way to go. As he neared the back of the first boulder, the ground began a slight downward slope. Smaller boulders and squarish chunks of dark brown rock were piled to the left. He wondered what loathsome inhuman figures crept past the range of his senses.

Charles looked ahead curiously. There was a sound nearby, a skittering of small rocks. Then the creature appeared. It had four clawed feet and was shaped somewhat like a large dog, but it had no ears, and its bare grayish skin glistened. There were dozens of scars on its body. Its large unblinking eyes conveyed obscene viciousness and bloodlust. It growled and ran swiftly, directly toward Charles. Double rows of fangs protruded from its massive jaws.

Fighting an instinct to run, Charles stood his ground. There was no way he could outrun the thing, and he'd rather face it than have it jump him from behind.

The beast slowed down as it approached Charles, its thick tail swaying, then lunged at him. Charles struck it in the snout with the wand. The animal whined and turned about, lowering its head. It growled horribly and lunged at Charles again, its gaping mouth filled with froth. Only then did Charles realize he had forgotten to activate the wand. He pressed the stud on its hilt. At once the shaft acquired a silver sheen and emitted a hissing sound. But the beast's jaws were already closing on Charles' leg.

The pain was unbearable as the sharp teeth cut through the flesh and into the bone of his leg. "Ahhrrgh!" Charles screamed in agony. He hit the animal's head with the back of his left hand. The creature was not fazed and sank its fangs deeper into Charles' leg. Blood spurted from torn arteries. In desperation, Charles swung his right arm in an arc.

The tip of the hissing wand struck the back of the beast. It cut right through the gray hide, filling the air with the sickening smell of burnt flesh. There was a final whimper from the animal and then it ceased to live. The jaws crushing Charles' leg went slack.

Esandos and another myrmidon came for him in a small vehicle that seemed to float in the air and took him back to the staging area. Charles was only partly conscious and saw everything through a red haze. His leg ached terribly. Soon other persons appeared. One of them was Rathiz; the others, a Bithian man and a woman wearing Indane-Aliemt green, Charles had not seen before. The strangers did something to Charles' leg and the pain stopped.

The red haze gradually wore away. Charles lay on an elevated white surface. He raised his head to see Rathiz, Esandos and the two officials he had noticed earlier: a short but burly man and a fine-featured woman with flowing white hair.

"You were careless," stated Esandos.

The graceful Indane-Aliemt woman introduced herself as Cirsegas Austir and the burly Bithian as Eberenze Reumonh. The two were physicians and had treated his leg. Charles found curious that such high-ranked officials had tended to him. He would have expected Drimtul or Kneth Karyprit. "The healing will be complete later today," the Cirsegas said. The woman pressed a short rod against Charles' arm, its surface cold and gleaming. "Rest for a moment. You have suffered no permanent harm."

Charles propped himself up on his elbows. The haze in his mind had cleared. "Thank you, Lady," he said. Cirsegas Austir nodded slightly, and then she and the Eberenze turned and left the room.

"Yes, Esandos," said Charles, fixing his gaze on the myrmidon, "I was careless. I didn't know you were setting that monster loose on me."

Esandos almost smiled. "You were warned," he said, grimly.

"Please call my attendant, Kliettaes," said Charles.

"She has already been called, Chasrydel." Rathiz glanced at Charles' leg. There was a rapidly diminishing redness on the skin where the wound had been. "She is on her way," he added.

"Why did you do that to me?" Charles asked, controlling his anger.

Esandos began to answer, but Rathiz interposed his own statement. "The tests expose you to adverse situations so that your capabilities may be better evaluated. You were not materially endangered."

"Not endangered! That thing, whatever it was…"

July entered the room. Charles saw her and sighed in relief.

She smiled and approached him. "Do not disturb yourself, sir," she told him, "everything is all right." Reaching him, she propped his back with her arm and helped him sit up. Her green eyes looked into his reassuringly.

July helped him stand up. She was surprisingly strong; her supple body initially bearing most of his weight. After a while, he felt strong enough to stand unassisted.

Charles limped a bit at first and walked close to July just in case he lost his balance, but before they reached his rooms he felt almost normal. "I need to get out of here," he told himself.

5

The wound soon healed so perfectly that there was no trace of it left. But that night Charles awoke from his sleep screaming, drenched in sweat. He had barely opened his eyes when July entered the small triangular room. Instantly, the ceiling and walls glowed, raising the level of illumination.

"I had a bad dream," he said, propping himself up by his elbows on the floor-level soft pad that was his bed.

July sat on the pad next to him and touched his brow lightly.

"I will stay with you, sir, and the bad dream will not return," she told him.

"Oh, don't bother, July. I'll be all right."

"You should allow me to help you, sir. It is my function."

"Must you call me sir all the time?"

"It is the proper form of address."

"Well, from now on I want you to call me Charles, not sir."

"We do not use your American name, sir."

"Well, at least call me Chasrydel, like the others," he insisted.

"It is not customary for an attendant to address her master in that way, sir."

"I don't care, July," he said, irritated. "Aren't you supposed to follow my orders?"

"Of course, sir."

"Well, do as I told you."

July regarded him tolerantly. "Very well…Chasrydel."

Charles permitted himself a smile. It was the triumph of man over machine.

"Lights off," July said. The room darkened immediately.

July slid on the mat until she lay lengthwise next to Charles. He started to tell her to go away, but was too tired to argue. Instead, he turned over and closed his eyes, his head nestling on her yielding breasts. A moment later he was fast asleep.

The next day Liaser, Cupahr's attendant, took him and July to a work area in the twelfth level. The hexagonal room was fitted with several machines. It appeared to be a small laboratory.

Liaser, her bright yellow eyes regarding Charles appraisingly, indicated a squat rounded machine. It was similar to the one that had administered the tests the day before.

"The monitor will provide you with all the information you need," she said. "Sit down, sir."

Charles took a seat facing the central screen. Liaser and July sat down at either side of him.

"Monitor," said Liaser, "project a plan of this level."

Instantly, a 3-D perspective view of the twelfth level appeared in front of them. It showed a semitransparent view of the level, like a thin slice of a cylinder. The disk showed four clusters of hexagonal cells, grouped around a central open area and separated by wide corridors that angled away from the center, forming an X that extended all the way to the circular outer wall.

"Highlight the transportation system area," Liaser said.

Two cells, on opposite sides of the central area, took on a pink hue that contrasted with the aqua and white tones of the rest of the projection.

These cells were truncated hexagons. A triangular piece had been deleted from each, so that the truncated cells presented flat faces toward the central open area.

Within each of the pink cells were four small square cells. The square cells represented shafts through which the transportation modules coursed.

"What is the total number of transportation modules?" Liaser asked.

"There are fifty-eight modules in this structure," the monitor said in a soft female voice. "The facility has two hundred and thirty-six."

"How many are presently operational?"

"Forty-one in this structure; one hundred and fifty in the facility."

Liaser turned to Charles. "Do you understand the operation of the monitor now, sir?"

"Yes, it responds to verbal commands."

"Kneth Cupahr requires a determination of the effect of the recent earthquake on the transportation system," Liaser said.

"I understand," Charles said.

Liaser stood up. "Contact me if you need further assistance, sir." She gave Charles one last look, as if assessing his ability, and left the room.

"July," said Charles, "I would like to see the Resseps Scahn. Would you arrange for an audience with him?"

"Yes, sir," she said, rising.

"Chasrydel."

"Yes, Chasrydel," July said, offering him a smile.

Charles saw July disappear through the doorway and turned to face the monitor.

"Display the facility," he commanded. "Highlight all exits."

CHAPTER 13
TRACING WORK

1

Cicely hurried past gray buildings along Cavendish Square. A heavy drizzle had just started, and she had left her umbrella in the MG. She was narrowly missed by a lorry when she dashed across the street, trying to escape the sudden rain. The driver, rolling his window down, yelled at her: "You ought to keep your eyes wide open, luv."

It was late afternoon, and office workers were still leaving the city. Rain drummed on the roofs of black cabs adroitly maneuvering their way around pedestrians crossing the road. Cicely strode on along Harley Street. Finally she saw Dr. McClellan's brass plate. Taking quick steps up the stairs, she pushed the heavy door open.

Dr. McClellan was just inside the door, hanging up his raincoat. He looked briefly at Cicely's damp clothes.

"Come in, Cicely. Just missed it myself."

"Hello, Doctor."

"Went out for the paper." He held up a folded copy of The Times.

Cicely walked into the consulting room and took a seat in her usual chair. Dr. McClellan followed her in and seated himself across from her at his desk.

"I had thought for some time, Doctor," she said without preamble, "that somehow I was receiving my dreams from Charles and Vivian."

Dr. McClellan regarded her owlishly. He took an envelope from his pocket and wrote something on its back, then returned his gaze to his patient.

Cicely crossed her legs and adjusted her skirt. "I don't mean receiving a radio broadcast or something like that. We talked about how silly that would be." She sighed, lowering her eyes. "I don't know how, perhaps ESP or something."

She looked at him then, meeting his dark eyes. "I know you don't agree with this, but that's been in the back of my mind all along." Cicely smiled. "Now something's happened to change my opinion."

She broke into a nervous chuckle. "I had another dream of Charles. One of a different kind."

"No monsters this week?"

"Oh, I had one of those too." Her eyes clouded. "They made him fight horrible animals…" Her voice broke.

"Stay calm, Cicely. Relax."

She took a couple of deep breaths, her hands grasping her chair.

"But it wasn't that," she said. "I'll tell you. I had this dream the night before last."

Dr. McClellan nodded and wrote down a reminder.

"It was hazy at first," said Cicely. "I heard party noises in the background. Young people. It was a birthday party."

Cicely closed her eyes. "I was Charles. There was a girl with me, awfully young, maybe twelve. We walked onto a balcony and stood alone with each other. It was Fall and the sun had nearly set. We looked down on a garden."

Her voice grew softer. "The air carried the sweet smell of flowers. Violets. I was about her age. The sky was beautiful: gray and pink."

Cicely paused, immersing herself in the memory of her dream. "I said

I would kiss her. She lowered her eyes and offered me her cheek. I kissed her on the lips, but she didn't dare glance at me. It was my first kiss. I told her that I loved her and she looked into my eyes, wondering. She looked so earnest..."

She drew a deep breath, opened her eyes and looked at Dr. McClellan. "Charles must have been in his early teens then," said Cicely. "I'd say thirteen or fourteen. It must have happened years ago."

Dr. McClellan watched her closely. "Do you think there really is a Charles?"

"Yes," she said firmly.

"But you don't think his thoughts are being transmitted to you."

"No, that can't be. His kissing that girl, that happened in the past."

"Maybe he remembered," Dr. McClellan suggested.

Cicely shot him a glance. "What do you mean, Doctor?"

"I was pursuing your notion that he transmits his thoughts." He rubbed his chin. "Don't you think these are your own thoughts, Cicely?"

"They are my dreams. I didn't feel like I was thinking about something. I was there."

"Do you ever think of yourself as Charles?"

"Only in my dreams."

"Does he remind you of someone you know?"

"No. Neither does Vivian, or any of the others."

"Your point of view is never one of the others, is it? Robinson, and so forth."

"No. It's always Charles or Vivian."

Dr. McClellan leaned back in his chair. He observed Cicely across the wide desk.

"I want to try hypnosis," he told her.

"Whatever you think is best, Doctor," she said resignedly.

"You sometimes look at my pictures," he said, gesturing toward the paintings on the wall behind him.

"Yes."

"Which one do you like the most?"

Cicely lifted her eyes and considered the four paintings. "The one with the lake and the pine-covered hills."

"I want you to lie back and relax."

Cicely adjusted her position in the easy chair. She took a deep breath and slowly exhaled.

"Now look at the painting with the lake. Fix your eyes on it. Try not to blink." His voice assumed a soothing quality.

She looked up at the landscape on the wall.

"Look at the lake, Cicely. The calm blue lake. The lake is deep and quiet. Think of nothing but the lake. You are right there. You feel more relaxed already. You can see the ripples in the water, on the surface of the lake…"

2

"Wait, Chasrydel," July said.

Charles stopped a short distance from the doorway and turned to face her. They were in the lounge area of Charles' quarters.

A form materialized above the pale yellow shape of the communications device at a corner of the room.

Kneth Cupahr's image glanced about the room briefly, and then directed itself at Charles. "Remarkable event, Pagres Chasrydel," said Cupahr.

Charles looked at the image hovering above the yellow hemisphere and returned the greeting.

"There will be a dramatic presentation at the theater in the Indane-Aliemt compound. The Resseps invites you, Chasrydel."

Charles glanced at July, uncertainly. "Thank you, Master," he said. "May my attendant accompany me?"

"If you wish," said Cupahr. "The presentation will begin at 900 milicycles. Chance favor."

The image vanished.

"Attendants are seldom present at the theatrical functions, Chasrydel," July said.

"Well, the Kneth approves. I want you with me. To keep me out of trouble."

Charles glanced at the time display unit on his sleeve. The function would start in 80 milicycles; about two hours.

The transport module shuttled them up to the sixth level and then accelerated horizontally. Soon they reached the Indane-Aliemt compound. The machine decelerated as it neared the amphitheater.

July tugged at Charles' shirt, adjusting the fit of his collar. She brushed back a lock of dark hair that had slid over his forehead. Her grin had a hint of smugness. He was about to tell her to quit fussing over him when the transport module came to a halt.

They crossed the portal and looked ahead at a large open space. Three tiers rose about the circular central area. At least a hundred people were moving about or had already assumed seats on the terraces.

Charles judged the area to be at least a hundred yards across. A huge glowing ball hung over the middle of the room, suspended from the white domed ceiling by a thin wire. Directly under it, at the very center of the room, there was a brown hemispherical mound twenty-five feet across.

They walked ahead. Others behind them continued to emerge from transport modules.

About half the people in the room wore the white outfits of Bithian personnel; the rest wore Indane-Aliemt green. Charles spotted the Resseps Scahn on the first tier, standing with a few others in a group surrounding two seated figures in green. A small rounded object hovered near one of the seated Indane-Aliemt officials.

"I see the Resseps," Charles said. "Should I go and greet him?"

"No, sir," stated July. "This is not an appropriate time."

"Who are the people he is talking to, the seated couple in green?"

"The male with the round face and the short gray hair is the Supracetor Breslui, the highest official in the mission. The female sitting next to him is the Intuger Sinderc. She directs Indane-Aliemt operations. Sinderc and the Resseps report directly to the Supracetor."

"What is that gray thing hovering over her shoulder?"

"It's an *emkenud*, a remote sensor responding to the Intuger's will. It extends her senses and incorporates a voice projection capability."

Charles stared at the gray disk. "What do you mean—responding to her will?"

"The device acts at her direction. It communicates sight, sound, smell and temperature directly to her brain. *Emkenuds* are rarely employed. Their use is difficult to master."

July led him swiftly away from the central area and up onto the third tier.

Moving around the perimeter, following July, Charles looked down on the central area. People were still arriving. There were nearly two hundred in the spacious room. Finally, July stopped and produced seats for Charles and herself.

Suddenly, the Intuger's *emkenud* flew from her shoulder to the center of the amphitheater. It hovered under the great luminous globe for a few moments, perhaps allowing Sinderc to scan the room. In an amplified voice the device said "Commence," and returned to her.

"We are near the main projection axis," said July in a low voice. "Viewing is optimal here." As they took the adjustable seats, the suspended globe began to dim.

"What happens next?"

"Scenes will be projected in the central field. The story takes place four thousand major cycles ago, on a planet called Dictos. It concerns two lovers, Emtor and Aliese, who are put in jeopardy by the financial machinations of Sentelleg."

Gradually, the domed ceiling darkened. The murmur of voices died and the silence fluttered with indrawn breath and the final adjustments of position. Then, suddenly, a scene took shape at the center of the darkened chamber.

A stately man sat on a carved bench at the center of a room encircled by iris doors, his chin resting on his joined hands. "Without her, my life is without ease," he said, sadly. "If I could find where she is…"

A young woman stood by him. Her features were plain, but she had the poise and bearing that marks people of significance.

"Excellency, nothing is to be gained by dwelling on the past. Forget Penferet. She's gone. There are state matters at hand that require your attention. As Supracetor, you cannot ignore them."

Charles marveled at the lifelike quality of the three-dimensional projection. He heard the words as if they were being uttered a few feet away. The sense of presence was overwhelming.

The scene changed. A young man, Kneth Emtor, was shown accidentally overhearing two others discuss the arrival of a spaceship.

"When will it arrive, Socusar?" asked one of the strangers.

"Three cycles from now. The Captain will have to sell the green milnay to pay for repairs."

"How much will the repairs cost?"

"I just obtained an estimate from the Berenz—three thousand credits. One of the drives was damaged by the Bith raiders."

Emtor next met with a taciturn man, Vadycrel Sentelleg. There was a tension between them.

"How large a loan do you require, Kneth Emtor?"

"Three thousand credits, Lord."

Sentelleg eyed the younger man calculatingly. "You offer little in the way of security. I have to decline. You have not done well, since leaving my employ."

"But I assure you," persisted Emtor, "I will be able to repay you fully in six cycles."

The Vadycrel considered for a moment. He consulted a computing device, then made an offer. "Three thousand credits on loan for six cycles. If you do not pay back the sum, plus four hundred credits, you must agree to place yourself under unrestricted contract to me for a fee of one credit per major cycle."

For a moment Emtor's confidence seemed to reel, but he steeled himself. "I agree."

Emtor meets with his lover, Kneth Aliese. They embrace by an indoor pool festooned with alien ferns. Later, they approach the ship owners and, pooling their resources, buy the shipment of green milnay for five thousand credits. They figure to sell it for twelve thousand and buy a ship of their own.

Emtor and Aliese travel to a spaceport, huge metal structures set on a vermilion plain.

Charles grasped July's hand. "The sky is green," he observed.

"That is correct, Chasrydel," she whispered. "The atmosphere on Dictos is highly stratified and has that effect."

Sentelleg learns of the deal and manipulates the market so that all green milnay orders are fulfilled. Emtor cannot sell the shipment. In desperation, he offers it to Sentelleg in exchange for cancellation of his debt, but the Vadycrel declines. Sentelleg intends to challenge Supracetor Vintersla's rule. Emtor's contract would force him into mortal combat on Sentelleg's behalf.

On the sixth day, Sentelleg attaches Emtor's possessions, including the shipment of green milnay. Emtor contests the Vadycrel's action, and the Supracetor is called to appoint an arbiter.

The scene changes once more. Supracetor Vintersla, wandering about in a park lined with strange blue-green trees, meets a brooding Aliese and mistakes her for his beloved Penferet.

"Let me hold you," he pleads. "So much time lost, dear."

Aliese retreats at first, but then, inspired, declares herself to be Eberenze Liseie, a cousin of Penferet, and by vocation an arbiter. She maneuvers a fawning Vintersla into installing her as arbiter in his domain and assigns the dispute between Emtor and Sentelleg to herself.

At the arbitration, Aliese, as Liseie, rules Sentelleg's contract with Emtor invalid, since Sentelleg has manipulated the price of green milnay, and confiscates one half of Sentelleg's property, awarding it to the Supracetor.

Kneth Emtor, now Eberenze Emtor, his lover Aliese, and their closest friends form a mercantile guild which they call *Aliemt*. The presentation concluded with Emtor and Aliese happily setting out on a voyage to a neighboring planet, aboard their own ship.

"Is Dictos a planet in the Epsilon Eridani system?" Charles asked.

"No, sir," replied July. "It orbits a different star, Ertugral, known on Earth as Lalande 21258."

3

The jet arrived at the Seattle-Tacoma airport at 12:45. Vivian had already determined that Charles had not reported back to work at his office, so she didn't bother checking there. She placed her carryon bag in a locker and took a cab straight to his home address in Edmonds. It was nearly two o'clock when she reached the two-story brick building.

She walked briskly along the court at the front of the building, looking for the manager's office. There was a light drizzle. Finally, she saw the sign and walked up to the door. She pressed the doorbell and a moment later a stout man in his fifties opened the door. He held a half-eaten sandwich in his hand. His dull eyes swept over her figure, while his tongue picked bread crumbs from the corners of his lips.

Vivian smiled at him. "I'm here regarding apartment 209, Mr. Ryder's apartment."

The man shook his head. "Can't let you have it yet. Papers haven't gone through court."

"Papers?"

"Eviction notice. Hasn't paid rent in over two months. The guy pulled a disappearing act on me." The manager took another bite of his sandwich. "I have two other apartments available," he added, looking at Vivian hopefully.

"I am an attorney with Strauss, Bosworth and Holley," said Vivian, handing the manager a printed business card. "Mr. Ryder has recently inherited a rather sizeable fortune and is currently traveling in Europe. My firm is handling his affairs here in Seattle."

The man eyed her dubiously. "Does that mean I get the back rent?"

Vivian smiled at him. "Of course. How much is owed?"

The man gulped down the last of his sandwich. "Please come in," he said, retreating into his living room. He took a seat at a tall padded arm-chair and invited Vivian to take the florid couch.

"It's two months' rent," he said, once she sat down, "plus the deposit." He looked at the ceiling while he performed a mental calculation. "That'll be around eighteen-hundred and fifty dollars. I'll also have to charge you extra for the late payment."

"That's fine," Vivian said. "I'll arrange for a moving company to pick up Mr. Ryder's furniture within the next few days. Could I take a look at the apartment now? I need to inventory his belongings."

"You'll have to pay before you move anything out," said the manager. He got up from the easy chair and took a key from a hook in a recessed bin on the wall. Vivian stood up and smoothed down her skirt.

"Here," said the manager, "let yourself in. It's right upstairs." He handed Vivian the key.

"I'll also need the mailbox key," said Vivian. "You may want to figure out exactly how much is owed and draw up a bill while I look over the furniture."

Vivian walked to the mailbox first. She opened it and found it full. Taking care not to drop any of it, she carried the thick pile of mail up the stairs to the second floor.

There was a short tense moment when she opened the door. She looked through the apartment quickly. Paperbacks were lined up neatly in a teak bookcase in the living room. A bicycle leaned against the wall in the smaller bedroom, between a workbench topped with model airplanes and a small desk. The bed in the master bedroom was made up. Coins, a comb, theater tickets, and an address book lay on top of the dresser. Nothing had been disturbed. Whatever had befallen Charles had happened before he returned to his apartment. And yet Robinson had told her that he had driven Charles to the airport in Miami; had seen him board the plane.

Methodically, she searched through Charles' papers and found his checkbook, his apartment lease, and the title to his car. She put them in her purse.

Then she sat at the dining table and went through his mail. She set aside rent and telephone bills and copies of Road & Track and Science News, then sighed when she found her own letters from Medellin and Miami, unopened. Very carefully, she scanned the statements from Charles' bank and credit card companies. There were several credit card receipts from the Los Angeles area dated the day Charles had left Miami and on two successive days later. The accounts had been inactive since then.

4

Vivian returned to Miami that evening. She met with Robinson the next morning, at his office.

He sat behind his desk and looked up at her, standing with a hand on her hip and the other pointed at him, her dark brown hair carelessly parted.

"You didn't tell me everything. Charles went to Los Angeles. You sent him there, didn't you?" Her blue eyes sparkled.

Robinson put down the report he had been reading. He was neatly dressed, but there was a vague and unkempt look about his face. "I did not," he said.

Vivian went a step closer to the desk. "I want to know what happened to him." She spoke quietly, but with a trace of danger in her voice. "He never reached Seattle. He didn't show up for work. His BMW is still parked near his apartment. His mailbox was full with ten weeks' mail. No one of his description has been reported dead or injured in Seattle or Los Angeles."

The look he gave her was more like a glance turned inward. "I don't know what happened to him."

She glared at him. "Don't you care?"

"Of course I care. There's just nothing I can do." Robinson looked uncomfortable. Unconsciously, he began to tap a finger on his desk.

"You must have given Charles another task to do. It was something to do with the Arteaga document, wasn't it?"

The color rose in Robinson's cheeks.

"Ryder no longer works for me," he said, his voice louder but tightly controlled. "We are not investigating the Arteaga case. Persons in the highest authority want the matter dropped. I have already forgotten it."

"You are a coward," she said scathingly.

Wariness showed on his tanned face. "You are upset. Take a few days off. I'll make some inquiries if you like."

"What was Charles doing in Los Angeles?" She tried to control her fury but her voice shook. "It will save me a lot of tracing work if you tell me."

Robinson blinked. He took a sheet of paper from a yellow pad on his desk, wrote briefly on it, and then handed it to Vivian.

She looked at it. There were five words printed on it: KATHRYN RED CHALICE KNEW ARTEAGA.

Vivian glanced at Robinson and then turned to go.

"Miss Venables." Robinson held out his hand, palm up.

She handed the note back to him.

"I'm sorry about Mr. Ryder," Robinson said. He crumpled the sheet of paper in his fist.

She turned on her heel, flung open the door, and walked out.

5

The taxi drove around the Queen Victoria Memorial and followed The Mall past the trees of St. James's Park. Then it turned into Marlborough Road, artfully dodged traffic near St. James's Palace, and stopped in front of a nineteenth century Georgian building in Pall Mall. Three men emerged from the car under a warm summer drizzle. Talking animatedly, they walked hurriedly past the imposing stone facade into Fallan's Club.

Dr. McClellan, who was a member, invited the others to join him for lunch. They took a secluded table in the lounge, a brown-paneled room of bay windows and stone carvings. A portrait of the founder, impeccably attired in a blue coat, hung above the stone fireplace. Sir Edward Fallan looked arrogantly down at the three men.

They shared an interest in the collection of books, those dealing with scientific or engineering subjects, and published prior to the twentieth century. Their first meeting had occurred eight years earlier, in New York City, at an antique book auction. Since then they had corresponded irregularly, occasionally exchanging or selling books among themselves. Commander Sifford's duties often took him to cities in the European Continent, where he frequently searched antique book stores for rare scientific and engineering texts. Mr. Drake had similar opportunities in North America.

Dr. McClellan seldom ventured out of Great Britain, but he devoted his Saturdays to searches through London's many antique book stores, and occasionally extended his explorations to other British cities.

During the taxi ride they had agreed to pool their resources in bidding for a well-preserved copy of a 1704 edition of Newton's *Opticks*. While waiting for their meal to be served, they settled on a limit bid and on Commander Sifford as the one who would actually carry out the bidding.

The dour but punctilious waiter slowly served the pheasant they had all ordered.

"Burton," said Drake, "I was told today that Newton had several mental breakdowns." The American deftly cut a slice of pheasant breast. He raised his dark eyes to Dr. McClellan. "How did they treat that sort of thing in those days?"

"Rest," replied Dr. McClellan. "Fairly effective." He turned to face Commander Sifford. "How's the spy business, John? Anything interesting going on that you can share with us?"

Commander Sifford smiled, shaking his head. "It's terrorists. You don't want to know." He tilted his head toward Drake, a lock of blond hair falling across his forehead. "Let's ask Carlos. What are you working on now?"

"It's a detective story, set in Holland," replied Drake. "I'll fly there after the auction to get some local color. I'm still working out the plot." The dark-haired man took a sip of the excellent white Cabernet. He fixed Dr. McClellan with an appraising glance. "Any interesting cases, Burton?"

Dr. McClellan pursed his lips. "As a matter of fact, I am working on a peculiar case. Puzzling." He carefully cut into a portion of pheasant. "It is a possible multiple personality. She first came to me about eight months ago."

The other two looked at Dr. McClellan with interest. Then, in general terms, he told his friends of Cicely Denfeld's case. The story held their attention throughout the meal.

They declined dessert, but agreed to a glass of port.

"It occurs to me," said Dr. McClellan, "that you two chaps might be able to do me a favor."

Commander Sifford and Mr. Drake looked at him expectantly.

"My patient's dreams are so detailed that they suggest familiarity with people and places that she claims to have had no contact with. It is unlikely that these people are real, but…"

"But you would like us to check them out," said Sifford.

Dr. McClellan took a sip of the strong wine. "Robinson is supposed to have a British background. There should be records of him. And if M.I.5 reaches that far, perhaps you could check on that fellow Gary Smith in the Bahamas."

"I'll do it," declared Sifford enthusiastically.

"And I'll check out Charles Ryder and Vivian Venables in the States," said Drake. "I have to go to Miami soon anyway."

"Don't forget Robinson," Dr. McClellan said.

"Oh, no. I'll look him up. And the other guy; the wise man."

"Alden Swan," Dr. McClellan said. "It's jolly decent of you two to agree to help. I'll go through my notes and get other details that might help you. And I'll talk to my patient."

"To the search for truth," said Sifford, holding up his glass.

The others joined him in the toast.

CHAPTER 14
THE PICARIEL CRYSTALS

1

Charles stepped into the transport module. The doorway closed behind him and he directed the vehicle to the sixteenth level.

The module took him down swiftly. He had been working at the room in the twelfth level that he had come to regard as his office. The assignment Cupahr had given him, investigating the effect on the transportation system of the earthquake, had proven more difficult than he had first thought. Working with the monitor, he had soon determined that the incidence of problems with the transport modules had increased since the time of the earthquake. Finding where the problem lay had proven more difficult.

He had eliminated problems in the drives within the Bithian and Indane-Aliemt compounds as possible causes. Modules in the Bithian system were being damaged more frequently than before the quake, but they were being damaged outside the Bithian compound. The modules shuttled back and forth throughout the entire transportation system, suspended and driven by electromagnetic rails. At some point in the system, thought Charles, the rails had been damaged by the earthquake.

His module came to a stop and Charles stepped out into the sixteenth level. Two female Kliettaes, wearing the green uniforms of Indane-Aliemt, hurried past him to board the vacant vehicle.

Charles walked across the bay and followed the corridor to the left. A Pagres, with the tall muscular physique of a myrmidon, stood guard by the doorway to Resseps Scahn's quarters. Charles approached him.

"Pagres Chasrydel to see the Resseps. My visit has been arranged."

The myrmidon took a small disk from a pocket in his white shirt and held it in front of a panel by the doorway. The blue portal's dark outline turned clear, and Charles entered the Resseps' quarters.

The reception room was large. The entry door led directly to a hexagonal room fifty feet across. It was, in Bithian fashion, devoid of permanent furniture, but its walls were illuminated in soft crimson and violet hues. At its center a large, intricately decorated violet and white globe slowly rotated, floating ten feet above the white floor.

Across the empty room, partially blocking the view into an adjoining chamber of similar size, stood a gleaming sculpture of metal and light, a helix that continually turned, its changing pale colors melting into one another. It made a soft, pleasant sound, like a distant waterfall. Charles walked towards it.

Looking at the alien sculpture, his thoughts turned to the world he was being kept from. A wave of nostalgia hit him. He missed leaf-strewn streets, trees, the sea, rain, the open sky, crowds; and most of all Vivian.

He heard voices. They came from the adjoining room. Charles couldn't quite make out what they said. Then, as he continued to approach, he heard a single voice clearly: "*Eke inverat.*"

Another voice joined the first. The words were spoken slowly, with a cadence. He could not understand them. They were not standard Galamic.

"*Eke inverat esder, eke inverat sudrals…*"

Charles held his position. He could not see the others.

A third voice joined the first two: "*Eke inverat dareske…*"

Charles moved cautiously closer to the sculpture. A fourth voice joined in: "*Eke Inverat.*"

After a moment the chorus repeated, "*Eke Inverat!*"

There was silence for a moment. Then the others began to talk, using words Charles understood.

"How is number forty developing, Berenz?" Charles recognized Scahn's voice.

"The process remains within nominal bounds, Lord."

Charles did not want to be caught eavesdropping. He resumed his progress toward the others, acting as if he had just entered the Resseps' quarters. Walking around the gleaming sculpture, he passed into the other section of the chamber.

The four sat around a circular dais bearing several translucent drink globules. From the insignia on their collars, Charles could tell they were all of high rank. On either side of the Resseps were a Bithian Berenz and a Vadycrel and across from him, in Indane-Aliemt green, Cirsegas Austir. The two small red squares on her collar glinted in the light of the rotating sculpture.

"Lords, Lady," Charles said tentatively. The others looked up at him.

The Resseps swung his seat about. His face showed controlled emotion and brilliant, all-pervading intelligence. "Remarkable event, Chasrydel. Approach us. We were expecting you."

"Yes, Lord," Charles said.

The Cirsegas tilted her handsome head slightly, her fine white hair spilling over her shoulder, and commanded a seat to appear. It rose from the floor next to her.

"Join us, Pagres," she said.

Charles took the seat. It adjusted swiftly about him.

The Resseps introduced the two distinguished-looking men as his aides, Vadycrel Exlof and Berenz Compcenlu. They carried about them the indefinable aura of persons used to making successful decisions. Charles bowed his head deeply in their direction. The others looked intently at him.

"We were discussing the latest crystal," said Scahn, smiling.

"The crystal, Lord?" Charles asked.

The Resseps nodded his bald head. "The fortieth Picariel crystal," he said. Then he exchanged a quick glance with the Vadycrel. "Perhaps you do not know about the crystals yet," he added, returning his attention to Charles.

"I have only just heard about them, Lord," Charles admitted.

Charles noted that the others watched him closely. Their expressions were friendly, but he found their attention vaguely disquieting.

"The crystals are used in the drives of interstellar ships," explained the Resseps. "They are the primary reason for our installation here." He made a sweeping motion with his hand.

"They are perfect crystals of cubic boron nitride," said Vadycrel Exlof, with an air of bemused detachment. "About three meters in length. It takes, on average, a major cycle to manufacture each Picariel crystal."

"Boron," Charles said, his brow wrinkled in thought.

"We extract it from kernite," Exlof said. "The deposit nearby is the largest known bulk accumulation."

The Bithians were after boron! It must be extremely rare in the Dramtes worlds, thought Charles. And on Earth they had found tons of it.

"I have some good news, Chasrydel," the Resseps said.

Charles pushed back his thoughts and looked at Scahn.

"Kneth Cupahr reports that you have performed very well in your short stay with us," said Scahn. "Effective immediately, you assume the degree of Kliettaes."

With a smile, the Resseps took one of the translucent globules from the raised platform around which they sat. He held it in his hand. The Berenz Compcenlu imitated Scahn's action and then the others followed suit.

"The Kliettaes!" they all called out, and drank the liquid, turning admiring eyes toward Charles.

2

Cicely Denfeld finished brushing her teeth. She washed the toothpaste from her mouth and dabbed at her face with a towel. Forcing a wide smile, she looked at herself in the mirror. Her teeth were bright and clean.

She turned off the bathroom light and went into her bedroom, humming fragments of an old love song.

With practiced movements, she pulled back the covers of her bed and set out the clothes she would wear to work the next day. There was something of the fawn in her graceful motions, a self-aware vulnerability.

Her last act, before slipping into bed, was to place the notebook and ballpoint pen on the small table by her bed, next to the portable voice recorder. It had become a part of her routine. She set the alarm clock, turned off the bedside lamp, and settled into her bed. Before closing her eyes, Cicely did one more thing. She whispered a prayer. Life had been terribly difficult recently. She prayed that she would be well soon. A moment later she was asleep.

The Mustang's red hood gleamed briefly in the sunlight as Vivian drove across the intersection. It was soon shaded again by rows of elms on either side of the empty street. A wistful smile came to her lips, as she remembered the last time she had visited Swan, together with Charles. It was Charles, the missing Charles, that brought her back.

She drove ahead on the leaf strewn street and parked the convertible in front of the white stucco house. A moment later she was across the lawn, banging the brass knocker on the sky blue door.

The girl, Gisela, let her in.

"Please come in, Miss Venables," said the young girl in her clear voice. "Alden is in the study. He asked me to bring you to him."

"I brought you a present, Gisela," said Vivian, entering the house and following the girl along the hall.

Gisela's face lit up with a smile. "You did?"

"I've been to Colombia." Vivian returned the smile and brought out a small object out of her purse. "I thought you might like it."

It was a small carved stone figure, about two inches high.

The girl, her eyes wide in admiration, accepted the green effigy. She ran her fingers over the smooth stone. "It's beautiful." Smiling, she turned and kissed Vivian's cheek. "Thank you, Vivian."

They walked through the gold room that held Swan's Chinese porcelain collection, and then followed a short hallway into the book-lined study. Swan was just inside, replacing a thick tome on the lowest shelf of a recessed bookcase. He rose as the others arrived.

Gisela could not contain her enthusiasm. "Look, Alden," she exclaimed, holding out the green figure for his inspection, "Vivian brought me a present. It's a little Indian god."

"Good day, Miss Venables," he said, taking the figurine in his hand.

Vivian nodded. "Mr. Swan," she said, in greeting. "I picked that up in a little shop in Cartagena. The proprietor, an old Indian, told me that it came from Nicaragua." She smiled. "He said it was Mayan jade."

Swan held the small object up to the light, then hefted it in his hand. "The Mayans had jadeite," he said, "not the Chinese *laoyu*, but just as valuable."

He examined the figurine closely. "This is not jadeite," he announced. "Probably diopside. But it is quite old, and the style is Mayan. It is difficult to gauge its authenticity without knowing more about its provenance, but the Mayan influence did extend as far south as Nicaragua."

Returning the object to the girl he told her: "It is a rare and valuable carving, Gisela."

"And beautiful," she added, admiring the figure for a moment and then holding it tightly against her breast.

"Yes," Swan said, looking at her fondly. "That most of all."

Gisela smiled, thanked Vivian once again, and stepped lightly away from the room.

Vivian sat down on a comfortable couch. Across from her, Swan leaned back on his high-backed stuffed chair, his unsteady eyes examining her in a direct way that she found slightly uncomfortable.

"I expected you back earlier," he said, taking his gaze from her.

"I have been abroad on another assignment."

"And Mr. Ryder?"

"He was also called away," she said. "But I'm back on the case now." With a quick motion of her hand she pushed back a lock of flowing dark-brown hair, away from her face. "Have you made any progress?"

Swan picked up a manila folder from the low table between them. He idly turned over sheets of closely-typed notes.

"My dear Miss Venables," he said, "we must trust each other more. You are holding something back from me. Are you not?"

Vivian sighed deeply, her rising chest attracting a glance from Swan. "Charles is missing. He was in Los Angeles."

"And there was an attempt on Mr. Robinson's life," said Swan. "The day you were here."

"Yes," Vivian admitted.

"There is risk involved in this that you did not tell me about."

"You were paid well."

"Mr. Lawrence stopped by a month ago and paid for my services to that date. Any additional services will require an additional compensation."

"How much do you want?"

"For today's work, my fee is five thousand dollars," he declared.

"Oh, come on Swan. I don't have that kind of money."

"Mr. Robinson won't be paying for this?"

Vivian took a check book from her purse. Using the check book that she had found in Charles' room, she had during the past few days forged his name to several of his checks, transferring most of his funds to her own account. But her trip to Seattle had been expensive, and her planned trip to Los Angeles still lay ahead. Robinson had refused any further involvement.

"I'll give you two thousand," she said firmly.

"That is not enough."

She ignored him and started to write out the check. "You didn't even offer me chocolates this time," she quipped.

"Two thousand is not enough," Swan repeated. "There is great risk." He smiled thinly, his unsteady gaze watching her finish writing out the check. "Besides, where else can you obtain a consultation like mine? If you do not have the funds, you can always investigate on your own."

Vivian tore the check off and held it out to Swan. He momentarily leaned forward, but stopped himself and did not take the proffered check.

Annoyed, she gave him a hard look and placed the check on the table. "What is your relationship with Gisela?" she asked.

Swan pulled back into his chair. "Why do you ask that?"

"You are a very wise and intelligent man. I want you to appreciate my circumstances. I very much want to find out what happened to Charles. If he still lives…" She took a deep breath and went on in a tight hard voice. "I am not as good at thinking through things as you are, Swan, but I am a good investigator. Would you like me to investigate you?"

Swan's watery eyes crossed Vivian's for a moment. He leaned forward, picked up the check from the table, and, without examining it, folded it and placed it in his shirt pocket.

He looked at her grudgingly. "Colonel Nester was an Air Force intelligence officer. He was found dead in a motel room in Palmdale, California, about two years ago. There was no previous illness and he was not in the care of a physician, so an autopsy was performed. The coroner concluded Nester died from massive trauma to the thorax, inflicted by person or persons unknown, via undetermined means. There were first and second degree burns in the chest surrounding a deep wound. This initially suggested a gunshot injury, but no projectile was found and there was no exit wound."

"Was he robbed?"

"No. And his room appeared to be intact."

"I saw a wound like that once," Vivian said quietly. "On Arteaga, the man who stole the document. I thought it was a shotgun wound, although Charles said a handgun had been involved. There was a fire at the site…" She looked at Swan directly. "What would make a wound like that?"

He rubbed his chin. "If a single projectile is involved, it would have to be of an explosive nature. Something like a flare or a small rocket-propelled grenade. Otherwise, well, something along the lines of a laser, or a very large electrical discharge."

Vivian shook her head.

Swan flipped a few pages in the manila folder he held. "The Tieck thesis dealt with an anomaly in background radiation. He noticed it while collecting data for a space-based sensor registration study. It suggests the presence of an underground thermal source approximately 70 miles north of Los Angeles. That's fairly close to Palmdale, where Colonel Nester's body was found."

He pulled a glossy eight-by-ten photograph from the folder and placed it down on the table. "This is the location of the anomaly," said Swan, pointing at an area in the photograph. "It's from Tieck's paper."

Vivian examined the photograph. "What do you think about this?" asked Vivian, tapping the photograph.

Swan pursed his lips. "Tieck dismissed it as a geothermal source," he stated. "I think it's an underground installation. It must be huge to generate so much energy. And it has been kept secret for several years, which is astounding. Tieck's basic data was collected many years ago."

"A Government installation?"

"That is most likely." Swan turned another page over in the folder. "I found little of interest in the Ozma project. They mostly scanned the sky for radio frequency transmissions of an unusual nature. As far as I can tell, they found nothing they considered worth reporting. Except…"

Vivian inched forward on the couch. "Except what?"

"The project started rather spectacularly. They detected strong emissions from the direction of a nearby star." He glanced at the folder. "In the constellation Eridanus. They thought they really had something. All of a sudden, a lot of people got interested in the project. But when checks were made, the emissions were identified as signals from Air Force installations. Radar interference. The project was cancelled two months later."

"They were looking for extraterrestrial transmissions?"

"Yes. For patterns indicating an intelligent source."

"But perhaps they got something else. Something related to," she again tapped the photograph, "to whatever this is."

"That's a plausible theory, assuming that the two subjects are related. If the Government is involved, when the Ozma people inquired about their peculiar data they could have been told it was caused by a military experiment, a spy satellite or some such thing."

"Anything else?" Vivian asked.

Swan sighed. "The Gilgamesh project conducts privately funded research into ways to extend life. It has been going on for almost five years at the Baylor College of Medicine in Houston, Texas. They can make rats double their life span by altering their diet and exercise schedules; that sort of thing. I can find no plausible relationship to the other items in the Index."

"What does the name stand for?" Vivian asked.

"Gilgamesh was a Sumerian demigod, the king of a city-state called Uruk. He appears in many epic stories. In some of them he searches for immortality."

Swan cleared his throat. "I was able to make some sense of the last item. The one mentioning 'Ames' and 'automaton device.' Ames may not refer to a person's last name, but to an organization—one of the NASA centers. There are actually two sites. Ames Moffett is in the southern end of San Francisco Bay, adjacent to the Naval Air Station, Moffett Field. Ames Dryden occupies 520 acres in the high desert about 70 miles northeast of Los Angeles, next to Edwards Air Force Base."

Swan closed the manila folder. He dropped it on the table.

"What do they do there?" Vivian asked.

"They have a long list of interests: aerodynamics, infrared astronomy, space sciences, automation and robotics."

"That last would explain the 'automaton device' reference. And Ames Dryden is near Tieck's anomaly."

Swan nodded.

"May I keep the photograph?"

"You can keep the whole folder." Swan paused for a moment, his eyes locking on Vivian's. "I have formed an impression as to what the source document might be."

He looked at the folder for a moment, and then returned his gaze to Vivian. "It could be a risk assessment study. An effort to identify possible means by which the main project could be compromised. The index to the first part of the document—really all that we have—lists the known exposures, which presumably are described in the missing text. The second part of the document may have assessed the risk, and perhaps recommended risk reduction procedures."

Vivian picked up the folder and placed the photograph inside. Then she directed a troubled glance at Swan and rose from the couch.

Swan stood up. "Someone has given this project the deepest cover. You place yourself in danger by attempting to unveil it," he said quietly.

Vivian's chin came up and her face was tight. "I just can't walk away from him, Swan. I just can't."

3

Charles and July sat in front of the squat white machine in the work area at the twelfth level. They had been conducting a series of statistical analyses, directed at identifying a relationship between the damaged transportation modules and a particular section of the transportation system.

So far they had eliminated the Bithian and Indane-Aliemt quarters and the tunnels linking them to each other and to the space port. July had recorded their results in a *hripitur*, a tablet-like device that she held in her lap.

"Correlation between unscheduled maintenance events and travel itineraries involving the port facility is 0.08," announced the monitor.

Charles shook his head. "Repeat analysis with respect to factory structure and its connection to port facility," he said.

A blue dot on the center of the monitor's display indicated it was processing the request. Seconds later, the display went momentarily blank.

"Unscheduled maintenance correlation with itineraries involving the factory structure is 0.16," said the monitor. "The correlation falls to 0.10 for itineraries involving the factory to port facility tunnel."

July made an entry on the hripitur. A small electronic eye at the tip of a wire-thin sensor stalk projected itself from the top of the device and rotated to view the figures appearing on the monitor's display.

Charles thought for a moment. "Repeat analysis with respect to kernite mining facility and its connection to the factory."

The blue dot returned to the monitor display.

"That was the highest correlation yet," observed July. She pressed a stud on the hripitur and a 3-D graph of the transportation system was displayed on its small screen. The various sectors were tinted in different hues according to their maintenance correlations. She tilted the device so that Charles could clearly see the display.

The blue dot disappeared from the monitor's window. "A correlation of 0.47 exists for itineraries involving the tunnel between the factory facility and the mining facility," said the monitor. "This is a significant correlation. The correlation for itineraries limited to the mining facility itself is 0.11."

"Done!" July said, her green eyes glinting.

"We still have to find where in that tunnel," said Charles, smiling, "but we're getting close."

July returned his smile. She recorded the monitor's data in the hripitur.

Charles began to rise, then remembered something that had been puzzling him since his visit to Resseps Scahn.

"July," he said, turning to face her, "what does the word *inverat* mean?"

"I do not know the word, Chasrydel. It is not standard Galamic or English," she stated.

A blue dot appeared briefly on the monitor's display.

"Inverat," said the monitor's soft female voice, "means empire. It is an Uncial Galamic word."

Charles turned to face the monitor. "Uncial Galamic?"

"The language of the ancients," explained the monitor. "The Galams. Their empire was destroyed in a conflict between them and races from the core of this constellation."

"When did this happen?" Charles asked.

"Sixty thousand major cycles ago," replied the monitor.

COUNTERTRANSFERENCE

CHAPTER 15
MAINTENANCE PROBLEMS

1

Charles and July stepped out of the transportation module onto the training area anteroom in the fourth level. Kliettaes Rathiz, waiting nearby, greeted them.

"I will lead you to the exercise plain, Chasrydel," he said. "Kneth Cupahr is already there. He and Esandos have prepared the session."

Rathiz started toward the portal across the room. Charles and July followed him. They crossed the doorway and walked along the stark corridor.

"You are not required here," Rathiz said, half turning to address July.

July continued walking at their side. "I would like to accompany you, sir," she said to Charles.

Charles nodded. "Yes, please come along, July."

The shadow of a frown crossed Rathiz's face, but he said nothing. In a moment, they came to another portal, flanked by two myrmidons.

One of the two identical tall men smiled. "Remarkable event, Kliettaes," he said.

"Remarkable event, Esandos," answered Charles and Rathiz. July inclined her head slightly toward the myrmidon. She stood by Charles as Rathiz handed the cipher disk to Esandos and he unlocked the portal.

"Chance favor," Rathiz called out, as the others crossed the doorway.

They walked along the dun-colored corridor, July a half pace behind the two men. There was a warm breeze as they approached the training area, and it lifted wisps of her blond hair.

"What is it today, Esandos?" Charles asked.

The myrmidon's harsh face softened for a moment. "The Kneth will instruct you first," he said. "Then you will face a new trial."

Charles shuddered. The last "trial" had been a four-armed red-skinned monster that had almost torn him apart. As if sensing his anxiety, July took his hand and held it. A few paces further on the wall to their right ended, and they looked at the wide plain twenty feet below. They heard the roar of beasts in their cages close by.

July released Charles' hand. "I will wait for you here, sir," she said, as Esandos led Charles down a rough ramp to the barren field below.

There was a chamber at the foot of the ramp. A cavity forty feet across and almost that deep had been cut into the rock wall. A man, wearing what appeared to be light body armor, waited there.

"Remarkable event, Kliettaes," the man said, as Charles and Esandos approached. Charles began to identify the man when he heard his voice, but it was only a moment later, when the man unfastened his helmet's face guard, that he fully recognized him.

"Remarkable event, Kneth Cupahr," Charles responded.

Over his white tunic, Cupahr wore a set of gray pieces of apparel. A harness held shoulder, breast and rib protectors over his torso, and other gray sections covered his hips, thighs and knees.

Cupahr pointed at a set of the gray body armor lying in a pile nearby. "Put those on, Kliettaes," he told Charles. "Pagres Esandos will assist you."

As he donned the gray articles, Charles noted they were stiff and very light. The whole outfit weighed about four pounds.

Esandos helped slide the tight helmet into place over Charles' head and adjusted the face guard. With the heel of his hand, the myrmidon hit at

Charles' midsection. The blow landed with a reassuring thud, and Esandos nodded his approval as Charles rocked backwards, unhurt.

"Today we will practice defensive and offensive unarmed combat," said Cupahr.

"The Kneth and I will demonstrate a sequence," Esandos added, "and then you will repeat it with one of us." He handed Charles a pair of stiff gloves and helped him put them on.

"I don't want to do this, Master," Charles declared.

Ignoring Charles, the Kneth helped Esandos don a set of body guards.

A moment later, the three walked a distance away from the chamber, until they stood on the sandy terrain, at the edge of the seemingly vast plain.

"Watch, Chasrydel," Cupahr said, as he wheeled to face Esandos.

The myrmidon approached him slowly, half crouched, his arms held slightly forward. Suddenly he leapt toward Cupahr, a long arm swinging toward the Kneth's head. But, just as rapidly, Cupahr moved. He ducked under the myrmidon's hand and drove his right fist into Esandos' belly.

The myrmidon stepped back, air rushing from his mouth.

Then the two looked at Charles.

"It's your turn, Kliettaes," Esandos said, ignoring Charles' protest and squaring to face him.

Without waiting, Esandos started toward Charles, half crouching, his arms slightly forward. Charles turned to face him. Esandos took a step forward and Charles drove his left fist toward the myrmidon's head. Esandos grabbed the forearm in his powerful hand. Charles swung with his right hand, scoring a glancing blow off Esandos' breastplate.

Then the myrmidon pulled down on Charles' arm and, as he fell, clipped him on the chin with a driving knee. A moment later, Charles lay on his back, stunned.

Cupahr gruffly pulled Charles back to his feet.

"Esandos did not hurt you, did he?" Cupahr asked, a gleam of playful malice in his eyes. "Your response must be automatic, spontaneous."

Charles felt the back of his neck. For a moment, he had thought his head had been snapped off.

"You were too tentative," Cupahr said. "Spontaneity will cut your response time and rob your opponent of a warning."

Charles dusted himself off. He moved his left arm tentatively. His wrist hurt.

Esandos took a few steps back. He turned and faced Charles. He lowered his head, bent his knees and extended his arms. Slowly, he moved closer to Charles. Cupahr stepped back from the other two.

Esandos grinned. "Let's try it again."

They practiced for a long time, Esandos and Cupahr taking turns as instructors. Occasionally, they allowed Charles time to rest and to recover from the continued exertions. Gradually, Charles learned to parry the other's blows and to deliver his own more effectively.

"Well done, Kliettaes," Cupahr said, slapping Charles sharply on the back. "It's time for the trial."

Charles moved cautiously along a dusty trail bordered by rounded boulders. He was utterly exhausted, and his left side hurt, where Cupahr had delivered a particularly vicious kick. Based on previous experience, he expected one of the animals to attack him soon. They had given him no weapons this time, but he had picked up two fist-sized stones and held them tightly in his hands.

He heard a noise behind him and wheeled to see a massive humanoid form approach him at a run. The being was over six feet tall, hairless, with powerful muscles that rippled under gray skin. Its reddish sunken eyes glared at Charles with feral viciousness.

In one swift motion, Charles threw a stone at the being and crouched, arms outspread. The gray brute ducked, but the stone still hit its shoulder.

It winced in pain and almost fell, but soon recovered and lunged ahead, grunting defiantly.

Charles transferred the second stone to his right hand. It was too late to throw it. He held it in his gloved fist as he rammed it at the beast's chest. The blow landed with a loud thud. Shaken, the humanoid dropped and rolled away. Charles drove a powerful kick at its head, but the creature jerked sideways and suffered only a glancing blow. Then, moving with prodigious speed, it wrenched the stone out of Charles' hand and dragged him forward.

A desperate cry burst from Charles as huge four-fingered hands closed around his neck. Powerful muscles bulged in the creature's stout forearms. Charles experienced unbearable pain as his neck was gradually crushed, his body sagging in the overpowering grip that held him up, suspended.

It felt like he was at the bottom of a dark well. There was a point of light above, far away. He felt a coldness touch his arm. The light became a small circle and then it grew rapidly as he traveled up the well.

He opened his eyes to see the familiar blue walls of his triangular bedroom. A short, burly Bithian stood above him, Eberenze Reumonh. Charles' gaze dwelled on the four small red circles on his collar. His sight blurred for an instant. Then he noticed July's fair head. She smiled reassuringly.

Charles lay on his sleeping pad. His white uniform and body armor had been removed and someone had clothed him in a shiny silver frock.

The Eberenze held a gleaming rod in one hand and an ovoid instrument in the other. He pointed the latter at Charles' chest. It clicked faintly. "How do you feel?" Reumonh asked.

"Tired, Master," Charles said. "My vision..." He blinked. "But it's all right now."

Charles tested his neck by turning his head from side to side.

"Any pain, sir?" July asked.

"No." Charles wondered how they had brought him back to his quarters.

Reumonh consulted an indicator on the ovoid instrument. He put the device in a pocket of his tunic and turned to face July.

"Kliettaes Chasrydel is fully recovered now," he told her. "I will inform Berenz Compcenlu."

Reumonh patted Charles on the shoulder. "Chance favor, Kliettaes," he said. "All you need now is rest." Then he turned and left the room.

Charles closed his eyes and quickly sank into a slumber. He had to find a way to escape, before the damned monsters killed him. But every exit to the facility was guarded by semi-intelligent automatic sentries with enough firepower to stop an armored regiment.

Vaguely, he heard July moving about; the rustling of clothes and the whisper of a drawer retracting into a wall. A moment later he felt her nude body press lightly against his. He put his arm around her.

2

Charles directed the transport module to take them to the factory structure. It lifted them to the sixth level of the Bithian compound, shuttled through a channel interchange, and then moved them quickly along the tunnel to the space dock. There the module slowed down again.

"Cupahr rejected again my request to stop the training—the encounters with the beasts," Charles said.

July's green eyes met his. "His orders come from the Resseps," she said after a while.

"Where do the creatures come from, July?"

"Some are reproductions of animals from various Dramtes worlds, others are induced mutations."

"Reproductions?"

"Biological constructs."

"I don't understand why they insist on those insane stunts. I could get killed."

"You must do as they ask, Chasrydel," July said. "You are protected. No permanent harm will befall you."

Their module lurched imperceptibly and then accelerated along the tunnel leading to the factory. A moment later it came to a stop. The rim of its doorway cleared, and Charles and July walked through to a gray platform.

It was Charles' first visit to the factory. He watched as a slender bronze-skinned man in a blue uniform, trailed by a levitating chromium cylinder, entered the transport module they had just left.

"I had not seen anyone in blue before," Charles said.

"He is a Nesdelsen technician," July said. "A few of them work at the crystal farm."

July adjusted the fit of a small white bag she carried slung over her shoulder. It contained instruments they would need later on.

The platform stopped abruptly fifty feet ahead. Beyond was a vast open space. A cluster of people stood a short distance away, near the edge of the platform. Two wore white, the other two green.

"Remarkable event, Kliettaes Chasrydel," one of the four called out.

Charles recognized the short, wiry body and long gray hair of Eberenze Fermilo. He and July returned the greeting and approached the waiting officials.

As they neared the group, Charles noted the chasm beyond. Huge cylindrical shapes rose to meet massive girders one hundred feet above. They plunged hundreds of feet below, amidst spherical shapes and dozens of small platforms. He could see workers milling about across the enormous cavity, four hundred feet away. Some whizzed by on air cars that flew between platforms. His ears were assaulted with the strident sounds of numerous machines.

Fermilo introduced the Indane-Aliemts as Obiredes Dahlgers and her aide, Kneth Fernoch. Dahlgers' bronze skin had more gold in it than any of the other aliens Charles had met. Her narrow face held harsh angles softened by a permanent smile and flowing gray hair. Fernoch was tall and athletic, with inquisitive yellow eyes.

Fermilo's attendant was a statuesque android with neatly cropped white hair. She carried a hripitur in her hand and a light rod, an imdermi, clipped to a silver belt. Her name was Roxelan.

"We are ready to proceed, Kliettaes," Fermilo said.

"I have made arrangements for our transportation, Master," Charles said. "Please follow us."

They walked in a group to the transport area and boarded a waiting module. July brought out a hripitur from her bag and pressed a sequence of keys on the recording device. It emitted a series of beeps and musical tones. At once, the doorway edge darkened and the transport module was set in motion.

"Where are we heading?" Obiredes Dahlgers asked.

"The transport module will take us to a location about one kilometer from the factory structure, Lady," Charles stated.

"We will exit the vehicle at a maintenance station there," July added, "and proceed on foot along the tunnel leading to the mining installation, Lady. Kliettaes Chasrydel has determined the location of the damaged levitators to within a few hundred meters."

They sensed the turning motions of the vehicle as it shifted channels within the factory structure. Then, as they entered the tunnel that connected the factory to the mine, they felt a steady acceleration.

———— ⌘ ————

The group moved single-file along a narrow platform at the edge of the tunnel, halfway up its side. The tube was a huge structure, one hundred feet across. Three twenty-foot rectangular ducts, suspended side-by-side at the center, enclosed transport module pathways. A series of smaller round ducts were strung above, dimly visible in the red light emanating from narrow strips set on the curving walls. Forty feet below was a wide roadway along which self-guided wheeled vehicles occasionally sped by, pulling trains of boxy containers. Theirs was the only noise in the otherwise silent chamber.

Roxelan made an adjustment to her imdermi and the rod-like device cast a bright beam on the wall of the tunnel. She moved the bright spot about as the group moved along.

"There," she said, her voice echoing eerily. "Ahead."

A moment later Fernoch called out: "I see it too. A great bulge." His yellow eyes glinted in the imdermi's light.

July brought out her hripitur and held it so that its electronic eye could record the scene. The tunnel wall showed a marked indentation. Its remarkable strength had allowed it to retain its integrity despite the tremendous pressure of dislocated rock strata, but it had yielded at this place.

They moved slowly ahead. Charles pulled out an imdermi from the bag that July carried and added its light to Roxelan's, illuminating the bent structures. The intrusion had deflected the transport module ducts, forcing one of the outer ducts against the center one.

"The damage is not noticeable from within the transport module pathways," July said.

"That explains why the inspection mechanisms did not detect it," Obiredes Dahlgers said. She turned to Fermilo and added: "What will it take to repair this, Eberenze?"

Fermilo studied the intrusion a while longer. "We can realign the pathways right away, Lady. That will stop the maintenance problem with the modules. Correcting the intrusion will take more effort. The pressure from the dislocated rock will have to be relieved, probably by disintegration."

With a glance to Charles, Fermilo added: "Kliettaes Chasrydel will analyze the problem and recommend a specific procedure."

"I have seen enough," Dahlgers declared.

July accompanied Fermilo and the Indane-Aliemt officials back to the transport module, while Charles and Roxelan continued the inspection. They displayed plans of the area stored in the hripitur, and figured out a way to approach and enter the damaged transport module ducts. The levitator rails inside appeared intact, but Roxelan took measurements that showed them to be slightly bent. Finally satisfied, the two climbed out to the platform and started to walk back to the maintenance station.

Suddenly, an extremely loud noise broke the sepulchral silence. It rose and fell at irregular intervals, filling the place with a rapid staccato.

Roxelan leaned over the side of the platform and directed the imdermi's light toward the zone where the noise seemed to come from. A puzzled expression grew on her face.

Charles joined Roxelan in peering into the dimly-lit area below. There was a side entrance to the roadway. They both saw the gloomy opening.

"I cannot identify that noise, sir," Roxelan said.

Charles recognized it at once. It was the sound of an automobile engine being revved up and down.

"Let's go down and look, Roxelan," he said.

They used a small elevator to reach the roadway level and then moved cautiously along the side of the tunnel toward the side opening. Once, a train of vehicles passed them, the huge containers whizzing by a mere ten feet away. For a while, the roar of the vehicles overwhelmed the engine's sound.

The side opening was a forty foot square, cut into the lower part of the tunnel. As they turned into it, Roxelan held out her hripitur.

"The sound appears to be caused by a series of explosions, sir," she said.

"It's an internal combustion engine," Charles said.

Roxelan looked at him quizzically, her short white hair tinged with red from the overhead lights.

"Probably made on Earth, Roxelan," added Charles with a smile.

Ahead, they saw a dark shape. As they approached it, the raucous sound suddenly stopped. Two figures emerged from the reddish dusk. One of them wore Indane-Aliemt green, the other was Chadwick.

3

The CIA man approached Charles with hand outstretched. There was something vaguely menacing in his brisk steps and inquisitive look. They shook hands, Charles finding himself surprisingly pleased to meet the man again.

"Hello, Chadwick," Charles said, in English.

"Hello yourself, Ryder," Chadwick said. He glanced at Roxelan. Then, noticing the two red circles on Charles' collar, added, "I should say Kliettaes, eh?"

Roxelan stood by Charles for a moment. She could not understand their speech, but recognized it as an Earth language. A moment later she approached the Indane-Aliemt and spoke to him.

"We heard the sound," she said. "What do you do here?"

"We work on the vehicle." He pointed with a thick finger at the dark shape nearby, and Roxelan unclipped her imdermi from her silver belt and activated it. A beam of bright light illuminated the entire area.

They all looked at the vehicle. Its black paint added a sinister touch to the wildly curved form. The bodywork wrapped itself tautly around huge tires. An airfoil blended smoothly with the rear fenders. Slots and vents were inset into virtually every panel. Only the roof retained a familiar shape.

"It's the Supracetor's toy," Chadwick said, speaking in standard Galamic for the benefit of Roxelan. His brown eyes darted over her shapely figure, then returned to the car. "A Porsche 959. One of the few in the country. Only two hundred and forty were made."

They approached the coupe. The cover over the rear engine was open, revealing a mass of complex mechanisms dominated by a large ducted cooling fan and a shiny intake manifold.

"The engine has two turbochargers," Chadwick commented. "The factory claimed 444 horsepower." He patted the glossy black fender. "It has four-wheel drive, a six speed transmission, and will do 200 miles an hour. Supracetor Breslui takes it outside every once in a while, so we put a polymer-based paint on it from the Stealth program that makes it invisible to radar. We don't want the cops to spot him, even though they sure aren't going to catch him."

Charles walked around the car, admiring the brutally sensuous shape. He glanced at the man in green. He had a studious look and was the first human, other than Chadwick, that he had seen in the site.

"Where's your attendant?" Chadwick asked.

"We came in a group, to inspect a section of the transport system," Charles replied. "July went back with the others."

"I could have used her. This beauty's got an electronic fuel control system that's slightly off. We've been trying to adjust it for hours."

"I can ask Roxelan to help you, if you wish."

Chadwick glanced briefly at Roxelan, who was peering inside the passenger compartment. "No," he said, reverting to English, "she's a type 47. That's not much better than Kanuner. He's been of some help to me. But your attendant is a type 63, which should make her a whiz at just about anything."

Charles glanced at Kanuner's collar. It bore the Galamic numeral 45. "Kanuner is an android," Charles said.

"He is," Chadwick said. "His appearance allows him to accompany me outside without drawing undue attention."

Giving Charles an appraising glance, Chadwick added: "I'm still amazed that they assigned such a model to you. Even Breslui's attendant, certainly a command-grade android, is only a 52."

Charles shrugged. "She had to have some special knowledge, so that she could teach me to get about, and so that she could communicate with me when I couldn't speak standard Galamic. Why are you so concerned about it?"

"It's part of my job," Chadwick said. "I evaluate their technology and their capabilities." He fixed his brown eyes on Charles'. "I play chess at the grandmaster level. Sometime back I taught Kanuner the game. He likes it, and seems able to recall every move of every game we've played. We play often, when we take a long break. On the eleventh game we played I got careless and we had a draw. About two weeks later he beat me for the first time."

Chadwick shifted his gaze to Kanuner, who was showing a device to unfasten the car's central-locking wheels to Roxelan. "He's almost even with me now. I win most of the time, but he makes me stretch. He doesn't play like a computer; he plays like me."

"But he's not a great mechanic," Charles ventured.

"No," Chadwick sighed, "not yet." He folded his arms across his chest, displaying a grease smudge on his white sleeve. "At the highest levels, chess is a game of associative memory as much as it is of pure intelligence. Kanuner's rapid progress makes me wonder just how intelligent these androids are."

"Maybe it all depends on what you define intelligence to be."

"Oh, I think it's quickness in seeing things as they are."

"I wonder if you could tell me something," Charles said. He was about to ask Chadwick how the Supracetor got outside with the car. But he decided not to bring up the subject. Instead, he posed a different question. "The Picariel crystals. What are they used for, exactly?"

Chadwick rubbed his chin. "Well, I don't know exactly," he grinned. "Have you asked the Bithians?"

"No. I heard about them only recently."

"I don't think they will refuse to discuss the crystals with you," Chadwick said. "But if you can settle for an inexact explanation..."

"Sure. All I know is that they are used in their starship propulsion system."

Chadwick leaned against the car's fender. Charles joined him.

"Be careful, Ryder," Chadwick warned, "It's pretty thin aluminum."

Charles was very careful. He didn't want to dent the Supracetor's car.

"The way I get it," Chadwick said, "the crystals aren't really used for propulsion. They use a fusion-powered ion drive for that. What the crystals do is to control gravity. They act as magnifiers of an antigravitational force that is inherent in all matter—a force proportional to atomic composition. The crystals reduce the effective inertia in a volume encompassing the ship, so that it offers little resistance to acceleration."

"An antigravity force?"

"At the atomic level. Something Einstein seems to have missed. It's normally very weak, and it fades out within a mile or so. The crystals induce a strong field of antigravity. The ship's drives don't really generate all that much power, but with the field effect on, they can make it move pretty fast."

"How fast?"

Chadwick raised his hands, palms up. "I'm not sure. As fast as light, maybe."

There was silence for a moment, except for the clicks caused by some mechanical component in the engine compartment cooling off.

"Kneth Cupahr said you were wrong about the Bithians fighting commercial wars, Chadwick. According to him there has been no fighting for centuries."

Chadwick slid away from the Porsche and turned to face Charles, giving him a shrewd look. "No armed conflicts for a few centuries does not mean much to a civilization thousands of years old. I think they'll go back to it, although Cupahr may be right. Their society seems to have changed significantly in the last four or five hundred years. They have begun to expand. But they would take us by force if we opposed them. There's no doubt about that."

Charles frowned. "So our government just sits and lets the Bithians do whatever they want," he said.

Chadwick lectured him in a firm, mechanical tone: "We act with caution and restraint. We learn as much as possible about the aliens. A lot of time and effort is put into looking for alternatives. So far, our course has been to keep their impact to a minimum. Once, we asked them candidly: what would they do if we took Site One? This happened at a meeting with Intuger Sinderc and Vadycrel Exlof, two of their big shots. First, Exlof said that was impossible, that their defenses were impregnable. Then Sinderc added that if we somehow managed, they could do something like spray a colloidal dust on the upper atmosphere. It would increase the temperature worldwide a few degrees and, among other things, raise the ocean level twenty meters. The bitch smiled when she said that. Can you imagine what that would cost us?"

"Isn't freedom worth the risk?"

"Freedom is overrated. There are many who are totally free and also totally miserable. They lack direction to their lives. And there are contented people who lead highly restricted lives."

Chadwick smiled wryly, "It's the story of the satisfied, dutiful servant and his carefree but discontented master. There are many dimensions to life, and happiness and freedom are just two of them."

Charles thought for a moment. "Have you considered telling our people about the aliens?"

"There would be chaos," Chadwick said. His face tightened, as if entertaining a dark thought. "In any case, they would not allow it. They deal harshly with any action that undermines their position."

"There's so few of them. I can't believe the Army couldn't take them."

With his hand leaning against the edge of the car as if it were a short lectern, Chadwick spoke in a schoolmaster's voice. "In the early sixteenth century, the Inca Empire stretched 3,000 miles down the west coast of South America. The Inca were not tame or disorganized. They had 14,000 miles of roads. The emperor Atahualpa commanded an army of 100,000 fierce and disciplined warriors. But, in 1532, Francisco Pizarro led 150 Spaniards to conquer the Inca. It took him about a year to finish the job."

Chadwick stepped away from the car and clasped his hands behind his back, his eyes not leaving Charles. "Pizarro and his men had courage and ambition, but their real advantages were superior knowledge and tools. Atahualpa's generals used technology less advanced than that available to the early Pharaohs. A few Spaniards used top notch tactics, steel swords, muskets, and cannon to crush the Inca armies. The technology gap between us and the Dramtes is much greater than that between the Incas and the Spanish. We wouldn't have a chance, Ryder."

"Has anyone actually acted against them?" Charles' voice was raspy.

"The Air Force intercepted and attacked their initial probes. That was long before my time. I am not sure what the Dramtes response was, but it was brutal enough to ensure that their landing here was undisturbed. Since then, no one has tried to tell them to pack and go home; that would be suicidal. But Presidents and top Cabinet members are not accustomed to restraints. Sometimes they go too far, and bad things happen to them."

"What bad things?"

"Remember the Apollo Program? Trip to the moon? President Kennedy announced the project without consulting with Site One. I'm told that Sinderc was livid when she learned of it. They want to limit our activities in space. Those constraints are part of a secret treaty dating from Eisenhower's time. Anyway, Kennedy was told to call it off—cancel Apollo." Chadwick's countenance grew increasingly somber. "Kennedy tried to negotiate some sort of compromise, but Sinderc got the Supracetor to back her and there was no agreement. On November 20, 1963, Sinderc sent an ultimatum. Kennedy chose to ignore it. Two days later he was dead."

Charles stared at Chadwick, shaken. "You mean to say they killed him? They killed President Kennedy?"

Chadwick shrugged. "One theory is that a Dramtes agent, perhaps a myrmidon, planted the plan in Oswald's mind; something like a hypnotic compulsion. Or maybe a lookalike android did the actual shooting."

"That's monstrous."

"They denied any involvement," Chadwick said, sighing. "It's possible we could be wrong. They prefer acting in subtle ways. There is no proof. But coincidences bother me, and our progress in space has been much slower than originally projected. Reagan took a big chance when he announced SDI, the missile defense program. Soon afterwards he started to have memory problems."

They paced away from the car and leaned silently against the rough textured wall of the tunnel.

"When the Galams were destroyed," related Chadwick, "all that apparently remained were a few commercial outposts and the remnants of provincial garrisons. I've made inquiries through the monitors. There are no records from that far back, but it is what many of their scholars think happened. The rest think that the Galams were totally annihilated; that the Bithians and the rest evolved separately. So, if the Galams didn't altogether disappear, they at least came pretty close to extinction. In any case, the earliest records are of a society based on a ragtag blend of merchant and military personnel, organized in loosely-coupled groups."

Chadwick and Charles watched Roxelan and Kanuner scrutinize the Porsche's engine.

"It was many centuries before they recovered enough to attempt interstellar travel and by then they had made it a habit to settle commercial disputes through fierce battles and raids on their opponent's installations. That went on for ages, as far as I can tell."

"Then the Bithians and—"

"The Bithians, the Indane-Aliemts and the Nesdelsen were the largest commercial groups. They absorbed or destroyed the rest and competed with each other. Then, a few centuries ago, they joined in a loose federation."

"The Dramtes."

"Yes. The Trinity. Their leader, the Exaege, is selected in rotation by each of the three member organizations. They control a dozen inhabited planets on six star systems. Seven if you include our own."

"Do you know why they make me fight those beasts?" Charles asked.

"No. I'm surprised the Resseps condones such activities. He doesn't strike me as a sadist. On the whole, he seems more trustworthy than his Indane-Aliemt counterparts."

"There must be a reason," Charles said patiently. "They also give me psychological tests. In fact, the whole activity appears to be a test."

Suddenly, they became aware of a growing brightness. They heard a faint buzzing sound. Something was approaching from the direction of the main tunnel.

By the car, Roxelan and Kanuner raised their heads and looked in the direction of what approached. Charles and Chadwick walked toward them.

"There's something I want you to find out for me," said Chadwick urgently. He ran his fingers through his wavy black hair. "They should be making a run of their transfer ship soon. We'd like to know the flight schedule as early as possible; the date and time."

Under raised eyebrows, Charles' gray eyes fixed on the other man. "You plan to intercept it?"

"Of course not." Chadwick made a face. "They can make the ship invisible, optically and to radar; much better than our stealth technology. The Joint Chiefs are trying to find out how they do it."

The buzzing sound grew louder. In the red light, they saw a small uncovered vehicle approach. It glided a foot above the surface. A moment later its broad gray shape came to a stop in midair. It then sank slowly to rest on the tunnel floor. July sprang from it and walked briskly toward them, her blond hair curiously lustrous in the red light.

"Here comes my mechanic," quipped Chadwick.

July glanced at the car and, ignoring the others, told Charles: "We must return at once, sir."

Charles did not know if androids could be breathless, but that was the impression he got from his attendant.

"I thought you might stay for a moment and help me tune the engine," complained Chadwick.

July glanced at him. "No, sir," she stated. Then, turning to face Roxelan, she said: "Come with us."

"What's the matter, July?" Charles asked.

"Berenz Compcenlu requires you to accompany him to a meeting with Intuger Sinderc, sir. He waits for you."

Chadwick's eyebrows rose.

"Come," July said, taking Charles by the arm. Chadwick's eyebrows rose higher.

"I'm coming," Charles said, slightly annoyed. To Chadwick he said: "I'll see you around." Then, with July and Roxelan, he walked rapidly toward the gray vehicle.

July leaped inside and took the controls. Charles took the seat next to her and Roxelan jumped into the rear. An instant later the vehicle rose from the floor. It immediately started to turn.

Chadwick and Kanuner stood by, watching as July deftly manipulated the controls. "Chance favor," they said in unison. The vehicle continued to turn and dipped its front slightly.

"What does the Berenz want with me?" Charles asked. A broad red belt wrapped itself automatically about his midsection.

The vehicle completed its turn and rose higher. It accelerated swiftly, the tunnel walls rushing by in a blur.

"The Indane-Aliemts found another intruder, sir," said July, her keen eyes interrupting the watch ahead for an instant to regard Charles. "An earth-woman—they think you may know her."

CHAPTER 16
PLAY

1

The horses trotted smartly across the lawn, Cicely's bay colt trailing Angie's black mare. They slowed down to a walk as they entered a bridle path, the rich foliage of majestic plane trees shielding them from the October sun. The girls were both neatly turned out in boots, white breeches, red coats and smart caps. When the cover ended, the girls dismounted and let the horses cool off.

Angie brushed strands of black hair away from her face. "It's divine, this weather," she said, taking Cicely's arm. "I wish you could stay at Aylesbend longer."

Cicely looked fondly at her friend. "I wish I could, dear. But I have to get back to my form tomorrow. I'm lucky I was able to get away from London for the weekend."

Angie played with her short whip, throwing it up and catching it repeatedly, until her black mare neighed nervously and bumped her lightly with her nose. Cicely giggled. "Stop, Angie, you'll spook them." She tried to get the whip away from Angie.

"Oh, nooo," responded Angie, her ironic brows rising in mock anger, "I cannot restrain myself. I shall use the whip on you instead."

Angie raised the whip menacingly, the sharp planes of her face arranged in an exaggerated leer. She chased a cowering Cicely a few steps.

"Angie, quit," cried Cicely, her straw-blonde hair spreading out from her face as she gyrated away from the approaching whip. "You are being silly."

"Silly, eh," said Angie, catching Cicely and delivering two rapid taps to her rump.

But the bay colt reared on his hind legs and they had to restrain their game. They resumed a steady walk.

"Did I tell you about the German count?" Angie asked.

"No."

"I met him last summer, in Antibes. Real looker. Very proper, very precise. Asked me and Meg Arundell over to his villa, a rented place, but nice. We had drinks and snacks, fabulous, particularly the fruit. Then he takes us to a room upstairs and pulls out this whips and ropes stunt."

"What?"

Angie burst into laughter. "He wanted to tie us up and whip our butts. After removing our clothes, of course."

"No!" cried Cicely, horrified. "Angie, what did you do?"

"We explained to him we were not into that sort of thing and respectfully declined," Angie stated.

"And what then?"

"Nothing. He looked disappointed. We didn't stay much longer after that."

"I should expect not!" Cicely shook her head. "Angie, you must quit running around with such weird people."

"I didn't know the fellow was that way, Cicely."

"I never thought much of Meg. She'd be the type to go for that sort of thing."

"Cicely! Meg is a nice girl," protested Angie.

"Oh, sure. A nice call girl, maybe. I say, Angie, sometimes you are just too wild for your own good."

Angie turned and looked levelly at her friend. "Well, I'm not the one that's seeing a shrink."

She regretted saying it instantly, even before she saw the moistness grow in Cicely's eyes. "I'm sorry, Cicely."

"I don't think it will ever go away," said Cicely, tears welling up in her eyes. "I so wish I were normal."

Angie hugged her friend. "Oh, Cicely, forgive me. Of course you're normal."

"The dreams go on and on. Dr. McClellan says I'm better," said Cicely. "But at times I get so scared, Angie. Scared of losing my mind. Of going to sleep some night and having one of the dreams and never coming back; never being myself again."

"I'm a brute," Angie said. She forced the short whip into Cicely's limp hand. "Here, hit me. I deserve it."

"You fool," Cicely sniffled. "Perhaps I shall do just that."

Cicely drew away from Angie and raised the whip above her head, the shadow of a smile breaking through her tears.

"Oh, no," cried Angie, cowering exaggeratedly, "have mercy."

Later, while the butler finished stuffing Cicely's things into her MG's small trunk, the two girls looked for a moment toward the setting sun. They saw a huge orange ball, sinking slowly behind the distant tree line.

Their reverie was broken by Angie's young Dalmatian, Toby, barking as he happily chased a field mouse.

Cicely climbed inside the car and shut the door. She rolled the window down and started the engine, hearing it come to life and settle into an unsteady purr. Angie leaned down and said to her friend: "Perhaps you should try another doctor."

For a moment, Cicely looked past her friend at the great Queen Anne house behind her. The setting sun painted it with swathes of gold.

"I've thought of it, but I think now that I'll stick with Dr. McClellan. He's taken a lot of interest in my case. Some of his friends are helping me too."

"Helping you? How?"

"They are tracking down Charles and Vivian and the rest. Finding out if they're real people."

Angie shook her head. "Of course they are not real, Cicely. They are dreams."

"I don't think so." Cicely blipped the throttle and the small engine responded with a roar. "But I'd like to know for sure in any case."

"Oh, Cicely," Angie said. She kissed her friend's cheek and pulled away from the car. "Take care, dear." Then, displaying a bright smile: "Work little and party a lot!"

"I'll ring you," Cicely said. She put the car in gear and set it in motion.

As Angie waved good-by, seeing her friend drive away on the leaf-strewn lane, a tear slid down her taut cheek. She stood alone for a while, until Toby joined her and licked her hand.

2

"Do you know the identity of the earthwoman?" Charles asked.

"No, sir." July answered. She looked at Charles calmly, recognized signs of the tension and anxiety he was trying to hide.

"What is her condition?"

"I was not told, sir," July said.

Charles, July and Roxelan stepped out of the transport module and onto a wide semicircular area in the Indane-Aliemt compound. They walked briskly across the bay and followed a curving gray corridor, July half a pace ahead of the others.

Charles' jaw was set, his mind racing through possibilities and coming up again and again with the same answer: Vivian. He had long before decided not to mention Robinson to the Bithians. His hopes for freedom were mostly pinned on Robinson's continued efforts. He feared that Robinson would be exposed through Vivian, if he had not already been exposed through the investigation of Charles' own background. But mostly he feared for Vivian's welfare. Had she been injured? How had she managed to get in? The new earthwoman, whoever she was, at least seemed to be alive.

"The next portal," July announced.

The doorway's outline was clear. They entered a round chamber. Inside, they met Berenz Compcenlu and an Indane-Aliemt Pagres.

Compcenlu left his seat immediately. "They are in the adjoining room," he said without preamble. "The Indane-Aliemts have indicated that the earthwoman is known to you—is this true, Kliettaes?"

"Can I see her?" Charles asked. July and Roxelan stood by silently.

"A young adult, tall, with white skin and dark hair. Her registered name is Vivenes. Do you know her?" Compcenlu pressed him.

"It's likely that she is someone that I know, Lord," admitted Charles. "A friend, Vivian Venables."

"Did you know she would follow you here?"

"No, Lord. She can't have known about the facility at the time that I found it. She must have found a way to track me...later."

"She somehow managed to follow a maintenance android into the port facility. When she crossed the iris gate she triggered an alarm." The Berenz drew back his head and added accusingly, "She destroyed two androids and badly injured a sentry before she was subdued."

Compcenlu indicated a doorway at the opposite side of the antechamber. "Let's meet them now," he said to Charles smoothly. "Eberenze Fermilo is with them." Then, glancing momentarily at July and Roxelan: "You two wait here."

Vivian sat quietly in one of the blue adjustable chairs. She regarded the aliens in turn. The wiry male in white sat across the raised oval surface. He had arrived a few minutes before and had spoken in their incomprehensible language to the two females. The one that they had originally taken her to, Karyprit, had been relaying questions from him, until the other female had arrived.

The green-clad newcomer, slender and leggy, with a short-nosed face that looked thoughtful and intelligent, had taken over the questioning. She spoke perfect English with a lilting, well-modulated voice. A small steel-gray machine shaped like a thick disk hovered over her left shoulder.

"You had several instruments in your possession, Vivenes." The alien woman indicated the group of objects laid in a neat row upon the beige oval slab. "Describe their function."

The imperious tone should have rankled her, thought Vivian, yet she felt little emotion. The physician, Karyprit, must have administered a tranquilizing drug while she was unconscious. Vivian sensed a twinge in her belly. She still felt a bit lightheaded.

"The rectangular object with the dial at the center is a lensatic compass; a direction finder. I can show you..." Vivian leaned forward.

"Do not touch the objects!" Karyprit commanded.

Vivian sat back. She adjusted the fit of the clinging green outfit they had given her to wear, determined not to let them see her distress.

"Vivenes," added Karyprit, "the official questioning you is Intuger Sinderc. Address her as *Lady*."

Noiselessly, the disk-shaped machine left its position over Intuger Sinderc's shoulder. It moved slowly toward Vivian, its clear rim glinting.

"The second object, Lady," said Vivian, "is a Geiger counter. It is used to measure ionizing radiations." Vivian paused for a moment, her body tensing as her eyes tracked the motion of the hovering disk. It came to a stop in midair, two feet above the oval slab. "The third," she continued, "is an automatic pistol."

"A weapon," Sinderc stated.

"Yes, Lady."

Vivian saw something move at the edge of her vision. A figure in white walked through a portal in the gray wall behind her. It startled her. She turned to face the entering alien, garbed in white, with sensitive features under a hairless round head.

"*Ucilaum mudipe*," he said.

Then someone else appeared, the white-clad figure gradually emerging into view. Lean, with dark hair and gray eyes. Vivian's heart leaped in her chest. It was Charles!

Suddenly events and memories closed in. She sprang from the clasping seat. Charles stepped through into the room and saw her instantly. "Vivian!"

He held out his arms and she ran into them, beginning to cry against his shoulder, holding him tightly. "Oh, dear, dear Charles."

"I'm so glad to see you!" he blurted, helplessly feeling tears come to his eyes. His lips softly, then ardently, kissed her neck, her cheek, finally found her trembling mouth.

3

Charles and July wended their way through a crowd of Bithian and Indane-Aliemt functionaries. They crossed the lower area of the amphitheater, passing under the huge glowing ball suspended over its center.

They were climbing a broad ramp rising to the elevated tiers when Charles held July's arm lightly. She slowed down her pace and turned to face him.

"Wait a moment, July." Charles looked about, his eyes first examining the faces immediately surrounding him, then darting across the large room.

"Chasrydel, we must take our seats."

Charles finally spotted Vivian, on the second tier, to the right of where he stood. She walked behind Karyprit and Drimtul.

"Let's sit there," said Charles, gesturing broadly to the right.

"That is not a very good viewing position," July said.

"I want to talk to Vivian, uh," Charles corrected himself, "Pagres Vivenes."

July followed his gaze. "The new earthwoman," she observed.

Charles started to walk toward Vivian. "Hurry."

"Yes, sir."

They walked swiftly along the broad curving aisle. About them, people were assuming their seats in preparation for the entertainment.

Vivian had been admiring the domed amphitheater when she noticed Charles. Her countenance shifted quickly from wonderment to joy. She moved past Karyprit and produced a seat nearer to the approaching Charles.

The suspended globe began to dim as a smiling Charles took a seat next to Vivian. They held hands for a moment. Vivian whispered: "Being with you, Charles, is like home in this strange place."

Karyprit, on the other side of Vivian, gave Charles a cold smile. July produced a seat for herself next to Charles, to his right. She glanced at the still-touching hands of Charles and Vivian, then examined Vivian closely.

Noticing her attention, Charles said to July: "This is my friend Vivenes, July."

The two nodded to each other. Vivian inspected July just as closely as she had been inspected earlier. July returned her gaze impassively.

Vivian leaned closer to Charles. "July?" she whispered.

"She is my attendant," explained Charles.

Vivian's stare grew colder. "She's a...robot?"

"An android, Pagres," July stated in her clear voice.

Charles broke the ensuing silence with a question: "What is the presentation, July?"

"It is a historical dramatization, sir." July shifted her gaze to Charles. "It concerns events leading to the Yor-Hoerri, the legendary war between the Galamic Empire and powers from the center of the Galaxy, the Yorj.

The conflict is said to have lasted for 800 major cycles and to have spanned hundreds of star systems."

Vivian leaned close to Charles. Her breast touched his arm. She whispered in his ear: "We must arrange a meeting soon. There's something I must tell you."

Charles nodded.

Suddenly, a scene was projected at the center of the theater. Vivian jerked in her seat, taken aback by the utter realism of the three-dimensional tableau. A dull, humming sound surrounded them.

The far side of the area shown was semicircular, the near side a shallow arch. All around was a curved wall four meters high, its surface interspersed with tabular and graphic displays in hues of green and blue. At the farthest end was a large oval screen displaying a star field.

About the periphery of the chamber were six stations manned by men and women in gray-and-white outfits. Two of them stood, the rest reclined on compound-curved form-fitting seats. Each work station was crowded with small control stalks and knobs of various shapes and sizes. There were small round screens between the work stations.

Four officers reclined in seats set toward the center of the chamber, one facing a free-floating semi-transparent screen, two side-by-side at the very center on instrumented seats, and another on a throne-like seat closest to the audience. In addition, two men stood by the central seats, holding tablet-like devices in their hands.

On the far right of the control room a crewman stood in front of a rectangular display about two meters high. It was made up of several dozen smaller oblong displays, each bearing written inscriptions or graphics. The data presented in one of the indicators shifted rapidly, and two others started to pulse in a soft yellow light. The crewman's attention was drawn to the pulsing displays, a puzzled look growing on his face. He said something to the female officer at the station next to him. She swiveled her complex reclining seat and looked at the pulsing display. With a frown, she manipulated several stalks in the console facing her and pressed buttons on the arm of her seat. Several dials took shape on the curved wall ahead of her.

"Long range sensors indicate a moving object ahead, Commander," the woman said, seeing the dials light up.

Near the center of the control room, the officer in the throne-like seat interrupted a conversation with a man standing by him and swiveled around to face the sensor stations to his right.

The men and women on the control room were physically different from any Charles or Vivian had seen previously. Their skin was an odd dark tan with a tinge of green in it, the eyes slightly protuberant. The two officers at the sensor stations had yellow irises like many Bithians, but the Commander's were a dark brown. None was hairless, and their hair varied from white to lustrous gray to light brown. They appeared to be fairly tall, and their heads were less broad than the Bithian norm. Their nose structure showed a more radical version of the Bithian nose-blending-with-forehead characteristic.

"What type of object?" asked the officer at the throne-like seat.

"Not a natural object, Commander. It is moving faster than light speed."

"It may be an Imperial warship. Identify friend or foe," said the woman in one of the instrumented seats at the center of the room.

Without exception, the crew exhibited the quiet competence of those performing routine tasks. Most did not seem concerned by the detection of the approaching object.

A man sitting by a console across the control room responded: "Object does not identify itself, sir."

"Attempt communication."

"Aye, sir."

On the far right, several additional rectangles on the sensor board showed increased activity. About a third of the board pulsed at varying rates. The crewman monitoring it announced: "There is a change in the object's course." He pressed a series of studs on the device he held in his hand. The board ahead of him displayed the results of computations. "Unidentified object is now on a close approach trajectory," he stated.

"Long range sensors confirm object characteristics not those of an Imperial warship," said the officer on the next station. "No match obtained to any reference configuration." She placed the knuckles of one hand against her lips, then manipulated a set of thin levers on her console. Two additional rectangular displays formed on the surface of the wall ahead of her. Soon they started to pulse. She studied them for a moment, then swiveled around rapidly to face the Commander.

"Sir," she said, "Master Control has completed analysis of available sensor data." Her voice grew increasingly fragile and taut. "It assesses unidentified object as probably alien."

From across the room: "Target is designated White Prime. The standard procedure—"

"I know the standard procedure," cut in the Commander. He pondered for a moment. "Plot an intercept course," he ordered.

The navigation officer facing the free-floating semi-transparent screen busied himself at his console. The Commander conversed briefly with the man standing by him, then said: "Place the ship on full alert, Sub-Commander."

"Done."

An intermittent blue light appeared overhead and a throbbing whistle sounded.

"Display target," the Commander said.

The stars on the large oval screen wavered for an instant. Near its center, an amorphous reddish blob appeared.

"Master Control confirms White Prime as alien, of unknown origin."

"Extreme magnification," said the Sub-Commander, manipulating small levers in her instrumented seat.

The projected image wavered, became duller overall. At the center of the oval, the alien object gained in size, its shape shimmering, never quite settling down. The image that evolved was that of two flattened spheroids, joined together by a thick axle. The larger of the spheroids was of a delicate pale violet color. The stubby axle and the smaller rounded shape were a pearly rose.

"White Prime does not respond," announced the communications officer.

"Continue to attempt to communicate," replied the Sub-Commander. "Evaluate target," she added, addressing an officer to her left, at a very heavily instrumented station.

"Insufficient data for further analysis. Request permission to engage active sensors," the officer said.

"Proceed."

The analysis officer manipulated stalks on his console and new displays became active on the wall facing him.

On the oval screen, the alien ship turned slightly. Part of the smaller rounded structure became obscured by the violet spheroid.

"I have an intercept course," stated the navigator.

"Execute intercept course," said the Commander. "Transmit ship's log continuously to home base."

The communications officer and the navigator performed as directed. On the large oval screen, the alien ship again shifted slightly. The Commander's brown eyes were riveted to the strange object, its fuzzy shape growing marginally more distinct.

"White Prime changing course," reported the sensors officer.

The commander took his eyes from the oval screen and consulted a small panel inset on his seat's arm. After a moment he said: "Pursue."

"Aye, sir. Increasing speed to operational maximum," announced the navigator. The dull enshrouding humming sound grew louder. On the oval screen, the background stars became streaks.

A moment later the long range sensors officer announced: "Second target detected at extreme range, same characteristics as White Prime."

"Designate new target White Second."

The Sub-Commander and the officer next to her swiveled to face the Commander. The three exchanged concerned glances. The Commander ordered: "Enable automatic defenses."

"Aye, sir."

A moment later, a ragged sector of the large sensor board on the ship's wall lit up. The crewman standing in front of it took a step back, surprised. "White Prime is scanning us. Broad spectrum, at extremely high energies."

Across the room, the analyst manipulated various knobs and levers, his hands moving rapidly across his control panel while he observed the data displayed on the wall in front of him. Without turning to face the Commander, he stated: "Analysis indicates alien intent possibly hostile. Master Control advises extreme caution. Their technology appears..."

On the oval screen, White Prime flickered. A bright dot appeared at the center of the pearly rose axle. It grew rapidly in size and brightness.

The entire sensor board lit up. The crewman cried out, "A beam——"

"Take evasive action," the Commander ordered.

The great oval screen grew totally white. There was a flash of the most intense light.

4

Dr. McClellan pressed the button on the voice recorder and watched as the machine began to operate. Across his desk, Cicely leaned back on the easy chair. She took a deep breath and straightened the cuff of her shirt.

"An image came to my mind while I was waiting at a stop light this morning," Cicely said. "A vague field of tiny lights flickering yellow, violet, emerald; many different colors. I could not reckon what to make of it. I forgot about the figure during class, but then at lunch time it came back, razor sharp." She leaned toward Dr. McClellan. "It was an unfinished bust made up of hundreds of delicate glass fibers. Charles went into July's room, looking for her, and saw the sparkling shape turning in midair, next to a stack of small black cylinders. At first he didn't realize it is his own image she has been forming, although it is a fine likeness."

"It must take meticulous effort to build such an elaborate framework. Why do you think she went to all that trouble?"

She shrugged. "Maybe she's in love with Charles."

"I want us to try something different today, Cicely," said Dr. McClellan after a moment.

"All right," she said, her eyes considering him steadily.

"I want you to try to bring forth a scene involving Vivian or Charles. Not something you have previously dreamt about. Something new."

"What?"

Dr. McClellan's eyes regarded her unblinkingly. In his steady voice he told her: "It doesn't matter. Anything that comes to mind."

Cicely frowned. "That's not the way it works, Doctor. I can't just bring the dreams forth at will. They just happen."

"I don't want you to dream. I want you to experience the scene while awake," he said calmly.

"It won't work," she predicted. "This is for you," she added, handing over an audio cassette to Dr. McClellan, who placed it in the desk drawer he had dedicated to storing Cicely's dream recordings.

"You are probably right, but I want you to try it anyway. We have plenty of time." He settled back in his seat.

"You are sentencing me to an hour of boredom," she said accusingly.

"Not at all," Dr. McClellan said. "Think of it as a game." He pulled a sheet from the prescription pad on his desk and made a notation on it. "Close your eyes now, Cicely. Relax."

Cicely shook her head. She leaned back on her chair and closed her eyes.

"Who do you think you might include in the tableau, Cicely?" he asked casually. "Charles or Vivian?"

"Why not both?"

"Yes, that would be nice," he said, ignoring her sarcasm.

Involuntarily, a smile came to her lips.

Cicely was silent for a long time. Dr. McClellan busied himself at first by reviewing his appointment calendar, and later by leafing through a digest of several of Freud's letters dealing with the Seduction Hypothesis.

Then, in a weak, tentative voice, Cicely said: "I'm at a hexagonal room, the work area in the twelfth level. July is with me. We're sitting by the white rounded shape of a monitor. I'm telling her..."

Charles gave July enough work to keep her busy for a day, then waited patiently for the report he had previously asked the monitor to produce. He went through the motions of reviewing stratigraphic data on the region surrounding the damaged tunnel. Then the monitor cut in: "The vibration analysis is complete."

"Hold the output," directed Charles. "I will review it in my quarters."

He rose from the adjustable seat and glanced over at July. She was asking her monitor for an expanded view of a section of tunnel wall. There was a satisfied look on her face. She enjoyed the opportunity to do technical work.

"I'm going to my rooms, July," announced Charles. "I'm bushed. I'll take a nap and then have this report displayed there."

July looked up from her monitor and put down the hripitur she had been holding in her hand. "This will take a while to complete, Chasrydel. Do you wish me to come with you?"

"No, I think it will be better if you go ahead with the conceptual design now. I'll check with you later."

She showed the barest trace of disappointment, then smiled. "Enjoy your rest," she said, and turned again to her work.

Charles walked across the room and crossed the doorway.

Vivian exited the transport module on the twenty-first level of the Bithian complex. She crossed the bay area rapidly. The corridor yawned at her, empty except for a tall machine that patiently cleaned its blue walls. She went along, surveying the portals for number 2114, glad that the recently-fitted limnen gave her an understanding of the Galamic numerals.

Soon she found the portal, its edge clear. With a quick glance, she made sure no one was about, then crossed the doorway.

Charles was just inside. Her blue eyes went wide with excitement. She briefly took on the angular layout of his quarters. "Oh, my love," she said, and walked into his arms. They kissed, at first softly and then with fierceness. Her mouth yielded to his and when she felt his hand on her breast she moved strongly against him.

"Did you miss me a little bit?" she asked.

In answer, Charles found the catch that undid her outfit. A moment later, the green garment had fallen at her feet. The soft warmth of her body was now all his.

They went into his triangular bedroom and lay down on his sleeping mat. She stroked the side of his face, ran her fingers through his soft dark hair, and moved swiftly to strip him of his white uniform. She kissed him with passion, urgently.

His arms surrounded her and he felt her firm breasts press against his chest. The deep kiss went on and they rolled on the mat, so that she was lying on top of him. She pushed back, the tips of her breasts brushing his skin, looking at him with a mischievous smile.

Charles studied Vivian's expression. Her eyes and teeth shone in the indirect light. His hands moved down her flanks until they came to the curve of her hips. "The look on your face."

Vivian straddled his long legs, looking down on him. "You have lost your tan." She leaned forward to kiss his neck, then traced a moist path down his chest to his taut stomach with her lips. Playfully she reached down with her hand.

"Mmmmm."

There was intense pleasure in their lovemaking. Their mutual desire was satisfied by shared delight.

Later, when they lay drowsily in each other's arms, they felt a safety and a contentment neither had experienced in a long time.

She turned over on her side, facing him, her naked body inches from his. They had not been awake long. This was the time, she thought, to tell him about the child she carried—his child. But before she spoke he lightly kissed her lips and said: "It's going to be very dangerous, but we must try to escape. I think I may have found a way, but it requires two people. Until you came, that made the plan unworkable."

He kissed her breast. "Do you think you are up to it? Lately I've had dangerous thoughts: To accept our predicament, to stay here as a Bithian, to see Omver someday. Just notions that tease at the edges of my mind, but I realize that the longer I wait, the more serious they will become."

Vivian looked into his eyes, was surprised at the pain she saw lurking there. She kissed him. "I'm up to it, sweetheart."

CHAPTER 17
PREPARATIONS

1

Dr. McClellan unfurled his umbrella. Right away scattered drops plopped against the black cloth. He walked on steadily. The odor of cold wet pavement reached him swiftly, carried by a palpitating gust, harsh with static electricity. He was one of several Saturday night strollers on Brompton Road. The familiar terracotta brick shape of Harrod's loomed behind him.

He peered through the earthbound cloud and crossed Walton Street, turning back toward home. His apartment was only a few blocks away, but he could not avoid catching a few wind-driven raindrops on his trousers.

A few minutes later, when he reached his home, he expected to be scolded by his wife for being out in the rain. But there had been an overseas call for him, and her attention, upon hearing him enter the apartment, was concentrated on relaying the message just received.

"You just had a telephone call from America, dear," she said. "Carlos Drake, from Houston I believe. He said he would call back. I think I met him some years back, when we first went to New York."

McClellan closed the outside door behind him and shook the rain from the umbrella.

"Sort of tall, dark hair?" said his wife. She glanced at him from the kitchen, at the other end of the hall. "Your friend Sifford was there too. Carlos took us out to dinner, I believe."

McClellan put up his coat and his umbrella and ambled into his den. "Yes, that's the same fellow. I'll call him back." He sat down by a small escritoire and started going through a leather-bound address book.

His wife, a short blonde in a white dress, walked into the room and kissed him lightly on the cheek. She stood behind him, watching as he flipped the pages.

"Can't it wait until after dinner?" Her hand rested easily on his shoulder.

"It will only take a moment. It must be just past noon in Texas. He may be home still."

McClellan finally found the telephone number. It included a long string of overseas call codes. He dialed them carefully.

"Hello?"

"Carlos? This is Burton McClellan."

"Oh, hi, Burton. How is it going?"

"Fine, Carlos. And you?" A smile came to McClellan's face.

"Real well. Listen, I found a journal with an article by Faraday. I'll write to you about it. I also have some news for you about the people I was supposed to look up."

"Yes?"

"I've found some of them. The names and town match."

"Which ones?" McClellan's hand tightened around the telephone receiver.

"Lawrence and Swan."

There was a pause. "Are you sure they are the right ones?"

"Well, there are some inconsistencies. Swan doesn't quite match in some respects, but I think it's the same guy your patient is talking about. I talked to him, in person."

"Does he know our girl?"

"I don't think so. Her description drew a blank with him. Same for Lawrence. But they know each other, and I think they know some of the others, Burton."

"Charles and Vivian?"

"Yes. Lawrence said he didn't recall, but I think he was just being cautious. He became very guarded after I mentioned them."

"An appropriate response for a lawyer," McClellan remarked.

"I had less luck with Robinson."

"No such person?"

"I think I found the man, but he doesn't live in Miami. That part of the story doesn't check out well."

"I didn't expect this," McClellan declared.

"Is it possible your patient is holding something back?"

McClellan thought for a moment. "It's possible, but I'd say very unlikely. She is desperate to learn what's causing her dreams."

"Burton, I'll be in Amsterdam in about three weeks. Early November. I can stop in London for a couple of days. We can go over this matter then."

"Splendid!"

"Are you interested in the Faraday monograph?"

"Yes, very much. Please bring it with you. I'll tell John that you are coming."

"OK, Burton, bye."

"Good-by."

2

It was a circular room. The walls, the high domed ceiling and the floor were eggshell-white. Two figures in green stood at its center. Vivian found it difficult to perceive distances in the chamber, it was so featureless. She had arrived with Drimtul a moment before. Kneth Karyprit and another woman had been waiting for them.

Vivian let Drimtul walk ahead while she inspected the woman standing by Karyprit. The stranger was a good three inches taller than the Kneth, with snow-white hair that flowed over her shoulders. On her collar was the blue metal cross-inside-an-ellipse emblem that all Indane-Aliemts wore, and next to it the two small red squares of a Cirsegas.

Without preamble, the Cirsegas voiced a command and a chromium slab rose from the floor. There was a figure on it. A naked male body of indeterminate age, with gold-bronze skin and short gray hair.

"Come closer," Karyprit said. She wore a glossy translucent gown over her skintight green outfit. A hripitur dangled from her belt.

Vivian and Drimtul moved forward. As they approached the body, Vivian watched Karyprit manipulate one of the arms. It broke off cleanly at the elbow. Vivian gasped, surprised. A moment later, after examining it casually, Karyprit reattached it.

The tall Indane-Aliemt woman looked briefly at Karyprit and Drimtul. She spoke directly to Vivian: "I am Cirsegas Austir, Pagres. Kneth Karyprit reports directly to me. For the time being, you will continue to be assigned to her, as part of the medical staff."

"Yes, Lady," Vivian said.

Cirsegas Austir glanced at Karyprit. "Proceed."

"Yes, Lady," responded Karyprit. Then, directing herself to Vivian and Drimtul: "You two will be temporarily assigned to the mining facility. Several mine workers have become ill recently. Nothing serious yet. They come here, we treat them, and they get well. A few cycles later some of them return."

Vivian looked closely at the body on the chromium slab. It was a model, but one so accurate that it defied identification. She touched its shoulder. It was cold, the texture just like skin.

"Pay attention, Pagres Vivenes," said Karyprit, her white eyes fixing on Vivian.

"Yes, Mistress."

Karyprit pressed a stud recessed on the side of the chromium slab. A gray structure, about two feet wide and an inch thick, rose soundlessly from the table's top. When it reached the top of its traverse it emitted a chirping tone.

"Display illness profile," Karyprit said.

The gray device's surface turned a light blue. A moment later, multi-color graphs and data tables covered the revealed screen.

Karyprit's delicate finger indicated one of the tables.

"None of the patients were suffering from viral, bacterial or protozoan infections," she stated. "There is no evidence of contagion."

Vivian and Drimtul crowded closer to the screen. They studied the data. Austir took a step away from the chromium structure and looked obliquely at the display.

"I have also considered chemical agents," went on Karyprit. "Poisons of some sort." She glanced at Austir and indicated a series of graphs. The amounts of various chemicals in the blood were plotted as a function of time. The different chemical elements and compounds were color-coded. "The data show no significant trend in this case, either. I am inclined to think that the pathological agent is something in the mine environment," concluded Karyprit.

"Only mine personnel have displayed the symptoms, Mistress?" asked Drimtul.

Karyprit glanced at the display device and pointed at one of the charts near the bottom. "When they are reassigned away from the mine, the illness does not recur."

"They may be allergic to something," offered Vivian.

"It is likely," agreed Austir.

"The symptoms are well defined," said Karyprit. She touched the model under the chin and at the bridge of the nose. The head split into two halves along its axis of symmetry. The inside revealed lifelike tissues, seemingly moist and textured like bone and flesh, but there was no blood.

"The nasal passages, sinuses and throat show inflammation in varying degrees. There is increased fluid secretion in most cases. Body temperature is elevated, but not greatly so," she said. She indicated the appropriate areas in the model, then again pressed the recessed stud and the display panel became gray again. Slowly, it retracted into the chromium slab.

"There is an immunological response," said Cirsegas Austir, turning to face Vivian and Drimtul squarely. "I want you to examine the mine environment and the workers there and to identify the cause of the ailment. Vivenes, you are to assist Pagres Drimtul."

"Yes, Lady," the two responded.

"Take whatever equipment you need," Karyprit said. "I have arranged for temporary quarters for the two of you at the mine facility. It will make traveling back and forth unnecessary."

3

Charles leaned back on the adjustable chair. The complex mechanisms within it compensated immediately for the shift in the position of his center of gravity. He looked idly at the monitor's viewer. His work at the laboratory was done for the day, but in a few milicycles he was due at the training area. He felt anxious, as he always did before the sessions with Cupahr and Esandos.

July stood a few paces away, viewing tunnel repair plans being projected on a mauve horizontal slab. In a barely audible voice, she dictated comments to a hripitur held loosely in her hand.

Turning to face her he said: "July, what do you know about the old Galams? To what extent was the presentation we saw at the theater based on fact?"

"My programming is not extensive in that area, Chasrydel," she said, turning her blond head to face him. "But I know that there are few facts known about them."

She glanced back at the plans on the display slab for a moment. "Suspend," she commanded. The plans immediately disappeared from the viewer, its surface turning into a purple mirror.

"There is anecdotal evidence that the Galams had a civilization that spanned hundreds of star systems," she said, returning her attention to Charles. "But aside from several ancient artifacts, there are few records of them. The presentation we saw was a reenactment based on an ancient record that is thought to be of Galamic origin. On Thesencerel, a planet circling the star Risper, a fortified trading facility exists which is thought to date to the time of the Galams."

Charles swiveled to and fro in his chair. "A remnant of the Empire," he mused, glancing at the time display on the cuff of his tunic. It was almost time to go to the fourth level.

"In this case, no," July said. "It appears that, long before the Yor-Hoerri, the Galamic Empire had lost control over several of their colony worlds. To maintain its integrity, the Empire was forced to build fleets of starships, and to fight colonial wars. The installation on Thesencerel was not originally under Imperial control. Those that built it joined forces with the Empire during the latter stages of the war against the Yorj."

Charles stood up. "I must go to the training area."

"Do you wish me to come with you?"

Charles shook his head. "No, it's best if you finish the design review." Lately, he had been doing better against the beasts Cupahr put up against him. "I'll be all right," he added. "I wish that I could do better during the exercises. I've yet to have a perfect session."

"Perhaps you will have a better experience today. The Kneth has told me that you have already mastered a variety of reflexive responses."

"I shudder every time the beasts appear. My concentration is poor," Charles said, introspectively. "At the worst of times, I get rattled."

"It is rare for individuals to be sufficiently critical of themselves, Chasrydel," she told him, taking a step toward him. "But perhaps you judge yourself too harshly. It is only a game."

Just then, across the room, above the hemispherical communication module, a shape materialized. It was Berenz Compcenlu.

"Remarkable event," said the Berenz, his lifelike image turning to scan the hexagonal room.

Charles turned to face the urbane official. July, placing her hripitur down on the mauve display surface, did the same.

"The Resseps requires your presence at his quarters, Kliettaes," said Compcenlu, his eyes settling on Charles.

"Yes, Lord."

"Please come at once," Compcenlu said.

"Yes, Lord," Charles replied.

"Chance favor."

The Berenz's image vanished.

Charles took a deep breath. "Curious," he thought.

"Inform Kliettaes Rathiz, July. I'm likely to miss my training today," Charles said, in his heart welcoming the turn of events.

"I will explain to him, Chasrydel."

As he turned to go, July made a gesture with her arm, as if to touch him, but he had already turned away, and she lowered her arm slowly to her side.

4

The Pagres facing Charles turned slightly and held the key disk in front of the panel by the doorway. Instantly, the portal's dark outline turned clear. With a nod to the guard, Charles entered Resseps Scahn's quarters.

At a brisk pace, he crossed the reception room, empty except for a decorated violet and white globe, slowly rotating a few feet above the white floor. He came to a gleaming metallic sculpture. Charles paused to admire the helix, its shape and color continually changing in subtle ways. The complex form made soft sounds as it turned.

"I find it soothing and intriguing at once," said a voice behind him. Charles turned around, startled.

It was a woman wearing Indane-Aliemt green. Tall, with flowing white hair. She added: "Does it appeal to you in the same way, Kliettaes?"

Charles recognized Cirsegas Austir. "Yes, Lady," he said. "I find it perhaps even more intriguing than you do. I do not understand how the changes in color and shape are accomplished."

The Cirsegas approached Charles slowly, glancing alternately at him and at the sculpture. "The dynamic effect is obtained partly through chemical changes—the moving parts are huge molecules—and partly through clever use of lighting."

She took his arm and led him past the gleaming form into the adjoining chamber. Three figures in white stood in front of a circular dais: Resseps Scahn, Vadycrel Exlof, and Berenz Compcenlu. "Remarkable event," they said in greeting.

"Remarkable event, Lords," Charles replied.

"Please join us," said the Resseps. Soft indirect light glinted momentarily from his bald head.

Scahn produced adjustable seats for all of them. A moment later he sat down and the others followed his cue. Charles ended up to the Resseps' right. Exlof, Compcenlu and Austir completed the circle around the dais.

The Vadycrel voiced a command and five translucent drink globules rose to the surface of the table. As Charles watched, the others traded brief glances and then turned attentive eyes toward him.

"We are very satisfied with your performance, Chasrydel," said the Resseps.

"Thank you, Lord."

Scahn smiled as he grasped a drink globule. "Let us join in a drink."

As the others grasped the translucent globules, other limpid spheres automatically replaced them on the dais.

"Success to us all," said the Resseps, raising the small globe to his lips. The others did the same.

Charles felt the delightful liquid warm his throat.

"You are being temporarily reassigned," said the Resseps, his orange eyes steadily regarding Charles.

"Outside the facility, Lord?" Charles had become an expert on the transportation system. He had hoped to obtain an assignment leading the tunnel repair work just getting started. It would facilitate his escape plans.

"Far outside," the Resseps stated.

There was an elusive element in Resseps Scahn's voice that made Charles unconsciously raise his eyebrows. "How long will the reassignment last, Lord?"

"Approximately twenty cycles. The first seven cycles will be spent in training. Then the mission and, after its completion, two cycles of debriefing."

An eleven day mission. Charles was familiar with the work to be performed at the tunnels. There should be no need for him to train, he thought.

"What is my assignment, Lord?"

"You are going to Sol-8."

Charles was stunned. "What?"

"The planet Neptune," the Resseps said. "You will be part of the crew of a transfer craft."

"But, Lord," muttered Charles, "what can I do there?"

The Resseps patted Charles on the shoulder. "You will accompany Berenz Compcenlu and three Indane-Aliemt officials. The Berenz will explain the details."

"I don't know if I am qualified. Besides, I am at a critical phase in verifying the new tunnel designs."

"We all think you are quite suited to the task," said Vadycrel Exlof. "Eberenze Fermilo will temporarily take over the tunnel maintenance task. Your attendant will assist him." Exlof's expression changed gently from detachment to amused reflection. "It will be an interesting experience, Kliettaes. You will be the first earthman to visit Neptune, the blue planet."

"We will rendezvous with our two starships, in orbit around Neptune," said Compcenlu, glancing at Charles across the dais. "The trip is usually made every major cycle. Transit time to Neptune is 3.5 cycles. The return will take slightly less time."

Thoughts raced through Charles' mind. A trip to Neptune. Starships!

"It is a task of great importance, Chasrydel," said the Berenz. "The necessary training will be of short duration, but it will be intense. The transfer craft will carry the Picariel crystal, which has just been completed."

The Resseps leaned forward in his seat. He placed his hand on Charles' shoulder again. "On the successful completion of your training, you will be promoted to Kneth, Chasrydel."

Exlof bent his spare frame and grasped a drink globule. With a slow, deliberate motion of his hand, he raised it to his lips. The others followed, lifting translucent spheres from the dais. "The Kneth Chasrydel," said Exlof.

"The Kneth Chasrydel," repeated the others.

Charles, disconcerted, bowed.

"*Eke Inverat*," said Austir, a smile on her thin lips.

Charles remembered the meaning of the Uncial Galamic words. The Empire.

"*Eke Inverat!*"

Charles bit into the globule and the pleasing fluid filled his mouth. He glanced at the others. There was fire in their eyes.

5

The ship was called Xartekres 3. The third of four transfer craft associated with the Indane-Aliemt starship Xartek. It had the shape of a huge flattened egg. Only vestigial horizontal fins protruded from its smooth rounded form.

Xartekres 3 was 150 feet long, and at its widest, its blue-black hull spanned 50 feet. For six days, Charles did little but train on its operation.

He was issued a new limnen on the first day. It had provided him instantly with a wealth of information about the ship. But the drills helped him learn appropriate responses to a number of emergency and routine conditions that might be experienced during a voyage. His designated responsibility was cargo master, but he also trained in the other disciplines needed aboard the Xartekres 3: communications, sensor management, defense, navigation, and piloting.

The seventh day was devoted to final preparations, primarily loading supplies and cargo. For the first time, Charles found himself involved in an operational task involving the ship. With July and a crew of myrmidons led by an Indane-Aliemt Kliettaes, he traveled to the factory facility and supervised the encapsulation of the Picariel crystal in a thermoplastic cylindrical container.

Charles watched as the 20 foot long container was carefully hoisted onto a levitating pallet.

"I want to attend to some other details," he told July. "Can you make sure they get the crystal back to the ship?"

"Yes, sir," she answered, and walked toward the group of myrmidons. A moment later July was directing the Indane-Aliemt crew to attach the pallet to an open-top tug.

Charles watched for a few seconds, then turned and strode away.

He met Vivian at a maintenance station on the tunnel linking the factory facility and the mine.

"I missed you," she said. He nodded, knowing. He had missed her too.

"I had trouble reaching you," Charles told her. "How long have you been at the mine?"

"About a week," she said. "I tried to reach you also. That attendant of yours told me you were being trained, but she wouldn't tell me where you were."

Charles looked puzzled. "I suspect my assignment is somewhat sensitive," he said. "But I'm surprised July didn't tell me that you had tried to contact me."

Vivian glanced at him, her chin up and her eyes slightly narrowed. With only a hint of a smile she said: "I think that mechanical wonder is in love with you."

Charles frowned. "Don't be silly."

They were alone in a rectangular room flanked on one side by transport module portals. On the opposite side, other doorways led to maintenance facilities.

He took Vivian by the arm and led her through a portal. It opened onto a square-section tunnel. Overhead, light strips cast a dim red glow on the floor and walls.

"Where are we going?" she asked.

"I only have a few minutes, Vivian. I must see Chadwick for a moment."

They walked rapidly along the side of the tunnel, their matching footsteps echoing in the empty space.

"Who is Chadwick?" Vivian asked.

"A Government man. Liaison with the Dramtes mission."

"What are you seeing him about?"

Charles slowed down slightly. "They are sending me on a trip to Neptune."

Vivian grabbed Charles' arm and wheeled him about, forcing him to stop in his tracks. "Neptune!"

"That's why you couldn't reach me," he said. He placed his hands on her shoulders. "I've been in training all week. At the port facility. They practically made me live on the ship."

He noticed a growing moistness on her eyes. "I will only be gone ten days," he said.

She leaned her head against his shoulder. "Neptune. Damn it, Charles! What are you supposed to do there?"

"Our ship takes a Picariel crystal, local wares, and biological specimens to a Dramtes starship orbiting Neptune. On the way back we'll bring supplies."

"Why such a distant rendezvous?"

"The starship is enormous—a mile long. It would be very difficult for them to keep it hidden from observers on Earth if they brought it near. I'm eager to take a close look at it." Charles pulled away slightly. "We must hurry."

He started to move, but she held his arm. "There's something that I must tell you," she declared.

They looked at each other for a wordless moment. Then she said: "We are going to have a child."

Charles stood very still. There was puzzlement, then delight in his eyes. "A child…."

Vivian smiled wryly. "It must have happened the last time we were together in Miami."

Charles grabbed her, playfully attacked her face and neck with his lips. "You're wonderful," he slurred. She giggled, as his hands fondled her body. They kissed, alone in the reddish gloom, an embrace with groping and moaning that seemed to go on forever.

When at last they stood again apart from each other, they resumed their walk at a slower pace.

She patted her belly. "I'm surprised you didn't notice," she said. "I've gained a few pounds."

He placed his arm around her. "Why didn't you tell me earlier?"

"I almost did, but I thought it might make you want to delay our escape. I hate this antiseptic dungeon." She stopped, pulled away from him and fixed her eyes on his. "Let's go now."

"We are not ready yet. We'll only get one chance. If we fail and somehow manage to survive, they will be twice as vigilant."

"We can't wait for everything to be perfect, Charles. Let's leave now. Right now!"

"No. It's unwise to take unnecessary chances. We must have a plan that accounts for everything. I've been thinking perhaps we need a diversion of some sort. And we don't know enough about the external layout."

She gave him a frustrated look. "Oh, all right, but we must leave as soon as you get back. Don't let my pregnancy affect that, Charles."

"We'll talk…"

Her voice became hard, "Promise me!"

He regarded her for a moment. "I promise."

They walked on, and Vivian told Charles of her assignment at the mine.

"Have you found out what's making them sick?"

"We've narrowed it down to something airborne. Larger than two microns. Probably a pollen, but we haven't identified it yet."

"Do you think they might let you go to the surface? Tell them you need to in order to identify the pollen."

She shook her head. "I already tried that. Austir put me in contact with an android that goes outside to do maintenance. He's the one that gets the air samples."

"Austir appears to have a relationship with the Resseps," Charles said.

"What kind of a relationship?"

"I'm not sure. They are both interested in the ancients—the Galams. It seems almost like a cult."

They saw a white figure move ahead.

"That's him," Charles said. "Be careful what you say to him."

"You don't trust him?"

"Not a bit. I think he would help the Dramtes hunt us down, if we ever manage to escape. But he can be useful. Tell him about the allergies. He's interested in that sort of thing."

As they approached him, Chadwick held out his hand to Charles. "Hello, Ryder. Got yourself a different girlfriend this time, eh?"

"Hello, Chadwick." Charles shook the CIA man's hand. He indicated Vivian. "Miss Venables."

"I know," said Chadwick, taking Vivian's hand. "News travel fast in our little community." His eyes swept across Vivian's tall, well-formed figure. "Green becomes you, dear lady."

Vivian inclined her head momentarily. Rich and glossy, her lips offered a cool smile.

"You are without your toy today," Charles observed.

Chadwick grinned. "We finally got it right. That is, Kanuner got it right. Evidently, he wheedled some advice out of Roxelan."

"What are you two talking about?" Vivian asked.

"The Supracetor's Porsche," explained Charles. "Chadwick was tuning it up last time I saw him."

"Is that what you do?" Vivian asked.

"Yes, I tune up cars," Chadwick forced a smile. "I'm a jack of all trades. Whatever pleases our masters."

"Does the Supracetor ever take the car outside?" she asked.

"Oh, yes. That he does do."

"Does he get ill? After going outside, I mean."

"Ill? No. Breslui's healthy as a horse," Chadwick declared. "All the aliens are. They never get sick and they live forever," he chuckled.

"Some of them get sick," said Vivian. "They have allergies. I've been assigned to a team trying to identify the cause."

"That is interesting," said Chadwick. "Tell me more about it."

"Several technicians have been afflicted. An android has been collecting air samples for us, but I am having problems getting him to obtain specimens in the right places. Could you help me with that, perhaps? I'd like to examine the surface; in the area near the mine facility air intakes."

Chadwick smiled broadly. He raised his hands. "There's no way that I could get you topside. It would get me in serious trouble. But I might be able to help with the air samples. There are personnel—"

"What did you mean," interrupted Charles, "when you said that they never get sick and they live forever?"

Chadwick rubbed his chin. "Just that. I never heard of one of them getting sick before. They don't seem to age. Except for accidents, they are practically immortal." He fixed his probing eyes on Vivian's. "Tell me more about these allergies. How..."

They heard a faint grating sound and for a moment remained very still.

"We need to go right now, Chadwick," said Charles, "we're late for a meeting. But I have something else for you: The next supply ship flies off tomorrow."

"Are you sure?" Chadwick looked suspiciously at an approaching sonic broom.

"Absolutely; I'll be in it. Estimated departure time is 300 milicycles."

"How did you get the assignment? On your own initiative?"

"The Resseps' order." Charles took Vivian's arm. "We must go."

"Good-by, Mr. Chadwick," Vivian said pleasantly.

She and Charles started to move away.

"Wait," said Chadwick, following them. "What have you learned about the ship? Where is it going? Will it carry the crystal?"

Charles accelerated his pace. He spoke hurriedly. "The ship's hull is made of a metallic polymer sheet stronger than steel but lighter than paper. I'll tell you more when I get back. Remember you owe me one, Chadwick."

Once they lost sight of Chadwick, Charles and Vivian slowed down. During the rest of their walk to the maintenance facility they conversed in hushed voices, making plans for their escape.

CHAPTER 18
CAUSE FOR CONCERN

1

The dream began in darkness, with the sensation of motion and the feel of a light wind on her cheeks. Gradually, light appeared ahead, she distinguished others sitting with her, and she heard a humming sound. She was Charles this time.

The Xartekres 3 lay, like a squat blue-black egg, at the center of a vast circular bay. The bay itself, as wide as two football fields and 200 feet high, comprised the top half of the space port. Half a dozen technicians milled about the spaceship, making final checks. The crew approached the ship in an open-top platform that glided quietly a foot above the chamber's gleaming surface.

With July at its controls, the transport platform came to a smooth stop in midair, fifty feet away from the ship. She made the vehicle hover for an instant, humming, inches above the surface, then let it sink slowly to the metal floor. The crew stepped down quickly: Berenz Compcenlu, commander; Obiredes Dahlgers, pilot/navigator; Kneth Fernoch, communications/sensors; Kneth Chasrydel, cargo master; and Kliettaes

Lamiken, defense and maintenance. In fact, complex mechanisms and electronic devices within the ship would carry out most functions automatically.

The ship's monitor already knew its destination. It had prepared a flight plan, and now periodically updated its projected trajectory, basing its computations on the positions of the Earth and Neptune, continuously changing as the planets revolved around the sun.

An android in Bithian whites voiced an instruction to the ship and a wide ramp emerged from the dark vessel's side, near its bulbous nose. The ramp was strong enough to support the heaviest of cargoes, although rather than the material object it appeared to be, it was a force field projected and sustained by the ship.

Compcenlu and Dahlgers were the first to board Xartekres 3. The others stood about briefly as the technicians reported on the ship's status. July, the last to leave the transport platform, now came near the small group. She touched Charles' arm gently.

As he turned to face her, a small smile formed on her lips. She surveyed his face. "Chance favor, Chasrydel."

When he was about to board, Charles felt a gnawing qualm in his stomach. The ship was charged with the suggestion of strange things far off. Suddenly, spaceflight ceased to be the stuff of training exercises and took on the harsh attributes of unknown reality. He tried to fight off nervousness by being flippant.

"Are you going to miss me?" he said, returning July's smile.

Her glistening eyes held his for a moment. She nodded. "I'll find comfort in thoughts of you."

"I'll see you again soon. Chance favor," Charles said to her. He turned about and followed Fernoch and Lamiken up the ramp into the transfer craft's hold.

Inside the ship, the three crossed a narrow work area and rode a small elevator to the upper level. There they stepped directly into the control cabin. The chamber was forty feet wide at the rear and tapered to half that width up front, where Dahlgers sat at the pilot's seat. Charles sat on an instrumented chair next to Compcenlu, at the center of the cabin. The others assumed their stations at the rear.

As Charles was secured in his seat his mind stumbled on a worrying theme. Why was Chadwick so interested in the transfer craft's flight schedule? He had assumed the CIA man wanted to study the Dramtes stealth technology. Now he hoped the U.S. Government had not decided to blow the ship out of the sky.

"Initiate departure sequence," the Berenz said.

Dahlgers touched a symbol on her control panel and the ship became instantly immersed in a dull humming sound.

High above, huge iris doors opened rapidly. The projected image of a 700 foot wide section of the Tehachapi Mountains suddenly disappeared. A moment later, Xartekres 3 emerged into the evening sky. It rose swiftly ten thousand feet over the dark peaks, then moved rapidly west, its bulk made unnoticeable by electromagnetic jamming devices.

2

They met in Dr. McClellan's apartment in Knightsbridge, near Hyde Park. Commander Sifford was the first to arrive. He had come directly from his office and wore his naval uniform. In his hand, he carried a thin leather briefcase.

"Hello, John," Dr. McClellan said heartily. "How is it outside?"

"Bloody cold," Sifford replied, removing his cap, "and windy."

Dr. McClellan had arranged for his wife to be away. He was helping Sifford with his coat when Carlos Drake arrived, shivering, at the door. The three exchanged greetings.

After attending to his friends' coats, Dr. McClellan led them to the drawing room. Stained glass windows looked on a small garden. At one side of the room stood an upright piano, littered with musical scores and flanked by bookcases. The opposite wall held an enormous brick fireplace, its fire burning invitingly. In between, a long leather couch and three bucket chairs trimmed in red plaid were arranged around a low brass table.

"Please have a seat," invited Dr. McClellan. "Miss Denfeld will be here presently. She called to say she would be a bit late." He smiled apologetically. "Something to do with school and Guy Fawkes' Day."

"Where does she teach?" Sifford asked.

"I believe it is a primary school in Bromley."

"I've never understood why the British celebrate someone's attempt to blow up Parliament," Drake declared, sitting down next to Sifford on the plush couch.

His friends smiled benignly. "*Remember, remember the fifth of November, gunpowder treason and plot,*" Sifford intoned. "We celebrate the fact that tradition endures, that plotting against the King is just not done."

"Americans associate fireworks with the Fourth of July," said Dr. McClellan in a side remark to Sifford.

"And the whole month of November with Pilgrims celebrating survival in the colonial wilderness," Sifford commented slyly. "They are still really quite provincial."

Drake shook his head.

"Let me get you both a drink," Dr. McClellan offered.

They spent the next fifteen minutes discussing the Faraday monograph that Drake had brought from America and a book by Carl Linnaeus that Sifford had discovered in Vienna. Then the doorbell rang and Dr. McClellan left the others to answer it and take his visitor's coat.

He returned a moment later, with a young woman still attempting to tidy up the straw-blond hair that a gust of wind had disarranged. She wore a simple brown dress with a white bodice. Her face was long and delicate, with large, clear eyes that quickly swept over the room.

"Gentlemen," Dr. McClellan said, "Miss Cicely Denfeld."

John Sifford and Carlos Drake stood up and greeted Cicely as the doctor introduced them.

"Please have a seat, Cicely," Dr. McClellan said. Choosing the bucket chair closest to the fire, she smiled tentatively at the men.

"We have started on our drinks already," Dr. McClellan told Cicely. "Do you care for anything?"

"A glass of wine would be nice, Doctor," she said quietly.

"I have a nice Chablis," Dr. McClellan said, as he walked away to the kitchen.

Cicely looked in turn at the other two. "I can't tell you how much I appreciate what you are trying to do for me," she said, with obvious sincerity.

Sifford gave her a wide smile. "We are glad to be of service, Miss Denfeld."

She glanced at the stained glass windows. It was growing dark outside and the garden was barely visible through the lighter-colored panes. "Dr. McClellan has been wonderful to me," said Cicely, introspectively.

The doctor returned and handed Cicely a glass of white wine. He took a seat on one of the bucket chairs. With a gesture of his hand, Dr. McClellan indicated Commander Sifford. "John works for the government," he told Cicely. "He has been kind enough to perform certain inquiries on our behalf."

They all looked at Sifford expectantly.

The Navy man sat very straight, his shoulders not touching the back of the couch. Quietly, he took a sip from the brandy snifter in his hand, then placed it on the brass table in front of him.

He looked directly at Cicely. "Burton gave me the names and descriptions of two individuals. One of them, Gary Smith, was reported to live in the Bahamas, a Commonwealth member. The other, Reynold Robinson, was reported as having a British background. I made the necessary inquiries and was able to confirm that persons of those names and descriptions do exist."

Sifford paused. The others watched him closely, and for a moment the only sound in the room was the popping of logs in the fire.

"Smith is a common name," he went on, "but the population of the Bahamas is not large. On Andros Island, there is only one Gary Smith."

Cicely stared at him. Her hand went involuntarily to her throat.

Sifford regarded her solicitously. He leaned over to the side of the couch and retrieved the leather briefcase he had placed there earlier. He opened it and extracted a thin manila folder. From this he took a few sheets of typewritten paper. As he looked through them he said: "Smith is a British subject. Age fifty. Born in Bristol. Married, no children. Served in the Royal Navy. Saw action in the Falklands. Wounded in battle. Received a medical discharge and settled in the Bahamas six years ago."

He slipped the typewritten pages back into the folder and peered inside. Then he took out two narrow yellow sheets.

"He lived initially in Nassau, New Providence Island, but soon moved to Nicholls Town, on Andros Island. Active in the British community. Works on a part-time basis at a U.S. Navy installation nearby, as a security consultant. Evidently they have problems with smugglers. Has published a book on navigation for small craft."

Sifford replaced the papers in the manila folder and returned it to his briefcase.

"It all fits," Cicely said, her voice hoarse.

Sifford lifted his eyes from the briefcase for a moment and looked at her. "Yes, it does fit, Miss Denfeld."

He removed another folder from the briefcase. This one was thicker, brown, with a wide red stripe. Sifford took out a thin stack of sheets. As before, he glanced through them and read out some of the details.

"Reynold Robinson. Age fifty-one. Born in Leeds. Major in the Intelligence Corps. Detached to the Secret Service." Sifford flipped through several pages. Then he started again: "Lived abroad often. Naturalized American citizen. Married, one daughter. Owner and operator of an industrial security and investigation service. Ties to several foreign governments. Lived in Washington, District of Columbia, and Miami, Florida. Apparently quite well-off. Presently semi-retired. Resides in Basseterre, on the island of St. Kitts."

"That's him," Cicely declared, "Mr. Robinson." She leaned forward on her seat. There was a peculiar expression on her face, a mixture of anxiety and delight. "Except for the last part, about his being semi-retired and—"

"Let's wait, Cicely," interrupted Dr. McClellan. "We can get back to this later."

"I am sorry," she said, settling back on her seat.

"Let's hear what Carlos found out," Dr. McClellan suggested.

The American reached into a pocket inside his suit and brought out an envelope. "Like John," he said, "I started with names and descriptions."

Drake paused for a moment, regarding the envelope. Then he continued: "I used the phone at first—long distance information—and assembled a list of likely name matches. I also used an online search outfit. Then I placed calls to the resulting list of possibles and ended up with three individuals."

He took two folded sheets of paper from the envelope and opened them flat. "Two Benjamin Lawrences that practice law and one Arlen Swan in the Miami metropolitan area. As it happens, I had business in Miami, so I arranged to meet them. I gave them my real name, just in case they wanted to check me out, but told them a story about trying to track down a mutual friend."

Drake was overcome by a sheepish grin. "It sounded weak to me, but it worked. They all agreed to meet me." He took off black-rimmed glasses and rubbed the bridge of his nose. "The first Lawrence was about thirty, short and chubby."

Across the brass table from him, Cicely slowly shook her head.

"But the other Benjamin Lawrence was a good fit," he glanced at the papers in his hand. "In his early forties, slender, brown hair."

Drake looked up at Cicely, who nodded approvingly. He went on: "He admitted to knowing Swan. Other than that I got very little out of him. Very careful fellow. Did not deny knowing Reynold Robinson, or Vivian Venables, or Charles Ryder. But he wouldn't actually confirm knowing them. He made vague references to client-attorney relationships or he claimed he didn't recall. My impression was that the names were at least familiar to him."

The American looked directly at Cicely. "He doesn't know you," he added. "I gave him your first name and a description. He said it didn't ring any bells. It was about the only thing he was emphatic about."

He glanced again at the sheets in his hand. "I asked around about Lawrence. The Bar Association, Credit Bureau, and so forth. He's legit. Practices by himself, mostly corporate law. Has lived in Florida for the last twelve years."

There was a short pause as Drake put his glasses back on and took a sip of brandy.

"Alden Swan," he went on, "was more cooperative. Middle-aged, thinning blond hair, about five-nine." Drake looked at Cicely and she nodded. "Admitted to knowing Robinson, but said he hadn't heard from him for some time, that Robinson was living somewhere in the Caribbean. Said that he remembered Benjamin Lawrence, Charles Ryder and Vivian Venables and referred to them as being in Robinson's employ, but he became suspicious of my questions and would say nothing further."

Drake removed his glasses and read from the paper in his hand. "Alden F. Swan, Director, Miami Museum of Fine Arts. I know that for certain, since I met him at his office there. The rest I got from an acquaintance at the Miami Herald." He paused for a moment, then added, "Undergraduate degree from Princeton, Masters in Physics from the University of Florida. Was conferred a Doctor's degree *honoris causa*, by the University of Miami. An expert in Chinese, Mycenaean and Pre-Columbian art…"

Taking a quick look at the others, Drake took the first sheet in his hand and placed it behind the other. "That is all I had on Swan, until I got a call from his wife."

"His wife!" Cicely interjected.

"She called my motel. Later that evening I met with her and Swan. They treated me to dinner at a Basque restaurant. She is quite a looker, dark hair, very well poised. Very young. The meeting was her idea. Apparently Swan mentioned his earlier meeting with me to her and she insisted on seeing me. She was full of questions about Vivian Venables and was very disappointed when I told her I had no information to offer. Neither of them appeared to know you, Miss Denfeld."

"What was the wife's name?" she asked.

Drake glanced at the sheet in his hand. "Gisela."

"But she's only thirteen!" Cicely shook her head.

"The young woman I met," Drake stated, "Gisela Swan, is perhaps eighteen years old. There was a silver-framed picture of her in Swan's office. She and Swan wore matching gold-and-platinum wedding rings. They seemed to be very taken with each other."

Cicely said nothing, but moved her head slowly from side to side.

"The next morning, Swan came to see me again. He brought two folders with him, one on Vivian Venables, the other on Charles Ryder. Said his wife had asked him to show them to me, evidently in hope that the information might help locate Miss Venables. Each folder held a single typewritten sheet, and each was dated five years ago. He wouldn't let me copy them or take notes, but as soon as he left I wrote down all that I could recall. I think I got most of the important bits."

The others listened closely as Drake read from the sheet in his hand: "Charles Ryder, age 28. Born in Macon, Georgia. Father Marine officer. Three year residence at U.S. Navy base in Guantanamo, Cuba. Engineering degree from the Georgia Institute of Technology. Resides in Edmonds, near Seattle, Washington. Participates in regional SCCA races. Unmarried. No criminal record. Employed by the Boeing Aircraft Company for past six years, but also recently by Robinson's organization in unknown capacity."

Drake looked up from the paper for a moment and glanced at the others. "There really wasn't much more," he said, apologetically, before continuing. "Vivian Venables, age 27. Born in Winston-Salem, North Carolina. High school athletics. Springboard Diving. Was first in state, 800 meter run. Attended University of North Carolina at Chapel Hill. Unmarried. No criminal record. Participates in area horse shows. Joined United States Air Force. Assigned Air Force Intelligence. Duty assignments at Eglin AFB, Fort Walton Beach, Florida; and Howard AFB, the Canal Zone, Panama. Holds a private pilot's certificate. Employed by Treasury Department's Bureau of Alcohol, Tobacco and Firearms after completing four-year tour of duty with Air Force, but resigned after one year to form own detective agency. This was later absorbed by Robinson's firm. Undercover agent. Resides Miami, Florida."

Drake refolded the sheets of paper and placed them back in the envelope he had taken them from. He again donned his glasses. For a moment, the room was silent, then Cicely said: "I don't understand." She raised a hand to her brow.

"Well," Dr. McClellan said, "these people came together, evidently some time in the past. We know that much now. So, some of your dreams seem to be based on facts. Facts that your conscious mind is not aware of. This gives us something to work with." He pondered for a moment, then went on. "For one thing, it appears that we are dealing with a fairly recent trauma, since the events are no more than a few years old."

"What events?" Cicely asked.

"Certain incidents in your dreams match reality. Some of the episodes involving Vivian, Robinson, Charles, Swan and the rest. The girl, Gisela, who was then thirteen and is now eighteen."

"But, it still doesn't explain…"

"I know, Cicely," Dr. McClellan said. "There is still work to be done. But I can tell you this is progress, real progress. Now I think the best thing for you to do is to go home and rest. Don't dwell on what you heard here tonight. Have a nice, quiet evening." He smiled warmly at her, "You will make very rapid progress now, you will see."

3

After Cicely Denfeld left, Dr. McClellan stoked the fire and served another round of drinks to his friends. He thanked them effusively for their efforts.

Sifford cupped a brandy snifter in his hands, deep in thought, while Dr. McClellan leafed through the Faraday monograph and Drake examined the contents of a bookcase.

"How do you feel, Burton," Sifford said, "about the result of our little investigation?"

Dr. McClellan lifted his dark eyes from the yellowed pages and looked searchingly at his friend. "It's a good, clean copy," he said, referring to the volume in his hand. Then he added: "I was initially surprised. The two of you seem to have gone some way to proving my null hypothesis."

"That there is some factual base to her dreams?"

"Well, the null hypothesis was that all her dreams are based on fact. Now we assume that is not true. No one has mentioned hard evidence of a hidden site, for example. But all these people are real," Dr. McClellan said. "I think this is a major breakthrough. Her dissociative reaction is not caused by a childhood experience. It stems from an overwhelming experience in adulthood, buried in her subconscious and seeking outward manifestation through her dreams. I think there is a subtle symbolism, and additional repressed material."

Sifford's brow wrinkled momentarily. "You believe, Burton, that she experienced a shock of some sort, somehow related to Robinson and the others?"

"It is likely," Dr. McClellan, said, nodding, "that her condition is a stress disorder brought about by a traumatic event, or a series of events."

Dr. McClellan waved an extended index finger at his friends. "I know my way now. I should have used free association earlier. Yes. Within eight weeks we will bring this traumatic experience out and deal with it." He smiled. "Then she will be free."

Drake shared Dr. McClellan's smile, but Sifford's face remained serious. "Most of Robinson's professional activities," he said, "have been of a highly secretive nature. How do you think Miss Denfeld came about such information?"

"We don't know that yet, John," Dr. McClellan said.

"Also consider this: How much of what she dreams is a recollection and how much is fancy? I see cause for concern here. We are dealing, on the face of it, with fairly dangerous stuff."

Dr. McClellan thought for a moment. "What, specifically, are you concerned about?"

"Well, to begin with, in some of her dreams, people die," said Sifford.

"And there is the mysterious document these people were involved with," added Drake.

"There may be some embellishments," conceded Dr. McClellan. "After all, these are dreams."

"And what if you unblock the woman's mind, or whatever it is you intend to do, and she starts spouting state secrets? She could get herself and others into a lot of trouble, if she mentions to the wrong people some of the things that Robinson learned while he worked for M.I.6."

"Let alone what he may have learned or done since then," Drake added, from across the room.

Dr. McClellan's index finger went up again. "Now remember that Miss Denfeld's case must be held in the strictest confidence," he said, seriously.

Sifford regarded Dr. McClellan for a moment, then sighed. "Nothing you told me will be revealed, Burton. But you must realize that I have duties with regard to the Security Service."

Dr. McClellan stepped over to where Sifford sat and patted his shoulder. "Don't worry, John. I'm sure nothing like what you fear will happen. Whatever trauma Cicely suffered will be disburdened when she and I become conscious of it. It will not be something that she would want to disseminate."

"I'm glad to hear that," Sifford said. But he had already decided to secretly inquire into Miss Denfeld's past, and into some of the people she knew about, but claimed never to have met.

"Could she be experiencing some sort of ESP?" Drake asked.

Dr. McClellan shook his head. "There's no such thing as ESP," he stated. "Cicely suffers from a neurosis." He pondered the status of the work of his friends, and how to proceed, given their enthusiasm. "I would like to share some additional information with you that may channel your inquiries beyond the individuals you have been concerned with," he said. "Assuming you are interested, of course."

"Certainly," said Sifford.

"So, has she dreamed of other documents?" asked Drake. "A different set of acquaintances? How are they different?" asked Sifford.

"There are other subjects," Dr. McClellan told them. "They are more… exotic. I will discuss this with Miss Denfeld and, if she agrees, I will share the additional material with you. It will be on a strictly confidential basis."

"I can hardly wait," said Sifford.

Drake stepped closer to the others. "Well," he said, "with that out of the way, why don't we let John show us the Linnaeus book? You did bring it with you, didn't you?"

"Oh, yes," Sifford said, "it's here." He leaned over the side of the couch and looked into his briefcase. "It's in fair shape. Not very handsome, but well bound. There is an inscription in ink on the flyleaf."

Their interest shifted to the new acquisition. For the next half-hour, they talked of nothing else.

INTERPRETATION

CHAPTER 19
ATTACK

1

Charles watched Obiredes Dahlgers as she viewed a ship status report on a virtual-image display in front of her. Occasionally, her monitor would make a remark, or announce the display of new data with a soft click. Other than that, and the remote humming of the engines, the ship was silent. The others had retired to their cabins once the ship had left Earth's vicinity.

He felt a dulling of sensation. Xartekres 3 supplied a comfortable but spiritless environment. A gravity close to Earth normal was provided, but it varied slightly in strength and orientation throughout the ship. Growing weary, Charles decided to once again make his rounds. "I will be going aft now, Lady," he said, "to monitor the cargo."

Dahlgers nodded. She consulted a projection above her console. "Kliettaes Lamiken is due to take over your station in twenty milicycles, Kneth," she said, her narrow face turning toward Charles. "I will notify you as soon as she reports for duty."

Charles rose from the control chair and walked to the elevator. The platform was set against the cabin's rear bulkhead, next to a narrow passageway that led aft to the upper crew compartments. "Down," he said, and the open platform took him away from the instrument-laden walls of the control cabin, to the lower deck.

He passed the work area and took a hripitur from a wall-mounted chromium receptacle, then followed a light blue passageway aft. On either side were crew cabins.

A moment later he reached the cargo bay. Smelling faintly of metal and ozone, it stretched the full width of the ship and rose all the way to the top of the curved hull. At its center, secured in an elastic cradle, was the Picariel crystal in its cylindrical container. To the sides were stacks of brown and yellow plastic crates, also carefully secured. Some of these were cryogenic devices and Charles, hripitur in hand, proceeded to check and record their functioning.

Then, abruptly, the voice of the ship's monitor said: "Return to the control cabin immediately."

Charles glanced at the time display on the cuff of his sleeve. Lamiken was not due for another ten milicycles. He completed verifying the functioning of a crate he had already started on and switched off the hripitur.

He was on his way toward the bow when he ran into a sleepy-eyed Lamiken, just emerging from her cabin, her green tunic still partly undone. It was the first inkling Charles had that something was amiss. Together, the two hurried forward to the elevator and rode it to the upper deck.

When Charles and Lamiken reached the control cabin, they found the others already there.

"Assume your stations," said Berenz Compcenlu, curtly. Charles and the now alert Indane-Aliemt Kliettaes obeyed quickly.

Kneth Fernoch, manning the sensors/communications station at the right rear of the cabin, announced: "We are being scanned."

Several displays surrounding Fernoch's station were alive with diverse types of information. His fingers flew over small levers and studs, adjusting various sensor devices that had been switched on earlier by the ship's monitor. Without lifting his eyes from the restless instruments, he pulled a small red device from a receptacle in his console and clipped it over his head.

The size and shape of a golf ball, the mechanism pressed against Fernoch's ear. It provided a direct communications link between his brain and the ship's monitor.

"Something is approaching us at relativistic speed," said Fernoch. "Current distance is thirty million stadia." A stream of new data appeared on the display projected ahead of him.

Fernoch watched the changing characters closely. "Direction vector is 10.2, 56.5, 0.3." He paused, straining to interpret the data. "It's on an intercept course," he added, his athletic body tensing perceptibly.

For an instant, it occurred to Charles that the United States or the Russians had somehow launched a missile at them. But it could not be. They were past the orbit of Jupiter, 750 million miles from Earth, and traveling at speeds that no Earth-made spacecraft had ever approached.

"Activate electromagnetic shields," Compcenlu commanded.

"Aye, Lord," called out Lamiken. With unpracticed, but deliberate and careful motions, she pressed appropriate icons on her console. Instantly, status lights on her control board announced the system's readiness. "Shields active."

"Range now twenty million stadia," Fernoch declared.

"Take evasive action," Compcenlu ordered.

At the forward station, Dahlgers busied herself at her controls. There were slight lurches and intermittent resonant sounds as the ship altered its course. "I am taking us out of plane," she stated.

Charles set switches on the arm of his chair to obtain control of the main display. In the forward cabin a volume of air suddenly flickered, then became almost totally dark as it provided a three-dimensional image of the surrounding void. Only small pinpricks of light interrupted the black well ahead.

"Show approaching object on main display," Charles requested.

"Object is outside visual range," responded the monitor. But it did its best to comply with Charles' request. The pinpricks of light on the projection momentarily became streaks, as the field of view was rotated and the magnification enhanced to maximum. When the image settled, the display showed a field of enlarged stars and, near its center, a small yellowish disk with a thin white band crossing it.

"Saturn," Charles said, recognizing the planet.

For a moment, they all looked at the main display.

"A backwards propagation of the approaching vehicle's trajectory indicates the ringed planet was its point of origin," said Fernoch. He pointed accusingly at the light yellow globe on the main display.

"But that is impossible," said Dahlgers, glancing back at Fernoch. "There is no one there. Nothing."

Fernoch's eyebrows rose very slightly. He turned his head for a moment to glance at his instruments, his hand darting to steady the device clipped over his ear. "The object is very small. It does not respond to communications." He closed his eyes for a moment, concentrating his attention on his mental dialog with the ship's monitor. A film of perspiration appeared on his forehead. "It is accelerating. Current distance ten million stadia."

"We must consider it hostile," said Compcenlu. He swiveled his seat around to face Lamiken. "Arm weapons! Set for automatic fire."

"Aye," said Lamiken, visibly shaken. Her hands moved hastily to release safety restraints.

"Object can now be resolved," announced the monitor. "It is not of Dramtes manufacture. This is the enhanced image."

The display wavered for an instant and Saturn's disk faded. A rectangle of gleaming metal appeared at the center of the projection.

"Five million stadia," Fernoch said, mechanically.

The ship vibrated, as Dahlgers performed more drastic maneuvers. The brutal acceleration pressed the crew relentlessly against their seats.

"Broadcast a final warning," Compcenlu said.

The object on the main display grew menacingly. It was a gleaming gray pyramid, its tip truncated, seen almost head-on.

"Firing sequence starts in one milicycle," announced Lamiken. "Protective screens are set to maximum."

"Six hundred thousand stadia."

"Transmit ship status to base," Compcenlu said.

"Aye, Lord," Fernoch said.

The gleaming image filled the display and, simultaneously, Fernoch yanked the red instrument from his head, grimacing in pain. The main display became blindingly bright, then disappeared.

A moment later, the entire ship shuddered, and a series of explosions racked its hold. Then the control cabin became totally dark and the synthetic gravity field ceased to exist. The crew experienced the queasy feeling of free fall.

"Report ship status," said Berenz Compcenlu, once light had been restored. There was a hint of acrid smell in the air, from a chemical spill or a small fire, and a distant hiss that suggested a gas, perhaps the precious cabin oxygen, was being vented to space. A series of mechanical clatters and rasping sounds accompanied the efforts of the ship's damage control mechanisms. Freed of the artificial gravity, a number of small objects floated throughout the cabin.

A feeling of stunned fear gripped the crew.

"Operational capability is retained," stated the ship monitor, "but substantial damage has been incurred. Two fuel tanks are ruptured and their contents are lost. There are leaks in one of the remaining three tanks. Long range sensor functions are impaired. The propulsion system can operate at one fourth rated capacity. Steering and attitude control are effective. The cargo is intact."

The monitor paused, and in an almost apologetic tone of voice added: "The synthetic gravity is operational, but has been intentionally shut off to conserve fuel."

Then it went on, using its usual unemotional voice. "The weapons system was damaged, but is operable. There is some damage to the environment support system, and communications capability is lost."

"Totally lost?"

"Yes. The equipment was crushed."

"The hull was breached?"

"No. It was permanently deformed by shock. Most of the damage was to externally mounted apparatus."

Compcenlu held his head in his hands. A bead of blood emanated from a cut on his lip, then flew off to float in midair. He raised his eyes to Dahlgers. "Can we get to Neptune?"

"No," Dahlgers said, her harsh features rigidly set. Pointing at the displays flickering above her station, she added: "We cannot go back to Earth either. The only planet we can reach is Saturn."

"We cannot land there," Compcenlu said. He looked at the main display which again showed the ringed planet. "It's a gas giant, mostly hydrogen. Like a dark star. The atmospheric pressure would crush us."

"There are several satellites," said Dahlgers. "None is habitable without life support equipment. Several have suitable gravity fields, but most of them lack atmospheres of any kind."

At her console, a shaken Lamiken repeatedly obtained status summaries for the life support system. She instructed the monitor to perform the calculation one more time. When it was presented she turned about to face the others, moving awkwardly in the weightless environment.

"The ship's air supply will last only one cycle," she told them. "After that we can don our space suits. They each have a 250 milicycle supply."

No one spoke for a while. "We are doomed," said Fernoch in a rasping voice, expressing a consternation that they all shared.

Dahlgers stared fixedly at her console, a muscle twitching in her jaw. Compcenlu sat still, his hands supporting his bowed head. Behind them, Lamiken looked jerkily from one to another, her hands visibly trembling.

"We can't give up yet," said Charles. "There is water ice in some of the satellites. We could rig up something to obtain oxygen through electrolysis."

"There is not enough time," Dahlgers stated. "It would take several cycles to construct the equipment. Besides, electrolysis needs power, and ours is rapidly dwindling."

The uncomfortable silence returned. Finally, Charles insisted, "We can't just wait here. There must be a way."

Compcenlu raised his head. His moist eyes glanced at Charles. Then he said: "Set course for Saturn."

Dahlgers swung about and worked at her console for a moment. The ship vibrated as it changed direction. The drone of the powerplant became more insistent. Without turning she spoke to Compcenlu. "We will reach the planet in 420 milicycles. Or we could orbit one of the satellite worlds."

The Berenz had been deep in thought. "Fernoch," he asked, "are you able to determine the exact origin of that interceptor?"

Fernoch consulted his monitor. "Yes, Lord," he replied. "It left an ion trail. The point of origin is on the surface of one of the large icy satellites, Dione."

Fernoch spoke inaudibly to his monitor and a few additional columns of data were displayed for his study. After a moment he said: "Dione is spherical, 1120 kilometers in diameter. Its rotation is locked, so that it always presents the same face to Saturn. The interceptor was launched from a location on the leading side."

"We will go there," Compcenlu said.

Lamiken fidgeted in her seat. "Why, Lord?" she blurted. "Won't they try to intercept us again?"

"They have not launched another attack yet," replied Compcenlu.

"Maybe they won't. In any case, there are no alternatives. If there is air for us to breathe on Saturn, the only possible source would have to lie with whoever assailed us."

The Berenz paused for a moment as the others looked at him, dismayed. "We will try to contact them. Make our needs known to them. Perhaps they will help us," he added doubtfully.

"At best, we will be prisoners," Dahlgers said. She glanced distractedly at an angry bruise on her hand.

2

Cicely sat on an antique straight-backed chair in a cozy wood paneled room. She had confessed to the fastidiously dressed little man that she only had two hundred pounds and could ill afford the Alfred Sisley sketch he had just shown her. He did not seem disappointed. A long career had taught him that people who love art would, when they could afford it, and sometimes when they could not, collect the pictures they admired. He was unhurried. He would be there six months, or a year or two hence, when the young blond lady saved the money, or married into it.

"Before you go," he said, beaming, "you must permit me to show you one more canvas." Then, with an enigmatic smile, he disappeared into the basement.

A moment later he returned, his pixieish face illuminated by a coy smile. In his hands he held a golden-framed painting, about two feet wide.

Kneeling in front of Cicely, he turned the picture so that it would catch the best light. It showed a young woman with regular features that oddly reminded Cicely of herself, sitting on a bench knitting, in front of a bed of white roses. The brush strokes were intense and luminous, the colors broken in the way a rainbow breaks sunlight. Tiny strokes made vital a commonplace subject.

Cicely's eyes widened. They danced gaily, taking in the offered treasure. Her mouth opened in a joyous smile. It was his reward.

"An early work of Berthe Morisot," he revealed. "We only received it yesterday." Then, secretively: "You are the first person I have shown it to."

A few minutes later, Cicely held her coat collar closed against the cold wind and walked hurriedly down the narrow sidewalk. It was late afternoon. She had come to the West End to visit Agnew's, her favorite art gallery. Just to look. The oils she liked were hopelessly beyond her means. But she had been tempted by some of the line drawings. Some day, she told herself, she would buy a Morisot or a minor Pissarro and keep it by her bed, where she could look upon the dappled brightness each morning.

On the way to the Underground she had to pass through a rather seedy area. She had never had any trouble before, but this time she was accosted by two carousing punks, their smelly hair lacquered into spikes. They tried to get her to go with them. Cicely walked around them, but they tagged along, one on either side of her. One of them offered her ten pounds: "Just to come visit for a half-hour," he promised.

Cicely's heart beat rapidly. She hurried on, looking for someone, some passerby that might drive off the boys, but all she could see were two old women in gray coats, helping each other across an alley at the end of the block. Cars drove by, their drivers blind to everything but other traffic. The punks sensed her fear; the way hyenas sense the presence of a hurt animal hundreds of yards away.

One, and then the other, looked nervously around. They needed a fix badly. And money. First they needed money. And perhaps some raw fun.

The shorter one, wearing a stringy blue corduroy jacket, moved first. He grabbed at Cicely's wrist, but she shook him off. Rigid with fear, she started to run, but the other, in red vinyl, lunged forward and pushed her against a grimy brick wall. Then, rapidly, the two were on her. They shoved her and pulled her a few paces ahead, into a narrow alley. Then, in stages, they forced her back into a blocked doorway.

"Please!" she said, "leave me alone." She was trembling.

Their coarse defiant mouths opened and they laughed in anticipation. A quick glance passed between the two thugs: This one was the begging kind.

Cicely screamed, clutching her handbag to her side. The one in the vinyl coat slapped her, hard. She tasted her own blood and saw a broken cross tattooed on his cheek. One of his front teeth was missing. He leered at her.

Backing away from them, Cicely held out her handbag. Her back pressed against the door. "Take it," she said, "please take it."

"Oh, yes, bitch," said the one with the cross tattoo. "We'll gladly take that too." He ripped the handbag from her hand and threw it down on the pavement. She ducked under his arm and started to run away, but before she had taken two steps she was caught again. His right hand went for her throat, grabbing her neck and slamming her against the alley wall, while his left searched for the buttons on her coat.

His accomplice watched with sly insolent eyes, blocking the view from the street and licking his bluish lips. He took quick steps side to side, as if containing bottled-up energy. Silver half-moon earrings swung sideways, framing his colorless face. His gauntleted hand touched his crotch. He would be next.

Cicely groaned, her head filled with pain. And then, in the midst of her agony, she suddenly acted. Her knee came up straight into the tattooed punk's crotch. As his fingers left her throat, her fist drove with unexpected strength three inches above his belt. He fell back, gasping for air. Her other hand, the fingers held flat and stiff, swung upwards with explosive power. It brushed his lips and moved up into the base of his nose, crushing the bone. Blood spurting from his face, he fell to his knees and then collapsed on his side.

The one in corduroy, eyes wide open, unbelieving, lunged at her, a leather-clad fist aimed at her head. "I'll make you pay for that, slut," he threatened viciously. But Cicely ducked aside. She slammed the butt of her fist against the side of his jaw. There was an audible pop as the bone cracked, and in an instant an angry red swell appeared on the side of his face. A tooth fell from his gaping mouth to the slick pavement, next to where a bloodied half-moon earring lay. Then Cicely's kick hit the side of his knee and as it popped too, the dazed would-be robber fell down, driven unconscious by the shock and pain.

Cicely stood for a moment looking at them, her chest heaving. Then she picked up her handbag, stepped over the body of the tattooed punk, and walked unsteadily away.

"That," she told herself upon reaching the street, "was not me."

CHAPTER 20
DIONE

1

"We are being monitored," said Fernoch, "by an object launched from the vicinity of the target feature." He peered at one of the virtual image displays near his console and then added: "An armed probe. It has assumed a fixed position above us."

The main display showed Dione's cratered terrain passing rapidly under them. Dark shallow ridges stood out over dim gray icy plains. Occasionally, the dull gray and brown surface was crossed by irregular wispy white streaks that glinted momentarily before being left behind.

"The feature is directly ahead," announced Fernoch warily, "just over the horizon."

They flew low enough now that they felt the tug of Dione's weak gravity.

The airless world's sky was a starry black, except for Saturn's huge butterscotch orb to the east. The distant sun was hardly recognizable; it seemed just an abnormally bright star.

"What kind of beings would live in a place like this?" Lamiken asked.

A ragged dark line came into view. It grew rapidly to become a wide ribbon crossing the surface near Dione's sharply curved horizon.

"Set us down now," Compcenlu ordered.

Dahlgers placed Xartekres 3 in a smooth decelerating descent. As they approached it, they saw the dark ribbon become a deep chasm, a fault that crossed a broad craterless plateau. Near its edge, two artificial features could be discerned. A shallow white dome and an object like a truncated pyramid, one of its visible faces a delicate blue, the other at first seemingly gray, but eventually resolving into a perfect mirror.

Handling the controls delicately to overcome the ship's impaired capability, Dahlgers maneuvered it to a smooth touchdown on a beige terrace. The white dome and the mirrored pyramid structures loomed enigmatically a kilometer away.

In their spacesuits, three of the crew assembled outside the ship. Charles and Fernoch walked around, inspecting the external damage. There was a large dent along the left rear of the dark fuselage. A thin white plume streamed upwards from the area where the stubby horizontal stabilizer joined the body. It was their precious air leaking out.

Charles had directed the ship's monitor to study the two artificial structures nearby. The monitor had immediately concluded that the structures were not of Dramtes manufacture. Further analysis indicated that the pyramidal body very likely enclosed a massive set of sophisticated sensors within its seamless shell. A variety of very complex waveforms emanated from it. The white dome was heavily shielded, but various ports, vents, and multi-leaf doors suggested that it might be inhabited. Ship sensors had detected extremely high energies coursing within the round edifice.

Dahlgers and Lamiken remained with the ship. They would observe the progress of the others and keep watch on the two alien structures.

Dione's gravity was extremely weak, less than a twentieth of Earth normal. It facilitated their progress. The three moved swiftly toward the dome in a ragged line, taking high leaps that sent them soaring over the terrain, a mixture of glassy ice, coarse sand and rock. The temperature outside their suits was 190 degrees below zero Centigrade.

A minute later they had covered half a kilometer. It was then that they noticed the vehicle. It was an iridescent silver box, about two meters long, and it approached them at very high speed from above.

"Scatter," Compcenlu said. They all leapt in different directions.

Out of the corner of an eye, Charles saw the blue-black shape of Xartekres 3 rise and begin to move in their direction. The iridescent vehicle slowed its rate of progress, but continued to approach. It altered its course slightly, taking a heading toward Fernoch, who was leaping toward the mirrored pyramid.

A moment later a beam of purest light emanated from the Xartekres 3. The iridescent box exploded in a luminous burst. Myriad incandescent fragments fell to the surface, tumbling slowly against Dione's black sky.

The fortress responded swiftly and terribly. A port high on the white dome opened for an instant and a glowing ball emerged. With incredible speed, it streaked toward the Dramtes ship, itself now maneuvering in maximum-effort acceleration away from Dione.

The three men on the surface watched in horror as the radiant streak closed relentlessly on Xartekres 3. When the glowing missile reached the ship, the sky was momentarily bright, as if a new, intensely luminous sun had been created. Then the blaze faded and the sky was again black.

The Xartekres 3 no longer existed.

2

Cicely walked up the short run of steps and pushed the heavy door open, hurrying inside the building, away from the lashing cold rain. Dr.

McClellan's new secretary, a very tall blonde with slender good looks, helped her put up her coat.

"I'm Amy," said the young woman, after Cicely introduced herself. "Dr. McClellan is taking a telephone call. He will be ready for you in a moment, Miss Denfeld."

Cicely sat down on the leather couch across from the secretary's cluttered desk. She glanced at Amy, working industriously at a desktop computer, and assessed her age at twenty-nine or thirty. A moment later a buzzer sounded and Cicely was asked inside Dr. McClellan's office. She took her usual seat.

The psychiatrist peered at her from behind his heavy wooden desk. He replaced the gilt pen in its holder and said: "I have asked Miss King to change your next appointment so that we can have a two hour session. Please talk to her when you leave and choose a time convenient to you."

Cicely nodded.

"Is it still raining?" he asked.

"Relentlessly. But I prefer it to yesterday's snow."

Dr. McClellan waited for a moment. He prompted her. "Any new dreams?"

"Yes, but I must tell you about something else first," she said hurriedly.

He glanced at her with his dark searching eyes, then looked away and brought the fingertips of his two hands together, forming a steeple. "Go ahead, Cicely," he said mildly.

Haltingly at first, and then in a rush, she told him of her encounter with the two muggers.

When she finished, he remained silent for a moment, while he tore off a sheet from his prescription pad and wrote a note for himself on its plain back side.

"How horrible! You are fortunate to have escaped unharmed," he told her. "You performed remarkably well. Were you disoriented as to your own personality at any time during this occurrence?"

"No. It was as if, all of a sudden, I knew what to do."

"I wouldn't worry about it," he said.

"Perhaps there is a silver lining to my affliction," she said wryly.

She studied one of the landscape paintings on the wall behind Dr. McClellan until he said: "You had a new dream."

Cicely nodded. She met his eyes. "Yes, two nights ago."

"I want to record this," he said, starting the voice recorder on his desk.

"I'm a bit fuzzy about the beginning. Just darkness and silence. Then I heard a hissing noise, rhythmic like. It was my own breathing."

Cicely brushed a long strand of blond hair away from her eyes. "It was a cold, desolate place. I saw it through the transparent visor of my suit. Scattered rocks and sand of a light grayish brown. I felt lost. Abandoned. Then I noticed there were two others with me…"

They waited in hiding for a long time: Compcenlu, Charles and Fernoch. Their thoughts turned to suicide, as they watched the air quantity indicators in their spacesuits inexorably decline and contemplated the alternative of death by slow asphyxiation.

Avoiding each other's sight, they looked at the spectacular vista beyond the barren terrain.

Saturn's majestic shape loomed against Dione's black sky. Two of the inner satellites appeared as small silvery disks. The shadow of the rings showed as a narrow black stripe on the giant planet's faintly banded orange-yellow surface.

When his air supply was down to 100 milicycles, Charles rose from the sheltering rock outcrop they had adopted and bounded away from the others.

"Where are you going, Chasrydel?" Compcenlu asked.

"To the dome. It is our only hope."

Soon the others joined him. It took little time to reach the white structure. The withering bolt they all feared did not come.

Up close, the dome's 100 meter height proved daunting. They found small craters in the rock near the structure's periphery. Meteorites like the ones that had caused those craters must have bounced harmlessly off the white fortress, for its shape was unmarred.

"It must be incredibly old," said Fernoch, brushing off the dust coating the surface with a gloved hand.

"Let's look for an entranceway," Charles suggested.

Compcenlu bowed his suit in an awkward imitation of a nod.

They spread out, taking great leaps, then carefully examined the ancient white surface.

A few moments later Fernoch called out: "Hurry here. I have found something."

The others soon reached the spot where Fernoch stood, pointing at a place in the curving semi-metallic surface. It was a ground-level doorway, ten feet on each side, recessed a foot inside the outer wall. Red symbols flanked it on one side, partly obscured by tan dust.

Charles pushed against the door. It did not budge.

Fernoch slid his hands over the door's surface, looking for a recessed handle. Compcenlu regarded the symbols with interest. He brushed off the film of dust and ice.

Gradually, the stilted symbols became clearer. "Incredible," muttered Compcenlu.

The others looked at him.

"Are the markings a form of writing?" Fernoch asked.

"It is Uncial Galamic," said the Berenz. "It reads…" He brushed off more of the dust coating.

"*Alsriss monral duqs. Fecdar ed…*"

"But what does it mean?"

Fernoch and Charles brushed off the remaining dust from the red script.

Compcenlu haltingly translated. "Entrance number two. Field effect weapons sector. Press for manual…"

Just then, with a tremor, the multi-leaf door slid open, revealing a dark recess. A moment later, as the first of them tentatively stepped inside, a bright yellow light illuminated a vast chamber.

They walked in, their faces tight with apprehension and lit with the wonderment of gradual discovery. Their suits rustled about them, as air rushed by into the vacuum outside. The chamber was pressurized. Dark green metal walls surrounded them and a high ceiling glowed yellow overhead. An extraordinarily complex console was recessed in one of the walls. A mechanical pulsating hum came from the far end of the chamber. Then, suddenly, the multi-leaf door closed behind them. They were seized by panic.

3

Vivian was summoned by the Eberenze in charge of the kernite extraction operation. One of the workers had nearly died; an Indane-Aliemt Pagres assigned to equipment maintenance duties at the mine facility.

The Pagres, a lightly-built female with short white hair and a round face, was found slumped over the motor of a huge gray machine. An ore extractor, the machine used a giant screw to move the crumbly material from the immense deposits to underground tunnels. Its production rate, explained the Eberenze, had shown a marked decline, and operation had been suspended while the technician ministered to its mechanisms.

A sharp caustic smell pervaded the area.

Vivian placed her hripitur on the gray machine and instructed it to record her actions. The device immediately extended the stalk carrying its optical sensor.

Two deep purple trenches lay beneath the stricken Pagres' bloodshot and swollen eyes. Using a wand-like instrument she unclipped from a silver belt, Vivian gave the woman a drug to curtail the paralysis of the skeletal muscles. Then, with the aid of an ovoid diagnostic device, she evaluated the state of every major bodily function. Heart activity was impaired. There were runs of premature ventricular contractions. Throat constriction, edema, sinus congestion and other indicators of the allergy were present. In the Pagres' case the symptoms had been extreme. The fool had removed her respirator mask, presumably to perform close work on the motor.

Gradually, the Pagres' heartbeat became regular. Vivian administered an analgesic and a tranquilizer. Then she clipped the medical instruments to her silver belt and moved away from the woman.

"Will the Pagres be all right?" the Eberenze asked.

"I believe she will recover, Master," Vivian answered.

From a blue pouch she extracted a shiny cylinder. She pressed a stud on its side and returned it to the pouch. Methodically, she walked about, taking several air samples and sealing them in small hermetic containers while making a short inspection of the area.

Vivian, the Eberenze, an Indane-Aliemt Kliettaes, and the Eberenze's android attendant were in a large hexagonal chamber. Except for the android, all wore white respirator masks. Strip lights above cast a red sheen on the rough-textured gray walls. The mouths of three square-section transport tunnels and the round shaft that the ore extractor had dug opened darkly into the bay.

A container train stood by half-laden, its squat yellow cars covered with kernite dust. The oval shape of an airway opened at the far end of the chamber's flat roof.

Vivian gave the Eberenze's attendant one of the small cylinders and asked him to obtain air samples from within the airway. He used handholds to climb a side wall and entered the oval duct.

"Your people must wear respirators at all times, Master," Vivian told the Eberenze. "Until we can determine the exact nature of the allergen and find a more convenient solution."

The Eberenze, a short man with a pensive countenance, nodded. "They will be reminded," he said, glancing at her with piercing white eyes.

"The Pagres should be taken to the clinic as soon as possible," Vivian said.

"I will arrange for her transport at once, Pagres Vivenes," declared the Kliettaes.

Vivian and Drimtul stood in front of a chromium structure at the center of a white-walled circular room. The device, a clinical monitor, presented an unadorned metallic face and waited patiently for instructions.

Vivian extracted a handful of small air sample cylinders from the pouch she carried. She set them in a neat row on a pink-colored square sector on top of the machine. "Analyze contents," she said.

At once, the pink surface vanished and the cylinders were drawn swiftly inside the artifact. A moment later the pink panel reappeared.

A flat 2-foot-square white tablet rose from the monitor. In a moment, its surface became clear and a few rows of data were displayed. The monitor summarized the information verbally: "The contents are primarily a mixture of nitrogen, oxygen, water vapor, and argon. There are trace amounts of—"

"We are interested in the particulate matter," interrupted Drimtul. "Potential allergens."

The information on the tablet was replaced with a new data table. "There are quantities of organic matter with allergenic potential, in varying amounts on all samples," stated the monitor. "There is also inert mineral matter in colloidal suspension."

"Display a typical organic particle," Drimtul said.

The three-dimensional image of something that looked like a hairy ball was displayed. The rounded shape slowly rotated, showing spiny geometric structures protruding from it.

"Identify," Vivian said, leaning forward to obtain a closer look.

The machine was silent for a moment. Then it said: "The particles are male reproductive cells from an indigenous flowering plant."

"Which plant?"

After a long silence the monitor said: "That information is not available locally. A query has been sent to an auxiliary data bank at a remote location."

Vivian glanced at Drimtul. "What remote location?"

"I do not know, Vivenes," he answered.

"The facility is located 2,400 kilometers east of this site," explained the monitor. "It is operated by the host government, which has designated it Gilgamesh. The communication link is inefficient."

"How long is this going to take?" Vivian asked after a few moments.

"The Gilgamesh facility has received the images and supporting data," the monitor said. "Their scientists are studying them now. They confirm the initial analysis. It is pollen from a plant of the class Dicotyledonae. A more detailed analysis should be complete within five milicycles."

Vivian tapped her fingers wearily on the monitor's shiny surface. Then she crossed the room and stood by the yellow mound of a communication device. Drimtul stayed behind, looking expectantly at the monitor.

"Contact Kneth Chasrydel," she commanded.

"Kneth Chasrydel is not at the site," answered the communicator.

Vivian frowned. She had been trying to contact Charles for three days. "Surely he's back by now," she thought.

"Contact Kneth Chasrydel's attendant."

"Attendant July is away from her work area."

"Find her," said Vivian impatiently.

A moment later the device announced: "July is at the 19th level of the Bithian facility, in Kneth Cupahr's quarters. The Kneth's communicator is directed not to accept summons at this time."

Vivian wheeled and spoke at the monitor across the room. "What is the status of the Xartekres 3 transfer craft?"

Drimtul looked at her, a trace of curiosity appearing on his usually expressionless face.

"Unknown," the monitor replied.

"What?" An alerting coldness coursed through her body. "Explain."

"The status of the Xartekres 3 is indeterminate. The starship Xartek has not confirmed its arrival at Neptune."

Vivian turned to the communication device. "Contact July at once. Override all previous directives. This is an emergency."

Immediately, Vivian found herself looking into the flat planes of a Bithian room. The hexagonal chamber seemingly rotated as the communication device altered its point of view. Kneth Cupahr's image and the shorter frame of Eberenze Fermilo passed by and then July's statuesque white-suited figure appeared.

"July, where is Chasrydel?" Vivian asked.

July's green eyes looked back cheerlessly. "We do not know. His ship is unaccounted for."

Vivian stared at July wordlessly.

"The last transmission from the Xartekres 3 was monitored twelve cycles ago. It was a ship's log transmittal, but it was interrupted. Only a few frames were received. They were slightly off course at that time, near the orbit of Saturn. Every attempt to contact them since then has failed. It is assumed that they met with a serious accident."

Vivian thought she could feel the walls pressing in to squeeze her breath away. She mumbled something and heard July say that a transfer craft from the Neptune base had reached the last known position of the Xartekres 3. Some debris had been detected in the region.

Vivian terminated the communication and turned automatically toward the clinical monitor's beckoning voice.

"The pollen has been positively identified," it reported, "as belonging to a plant of the family Cactaceae, genus Opuntia. Possibly Opuntia basilaris. A fleshy-stemmed desert plant, leafless and spiny."

4

Cicely closed the door to the classroom and headed toward the school's main entrance, her steps resounding in the empty hallway. She held her purse in one hand and in the other a notebook and an apple. The apple was a present from one of her boys, Jeremy. She had worked through her lunch hour and had forgotten to eat it.

She walked outside, closing her blue coat against the cold, blustery wind. Leaning against the wind, she hurried toward her car. Near the gate she passed the stooping form of the caretaker, bent over a hedge.

"Have a nice evening, Miss Denfeld," he called out to her.

"Good night, Mr. Prescott," she said, smiling at him.

She passed a man in a tan overcoat and heard the sound of Mr. Prescott's shears. A moment later she reached her car and started the drive home. The afternoon traffic seemed particularly heavy.

Famished, she decided to stop for a sandwich and a cup of hot tea at a restaurant on Bridge Road. She parked her car and was on her way when she remembered the apple. On impulse she decided to eat it just then, before she forgot it again.

Cicely turned around and walked back to the MG. As she opened the door she noticed a man leaning against a black sedan, twenty feet beyond. He wore a tan overcoat. It was the same man she had seen outside the school.

She took the apple and walked to the restaurant. Inside, she forwent her favorite table and took one that allowed her to keep an eye on the black sedan.

The man in the tan overcoat stayed by his car, occasionally taking short walks up and down the sidewalk. When she finished her meal he was still there, leaning casually against a dark fender.

Driving home, Cicely kept a keen eye on her rearview mirror. She spotted his car behind her, but she made a couple of sharp turns, and once she got on the M40, she didn't see the black car again.

CHAPTER 21
ASSOCIATIONS

1

Vivian looked around one last time, confirming she was alone in the hexagonal chamber. She walked swiftly to one of the walls and climbed up the ladder inset on the rough-textured surface, until she reached the oval entrance to the air duct. She detached the imdermi from her belt and illuminated the tunnel. It was about five and a half feet high and seven feet wide. Its metal surface shone brilliantly in the imdermi's light. Then, her head bent, Vivian entered the upward-slanting tube.

It would be winter outside, so cold rather than sunstroke would be the problem. And water. She may have to walk for a day.

Early on, Vivian and Charles had prepared and hidden packs for the eventuality of their escape. Inside each held an imdermi, which would provide light and could also serve as a staff, and an extra suit, a day's supply of water, and maps they had constructed from memory. Recently, Vivian had added a device like a slingshot that she had cobbled up out of medical equipment parts, and a surgical knife.

For a time Vivian had wondered, with desperate hope, whether Charles could possibly have survived. She had contrived to obtain clearance from Cirsegas Austir to examine the Xartekres 3's mission manifest. Her effort had merely served to confirm what the monitor initially stated: that the crew would have long ago exhausted the ship's air supply. Finally, Vivian had forced herself to seek out July, whom she disliked, hoping that the attendant had somehow obtained new information. But July had confirmed Vivian's own conclusion. Even if the crew had survived whatever accident befell them, they would have perished from lack of air and water. It was then, in Charles' empty quarters, in the presence of the icily courteous android, that Vivian accepted, with a cold grief, that Charles was irretrievably gone.

Once the loss of Charles sank in, Vivian had decided to attempt to get away at the first opportunity. She had begun to have bouts of morning sickness, and wanted to flee before her pregnancy made it physically impossible to endure the rigors of the escape.

Twice before Vivian had tested the first two stages of the plan: reaching, unnoticed, the mine facility tunnels, and then following a ventilation shaft to the surface. On those occasions she had spotted sentries patrolling the area outside and had turned back. But the attempts had allowed her to work out their watch patterns.

Vivian reached the end of the slanting duct and came upon a round chamber. A gentle but constant airflow tugged at her hair. She noted with disgust fittings and stenciled markings that showed this section of Site One had been built using American parts. The chamber's floor was a metal grate. Below lay a pit that would hold water overflow in the unlikely case of a heavy rainfall. The top was a shallow dome. The vent structure was shaped like the top of a mushroom, with the outside camouflaged to look like a rounded rock. It was early morning, and the light of day illuminated the brown wall of the air shaft. She turned off the imdermi and clipped it to her belt.

Vivian listened for a moment. She heard only the sound of her own breathing and the whisper of air flowing down the gleaming shaft. It was cold in the chamber. She opened a small hinged gate and peered outside. At first she saw just the coarse sand nearby, but then, fifty feet away, she saw the back of one of the sentries. The android walked away at a slow pace, systematically surveying his surroundings. He was too far away for Vivian to hear his footsteps, but she wondered how acute his hearing was.

If the sentry followed his usual pattern, he would walk to the next air shaft, four hundred yards away, and then follow a roughly rectangular pattern around four other vents before returning. At the farthest point in his circuit, he would be half a mile away.

From the pouch she carried slung over her shoulder, she extracted the extra suit and put it on over the one she already wore. It would help keep her warm. Then she undid the clasp that held the access door closed. Very carefully, she opened the door and looked outside. The sandy terrain was fairly flat, but Joshua trees and occasional boulders provided some cover. For the first time in months she smelled the scent of plant life and heard the chirping of insects. She could not see the guard, but she estimated that he should be past the second vent and still headed away from her.

Quietly closing the door behind her, Vivian looked up at the sun in the cloudless sky and then at the brown peaks of the Tehachapis to the west to get her bearings. She took a few deep breaths and willed fear away from her thoughts. Leaning low, with silent sleekness, she moved away from the air shaft. A moment later she was running, heading in a direction that she hoped would take her to State Highway 14.

She covered a mile in the first ten minutes, keeping her head as low as she could and avoiding the higher ground. Once, she passed a two-yard-wide clump of cactus, and a part of her mind deduced that they may be of the type the aliens were allergic to. The terrain gradually became flatter, with less rock outcroppings and fewer Joshua trees and scraggly bushes.

With fewer obstacles, Vivian found it easier going, but knew her exposure to detection had increased. She picked up her pace. It took her just seven minutes to cover the second mile.

Then she heard a humming resonance, above the sounds of her breathing and the rhythmic pounding of her feet on the sand. Without slowing, she glanced uneasily over her shoulder and saw a dozen broad gray shapes, gliding eight or ten feet above the yellowish-brown surface. They closed rapidly on her.

Desperately, she looked around for cover and broke into a flat out run. But there was nowhere to hide.

There were myrmidon guards or androids in the uncovered vehicles. She could see their shapes as they closed on her. They held narrow glinting devices to their shoulders and pointed them at her. Suddenly, a patch of ground in front of her exploded in a cloud of dust. She veered to her right and passed by a dark vitrified smear, still smoldering. Sliding to a stop, she unclipped her imdermi and twisted and pulled the rod, setting it to over-load. The device began to emit a pulsing red glow. A second blast hit just beside her, close enough that she felt its searing heat.

The closest of the hovering vehicles was a mere thirty feet away. Vivian threw the glowing imdermi at it with a powerful swing of her arm and again changed direction. A moment later she heard a jarring explosion behind her and felt the blast and shards of metal hit her back. She stumbled ahead. Another of the broad gray shapes passed overhead and wheeled about, circling toward her. One of the figures on it pointed a broad gleam-ing device at her, its end a flat maw. Abruptly, a blazing cage enveloped her. She fell down, driven unconscious by the overwhelming pain.

2

Cicely adjusted the skirt of her cream wool suit and glanced at Dr. McClellan.

"You are not going to like this," she said edgily.

Dr. McClellan looked fixedly at her. He turned on the voice recorder. "What is it?"

"Someone has been following me."

Dr. McClellan was silent for a moment. His hand rubbed his chin. "When did this start?"

"I first noticed it three days ago."

"Someone that you know?"

"No one I can recognize. I haven't had a good look at him."

He took a gold pen from the pen holder on his desk and turned it around slowly in his hand. "Do you know of any reason why anyone would want to follow you?"

"No."

"Were you followed here?"

She fidgeted in her chair. "I didn't notice anyone."

Dr. McClellan looked at her calmly. "It may be just a coincidence, you know. Someone just going your way. It's happened to me a couple of times." He wrote a short note on the back of an envelope and returned the pen to its holder.

Cicely looked at him dubiously.

Dr. McClellan thought for a moment. He took a deep breath. "If it happens again you might consider carrying one of those small autofocus cameras with you. I think one may fit inside a handbag. Then, when you next see him, take his picture. That would give you something to pursue."

Cicely frowned. He didn't believe her, she thought.

Dr. McClellan drew a notebook from a drawer in his desk. "I want to try some word associations," he said. "Just say the first thing that comes to mind when you hear the word."

Cicely adjusted her position in the easy chair.

"Road," he read from a list in his notebook.

Cicely thought for a moment. "Car," she said.

"Bird."

"Flight."

"Father."

"Love."

"Easy."

She hesitated, then said, "Pie. Easy as pie."

"Don't think too much about your response, Cicely. There are no wrong answers. Just say the first thing that you think of."

"All right, Doctor."

"Shirt," he started again.

"Coat."

"Winter."

"Cold."

"Friend."

"Angie."

"Knife."

"Sharp."

"Baby."

"Forget."

Dr. McClellan looked up from the notebook. "Why forget?" he asked, deliberately casual.

Cicely looked sharply at him, her eyes wide.

3

To Vivian, the sound seemed remote, barely perceptible. She found it significant only because, for a time, it was the sole intrusion on the feeling of total internal peace. Much later, a pinprick of light appeared in the comforting darkness. Then, gradually, but slightly detracting from the pervasive feeling of security, sound and light gained intensity.

Vivian floated inside a white cocoon. The machine surrounding her lay at the center of a round chamber, deep inside the Indane-Aliemt complex. Cirsegas Austir, Kneth Karyprit and Pagres Drimtul stood by the machine, intently observing status displays exhibited on its chromium surface.

Austir leaned forward and pressed a blue icon on the vitalizer's gleaming surface. The sides of the towering apparatus vanished and Vivian became visible to them. Her nude body, suspended between the upper and lower internal surfaces of the device, showed no trace of the injuries she had received during her escape attempt.

Austir's snow-white hair slid forward over her green tunic as she touched another icon on the machine. There was a satisfied smile on her lips. Vivian's body slowly descended and came to rest softly on the white pad.

"She should recover fully," said the Cirsegas. She glanced at Karyprit. "I will meet with Intuger Sinderc and the Supracetor and ask for an investigation of the poor performance of the perimeter security. They allowed Vivenes to almost slip away from them, and then used excessive force to stop her."

Resting on the white pad, Vivian looked up at the three Indane-Aliemt physicians. Still groggy, she offered them a faint smile. "I guess I did not make it."

"You placed yourself in great danger, Pagres," Austir said.

Vivian blinked, trying to clear the haze that still clouded her vision. "Danger," she thought. She raised her head and looked at herself. Her body seemed intact. Then, as she more fully regained consciousness, a strange dark feeling struck her.

Karyprit noticed a rapid change in the neural activity monitors.

A look of concern crept over Vivian's face. "Is my baby all right?"

Austir looked sharply at Karyprit. "Baby?"

"The natives still use placental reproduction, Lady. Vivenes was hosting an embryo."

"What was done?"

"It was withdrawn during treatment."

"What did you do to my baby?" Vivian cried.

Austir and Karyprit noticed the violent surge in the psychomotor readings.

"It had to be removed," Karyprit said.

With an effort that made her body tremble, Vivian began to rise. "Will I be able to have my baby?" She looked wildly at the three of them, her eyes darting from one to another.

"No, Vivenes," Drimtul said, kindly, "but you still may have offspring, later."

"No!" Vivian cried. A cold shock ran through her. She started to swing her legs over the side of the machine. "I want my baby back."

"Restrain her," Austir commanded. Karyprit and Drimtul held Vivian down for a moment, but, gaining strength, she shoved them back violently.

"You murderers!" Vivian cried, her eyes brimming with tears.

Austir withdrew a silver rod from a recess in the vitalizer and quickly manipulated a setting. She pressed it to Vivian's thigh just as she was about to spring down from the resting place.

Vivian quickly sank back to the white padded surface.

"Psychomotor activity reached critical levels," announced the clinical monitor, just as Karyprit and Drimtul picked themselves up from the floor.

Karyprit and Drimtul glanced nervously at Austir. The tall woman stood pondering for a moment, rapidly assessing alternative measures. Then she caused an adjustable seat to be produced and sat by the gleaming machine, studying the diagnostic displays.

Drimtul adjusted Vivian's position on the mat, aligning her body at its center. When he finished, Karyprit walked to the edge of the machine and observed Vivian's unconscious form. Gently, she ran her fingers over a flaccid arm.

"I did not expect such extreme distress," Karyprit said.

Drimtul shook his head sadly. "In her condition, she may not be able to withstand another shock."

"Instruments," the Cirsegas said. An oval section of the machine's gleaming surface vanished, revealing a recess studded with complex medical implements.

Austir took a thick red disk, its upper surface dotted with controls, and placed it against Vivian's forehead. She handled the controls, making delicate adjustments while the round instrument emitted a series of chirping tones. Then she leaned close to Vivian's ear. "Forget," she said in a soft voice. "Forget the baby." She repeated the suggestion many times.

<h1 style="text-align:center">4</h1>

Commander John Sifford walked up to the window and gazed down on the mid-afternoon street traffic from his vantage point high on Thames House. The massive building served as headquarters of M.I.5, the British Security Service. He held a brown folder loosely in his hand. Taking a seat on the window ledge, he opened the folder and read from the second page.

FROM SOURCE JONAH VIA TELEX / 12.02

DCRPT GCF / 12.03 / 0927

FOR JOHN SIFFORD EYES ONLY

OBTAINED POSITIVE ID SUBJECT "KATHRYN." INTERVIEWED 11.28 LAWTON, OKLAHOMA. SUBJECT NAME MRS. ANNETTE MENDENHALL, NEE ERICSON. ATTRACTIVE BLONDE, LATE TWENTIES. MARRIED BRUNO MENDENHALL, A RESTAURANT OWNER, SOON AFTER MOVING TO LAWTON THREE YEARS AGO. COUPLE HAVE ONE CHILD, NANCY, TWO YEARS OLD.

SUBJECT USED NAME KATHRYN PARKS FOR SEVERAL MONTHS IN LOS ANGELES, CALIFORNIA, FIVE YEARS

AGO. REAL KATHRYN PARKS SHARED APARTMENT WITH SUBJECT, WAS KILLED IN ATTACK SUBJECT THINKS WAS DIRECTED AT HER. (L.A. POLICE RECORDS CONFIRM "ANNETTE ERICSON" VICTIM HOMICIDE AT THE TIME, CASE CLOSED WITHOUT ARREST.)

SUBJECT STATED SHE WAS ONCE ENGAGED TO LEO ARTEAGA. SHE BELIEVES ARTEAGA "GOT INVOLVED IN SOMETHING DANGEROUS," AND PRESUMES HIM DEAD. CONFIRMS WORKING AT CLUB "RED CHALICE" USING ALIAS "KATHRYN" AND MEETING BRIEFLY WITH MAN ANSWERING DESCRIPTION "CHARLES." WAS LATER AP-PROACHED BY WOMAN FITTING DESCRIPTION "VIVIAN." BOTH QUESTIONED HER WITH RESPECT TO ARTEAGA. NEGATIVE RECOGNITION "CICELY." INTERVIEW TRAN-SCRIPT FOLLOWS.

Sifford looked up from the folder and gazed out the window for a moment. "So there was a Kathryn," he thought. Frowning, he walked back to his desk and threw down the folder. For a time he stared at a picture of the Queen, on the otherwise bare gray wall across the room. Then he opened the file and again read from it.

From Source Raphael via F.O. courier / 11.30
For Commander John Sifford Eyes Only

Robinson claims he is now retired. He established residence in St. Kitts two years ago. It is known that he runs small networks in Honduras and Nicaragua, presumably for CIA. He says he does not know the girl in the photograph and has no recollection of "Cicely."

Testimony: Admits setting up a freelance operation to obtain a document "that was being peddled by Leo Arteaga," more than five years ago. According to Robinson, Arteaga obtained a coded classified document from a U.S. Air Force contractor, evidently decoded it, and decided to sell the information. But someone made a series of attempts on Arteaga's life and he fled to Cuba. Robinson determined all records on Arteaga were being systematically destroyed and was unable to obtain identifying characteristics or photographs. He discovered a school acquaintance of Arteaga able to recognize him: Charles Ryder. Robinson told Ryder that he was working for the FBI and employed him to help locate and identify Arteaga.

Robinson states that Ryder and Vivian Venables (an associate of Robinson's) reported they were able to reach Arteaga in Cuba, but that Arteaga was killed "by unknown persons" without passing on any useful information. He says that he closed the investigation shortly after Ryder and Venables returned to the U.S. (via Bahamas). Robinson insists that "nothing ever came of it."

Sifford closed the folder. His eyes again rested on the Queen's picture on the wall. All his inquiries about Cicely Denfeld had failed to find evidence of her ever meeting Robinson. And five years ago the woman was attending college; her time was accounted for, almost day for day. Her passport showed no visa or stamp indicating a trip to the United States. He had found evidence of only two trips abroad, both to the Continent. She had traveled as a member of supervised tour groups.

He leaned back in his chair, his fingers tapping impatiently on the polished surface of his desk. Although Robinson was not saying much, something had actually happened involving a secret American project. Sifford discounted a great part of what Cicely Denfeld dreamed about. But what was her connection with Robinson? How could such a connection have come about? "Raphael" would have to contact Robinson again. There were additional pressures that could be brought to bear.

The telephone rang and Sifford reached across the desk to pick it up. It was Amy King.

"Dr. McClellan just started a session with her," Miss King said, hurriedly. "I have installed the bug, so from now on I shall be able to provide you with recordings of everything."

"That's very good. Have you been able to get at the files?"

"No, he always locks them up. I'll have to stay late and work out the combination on the safe." There was a pause, then the girl's voice went on, excitedly. "I almost forgot, sir. Are you having her followed?"

"Yes. Why do you ask?"

"She's aware of it."

"Drat!"

Sifford went over the entire case in his mind. He still found nothing to indicate a link between Cicely Denfeld and the others. Someone, he thought, had penetrated Robinson's organization at some time in the past. Since Cicely Denfeld had not traveled to America, it was likely that the person had come to England and somehow passed the information to her. Perhaps accidentally, in a way traumatic enough to provoke her mental problems. Whoever it was could still be in England. Still operational. But he was just speculating. There was so little to go on. Was he overlooking something? He felt dispirited. But he had the resources of the Security Service at his disposal, and he knew himself to be good at his job. He assured himself that, in time, he would work it all out.

CHAPTER 22
THE ANCIENT SOLDIER

1

The telephone was ringing when Cicely entered her apartment. She shut the door behind her and hurried to pick up the receiver.

"Hello."

"How are you, Cicely?"

She recognized Greg's voice at once, and it surprised her. It had been months since she had heard from him. A flurry of emotions coursed through her: delight, annoyance, affection, resentment. "Who is this?" she said.

Shifting the receiver from hand to hand, Cicely slipped out of her overcoat and laid it on the back of the couch.

"It's me, Greg. You haven't forgotten me already, have you, Cicely?" His laughter was natural and unfeigned.

She made her response icily polite, a cover for the hurt and anger that his voice evoked. Greg chose to ignore her distant manner.

He was telling her about the new manager of his polo team when Cicely at last interrupted him. "What do you want, Greg?"

The telephone was silent for a moment. "I have missed you, Cicely."

She said nothing.

"I have wondered how you were doing," he said.

She sat down on the padded couch, placed the telephone on her lap. "That's good of you. I am doing quite well."

"There is a new play at the Phoenix…"

"We cannot just start where we left off, Greg."

"Let me invite you to dinner, then."

She thought about it. Her first impulse was to just hang up on the inconstant dolt. It would be easier if he wasn't so damned good-looking, she told herself. Or if there were a dozen others for her to choose from. But the male teachers in her school were either married, bent, or revoltingly unattractive. She compromised: "Tea, perhaps. Call me next week."

After hanging up, Cicely remained at the couch, examining her feelings. Why had he called, after all this time? Maybe he had a fling with someone and it was over now. Her good times with Greg had been real. But they seemed so distant now.

She remembered a wonderful spring evening. The food at Lenoir's had been superb, and Greg had been delightful to be with. She had ordered chateaubriand with truffles and asparagus, and Greg had tried a honey-glazed duck suggested by *le proprietaire* himself. They had shared a bottle of Champagne. After dinner they danced at Stringfellow's. As Cicely recalled the evening she experienced a longing for times past. Times when presentiments of coming evil did not occupy her mind.

So many things that had touched her life were gone, except in her mind. Her school days. Her parents. She smiled wanly, remembering their drafty old house in Birmingham. The day of her ninth birthday, when she sat with her mother by the lone lime tree and watched her smiling father approach, bearing a yapping Airedale puppy. Her parents would never be totally gone. She could always bring back the memories; hear the words from the past spoken again.

Suddenly, she thought of a more distant place. A stark and capacious hall inside a formidable fortress built ages ago. The strangers that had become her friends. The emotionless and patient presence that was at once jailor and protector.

They stood before the projection zone, at the center of the great semicircular hall where hundreds of troops had once gathered. There were only three of them: Compcenlu, Fernoch and Charles. In the year since their arrival at Dione they had come to accept the ancient Galamic stronghold as their home and the machine intelligence they knew as the Keeper as their ubiquitous host. The Keeper had imparted them with knowledge of Uncial Galamic and of the performance of various tasks.

"We wish to view it one last time, Keeper," said Berenz Compcenlu. "The System Commander's address to his officers."

They had come to believe that they would die on this cold and desolate world. Food and drink was provided for them. But there was something, some vitamin or mineral, missing. Their health deteriorated. Then the Keeper, its vast instrumentalities unable to forestall their decline, had at last allowed them to contact the Neptune base. A transfer craft was underway and, if all went well, would soon return them to Earth. They would take a recording of the presentation with them, but it would never have the impact that the original had on them here, in the ancient hall where they had first experienced it.

The origin of the address had been forgotten many centuries ago. But, from data the Keeper had provided, it appeared that the presentation, and others similar to it, had been supplied to the long-gone garrison as a report of military events.

"As you wish, friend Compcenlu," the Keeper said in a sonorous voice.

The intensity of the illumination was subtly reduced, causing the stark, equipment-laden gray walls to fade from view.

A plain appeared before them, stretching to a horizon of snow-tipped mountains, lit by a red sun and a star so bright that it must also be a sun. Above them a delicate blue-green sky bore wispy yellow clouds. Their viewpoint zoomed in on a circular feature at the center of the emerald field. The smooth surface, dotted with the arcing branches and fronds of yellow ocher plants, seemed to race under them.

As they approached it, the circular feature became a large group of people arranged in a ring two hundred meters across. It was a curving row of men and women standing around a dais upon which a dozen figures could be discerned. The projection raced along the periphery of the circle. Hundreds of erect forms flashed by. Then, suddenly, the blurring traverse stopped and a single figure was shown up close. A woman of a beauty so arresting she could be taken for a goddess. The graceful posture of her slender body had about it something regal, and the perfect symmetry of her golden features disclosed intelligence and self-regard. Strands of fine silver hair showed under a jaunty cap bearing a gleaming emblem. Even after many viewings, the sight of her stirred the souls of the three onlookers.

The woman's lips parted in a refined smile and she said something to the man standing next to her. They both wore maroon uniforms trimmed in black, the shoulders displaying the insignia of general officers. The woman turned her head slightly, and the projection rushed ahead in the direction of her gaze, leaving her behind and then settling on the group of officers on the central dais. Wearing uniforms of various types (maroon, amber, white), they were the planetary commanders of a system-wide alliance. At their center stood a single man, younger than the others, in the slate-gray uniform of the Imperial Space Command. He was the Supreme System Commander.

The man in gray took a step forward and a hush fell on the vast group surrounding him, the general officer corps of the Arin Gridezi system. With penetrating eyes set below a noble brow, he scanned the assembled officers. Then he began the speech, his amplified voice clear and compelling.

"*Chisl eke liher. Rense ilmars ens…*" The words were Uncial Galamic.

"Consider the past. Four centuries ago Galamic vessels first reached Arin Gridezi. Your fathers fought cruel Nature and hostile beasts, gave their blood in taming the planets, and endured backwardness and isolation in the establishment of a system-wide nation. Their efforts made this system as strong and prosperous as any within the Empire and gave you the opportunity to live in liberty.

"This planet, this system, the Galamic culture, our very race, are now threatened by a vicious and destructive enemy of unsurpassed daring and ambition. The monsters pay dearly for their plunder. Our brothers have given and are giving battle to a heinous enemy: their blood, spilled in fighting overwhelming forces, has written our name in splendid fire across space.

"The dark forces our comrades faced will soon reach us. Our future holds danger, not an easy peace. We are destined not to be tempted by careless ease, but to be pitted against a mighty enemy in a struggle that will test us and will demand from us cunning and toil. I know you will not shrink from danger or labor, for your fathers and their fathers knew them.

"We shall face the enemy in our system, on our terms, and we will struggle not merely to endure, but to prevail. We will meet them in confidence and strength, for whatever the outcome of the next battle, ultimate triumph will surely be ours!"

The System Commander raised his arm. His hand swept over the general officer corps, in a benediction.

"Whom do you fear, knowing the Empire is with you?"

"We fear nothing!" the corps responded.

"The Vast Empire," he called out, his voice rising.

"The Mighty Empire," answered the corps, arms outstretched in proud salute.

The System Commander's eyes filled with fire. "The Eternal Empire!"

"The Empire!" Their cry rang across the emerald plain.

2

They assembled at sunset in the port facility, forming a few loose groups near the center of the vast circular bay. Supracetor Breslui, the Resseps, Vadycrel Exlof, Intuger Sinderc, and Austir made up the largest group. Nearby, Fermilo, Cupahr, and July talked to a Nesdelsen technician. Karyprit and Obiredes Nesadl looked about expectantly, next to Vivian and Kliettaes Salfors. A Bithian android standing next to a transport platform was the first to notice the motion of the iris door. He raised his arm and pointed at the opening gate two hundred feet above.

The last red glimmer of sunlight showed for a moment at the top of the dome, as the elements of the door, like retreating pincers, slowly withdrew. Then the lights of the space port dimmed and they looked on a circle of darkening sky. Soon a dark, whispering shape appeared at the center of the gate. It approached slowly, its descent accompanied by hissing noises from vents in its blue-black hull. As the transfer craft settled gently at the exact center of the bay, the iris gate above began to close.

A wide translucent ramp emerged from the side of the vessel, near its bulbous nose. The pilot, an Indane-Aliemt Nollecion, was the first to emerge. He was followed by Berenz Compcenlu. At his appearance, there was a cheer from the crowd. Compcenlu raised his hand in recognition and started to walk unsteadily down the ramp. Then, behind him, Charles and Kneth Fernoch appeared at the doorway, and were met by another cheer.

The Supracetor forced a smile on his round face and raised his right hand, middle and index fingers outstretched in a languid salute. Many in the crowd rushed up the ramp and greeted the three at last returning from Dione. News of their experiences had preceded them, but all at the Dramtes site wanted to know firsthand of their battle with the ancient fortress, of their internment by the Keeper, of their discovery of Galamic relics.

Charles felt the Resseps' hand grasp his arm and saw, beyond Supracetor Breslui's affected smile, the familiar form of a tall green-suited woman rush toward him. He held Resseps Scahn's hand for a moment, muttered a greeting, and then took a few more uncertain steps forward, not yet reaccustomed to Earth's gravity.

Vivian wended her way through to Charles and threw her arms around him, with tearful eyes and a joyful grin on her face. It was only then that he fully realized that he had come home. His arms circled her and then, helplessly, he began to sob against her shoulder, his face pressing against the softness of her brown hair. They held each other, alone in the midst of the milling crowd, until July approached them slowly and, with an uncertain gesture, gently brushed away a tear from Charles' cheek.

3

Fernoch's promotion to the rank of Nollecion was announced in a brief Indane-Aliemt ceremony. The group met in the anteroom of Cirsegas Austir's quarters, a semicircular room with rose walls and a vaulted pale gold ceiling. Charles and Berenz Compcenlu were among the few Bithian officials in attendance.

Vivian, Pagres Drimtul, Kneth Karyprit and Obiredes Nesadl were present. Intuger Sinderc and a few others left the function soon after congratulating the new Nollecion, leaving a dozen officials to chat, pay their respects, and consume food crystals and drink globules eagerly presented by two hovering servitors.

A taciturn Indane-Aliemt Kneth approached Fernoch, who stood among a ring of well-wishers, and commented: "It is said, Master, that the ancient war machine you found on Sol-6 possesses records of the Yor-Hoerri."

An uneasy expression appeared momentarily on Fernoch's face. He still associated the Galamic fortification with the destruction of the Xartekres 3 and the deaths of Dahlgers and Lamiken. "It would be more correct to say that the Keeper found us," Fernoch said, directing his yellow eyes at the Kneth. "The fortress does possess much information about the Galams and their wars against the Yorj." Fernoch glanced at Compcenlu. "The Berenz has become an authority on the subject."

Cirsegas Austir stood next to Fernoch. "Will we have to revise our history, Berenz?" she asked Compcenlu.

"When we entered the fortress we opened a door into another world, Lady," Compcenlu said. "What we will eventually find in that world, no one can predict. The Keeper will provide more information about the Galams than has been available before, from all other sources combined."

"That is intriguing. Tell us some of what you learned," Austir said. With a terse command, she caused a semicircle of red adjustable chairs to emerge from the gleaming floor. Then she sat down and gestured for the others to do the same.

Charles took a seat near Vivian. After the function was over, he hoped to steal a few moments alone with her, the first since his return. He noted the insignia on her collar: the three small red circles of a Kneth. She had received two advancements in grade during the year that he had been away.

Compcenlu, sitting near the center of the group, glanced briefly at the others and took a moment to consume a small violet crystal proffered by a glistening cylindrical machine.

"There is much data yet to be analyzed," he said. "But it seems that the Yor-Hoerri lasted longer than previously thought, perhaps as long as a thousand major cycles. The fortress at Dione was apparently built six hundred major cycles after the first contact with the Yorj. This system," Compcenlu waved his hand in an encompassing gesture, "was an outpost at the fringes of the Empire. The garrison that manned the fortress at Dione never engaged in battle with the Yorj, but, over time, they ceased receiving communications and supplies from the Galams. Eventually, they set their station on automatic mode and left it, presumably to search for others of their kind."

"Where did they go?"

Compcenlu shrugged his shoulders. "We are still investigating that."

A muscle knotted on Charles' brow. He had been with Compcenlu when the Keeper had told them where its ancient masters had gone. Why had Compcenlu withheld that information? Perhaps Compcenlu had not yet had an opportunity to discuss the matter with the Resseps. The two were careful men, with empires on their minds. Saying nothing, Charles deliberately looked away from the Berenz. He glanced at Vivian and then at Drimtul, sitting next to her. The Pagres had been quietly regarding Vivian, but now shifted his attention to Austir.

"Why did the war last so long, Lord?" asked the Kneth that had spoken to Fernoch earlier. "Were not the Galams obliterated fairly handily by the Yorj?"

"At first," said Compcenlu, "there were skirmishes. Imperial forces conducted probing raids into Yorj-controlled space, while continuing to fight colonial wars against their own wayward settlements. Then, realizing the severity of the Yorj threat, the Empire increased its effort against the invaders and withdrew from colonial campaigns, but to no avail. The aliens advanced methodically across a broad sector. When they approached the Imperial capital, the Galams mounted a massive counteroffensive. It proved to be a total disaster. The Galam home world, the Planet of Dreams, was destroyed, their Emperor killed."

Across the room, the air above the domed brown shape of a communications device shimmered. Pagres Drimtul left his seat and walked toward the coalescing image of a Bithian official.

"That is consistent with previous accounts," said Austir, her eyes briefly following the Pagres.

"Yes. But, soon after that great battle, something happened that changed the course of the war," Compcenlu said.

Austir and the others looked at him attentively.

"Evidently, portions of the Imperial armada survived the battle around the Galamic home world. A contingent escaped by vectoring past the attacking Yorj forces. They wandered about for a time and ventured into uncharted space. Then—"

"A message for you, Lord," said Pagres Drimtul apologetically.

The Pagres had just returned from the communicator and now stood next to the Berenz. Compcenlu looked up at him inquiringly.

"The Resseps Scahn, Lord, is meeting with the Supracetor and others at his quarters. He requests your presence."

Compcenlu stood up. "I must go now, Lady," he said, bowing rapidly toward Cirsegas Austir.

"You must complete your account at some other time, Berenz," said Austir, also rising from her seat.

"I will, Lady," he assured her, moving toward the portal. Charles stood up and started to follow, but the Berenz gestured for him to stay.

"Chance favor," Compcenlu said, leaving the room at a brisk pace.

The gathering started to break up, and, seizing the opportunity, Charles arranged to leave with Vivian.

4

They crossed the portal and entered the chamber, one of four intersecting circular rooms that made up Vivian's quarters. For a time, Charles just stood there and so did Vivian. They looked at each other, surrounded by the unadorned pearly white walls, until a broad smile overtook his face. He kissed her, and then their arms went around each other.

"It's been a long time," Charles said.

She took his hand and led him into the room. "You must take shorter vacations from now on."

"I'll remember not to take any without you." He smiled at her. "There are no girls on Dione."

"Is that the only reason you missed me?" She kissed his neck.

"Well, no," Charles said, placing a hand on her buttock. "Mostly I yearned for your deliciously witty remarks."

"I understand." She ran the tip of her tongue over his ear. "I missed your probing mind, too."

"You are the most wonderful woman in the world, Vivian."

"Does that mean you want to do it again?" She lay on her back, smiling up at him. A thin film of sweat covered their bodies. They lay on Vivian's sleeping couch, a cushioned pale green oval bowl inset on the floor of her bedroom.

Charles grinned, his fingers softly caressing her. Then his gray eyes clouded. "We must leave here," he said.

"I know, dear." She told him of her failed attempt to escape, and concluded with an admonition: "We must do better next time. They almost killed me."

Vivian tugged lightly at sparse dark hairs on his chest. "I may be able to pinch the pistol they took from me when I was captured," she said. "I've found where Karyprit put it."

"Remember the tunnel where we talked with Chadwick?" Charles asked. "That side tunnel has a concealed exit onto a secondary road. The Supracetor uses it when he takes his Porsche outside."

"That exit is certain to be monitored."

"There is an iris gate that can be manually operated via a wall switch near the exit, and a force field that is keyed to the Supracetor's car. The field should automatically deactivate when the car approaches it."

"We need to verify that."

They looked into each other's eyes, realizing the immediacy of the risk they were contemplating. A tingling of anxiety touched them both.

He kissed her lips and she reached up and ran her fingers through his tousled hair.

"Where's our child?" he asked.

"What?"

Charles ran a hand caressingly over her tightly-muscled belly. "Our kid. I should have asked earlier." He smiled. "Is it a boy or a girl?"

Vivian raised her shoulders slightly, propping herself on her elbows, and looked into his eyes. "What do you mean, dear?"

"Where's the kid?"

"Charles, I don't know what you are talking about. There are no kids here."

He saw that she was not smiling. A frown crossed his brow. "I have been gone a year, Vivian," he said, "and you were three months pregnant when I left."

Vivian slid back and leaned her shoulders against the side of the couch. The outline of an unpleasant thought crossed her mind, but she could not grasp it. Looking Charles straight in the eye, she said: "I have never been pregnant, Charles. I don't know what your joke is, but it isn't funny."

Charles felt a cold shudder run through his body. Vivian wasn't making any sense. He *knew* she had been pregnant. Why would she deny it? Unless...

"Did something happen, Vivian?" He regarded her steadily. "Did you lose the baby?"

Vivian stared at him resentfully.

"Stop this," she said, raising her voice in annoyance.

Charles grabbed her bare shoulders. "What happened? If we lost the baby; we'll have to get over it. We can have another. But I need to know."

Vivian grabbed his wrist and twisted his arm off her shoulder. She pushed him back. "I said stop, Charles! What's wrong with you?"

Charles shook his head incredulously. She was pretending that their child had never been conceived.

"There's nothing wrong with me," he said hotly. "But something is very wrong with you. Did you have an abortion? Can't you just be honest and say so? Why put on this stupid act?"

She looked at him angrily. He had never spoken to her like that before. In a tightly controlled voice she told him: "Cool off, Charles. I don't know what happened to you on Saturn, but whatever it is, don't take it out on me."

Charles blurted out, "I guess you just aren't cut out to be a mother." He saw her nude body tense, but mounting indignation drove him on. "Did you take a lover while I was away? Drimtul, maybe?"

Her eyes flashed dangerously. "I wouldn't say any more if I were you. I know what goes on between you and that mechanical bitch you live with."

"So it is true! You've taken up with that damned—"

Vivian slapped Charles across his face, hard. His head reeled from the blow and a droplet of blood appeared on his lip.

"I think you'd better go now, Charles." There was an edge of cruelty in her voice.

CHAPTER 23
WHAT LIES AHEAD

1

Cicely sat quietly in the armchair while Dr. McClellan took a look at her file and prepared the voice recorder. Her eyes traveled across the room, glancing at the familiar diplomas and landscapes. Some had been re-arranged to make room for a new picture, of green farmlands dotted with sheep, and a narrow beach bordering a deep blue inlet. A new item had appeared on his desk, a crystal vase holding a single flame-colored tulip. Cicely enjoyed the bright touch which, she was sure, was the work of the doctor's new secretary, Amy.

"A while back you mentioned that you thought a man had been following you," said Dr. McClellan.

"There have been a couple of times since then when he might have been there, behind me, but he was too far away for me to tell." She shrugged. "Perhaps it was a coincidence like you suspected."

"Does it still bother you?"

"No," Cicely said pensively, "although it drove me to spend extravagantly on a pocket camera." Then she added, casually, "I have seen Greg a couple of times recently."

Dr. McClellan kept silent for a moment, expecting her to add something. But she only looked at him, placidly.

"Any dreams?"

"Yes. Charles and Vivian had quite a row. I have remembered bits and pieces, where they have met later. They hardly talk to each other. And I keep getting these flashes, brief images, of something terrible. They——"

Dr. McClellan interrupted her. "You said you remembered bits and pieces…"

"Yes, brief segments."

"Memories. Not dreams," he said crisply.

"That's right, Doctor. It has been happening more often. I did have a long dream last night."

Cicely opened her purse and looked inside. "I was in a hurry this morning and could not record a summary," she said, extracting a small notebook, "but I did jot down some notes during the lunch period. I think I can recall most of it. Would you like me to go over it now?"

"Yes, let's do that first."

"It must have happened soon after Charles' return, but after his break with Vivian, for they avoided each other. Even though both of them were there."

"Where?"

"The amphitheater in the Indane-Aliemt compound."

Berenz Compcenlu stood near the central area, on the lowest of the curving aisles. He held a small white cube in his hand. Only a small group of functionaries had gathered. They sat in a cluster on both sides of one of the ramps that were arranged about the hall, like spokes of a great dished wheel.

Charles and July sat next to Kneth Cupahr and Eberenze Fermilo. Across the broad ramp, the Resseps murmured something to Vadycrel Exlof and Nollecion Fernoch.

Supracetor Breslui moved across the central area with an air of total self-assurance, of complete superiority. Intuger Sinderc walked serenely at his side, her emkenud gliding above her. They took adjoining seats on the second tier, a short distance away from the Resseps. Vivian sat one tier higher, with Cirsegas Austir and a group of other Indane-Aliemt functionaries. She and Charles had tried to ignore each other, but could not help occasionally exchanging furtive, resentful glances.

The Supracetor's red, piercing eyes took a hard, appraising look at the assembled group. Then, with an abrupt wave of his hand, he signaled for Compcenlu to begin.

The Berenz raised the small white box to his lips and spoke softly into it. Immediately, the glow of the great sphere suspended over the center of the theater began to fade. Soon the spacious hall darkened and a projection appeared at the center. A gray disk on a faintly banded yellow-brown background: Dione against the majestic orb of Saturn.

"The fourth major satellite of Sol-6," Compcenlu stated. "Where we found the Galam fortification."

Gradually, the projection zoomed in to show bright wispy streaks and shallow craters superimposed on the darker underlying surface.

"These images were recorded during our return voyage."

Closer in, the projection revealed narrow valleys crossing Dione's icy surface and the transition between the smoother, darker trailing hemisphere and the brighter, more heavily cratered leading face.

"The fortress," announced Compcenlu, just as the projection displayed the mirrored pyramid and white dome structures, set on the rough gray-brown terrain.

"We were not permitted to record more detailed images," Compcenlu stated. A moment later, the projection flickered and the view changed. A dozen gray figures appeared near the base of the white dome. They moved in great swift leaps past a massive, singularly threatening machine.

"The Keeper did allow us to copy portions of its data banks, including some recordings produced at Dione. The figures you see now are members of the Galamic garrison."

They wore close-fitting visored suits and moved across the craggy terrain with impetuous elegance. In their gloved hands they carried beautifully complex slender shapes that were in all likelihood deadly weapons.

"A unit of Imperial troopers on patrol," Compcenlu said. "These scenes," he added, "were recorded at Dione more than 60,000 major cycles ago, shortly before the fortress was abandoned."

"Did it occur to you to independently date this recording," Breslui's deep voice rang across the chamber, "or are you relying entirely on information provided by the machine that destroyed our ship?"

"We have not completed the study of the transcriptions, Excellency," Compcenlu said. "But a preliminary analysis of background star fields and of surface features allows us to calculate the time at which the scenes were originally recorded. Our estimates are consistent with the Keeper's account."

On the projection, a sculpture took the place of the ancient troopers. A glimmering figure of a man, sturdily built, with powerful limbs and broad square shoulders. The head rested on a muscular neck: a square jaw, a short narrow nose, hard eyes, a high forehead, and a fringe of untidy hair.

"Who is this?" the Supracetor demanded.

"We found the figure, Excellency, in a chamber that apparently was once used by the fortress commanders. It is the image of a Galam general named Vlaezerus. It is very similar to a fragmented statue found by Bithian archaeologists in the Galam ruins at Risper."

"I never heard the name Vlaezerus before," Breslui said.

"The Keeper provided the name, Excellency," Compcenlu said. "Along with the following account."

Compcenlu paused for a moment. He went on: "After a great battle in which the massed forces of the Empire were decisively defeated by the

Yorj, a fleeing formation under the command of General Vlaezerus ventured into uncharted space. The formation included elements of the 9th, the 82nd, and the 127th Imperial Fleets, units of the 8th Dharzi Squadron, and fragments of other detachments. In time, they reached the vicinity of an unknown Type-F star.

"The command ship detected various planets in orbit about the star as the formation approached it. The system was identified as part of the Yorj Domain and General Vlaezerus ordered a total communications blackout. He instructed the Science Adjutant to evaluate the system using only passive sensors. An analysis was soon forthcoming: There were five planetary bodies, one of them an artificial world. All were protected by spherical screens, and a defensive ring shielded the periphery of the system's orbital plane.

"General Vlaezerus immediately issued a command that was transmitted to each element of the formation: PROCEED AT ONCE ATTACK TARGETS OF OPPORTUNITY. It was a unique departure from Imperial military doctrine."

The image of General Vlaezerus rotated slowly in the central projection, but the eyes of everyone in the audience were riveted on Berenz Compcenlu. He continued his narrative in a steady unemotional voice.

"One by one, the fighting units of the Galamic force left the formation and directed themselves toward worlds of their own choosing. Without an integrated attack plan, the assault was carried out in an uneven fashion that the Yorj were unable to anticipate. Soon the outer ring shields were penetrated, with minimal losses to the Galams."

The central projection showed a distant yellow-white sun against an unfamiliar star field, and then, one-by-one, it displayed images of its planets. The artificial world shone with an uncanny metallic glow totally unlike that of the natural planets.

"The shell defenses were breached, and eighty per cent of the strike force effected landings in one or another of the Yorj worlds. Fortuitously, a disproportionately large number of commanders chose the heavily forti-fied artificial world as their target. For the first time in the Yor-Hoerri, a sizeable Galamic corps had landed on Yorj territory. And, on the ground, the Galams soon proved to possess the superior tactical instrument. The Yorj, despite their more technically advanced civilization, lacked the ac-cumulated practical experience that centuries of warfare and numerous planetary assaults had imparted to the Galams."

The Berenz paused for a moment, and the large chamber was impres-sively silent. All eyes were turned toward the central stage, where a suc-cession of brief scenes of extreme violence were projected: war machines of immense power swooped down on lofty spires and domed citadels, cut-ting a swath of fire and destruction.

"Despite desperate attempts by the Yorj to defend their positions, the Galams made swift progress. Plumes of smoke darkened the skies above the invaded worlds while violent battles raged below. With relentless, avenging fury, the advancing Galam forces destroyed the towering struc-tures in their path. Advance Imperial infantry units discovered that the artificial planet was a repository of knowledge, a library world, and they initiated the transfer of captured information to Galamic vessels. But the bulk of the invading forces pressed their attacks with methodical ferocity.

"The beleaguered Yorj leadership was forced to ask for a truce. But the Galams sensed a major victory would soon be theirs and ignored the Yorj appeals. The attack continued unabated, and one by one the Yorj posi-tions were overcome. Then one of the orbiting Imperial starships noted a rapid increase in neutrino radiation from the system's primary. Subsequent analyses revealed that the star was collapsing onto itself. In a final, hopeless act, the Yorj opted for self-destruction, rather than yielding their central knowledge banks to the Galams. They somehow managed to trigger a nova explosion.

"Vlaezerus ordered an immediate evacuation, which was completed barely in time to avoid the star's detonation. The Galams left behind thirty per cent of their numbers, but captured significant amounts of information about the Yorj, including several of their arthropod carcasses, and caused the destruction of an entire enemy planetary system. It was only after the formation reassembled, away from the nova's expanding wavefront, that they fully realized the magnitude of their accomplishment."

A smile slowly formed on Compcenlu's lips. With a wave of his hand, he gestured toward the glimmering figure which again turned behind him. "The commanding General was eulogized across the Galamic civilization. In each Galamic city and outpost, a monument or statue was erected in his honor. The Yor-Hoerri was not over, and the Empire had already been dealt a fatal blow, but Vlaezerus' victory hurt the Yorj deeply, and thereafter their incursions into Galamic space were more tentative, more conservatively planned."

Compcenlu spoke a command into the white control device in his hand, and the amphitheater was again bathed in the soft glow of the great overhead light. A moment later the General's projection vanished from the center stage.

2

"An interesting report," Supracetor Breslui said. "We must thank the Berenz for his effort."

"There is more," Resseps Scahn said.

The Supracetor had started to rise, but now stopped and turned to face the Resseps, his chair swiveling and adjusting itself to compensate for his motions. "We have heard enough from the past, Resseps," Breslui said, raising the index and middle fingers of his hand in a weary gesture. "There are present concerns we should attend to."

"Every shard of knowledge extracted from the past, Excellency, adds meaning to the present."

Leaning forward in his seat to look past Fernoch and Sinderc at the Supracetor, Scahn added, "My first observation concerns the Imperial garrison at Dione."

Breslui managed to place a fleeting smile on his thin lips. "Please enlighten us, Resseps," he said resignedly.

"They vanished ages ago," interjected Sinderc, directing a cool glance at the Resseps. Her emkenud moved away from her shoulder and approached him.

"Not quite, Intuger," Scahn said, ignoring the gray disk. "The Keeper's records indicate they traveled to a planet in this system."

The two dozen people in the amphitheater turned toward the Resseps. "They had lost contact with the Empire and had no interstellar ships. The expected Yorj raids never materialized. Taking as many supplies as they could, they went to the most hospitable planet in the system. They settled here, on Earth."

"They must have perished soon thereafter," Breslui ventured.

"There is evidence to the contrary, Excellency," replied Compcenlu. "For hundreds of major cycles they made periodic contacts with the Keeper."

"And then?" Sinderc asked.

"The contacts ceased. They did not respond to the Keeper's communications."

"So they *did* perish," Breslui insisted.

"No, Excellency," Scahn said, "they adapted. The current Earth population are their descendants. There were mutations, of course. Genetic drift accelerated by the harsh environment. Perhaps they manipulated the genetic structure of the local humanoids to make them more like themselves; perhaps they interbred; but more likely, over time, they just supplanted them."

Breslui stood up brusquely. "That is preposterous, Resseps. The local humanoids evolved separately." He glanced at Vivian, sitting a few meters away. "They trace their ancestry back for millions of major cycles. Straight back to extinct local apes. Their similar morphology is a case of convergent evolution. It is not even certain that *we* descend from the Galams."

"The physical similarity between the locals and the Galams is a bit too extreme, Excellency, to be ascribed to chance," noted the Resseps.

"You miss the point," Breslui said impatiently, his voice rising in volume. "We are at the tip of the evolutionary tree. There have been many starts to evolution, but they all lead either to humanoid forms very much like ours, or to something totally different, like the Yorj."

The Resseps smiled scornfully. "Genetic diversity among the earthlings is exceptionally low. The implication is that their ancestors went through a population crunch, which severely restricted the gene pool. The genetic difference between the two most different humans on the face of the Earth can be explained by genetic drift during the last 60,000 major cycles."

The Supracetor turned away from Scahn and started toward the adjacent ramp. Sinderc stood up and followed him, her emkenud trailing her closely. All the others stood then.

"I am not finished, Excellency," the Resseps said tautly. "My second point concerns the Yorj."

Breslui paused as he reached the ramp. Without quite turning around he said, "What about the Yorj?"

"They never came. Eons passed, but they never showed. Not even for a reconnaissance."

The Supracetor directed a disdainful look at Scahn. "Of course they did not show. They had no reason to return once the Empire was destroyed." Taking Sinderc's arm, he added: "You live in the past, Resseps. You always look back and fail to see what lies ahead. Chance favor, I have pressing matters to attend to."

Breslui resumed his walk down the broad ramp, but Scahn continued to address him, his voice rising in volume and assuming an admonitory edge. "I do know what lies ahead. The whole Galaxy is ahead. It is ours for the taking. The Yorj did not return because they could not. The Galams may not have realized it, but they destroyed them. We can duplicate the Galam war machines. Our men saw many of them at the Dione stronghold. And we have a planetful of Galam descendants with which to man them. Right here on Earth, billions of them."

"You are insane," Breslui declared, stopping cold in his tracks. His red eyes stared piercingly at the Resseps. "You would destroy us all."

"No. We have hidden in fear for too long. In fear of something that no longer exists."

"I WILL HEAR NO MORE OF IT!" the Supracetor shouted, his round face contorted in anger. He walked away determinedly, with Intuger Sinderc and Nollecion Fernoch in his wake.

Other Indane-Aliemts followed them, with two exceptions. Vivian held back for a moment and glanced at Charles uncertainly. His glance touched hers and for an instant he considered walking to her and letting himself take her in his arms, but the bitterness returned and he looked deliberately away from her, toward the Resseps. Vivian wheeled on her heels and walked away, across the central arena, leaving only one Indane-Aliemt official behind: Cirsegas Austir.

Austir now stood next to Scahn and Vadycrel Exlof, her face as taut as theirs. Compcenlu walked up the ramp and joined the other three.

Slowly, the other Bithians gathered around as the four at their center joined hands. Almost soundlessly, his large orange eyes shining, the Resseps' lips moved, voicing words Charles had heard before: "The Vast Empire, the Mighty Empire...."

TERMINATION

CHAPTER 24
ARENA

1

The sound of raucous voices and a wandering Robert Plant melody drifted from the living room into the red carpeted hall. Cicely and Greg had retreated there with another couple, a giggling Swedish girl and a gin-drinking man called Watkins.

"I say, old man," said Watkins, "do you know Lisbon well?"

Greg nodded his handsome head condescendingly, his arm casually encircling Cicely's waist.

"I'm being sent there." As Watkins spoke, he sent a wave of gin vapors toward the others. "I shall have to learn Portuguese," he declared, sipping from a very tall glass and leaning against his companion, who was two inches taller than he was and almost sober.

In the next room, a pair of very loud male voices started to sing Waltzing Matilda.

Greg took Cicely's hand and led her further down the hall.

"About time to go, eh, love?" he said.

Cicely glanced at her wristwatch and nodded. It was twelve-thirty. "Let me say good-by to Jennifer and Spence."

"Just don't go near that wild Australian. I think he's going bonkers."

"I shan't provoke him." She glanced at Greg with a rare salty directness.

Just then a very big man in a dinner jacket stumbled into the hallway, followed by an irate redhead in a sequined black dress.

"You bloody animal," the woman shouted, kicking at her retreating companion with shiny black shoes. "You can't say something like that to me!"

While Watkins and the big man attempted to reason with the red-headed woman, Cicely and Greg slipped into the foyer. "We better go before the killing starts," said Greg, chuckling.

Cicely nodded. "All right," she said, her expression suddenly troubled. She pretended to look for something inside a small purse that matched the color of her light blue dress.

The killing.

A wave of fearsome premonition touched Cicely. She shuddered as, for an instant, the image of something hideous entered her mind.

"I'll call them in the morning," she said, regaining her composure. She did not want Greg to notice. "Do you think you can find our coats?"

Greg glanced at Cicely. He thought she appeared a little unsteady, but attributed it to the whiskey-laced punch she had been drinking.

"Sure, I'll get them," he said, turning to go.

Behind him, Cicely started to tremble. Her handbag fell unheeded to the floor.

Greg had just reached the hall when he heard Cicely scream. He ran back to the foyer, closely followed by the no longer giggling Swedish girl and a disheveled Watkins.

They saw Cicely, squirming, back pressed against the wall, staring wide-eyed at something that was not there. She screamed again, her face contorted by panic, and sank slowly to the floor, her legs buckling under her.

"I am a nurse," announced the tall girl in a businesslike manner. She knelt by Cicely. "Please bring some water," she told Greg.

Cicely struggled with an unseen menace, her chest heaving with accelerated gasps. Then, suddenly, her contortions stopped and she lost consciousness.

2

The transport module hummed as it sped through the tunnel to the Indane-Aliemt compound. Eberenze Fermilo stood rigidly, flanked by Compcenlu and Cupahr, facing Charles and July. The collar of Charles' white tunic displayed a recently added fourth red circlet.

Fermilo straightened his thin shoulders into a more extremely erect posture. "The Resseps has formally challenged Breslui's authority as Supracetor. Under Dramtes law, Breslui must yield his rank, or be prepared to defend it in mortal combat. You will act as the Resseps' representative when the challenge is made, Eberenze."

Charles stared at Fermilo's strained face.

"It is unlikely that Breslui will offer a defense," Compcenlu said reassuringly. "He has lived for 433 major cycles. Barring a catastrophic accident he will live forever. He would not risk his life over a dispute such as this."

"I'm not eager to shorten my lifespan," Charles said.

Cupahr managed a smile that briefly displayed his small even teeth. "You have been trained for this, Master," he told Charles. "If it does come to a fight, just do as you were taught."

Charles stared at the three Bithians. "They have known about this all along," he thought. Charles' mind raced through a series of deductions. The Resseps must have conceived the plan to overthrow Breslui a long time ago, perhaps as far back as their chance meeting at the tunnel. The challenge was the reason for Charles' sessions with Cupahr and Esandos, and for the battles with the beasts. Because it was not only the Supracetor who was immortal. They all were. They did not want to risk their own lives.

With an almost imperceptible wobble, the transport module came to a halt and the doorway cleared.

They stepped outside and walked briskly into the amphitheater, Cupahr carrying a seamless tan box, long and narrow. The atmosphere was tense. More than two hundred Bithians and Indane-Aliemts stood or walked about the three wide terraces above the central area. Charles found himself walking between Compcenlu and July. Fermilo and Cupahr followed closely behind.

Charles glanced sharply at July. She must have known, just like the others. Her clear eyes returned his gaze steadily and her perfect features displayed an encouraging smile.

"How is your Uncial Galamic?" Compcenlu asked.

"Adequate, Lord," Charles replied. It was one of the advantages of having a limnen. The wearer never forgot anything.

"When you face Breslui, say *'Ae leskl Aeprestor'*: I would be Supracetor," Compcenlu said in a low murmur.

They walked past the sunken central area, under the huge glowing ball suspended from the white domed ceiling. The dull sound of many hushed conversations enveloped them.

On the first tier, to the right, they saw Resseps Scahn, flanked by Vadycrel Exlof and Eberenze Reumonh. Compcenlu led Charles and the others in their direction.

"Remarkable event," the Resseps said solemnly.

Charles and the others returned the greeting.

Scahn glanced across the ramp, where a stern-faced Supracetor Breslui stood surrounded by Intuger Sinderc and other Indane-Aliemt officials. Then he placed his hand gently upon Charles' shoulder.

"We made a pact some time back," the Resseps said, a faint smile forming on his lips, "in that caved in tunnel. We owe our lives to that agreement. Now we need to further our alliance."

"I have been told, Lord," Charles said. "But I do not intend to kill for you."

The Resseps' smile did not leave his lips. He nodded understandingly, his large orange eyes beholding Charles paternally. "It may not come to that."

"Since you mention our agreement," Charles said, "let me remind you that I never agreed to be kept here as a prisoner."

Resseps Scahn shook his head gently. "You are not a prisoner, Charles Ryder. You are a Bithian official, now an Eberenze, with powers and prerogatives that you still do not fully appreciate."

Out of the corner of his eye, Charles caught a glimpse of Vivian, standing grim-faced with Drimtul and Karyprit, across the adjoining ramp.

"Your opportunities are boundless," the Resseps said. He continued to talk with Charles for a time in a calm, singularly soothing voice. Finally, with a pat to Charles' shoulder, the Resseps added: "I continue to look for ways that will allow you to return to the surface. We will talk about that later." His voice then lowered to a mesmerizing murmur. "Now go stand in the arena."

Charles took a few uncertain steps back and stood alone near the edge of the central area.

The Resseps turned to his right and faced the Supracetor. Slowly, he approached Breslui. Throughout the great circular hall, suddenly, all conversation came to a stop. A stiff-faced Nesdelsen Berenz took a few steps forward and positioned himself near the Resseps. It would be his role to serve as arbiter in the impending confrontation.

Breslui regarded the Resseps with piercing red eyes, his round face set and his chin jutting out determinedly. Sinderc stood stiffly very close to him, her features severe. The steel-gray emkenud rested on her shoulder.

The Nesdelsen Berenz detached a hripitur from a silver lanyard about his neck and quietly activated its recording function.

Resseps Scahn took one last step forward, so that he stood directly facing the Supracetor. "I will lead the mission," he declared.

"No," responded Breslui, with the assurance of one who had reflected at length on the subject.

With a sweeping gesture, the Resseps pointed at Charles. "*Ae leskl Aeprestor,*" he said, adding, "The Eberenze Chasrydel will represent me."

Charles hesitated for a moment. *"Ae leskl Aeprestor,"* his words rang through the hall.

Breslui glared at Charles. "Your life is forfeit," he stated. Then he raised the index and middle fingers of his right hand and gestured toward the center of the arena. The brown shape of the projection dome slowly sank out of view. Momentarily, the glow from the overhead globe dimmed. A platform rose in the place where the projection dome had been, until it was even with the rest of the central area. Two indistinct shapes lurked in the darkness there.

"They will represent me," Breslui said, his deep voice echoing across the amphitheater.

The great globe's light regained its intensity. There was a collective gasp from the audience when they saw what was revealed at the arena's center.

The Supracetor's small mouth twisted into a satisfied smile.

They were identical nightmarish shapes. Gray, massively muscled torsos mounted on thick sinewy legs. Long, powerful arms that seemed to have one joint too many and ended in green-taloned paws.

Charles looked at the creatures and instinctively recoiled. Unlidded red eyes glared at him menacingly from under heavy brow ridges. Dark red cavities, the shape of an inverted Y, filled the places where nostrils and mouths should have been. The beasts were naked, but no genitalia were apparent.

While those about her still looked at the arena in horror, Vivian quietly assessed the situation. The monsters were biologic constructs, built, probably by Sinderc, for the sole purpose of physical combat. Charles, she thought, would not stand a chance against them.

Swiftly, unheeded, Vivian backed away around the circular terrace and left the amphitheater.

"I protest," the Resseps said, looking worriedly from the two ominous beings to Breslui. "You may not produce two substitutes."

But the Supracetor's smile only deepened. "Two challenges were issued," he said, "and two respondents have been presented. You may join your accomplice in the arena, if you wish."

The Nesdelsen Berenz held his hripitur tightly against his blue tunic. "The Supracetor's response is fair," he said.

The Resseps was silent, his bald head glinting and his lips a blanched slit as he turned toward his companions.

Slowly, without taking his eyes from the creatures, Charles stepped back to where Cupahr, Compcenlu and July stood, at the edge of the lower terrace. "I am not going through with this," he said, in a hoarse voice.

"The challenge cannot be withdrawn," Compcenlu said.

Cupahr laid down the tan box he had been holding and pressed a white mark on its side. The case opened longitudinally and revealed twin compartments full of body armor segments.

Cupahr chose a pair of white arm guards and an articulated head protector and set them down at the side of the case.

With a diffident wave of his hand, the Supracetor produced adjustable seats for himself and Intuger Sinderc. Then, looking with satisfaction at the Resseps' retreating back, he sat down. Sinderc, and then, gradually, others about the great hall, followed the Supracetor's example.

Two groups of Indane-Aliemt myrmidons marched in opposite directions across the highest terrace and started to descend along ramps on either side of the sector where most of the Bithians had gathered.

The Resseps walked to where Charles and the others stood. "It cannot be helped," he said, looking directly at Charles.

Cupahr took a breast plate from the case and held it out to Charles. With an abrupt move, Charles brushed it away.

"Don the equipment," the Resseps said, his face drawn. "It will protect you."

"Not against those things," Charles said, pointing at the gray creatures.

"Will you team with me?" Charles asked Cupahr.

The Kneth avoided Charles' glance, a flicker of dread showing in his grave face. He shook his head.

"I will join you, sir," July said, stepping down into the arena.

The Resseps looked pointedly at Cupahr. "What would the probabilities be, with her?"

Cupahr set down the breast plate and detached a hripitur from the inside of the tan case. His thick fingers danced over the control studs. A moment later, the machine's optical sensor deployed itself. Cupahr held out the device, allowing it a clear view of the two hulking shapes. The hripitur's small screen displayed a string of characters.

"The probability of success is thirty-two per cent for the two of them, Lord," Cupahr said. "Nine per cent for Eberenze Chasrydel alone."

"Not her," Vivian said, returning from her unnoticed excursion and striding purposefully towards the group, her head slightly thrown back. "I will stand with the Eberenze."

They turned to face her. "Do not involve yourself in this, Vivian," Charles said, surprised at her presence. "It's too dangerous."

"It's more dangerous than you think," Vivian replied. "And you don't know if she can fight."

"I am best qualified to assist him," July said, moving closer to Charles.

Vivian stepped down into the arena. She carried a silver pouch in her hand. Walking across to face July she told her: "Leave!"

But July stood still.

"You may not use the attendant, Resseps," the Supracetor called out, rising angrily from his seat forty feet away.

"Why not?" Scahn asked, turning to face Breslui.

"Only biological beings may be substituted," the Supracetor replied.

"The Supracetor is correct," the Nesdelsen Berenz declared. "The attendant may not join the challenger. But," he added, "the Kneth Vivenes may do so."

The Supracetor cast a glance of displeasure at the arbiter.

Four of the Supracetor's myrmidons walked along the edge of the first terrace and stepped down into the arena, to stand near Charles. As they approached, July backed away, looking worriedly at Charles. Vivian did not waver.

"Proceed," said the arbiter.

Vivian exchanged glances with Charles. She was turning to face him when one of the myrmidons noticed the silver pouch in her hand and suddenly snatched it away. Vivian tried to retrieve the pouch, but the other three myrmidons held her back while the first one extracted a dark blunt object from within. It was a Colt 10 mm automatic pistol.

Charles, realizing what was happening, joined Vivian in the struggle to regain the pistol. The myrmidon held the gun aloft, while other myrmidons rushed to his assistance and kept the Resseps, July and Cupahr at bay. "The weapon is not allowed," cried the Supracetor, as the myrmidons managed to hold Vivian and Charles within the arena. Then, suddenly, with a resounding clang, a ring of closely spaced rods sprung up along the rim of the arena to a height of about twelve feet.

Cupahr extricated himself from the myrmidons and lunged at the case of protective equipment. He hurriedly shoved the few outlying pieces of body armor into the case, closed it, and swung it over the newly formed fence. The tan box hit the top of the rods, flipped, and clattered into the arena before two of the myrmidons again slammed into Cupahr.

Charles and Vivian moved rapidly to the case, opened it, and immediately started to don the body armor segments.

3

"Do you still love me?" Vivian asked, kneeling as she helped Charles slip on an ankle brace.

Charles placed his gloved hand softly on top of her helmet. "I love you now more than ever, Vivian. I don't know what happened to us, but I suspect they had something to do with it," he said, casting a hostile glance at the crowd above them.

Vivian finished adjusting the brace and stood up. Their eyes met and they looked at each other intensely, wanting their love to endure, for a moment rejecting the growing sense of doom.

An unearthly feral roar issued forth from the center of the arena. Charles and Vivian, trapped within the circular fence, turned to face the approaching beasts.

"We must be absolutely careful," Charles said.

The constructs moved together with a curious, stealthy gait. Their initial steps were synchronized, as if they were performing a macabre ballet. Then they split apart and, while still approaching, started making small random motions. Charles and Vivian moved slowly toward them, not wanting to be penned against the fence.

As the two gray brutes continued their gradual approach, Charles and Vivian each faced one of them and continued to move away from the fence. The beings' hideous forms transcended mere bestiality. The gaping gashes that formed the lower part of their faces had not evolved in any sane world. The smooth oily skin that wrapped thickly around knotted, brawny muscles, had an unnatural flawless slickness. But it was the glare of the great hooded, lidless red eyes that projected their demonic hate. When they came within twenty feet, the two monsters charged simultaneously.

Charles had time to wheel and raise an arm in self-protection before he was struck a terrific blow. He was thrown headlong, and sharp green talons were sunk agonizingly in his flesh. With a desperate effort, Charles drove an armored fist into the side of the monster's thick neck and struggled to his feet. But the beast hooked a powerful leg behind Charles' and sent him sprawling, then rolled on top of him. Charles was enveloped in the construct's sickeningly rancid smell. His arms pinned, Charles drove a knee up with all his strength into the hateful face, but the blow glanced from the jaw it should have crushed.

A few feet away, Vivian backed away swiftly from the other charging construct. When it lunged at her, she ducked under its reaching arms and struck a two-handed blow to its midsection. The beast staggered, and Vivian used the moment to deliver a debilitating kick to its side. When the beast turned toward her, a glint of abysmal horror in its eyes, she turned and fled. The gray inhuman shape followed swiftly. In four rapid strides, Vivian reached the perimeter fence. In a single fluid motion, she jumped up, grasped two of the rods, and pulled herself up, out of the way of the approaching construct. The beast charged with such bloodthirsty fury that, ramming against the fence, its grotesque head became wedged between two rods. Vivian swung down, driving her heels forcefully into the construct's spine. The beast's back broke with a sharp loathsome sound. It died racked by reflexive spasms.

Vivian ran toward the center of the arena where, reeling from a blow and half-blinded by blood pouring from a cut on his brow, Charles staggered back, away from the monster pursuing him. He stumbled and finally fell, kneeling, at Vivian's feet. She placed a protective arm around Charles' shoulder and stepped forward to face the advancing construct.

The massive gray beast crept forward with fluid steps. It stood still for an instant, its vile eyes watchful. Vivian's body tensed. The monster started to crouch, then suddenly sprang forward, arms outstretched. But its taloned hands did not reach their target. With precise timing, Vivian released Charles and drove her gauntleted fist at the construct's head. The powerful blow landed squarely. Blood and fragments of bone seeped from the crushed temple.

The blow would have killed any man, but the beast still stood, staggering and uttering a soul shriveling bellow. With swift savage fury, the creature raked its sharp claws across Vivian's arm. She winced in pain and jerked back. The construct, its injured head unheeded, lurched after her.

Painfully, Charles stood up, wiping blood from his face with his forearm so he could see. He moved swiftly and struck a two-handed blow to the creature's back. The construct fell to its knees, but a moment later regained its footing. With a powerful backhanded sweep of its arm, it hurled Charles away.

Then Vivian wheeled, her right leg describing a rising arc as her extending left leg propelled her body in a violent release of energy. The heel of her right foot reached the monster's chest with blinding speed. There was a sickening crackle as her armored heel tore through flesh and bone. The construct fell backwards heavily, its last breath a gurgling spasm.

Charles came to his feet and saw an amber demonic shape emerge from the rising platform at the center of the arena. The beast moved with dazzling speed, approaching Vivian from behind. Charles called to Vivian, but his warning was drowned by the roar of the crowd. The Supracetor had produced a third construct!

At the last moment, Vivian sensed the approaching menace and turned to face it. She caught a glimpse of the amber shape and lifted an arm protectively, but the brute swept it aside and swung a massive fist at her. The club-like blow landed on her temple, a moment before Charles delivered a flying kick to the construct's side.

Charles rolled to his feet and saw the third monster writhe on its knees. He glanced at Vivian's still form. She lay on her side, a rivulet of blood seeping from her mouth. Charles approached her, oblivious of the inhuman growls of the monster, a desperate hope in his heart despite her continued immobility.

With anguish tearing at his heart, Charles sank to his knees by her side.

The unexpected appearance of the third construct evoked outraged cries from the Bithians, and the Supracetor's Indane-Aliemt myrmidons formed a protective ring about him, although only Kneth Cupahr actually lunged threateningly at Breslui. The myrmidons that had been guarding July rushed to restrain the surging Bithian throng.

July acted swiftly. She had seen the weapon that had been taken earlier from Vivian. The myrmidon that took it still held it in his hand. Rapidly, July approached the myrmidon and snatched the pistol away. Before he could react, July thrust her way through the wildly gesticulating mob, the weapon held tightly in her hand.

"Chasrydel!" July cried, as she approached the arena. The monster had just parried a blow from Charles and swung a mighty arm at Charles' head, the great taloned hand sending sparks flying from the protective helmet. "Chasrydel," she cried again, reaching the fence at the rim of the arena, "Charles!"

Several myrmidons converged on July, their harsh faces set, while others pinned Cupahr to the floor and restrained the Resseps and Compcenlu.

Charles at last heeded July's call and turned to face her. Instantly, she knelt and threw the pistol at him, sliding it through the fence, across the smooth floor. Charles barely evaded a pistoning blow that would have killed him had it connected and scrabbled to reach the sliding gun. He grasped it just as a great hand took him by an arm, the talons sinking painfully into his flesh. Furiously, Charles swung the pistol against the beast's glistening skull. It jerked away and released him.

Desperately moving away, Charles worked the pistol's action and chambered a round. The construct renewed its attack, diabolic hatred pouring from its great lidless eyes. Charles fired three quick shots into the monster's torso. It uttered a terrifying howl and sank back, tottering. For a moment the beast knelt down, but it soon picked itself up and stumbled backwards.

Catching his breath, Charles wiped the blood from his eyes and extracted the pistol's magazine. He took a quick glance at it and inserted it back into the gun's handle. There were four rounds left. He took careful aim at the creature, looking back at him ominously from thirty feet away, and pulled the trigger. The pistol recoiled in his hand as it sent a bullet through the construct's skull. The monster let out a powerful yell. Blood and gristle poured from a hole over a hooded eye, and it tumbled down.

Charles sighed bitterly. He felt very weak. Warily, he took his eyes from the construct and glanced at Vivian, her body still.

A cry from the encircling group made Charles look up to see the glinting shape of Sinderc's emkenud enter the arena and fly rapidly towards him. He barely had time to cover his head before the device swooped down on him. It hit his forearm hard, cutting through the arm shield and drawing blood. The machine flew on and up, hovering for a moment before turning around and accelerating, diving for the kill. Charles aimed instinctively and shot at the humming threat. The emkenud blew apart in a blazing shriek.

From the center of the arena came a loud feral roar and Charles turned to see the monster struggle back to its knees and fix its ghastly, malevolent glare on him. His jaw slackening, Charles realized the bullets may not kill the beast, at least not before it killed him.

The wounded construct staggered to its feet. Charles looked wildly around, saw a group of myrmidons holding a struggling July. He felt hopeless. Then he looked up, silently praying for delivery from the evil that faced him. He saw the great luminous globe that hanged from the domed ceiling and stepped back, just as the construct under it took its first threatening strides toward him.

Charles raised the pistol and aimed at the thin wire that he knew supported the globe. He could not see it, but he knew, from the shape of the globe, where it must be. He fired. Missing the wire, the heavy bullet sent sparks flying where it hit the ceiling. There was an excited, fearful cry from the surrounding crowd, as a few within it began to realize what Charles intended.

"Only one round left," Charles thought. He saw the construct look up questioningly, its mind racing to understand. With a pure, focused intensity, Charles again aligned the sights with the axis of the great glowing ball.

Merciful God, guide my aim.

The pistol recoiled in Charles' hands. The loud blast of the handgun was followed immediately by a resounding metallic clang, as the powerful shot severed the restraining wire. The huge glowing sphere fell down freely. For a moment, the construct's red eyes showed its final impotent understanding of what was about to happen. An instant later the luminous globe crashed down on the beast's huge yellow-brown form, spilling sparkling fire across the arena in a multicolored, thundering blaze.

Charles recoiled, his face singed by the heat of the conflagration. Except for the brightly smoldering ruin at the center of the arena, the amphitheater was in shadows. An acrid thick smoke quickly spread across the bay. There were terrified cries from the shaken crowd. Charles saw the encircling curtain of rods retreat into the floor, permitting the terrorized Bithian and Indane-Aliemt officials, some of them wounded by debris from the exploded globe, to cut across the arena on their way out of the amphitheater.

In the confusion, Charles backed out of the arena. People bumped into him, gripped by panic and trying to flee the fire. It was difficult to see through the sparks and the smoke, but Charles made out July's blond hair. A moment later, still wobbly from shock and exhaustion, he was by her side.

"Come with me," he said, firmly grasping July's arm. "I need your help."

CHAPTER 25
ESCAPE

1

The square-section tunnel was lit by the dim red glow of the overhead strip lights. Only a dull whirring sound intruded in the almost total silence. It came from beyond a turn in the wide passage. Charles and July approached the bend stealthily and peered ahead, pressing their bodies flat against the roughly surfaced wall. They saw, nearby, a single green-suited figure bending over a dark shape.

With July's help, Charles removed the pieces of body armor he still wore and laid them silently against the tunnel wall. After a moment's hesitation, he also set down the unloaded Colt pistol. There were blood streaks and tears on his suit, but there was nothing he could do about that now. Walking with a slight limp, his muscles stiff from the exertions and knocks of the fight, Charles gestured to July to follow him. They turned the corner and approached the lone figure by the Supracetor's car.

Charles recognized Kanuner, Chadwick's assistant. The android was methodically using a handheld device to polish a blue-black fender of the Porsche 959.

Doing his best to disguise his limp, Charles called out a greeting to Kanuner. The mechanic turned around to face Charles and July and returned the greeting. Kanuner's eyes regarded the two questioningly.

"Let me handle this, sir," July whispered. She stepped ahead briskly, the red light burnishing her blond hair, and addressed Kanuner authoritatively. A moment later, Kanuner set down the polishing tool and made a hasty departure.

For a time, the only sound was that of Kanuner's retreating footsteps. Charles looked tensely around, half expecting someone to appear in pursuit. But the shaft's stillness remained undisturbed and Kanuner's footfalls faded to silence.

Charles and July slipped inside the unguarded car.

"Are you certain you want to do this, Chasrydel?" July asked.

"Yes. Strap yourself in." Charles glanced over the unfamiliar controls and adjusted the seat. The shifter of the six speed transmission fell readily to his hand. He adjusted the rearview mirrors. The fuel gauge pointed to Full.

Charles started the engine. It came to life with a rumbling roar. He found the light switch and turned the driving lights on. Powerful beams illuminated the tunnel. Then Charles placed the car in gear and released the clutch pedal. The black coupe surged ahead.

Glancing periodically at the rearview mirror, Charles drove as quickly as he dared in the curving passage. Then he saw a white wall ahead. It totally blocked the tunnel. Charles slowed down the car, but did not bring it to a full stop. In the brilliant illumination of the driving lights, the wall ahead appeared seamless, impenetrable. It was a force field projection. Charles expected it to collapse automatically when the Supracetor's car approached it, but it remained steady, as rigid as a steel vault.

They braced themselves for a crash. Then, when they were within twenty feet of the wall, there was a muted beep from under the dash, and the white bulwark disappeared. A massive iris gate was revealed beyond. Above it, the slender shape of an articulated robotic arm slewed to point a gleaming weapon directly at the vehicle.

Without waiting for the car to stop, July jumped out and ran ahead to the side of the tunnel. She strode along the buff wall, searching for the hidden panel Charles had said would be there. A moment later she spotted it, a hand-size section of wall surrounded by a faint blue line. She pressed it and the virtual cover disappeared, revealing a set of recessed control keys. Her face broke into a smile.

July keyed in the unlocking sequence and the iris gate immediately responded. With a sharp whishing sound, the gray radial pincers retreated. A blast of cool night air swept into the tunnel as July ran back to the creeping car. Above the gate, the automatic sentry's arm returned to its standby position. The instant July took her seat, Charles launched the car forward. Tires smoking, fishtailing from the sudden application of power, the Porsche crossed the open gate, its lights piercing the external darkness. Outside, a lone myrmidon guard, porting a shoulder weapon, stared at them in surprise as they flashed by.

Charles turned sharply right into the unpaved road. The car was tremendously responsive, and, once the turbochargers kicked in, its engine seemingly provided unlimited power. Charles swept along the poorly surfaced road, white-knuckled, only vaguely aware of compensations that the variable-traction 4-wheel drive automatically provided. The road became a violently writhing silver band, snaking a tortuous path through the desert among briefly-glimpsed boulders and parched shrubs.

2

"You have to do something," Cicely said, glancing at Dr. McClellan, her eyes wet with long endured anguish.

"The experiences you are having," Dr. McClellan said, "the flash recalls, are bringing us closer to the causal event."

"What does that mean?"

They were in Dr. McClellan's office. Cicely sitting uneasily in her chair, Dr. McClellan glancing casually at her file. They had spent the first part of the session going over Cicely's breakdown at the party and her subsequent split with Greg.

"You are integrating more of the repressed material. It is a sign of recovery."

"I haven't noticed an improvement," she said acidly.

Dr. McClellan quietly regarded Cicely. "You are unable to consciously acknowledge your acquaintance with Charles and Vivian, perhaps because of an intolerably stressful situation you once faced. For a time, perhaps several years, you totally repressed the memories you found so distressing. Then, about fifteen months ago, the memories began to return, embellished and disguised. Initially, they took the form of fragmented dreams. More recently, you have experienced conscious recalls." He spoke in a neutral, unemotional voice. "You suffer from a type of dissociative reaction, a partial amnesia. I would like for you to search your mind for whatever triggered the initial dreams. Recognizing that event will help accelerate your recovery."

Cicely smiled bleakly. He made it sound so easy.

"I want you to think back to your first dream. The first dream that was different. Can you remember it?"

Cicely brushed a loose strand of blond hair away from her face. "I'm not sure, Doctor." She was silent for a moment. "It involved…Vivian. Most of the early dreams were of her. Charles was running with her on a beach. They were being chased by a band of men; Cuban soldiers."

Dr. McClellan peered into Cicely's file, then closed it smartly.

"I want you to try to recall the exact date of that first dream. You first came to see me on December six."

Cicely sighed. Her fingers traced a pattern on the arm of her chair. "I recall talking to Angie about the dreams the weekend before my first visit."

"I have an old calendar," Dr. McClellan said, bringing an appointment book out from a desk drawer. "That would be December third and fourth."

Cicely frowned in concentration. "I had several of the dreams before I went to Aylesbend Manor. The first must have come two weeks before."

Dr. McClellan again consulted the calendar. "Two weekends before. The Saturday was November 19."

"No, earlier. The first dream came on a Thursday. I remember, because I was upset and forgot to post homework assignments. I always do that on Fridays."

"Thursday, November 17. Did anything special happen that day?"

Cicely shook her head.

"What about the day before that? Wednesday, November 16. What did you do that day?"

"I can't remember. Nothing remarkable. I went to work."

"Was anything bothering you then? How did you feel?"

Cicely looked at one of Dr. McClellan's pictures. "I think I was having some problems."

"At school? What kind of problems?"

There was a long pause. "Nothing serious," Cicely said. She hesitated. "Cramps. My period was early."

"How about the day before that? Tuesday, November 15. Try to remember what you did. Did you go out that evening? Did anything unusual happen?"

Cicely shook her head, flustered. "I can't remember, Doctor."

Dr. McClellan returned the appointment book to his desk drawer. "It's not essential to remember right away," he said. "We'll talk more about it during the next session." Then he changed the subject. "You said you had another dream. After the episode at the party."

"Yes. It was just as awful…"

⌘

They came to a mile long stretch of paved road. Charles relaxed his grip on the wheel, letting the speed build up to 140 mph. The feeling of loss and failure that had dogged him since Vivian's death gained a stronger hold on him. He had dreamed of escaping with her, and knew they might die try-ing. But he had never expected to see her die and find himself surviving in a world without her. An intense anguish and the fatigue of the day overcame him, and his attention wandered from the advancing strip of road.

July's grip on his arm brought him back. A dip in the road following a gradual rise vaulted the 959 into the air. Airborne for a moment, the car hit the ground with a gut-wrenching crash. The headlights suddenly revealed a sharp turn directly ahead. Shaken, Charles spun the wheel vio-lently, throwing the car into a power slide and barely making the turn. The bent, spiny shapes of Joshua trees flashed by, only inches away. A moment later they came to a freeway entrance ramp.

After a few minutes Charles took his eyes from the road to glance at the fuel gauge. He had three quarters of a tank left. They were on State Highway 14, and the road sign they had just passed said 'MOJAVE 15 MILES'. It was imperative that they place some distance between them-selves and Site One. He needed a road map, clothes for himself and July, and food.

"Look around, July. There must be a storage compartment." He switched on the interior light to help her see better. "See if by chance the Supracetor kept some…" he shifted to English, "money about, and maps."

Charles kept the speed at a steady 120 mph, which he felt was not too conspicuous given the sparse night traffic.

July only found a small flashlight, fuses, and some manuals in the glove compartment. But, wedged behind the driver's seat, she discovered a flat metallic box, about the size of a hardcover book. She worked the catch and the lid sprang open.

Charles glanced out of the corner of his eye while overtaking an eigh-teen wheel truck. "Money?"

"No, Chasrydel," July said, examining the gleaming, elaborately curved object in her hand. "It is a weapon, a blaster, called an *aldui* in standard Galamic."

"We are going to have to steal some money," he told her.

She turned to face him. "To take currency secretly from others," she said coolly. "Will we require the blaster?"

"I hope not. Let's try to find an unattended vending machine. Look for a closed service station, or a diner."

"How can I determine…"

"The closed ones will be mostly unlit, and there won't be people about."

Soon they spotted a roadside stop that seemed suitable: a group of small single-story buildings, close but not adjacent to each other. Two service stations were open for business, but a curio store was closed. There were two newspaper racks in front of the store, and no one seemed to be looking.

The blaster came in handy. July set it at its lowest intensity level and lightly fingered the discharge stud, aiming the slender muzzle at the two coin boxes in succession. Quarters poured from the vaporized containers. Then they broke into the store. The heist yielded $22.75 and two Bear Flag T-shirts.

As they sped away through the desert, Charles appeased his conscience by reminding himself that the Bithians and the Indane-Aliemts posed a far more sinister threat to mankind. He had to expose the aliens, and the high officials that had betrayed public trust by concealing them. But first he had to survive the night. The Supracetor's myrmidons would already be quartering the area.

They stopped at a café-bar near Mojave, a metal-roofed stucco building with a red neon sign that said *Coors*. A rusty Ford station wagon and a white Dodge van were parked in front. Charles parked the Porsche on the side of the isolated structure, between a blue pickup truck and a VW Bug fitted with oversize tires, hoping it would not be visible from the road. They decided to leave the blaster in the car. Even locked in its metal case, the device would only have made them more conspicuous.

The place was almost empty. A man in a cowboy hat, jeans, boots, and a plaid work shirt sat on a stool by a redwood counter, talking to a pert brunette waitress that desultorily polished a row of glass beer mugs. Behind her, an Indian cook labored over a grill that shared the rear wall with a large refrigerator and a wine rack. The odors of grilled beef and beer filled the air.

Charles chose a booth at the far side of the room. Across from them sat the only other people in the place: a graying man in coveralls and a baseball cap, a pale and pretty woman, about thirty, wearing a red sweater, and a young boy more intent on a comic book than on his pork and beans. Above the front window, the clock's hands pointed to eleven-twenty.

Over coffee and hamburgers, Charles described his planned course of action, which involved leaving Highway 14 and traveling east to Las Vegas. He estimated that they had to cover about 200 miles.

July watched Charles closely as he drank his coffee. Very carefully, she picked up her own cup and took a sip from it, a pleased grin on her face. Charles smiled, realizing it must be the first time that July had drunk from a cup. "What do you do with the food?" he asked her.

"I process it in a manner similar to animal metabolism."

"In Las Vegas," said Charles, "I must find a way to sell the car. It must be worth half a million dollars, but I'll be lucky to get a tenth of that for it, without papers."

"Papers?"

It took a few minutes for Charles to explain how driver licenses and car titles and registrations are used to identify people and to establish automobile ownership. They had to assume, he added, that the FBI and the State Patrol would soon be searching for them. Then he mentioned

Social Security cards and was drawn into another explanation. July knew the book meaning of the words, but she only vaguely understood the way American society worked. Luckily, she was a very quick study.

They heard the loud roar of motorcycle engines. Through the front windows, they could see the lights of four or five cycles gathering in the parking lot.

"As soon as we sell the car and get some money, we must get fake identification. We'll buy blank baptismal certificates at a religious supply store, fill them in, and use them to get driver's licenses that will serve us for a while. Later we'll get birth certificates..."

Three young men entered the café-bar. They wore soiled blue denim jackets with their sleeves cut off, and matching pants. The jackets, bearing '1%' and '13' badges, were worn over T-shirts that matched the color of their red tennis shoes. They sauntered into the room. Two of them, wearing dark glasses, turned as they walked, looking the few customers over, bringing a sense of menace with them. The one in the middle, a short greasy-haired man aged about twenty-five, went directly to the bar and confronted the waitress.

"We need some money, mama." He withdrew a long barreled revolver from inside his jacket and waved it around as if it were a small dark flag. The girl cowered away from him, looking pleadingly at the cowboy sitting at the bar. The Indian cook stood paralyzed, his back flat against the white freezer.

Just then, four more entered, wearing the same colors, one of them a black girl with a particularly hostile scowl set on an oval face marred by a deep scar. She carried a sawed-off shotgun and took a position by the door. Two of the others brandished knives and surrounded the table with the couple and the young boy. The last one to enter, a red-bearded six-footer, walked threateningly toward Charles and July, an Army issue 9 mm pistol in his hand.

With an economical motion of his pistol, Red-beard ordered Charles and July away from their booth. Trading quick glances, the two slid to the edge of their benches and stood up.

One of the hoodlums in dark glasses reached across the bar and grabbed the waitress by the front of her white outfit. He pulled her halfway over the bar, yelling, "Get to the register, bitch, we ain't got all night." The desperate look of a chased doe grew on the girl's face, and she started to cry.

The cowboy swung a hooking punch at the bully in dark glasses, his fist slamming into the man's jaw. Released, the waitress screamed and began to scamper away. The short guy with the revolver took a step back, aimed, and fired two quick shots. The cowboy, hit in the chest and arm, groaned and slid to the floor.

Red-beard, with surprising swiftness for such a big man, tried to put an armlock on July. But she slipped away from his grasp and drove the heel of her hand at his exposed chin. Red-beard swayed sideways, clamped a meaty hand on her leg, and threw her. July fell against a table and the enraged hood started to bring his pistol to bear on her, but Charles unleashed a kick that shattered Red-beard's wrist. The pistol clattered to the floor.

There was a crashing sound from the entrance and two identical tall men entered, side by side. They wore well-cut dark blue suits, but Charles recognized them instantly—they were myrmidons. Next to them, the black girl swiveled her shotgun and fired a shot at the nearest newcomer. The myrmidon went down, blood pouring from his wounded leg, but he still managed to swat with an outstretched arm at his assailant's gun and drive it from her hands.

The short greasy-haired hood had been ready to fire at Charles and July, but now wheeled around and shot at the strangers by the door. While the wounded myrmidon tangled with the black girl and a knife-wielding hood, the other swiftly pulled a shiny object from under his coat. A blaster. There was a loud crack, and a blaze as bright as lightning filled the room. The gun arm of the greasy-haired hood was suddenly gone. For an instant, before dropping to the floor, the dying man stared at the cauterized stump.

The forty megawatt burst from the blaster had neatly sliced off a corner of the redwood counter and blown a four-foot wide hole in the side wall.

A pungent smell filled the room, and more shots were fired, as Charles and July scampered over toppled chairs to the smoking hole in the café-bar's wall and then through it into the cool night outside. Blue-white flames poured from a station wagon hit by the blast. They raced around the wreck to the Porsche, never looking back.

"I'll drive," July announced, simultaneously grabbing the keys from Charles' hand. She bolted into the driver's seat and in a slick motion slipped the key into the ignition and fired the powerful engine. Charles had barely settled into his seat when July placed the car in reverse and started to back out of the parking space, knocking motorcycles over as she went. He slammed his door shut as July shifted into first gear and, all four wheels smoking, the 959 shot out of the parking lot and veered into the road, the turbocharged engine's growl turning into a whine of ever-increasing pitch.

Thirty seconds later they were a mile away.

3

As soon as he walked into his office and saw the bookish man in the rumpled black suit standing at the window looking down to the River Thames, Commander Sifford sensed bad news. It was Jelen from Codes. The man turned slowly toward him and held out a red envelope, his serious brown eyes watchful.

"This came from St. Kitts via Foreign Office courier," Jelen said. "Highest security."

Sifford took the letter and signed the chit Jelen produced.

After the Codes man had gone, Sifford sat down at his desk and opened the envelope. Inside were four sheets of paper. He read the first, a troubled expression growing on his lean face.

From Source Raphael via F.O. courier / 3.05
For Commander John Sifford Eyes Only

Robinson received a single communication from Ryder, over two years ago: a letter postmarked in Boulder City, Nevada. It said this:

I FOUND MR. FROST 25 MILES NW OF LANCASTER.

> EE -10
> HR 56 8832
> LA 44 21258

ONLY A VERY FEW KNOW. TAKE CARE.

The reference to Mr. Frost was a recognition phrase that only Robinson and Ryder knew about. Robinson took the note to a person he called "the Wise Man", who told him that the alphanumeric character strings matched a part of the Arteaga document. In time, this "Wise Man" reported that the note referred to three stars, and their positions in the sky.

EE stood for Epsilon Eridani. The -10 indicated its declination, or distance from the celestial equator: minus 10 degrees. HR and LA were abbreviations for star catalogues. The other two stars were HR 8832, at a declination of 56 degrees, and Lalande 21258, at a declination of 44 degrees. All three stars are relatively close to the solar system.

There was a reference in the Arteaga document to a project Ozma. In 1960, the American project detected radio frequency emissions, seemingly from the direction of Epsilon Eridani. But the source of the emissions was later officially identified as ground based radar. The project was quickly terminated.

The Arteaga document alluded to something called COSPENC and the Wise Man found a reference to a Secret U.S. National Security Decision Directive, from the Eisenhower era, titled "Commercial Space Program and Extraterrestrial/National Cooperation Initiative (COSPENC)." Also, he found references to the crash of an unmanned spacecraft on December, 1950, near Catarina, in Dimmit County, Texas, close to the Mexican border. The wreckage was reportedly taken to what is now the NASA Ames Research Center, in California.

Robinson intended to pursue the investigation, but he received a threat from a person who described himself as a Government agent warning him to "completely forget the E.E. Project." This was followed by a tersely worded ultimatum and an infrared photograph of Robinson and his wife asleep on their bed. He moved to St. Kitts a week later.

Sifford glanced at the other three sheets. They were photocopies of Ryder's handwritten note and of Swan's report to Robinson.

"Great God!" Sifford shook his head and filed "Raphael's" report in the brown folder he had devoted to Cicely Denfeld's case. He would have to bring this up with his superiors.

CHAPTER 26
THE MEMORIES OF CICELY DENFELD

1

Cicely looked at herself in the dresser mirror, her hairbrush strokes gently arranging her straw-blond hair. A faint, pleased smile formed on her lips. She had gotten over Greg. The realization brought a sense of freedom with it. It was not that she no longer liked him, that she did not still find him attractive, or no longer enjoyed his company. But she was free of anxiety. She had become increasingly conscious of her own worth. She would enjoy her life; alone, with Greg, or with another. He might still see her if he wished. But if he did not; that would also be all right. Cicely's smile deepened and she put down the hairbrush. Her hair hung over her shoulders in a sheet of lustrous gold.

It was a bright Sunday morning and, on impulse, Cicely decided to walk to Hampstead Heath. She loved the park. It brought the feeling of the country to the center of London. Soon she was strolling along a street still damp from the evening's rain, feeling good, happy to be outdoors, passing a constable and then two young boys walking in the opposite direction. She crossed the road and was approached by a young couple who asked for directions to Highgate Cemetery in broken English. They were from Romania, and wanted to visit Karl Marx's tomb. Cicely walked with them along Hornsey Lane, past small Georgian houses and a pub, until they came to Waterlow Park. She directed them across the park toward the gate in Swain's Lane. Seeing them off, Cicely proceeded west past Lauderdale House, along Highgate High Street.

She walked along, enjoying the sight of a pair of pigeons taking flight from the still dewy green grass in the park, and marveled at people's preoccupation with tombs. It was years since she had visited her parents' graves. To Communists, she supposed, Marx's tomb was more than a grave, it was a monument. Like St. Paul's, where Nelson and Wren and Wellington were buried, and…Stonehenge, the site of ancient burials, where the Druids…

A powerful prescient feeling came upon her and she had to stop for a moment. Then, haltingly, she left the lane and sat down on a park bench, looked at the nearby hills and let her mind drift. The memories came gradually, in stages. Dr. McClellan had asked her about November, the year before last. She had taken the children to the ruined monument at Stonehenge. It was a Friday, and the site itself had been opened to visitors…

2

Charles drove the rented Rover with caution, being careful to stay to the left of the road, keeping his speed down. He had been in England for a week, staying in different hotels, moving every other day, like a tourist. Early that morning, he had checked out of the Pulteney in Bath. He had driven east on the A365 and A36 to Devizes, where he had stopped for a late breakfast, and had then turned south, taking the A360. The road veered gradually to the left as it crossed the shallow hills of Salisbury Plain, so that by the time it reached Shrewton it headed almost directly east. Charles checked his map. Stonehenge lay three miles ahead.

There were a few head of cattle about, grazing in the gently undulating grassy fields. Then, to the right, he saw the ruins. Imposing, somber, a double ring of massive stones stood broodingly on the side of a shallow rise.

Charles left the car on a car park lot to the left, across the road from the site. He wore a brown wool suit and a gray cable-knit sweater that offered some protection from the chilly wind. Walking past several cars and a bus, he wondered if July had already arrived. They had arranged to meet at the monument at noon. It was 11:37.

A path led past a grassy field and a concession stand. Following it, Charles felt a twinge of anxiety. He had not seen July in two weeks. He missed her. Walking on, he saw what appeared to be a ticket booth ahead.

They had been staying in Dallas, working at an automotive parts store during the day. Every night, and weekends, they worked in a lab jury-rigged in the cellar of their rented house, struggling to put together a portable mass-detecting device. It had to be sensitive enough to locate, from a distance of several hundred feet, an object that lay buried under the dust of 600 centuries.

After his escape, it had been Charles' first priority to let the world know of the Dramtes menace. He had contacted Robinson by letter, and later by telephone. They had exchanged few words, and Charles had shared only a portion of his knowledge. Just enough to make sure Robinson knew. But he had been told that the case was too hot.

Gradually, the vulnerability of Charles' situation had become clear. He was being hunted. Yet, in order to make a credible case, Charles would have to surface, and, once he was identified, a massive effort would be made to silence him. He had three pieces of evidence: the location of Site One, the Dramtes blaster, and July herself. But the entrances to Site One could be concealed and protected by the same Government officials that he was intent on exposing; and July, Charles, and the blaster could be taken into "protective custody," later to disappear and be dismissed as fakes.

They considered many schemes, and finally had settled on one that seemed perfect, if they could make it work. While on Dione, Charles had learned from the Keeper the approximate position of the Galamic garrison's landing site on Earth: 51 deg. North latitude, 2 deg. West longitude. The original settlement had been located in Great Britain, somewhere in Salisbury Plain. If they could find the exact location of the Galamic spaceship, a few telephone calls could set an unstoppable investigation underway. The British were renowned for their tenacity. And, in England, the long arm of the Dramtes would find it more difficult to suppress the news. Charles and July did not anticipate any substantial deterioration of the ship. An Imperial warship would be practically indestructible, like the Galamic fortress on Dione. Once the ship was exposed, Charles would come forth with the rest of the story. And then it *would* be believed.

A news item had appeared two months earlier, displaying composite drawings of Charles and July and describing them as a couple wanted by the FBI for questioning in relation to a suspected pro-Iranian terrorist group. It had encouraged them to travel separately to England, each shipping a copy of the detector they had finally assembled. Charles' machine lay snugly inside a suitcase-size box in the trunk of his car.

Charles followed an elderly couple to the ticket booth, a glass enclosure recessed in a masonry wall. He purchased a ticket and followed the couple down a path that led to a passage under an earthen bridge. Moving leisurely, he heard the swishing and roar of cars and trucks speeding by on the road above. The tunnel emerged on the other side of the road. Steps led up to a path that dipped gently down, over a shallow ditch, and then rose again toward the monument. A cold, grass-scented autumn breeze carried the smell of stone and ancient earthworks.

As he approached the structure, Charles became increasingly aware of the eerie, overwhelming presence of the awesome place. The stone monument appeared larger up close, the megaliths towering darkly against the sky. There were two dozen people at the site, walking about or standing by in wordless awe. July was not among them. Charles glanced at his watch. It was 11:53. Trust July to time her arrival for exactly twelve noon, he thought.

A group of school children were arranged in a loose group, just outside the outer circle of stones, around a young woman in a yellow dress and a man in a dark uniform, probably a guide. "Various burial mounds, or barrows, are found nearby, attesting to the religious significance of the monument. Some of these date from 5,000 years ago," the man said in a monotonous voice.

"Medieval legends describe the building of Stonehenge in the fifth century, and identify the builders as Uther Pendragon and the sorcerer Merlin. The name Stonehenge derives from the Old English word *Stanhengues* and means hanging stones, referring to the lintel stones that appear to hang in midair. The monument has been associated with the Druids, who were Celts concerned with pagan worship and astrology. But when the Celts and their Druid judge-priests arrived in England about 500 B.C., Stonehenge was already in ruins. We now know that the various structures you see about you were built in stages over a span of four centuries, starting around 2000 B.C."

The noon sun made the bracing cold almost pleasant. Charles placed his hand against a gray-blue stone and felt the ancient, coarse-grained surface. Some of the giant stones stood alone, some were capped by lintels. Many leaned precariously or had already fallen. Part of the structure appeared to be missing.

"The outer ditch and bank enclose an area 380 feet in diameter. The ditch is open to the northeast, where it leads to a 40-foot-wide approach avenue." The guide pointed to a large leaning block of gray sandstone, incredibly weathered, standing alone about 250 feet away. "At midsummer, the sun rises over the heel stone. Set within the avenue, the heel stone weighs 35 tons and originally stood 16 feet high."

Charles consulted his watch. It was 11:58. He looked in the direction of the path. A group of men and two young boys were approaching and a single older woman was walking away, toward the road.

The guide and his group strolled toward the center of the monument. "The outer ring of stones, called the sarsen circle, is 98 feet in diameter. There were originally thirty sarsen pillars, capped by stone lintels."

July was nowhere to be seen. Charles sighed and unconsciously started to follow the group of school children. He fought a wave of uneasiness.

"Arranged within the sarsen circle is a ring of smaller bluestones, which were brought here from the Prescelly Mountains in Wales, 130 miles away. At the center of the structure is the inner horseshoe of five trilithons, or stone archways. Each trilithon is made up of two pillars and a lintel. They originally varied in height from 20 to 24 feet. Individual stones weigh 45 to 50 tons and were transported here from Marlboro Downs, a distance of 20 miles."

The young woman with the school children began grouping her charges in rows in front of one of the great sandstone arches. Camera in hand, she turned to Charles pleadingly. "Could you take our picture, sir?" she asked.

Charles agreed and helped her position the children. He took several pictures of them, including one with the guide, who evidently had not fathomed the workings of a 35 mm camera. The young woman, the children's teacher, thanked Charles profusely. He consulted his watch again. It was 12:04. There was still no sign of July and, for the first time, Charles became really concerned. He paced nervously, glancing alternately at the approach path and at the great gray stones.

Then he noticed them. Two men standing side by side. One wore a tan overcoat, the other held a blue trench coat folded over his arm. Otherwise they were identical, like twin brothers. Myrmidons. Charles looked desperately around. Halfway along the approach path, near the circular ditch, stood two men in neat blue suits—one of them was the CIA agent, Chadwick. Charles started to move away, eyeing the surrounding fields, but the two myrmidons moved quickly to block his way.

"Please do not attempt to run away, Mr. Ryder," one of them said, holding Charles' arm firmly. "Or we will be forced to incapacitate you. We only wish to talk with you now." Charles looked at the man closely. He wore a hat to cover his bald head, and sunglasses masked his eyes. Something had been done to alter his skin tone. It lacked the characteristic gold-bronze sheen. It was primarily the exaggerated Greek nose that betrayed him as something other than a normal Englishman.

"Where is July?" Charles asked. Through an act of will, he managed to control a rising anxiety.

The myrmidon glanced at the car park area across the road. "In our van," he said. "No harm has come to her." Then, speaking with an iron politeness, "We wish you to come with us, sir."

Charles looked at the myrmidon, weighing his chances of escape. Then he noticed, almost concealed under the other myrmidon's folded trench coat, the outline of a blaster. The one holding Charles' arm caught his reaction and said: "He carries the weapon in order to protect you. You must not be harmed."

Noting Charles' hesitation, the myrmidon added, "I bring a message from Vivian Venables."

Charles stood still, shaken. Afraid that if he said or did anything the ray of hope that had entered his heart would fade away. He allowed the myrmidon to lead him away from the ancient structure, until they stood in the field nearby.

The myrmidons stood with their backs to the monument, shielding Charles from the view of the small group of sightseers. Without letting go of Charles' arm, the one in the tan overcoat pulled a hripitur from a vest pocket and held it so Charles could see it, then activated its playback mode.

An image appeared on the instrument's screen. The resolute features, the sparkling blue eyes, the dark brown hair were unmistakably Vivian's. And it was Vivian's voice which said: "I have missed you, dear. We have just learned that you are in England. I want so much to see you, but they don't think it's wise for me to go. Chadwick and a few of the others will meet you soon.

"I suppose you thought I was dead. I was, as were you a couple of times, after training with those other monsters. There were some things we were not told. They can reproduce any biologic organism, including us. When we were first captured, they stored complete scans of our bodies and our minds. The scans were updated periodically. Combined with the data stored in our limnens, the scans can be used to construct exact replicas, even if our bodies were totally destroyed. In my case, they only had to repair my broken neck and restore cells that were damaged due to asphyxia. When I woke up, I remembered everything, the entire fight with the constructs, up to the point where something hit me from behind."

She paused, as if to choose the right words, while her countenance registered briefly sadness and then joy. "Austir explained about the baby. I was hurt when I tried to escape. While treating me, they took the fetus and erased all recollection of the baby from my mind. I now understand why you were so cross. But the chromosome map of our baby was preserved." Vivian smiled briefly. She turned to face someone outside the screen. "I can't explain now, dear, but we could undo that dark chapter. Austir has said that they have the capability to bring our child to life." With her chin raised and her head thrown back, she said, "Imagine that."

On the screen, Vivian cocked her face slightly sideways, an impish smile forming on her lips. "Or we could make a new one," she said. "I have missed you so much. I can't wait until you come back." Then, more seriously, "I know we always planned to run away, to tell the world everything. But things have changed. You must come back. Breslui has been deposed. Resseps Scahn directs Site One now. And you, my dear, you technically are co-director. It was you who won the fight."

Vivian smiled openly, "I love you, Charles. I want to be with you." She raised a hand in a gesture of farewell. "I want you back."

The hripitur screen went blank.

"The message could be faked," Charles said after a while. His heart was racing. He did not know what to believe, what to do. It could be a trap. It probably was.

The myrmidon pocketed the hripitur and then brought out a small object in his hand. "Vivenes expected you to have doubts," he said, "so she asked us to bring you this." He held the bean-sized device out to Charles. "It is her limnen," the myrmidon added.

Charles took the limnen and held it speculatively in his hand.

"You will need some time," the myrmidon said, releasing his hold on Charles' arm and slowly backing away. "You may move about as you wish in the general area, but do not leave. We will keep you under surveillance."

Charles watched the myrmidons move off, to stand guard a hundred feet away. He wondered what they thought of the ruins. Then he took the limnen and inserted it into his left ear. Soon he was remembering scenes from Vivian's past.

<h1 style="text-align:center">3</h1>

It is easier to steadfastly exclude doubt than to control it, once it has been admitted. Charles was convinced that the limnen was Vivian's, and as he thought through what she had said in the recording, he had to admit that it could all be true. But he still doubted the Bithians' motives. And to turn himself in, without even a fight, was unthinkable.

And yet. His chances of evading the myrmidons and Chadwick's men were slim. He wondered how many there were. It would take at least one to guard July, unless they had—he quashed the thought. If there was any chance of Vivian being alive, of his gaining her again, of their child being born, he had to return. He could not live with himself otherwise, even if he managed to escape. But he must find a way to let others know. American Government officials, no matter how motivated, did not have the right to secretly yield control over Earth's resources to an alien merchant empire. Of that he was sure.

He was under surveillance. What he did, and perhaps what he said, would be monitored. It would do no good to blurt the whole thing out to someone. In the unlikely case that he was believed, whoever he told would be noticed and silenced. The facts had to be conveyed secretly and in such a way as to be utterly credible. Charles' mind worked furiously, trying to find a way.

He walked among the ancient stones, his mind racing, trying to remember the way limnens worked. There was an electromagnetic component that interfaced directly with the brain and a fluid part, based on nitrogenous organic molecules, like DNA, that stored information. If the organic chemicals were assimilated, they could transfer the user's memories, however imperfectly, to whoever had ingested the fluid.

Charles walked back along the path. One of myrmidons strode ahead. There was a reddish thimble-like device on the myrmidon's thumb; a pain inducer like the one Esandos had used. Charles watched him go down the steps to the tunnel under the road. He was not sure how much time he had. He had to find someone suitable. Not everyone would do. Children would be dismissed as having elaborate fantasies. And it would be hazardous...

Charles emerged on the north side of the road, walked past the masonry wall. The concession stand was to his left. Ahead was a field, where a few cows grazed. Then he saw the young woman. The schoolteacher he had met earlier. She smiled at him, pretty in a stock English way. Charles nodded at her.

"Hello again," she said. A puff of wind carried a hint of her perfume.

"It's an imposing sight, isn't it?" Charles engaged in small talk while he tried to work out exactly what he had to do.

She was about twenty-five, of medium height, slender, fair complected, with a long, delicate face and over-the-shoulder blond hair. Charles walked in step with her.

"Did you know," the schoolteacher asked, "that the stones are so arranged that they serve as accurate predictors of the seasons?"

"I didn't know much about the place until today," Charles confessed.

He glanced around. The nearest myrmidon was a hundred feet away, near the tunnel entrance. Chadwick stood watchfully on the west side of the field, where it butted against the car park.

"This was once a sacred temple to sun and moon gods," the young woman said enthusiastically. "They held festivals here. The priests had it built to display to their people their ability to predict solar and lunar eclipses and sun and moon cycles."

The school children had split into small groups and lay on the grass field in front of the concession stand. Three of the older boys began to chant heartily and very much out of tune. The cool wind carried the words: "From a point to a check, from a check to a view, from a view to a kill in the morning."

"I'm going to go for a Coke," Charles said, indicating the concession stand. "Would you care for one?"

"Oh, yes," she smiled. "I must stay and watch the children."

A jet plane flew low overhead, and Charles noted both Chadwick and the closest myrmidon raised their heads to look at it.

"I will be back in a moment," Charles said, walking away from her, his heart racing. He steeled himself. It had to be done now. He pulled his limnen from his ear.

CHAPTER 27
CLOSE YOUR EYES AND THINK OF THIS

1

Like never before in her life, Cicely felt rage. How could anyone have done this to her? To pour someone else's mind into hers! It was worse than any rape.

She could not stand still. Tears of indignation and hurt flowed down her cheeks. Raging mad, she screamed aloud her anguish, walking up and down her apartment, from her bedroom, through the living room, to the front door and back. She paced the rooms time and time again, until that was not enough and she grabbed a coat, slipped it on, and ran outside to a cool dry night.

Only a monster would perpetrate such an invasion. Cicely now fully remembered her meeting with Charles. The trip with the children to Salisbury Plain, their visit to the ruins at Stonehenge. The helpful dark-haired stranger she had met at the monument. He had helped her gather the children and take pictures of them in front of the great sandstone blocks. When they sat in the grass outside the concession stand, he had volunteered to go for refreshments. He had brought her a soft drink, and stayed with her while she drank it. All he had needed were a few moments to pry open his limnen and pour its liquid contents—the memory-storing nitrogenous chain molecules—into her cup. He had not thought of Cicely as a human being with her own life to lead. To him, the fresh-faced young teacher must have only been a convenient mouthpiece. A tool.

Charles had not only inserted his memories, his troubled mind, inside her skull. He had dragged there his lover's memories as well: the intimate moments he and Vivian had shared, and the horrible experiences they had suffered. Cicely felt used, defiled. Ruined by a stupid, heartless, incredibly cruel man. A stranger that had deliberately visited this curse on her.

Cicely ran for several city blocks, oblivious of the few surprised people she passed. Then, drained, she walked on, panting, muttering dully to herself. She would kill him! With a cold fury she pictured herself killing Charles. She shot him with a pistol, she stabbed him repeatedly with a knife, she pushed him over a cliff, she kicked the bloody bastard to death...

A red traffic light brought her to a stop. She would have to find him first, thought Cicely. Then a wry smile formed on her lips.

The light changed and Cicely strode across the empty street. Finding Charles would be no problem. She knew where he must be. Through her tears, she looked up at her surroundings: A dark winding road, poorly lit by a few dim streetlamps. To her right was a tobacconist's shop that seemed vaguely familiar, and across the way a blue neon sign announced Irma's Beauty Salon. Cicely recognized the shop. She was in Camden, a mile away from home.

Walking back to her apartment, Cicely made detailed plans. It was not difficult. She had his memory, and Vivian's. She knew exactly what to do.

Once home, Cicely threw down her coat and took a warm shower. She felt much better afterwards. As if not only her body but her mind had been cleansed.

Cicely splashed some brandy into a glass and brought her voice recorder to the living room. Ensconcing herself in an armchair, she dictated the events that had happened at Stonehenge a year before. She dashed off a letter to her uncle. While addressing it, a half-completed thought crossed her mind; something almost recalled. She tried to bring it back in the time it took her to take a sip of brandy, but failed. She wrote a long letter to Angie. Then, exhausted, she went to bed.

Her sleep was sound, uninterrupted. Cicely dreamt of herself, walking alone on a dusty country road bordered with fields of blue and yellow flowers. The sky above was dotted with puffy white clouds. A car drove by slowly. She was curious about it, but its windows were heavily tinted and she could not see inside. Ahead she saw a beautiful white house, by the side of the gently rising lane. As she approached the house, she heard the beckoning laughter of her friends inside. It was a simple, happy dream. Cicely soon forgot it.

2

She awoke with a song in her mind. A song from her school days. The remembered rhythm stuck with her as she washed up and made up her face.

At eight o'clock, Cicely called up Mr. Fortescue, the headmaster of her school, and informed him, with a few clearly stated words, that she was being called away on urgent family business. Then she made a number of telephone calls: to a travel agent, to her solicitor, to the American Embassy. Later, she slipped on a pink dress and put on a wide brimmed felt hat with a yellow band that set off the gold in her hair.

Cicely called a taxicab. It took her to Fleet Street and the office of her balding solicitor, whom she instructed to withdraw 6,000 pounds from her annuity. Later she bought a padded mailer and used it to post the cassette recording to Dr. McClellan. It described her meeting with Charles at Stonehenge and informed the doctor of her decision to discontinue her treatment. She also posted her letters to her uncle and to Angie.

Another cab took her to Cook's in Piccadilly: She made flight reservations to New York via British Airways, and from there to Dallas and Los Angeles via United.

Cicely then took the Underground to Marble Arch and walked to Grosvenor Square. The American Embassy took up the whole west side of the square. She hurried inside the great building, under the gold eagle poised majestically over the center of the facade, and found the proper place to apply for a visitor's visa.

Cicely emerged from the Embassy an hour later. She walked across Grosvenor Square, past a covey of pigeons and Franklin Roosevelt's statue, and went on to lunch at an expensive wood paneled pub on Brook Street. Afterwards, a cab returned her to her solicitor, where she picked up her money and made arrangements for her apartment.

It was past noon by the time she returned to Cook's to pick up her airline tickets, and almost tea time when she again stopped by the American Embassy, to get the visa stamped on her passport.

In the hurry of it all, Cicely had little time for deliberate thought. But, as the day progressed, she felt her attitude toward Charles and Vivian gradually change. Together with the horror, they had brought her a sense of wonder and discovery. The intense anger she had felt the night before faded and, in her breast, it was replaced by a dull resentment, and then by a curious void, a longing for something she had trouble identifying.

Once back at Highgate and her flat, she threw some clothes hurriedly in a suitcase and took a quick shower.

Cicely cast a last warm look at her apartment, took a big breath, and walked jauntily out the door, carrying a single white suitcase. She wore a beige coat over an ivory skirt and a print silk shirt in shades of brown. Life was good again. Ripe and satisfying. She walked to her car taking long strides, hurrying to make her eight-thirty flight out of Heathrow.

She slipped into her seat and started the MGB's engine. There was a Brahms cassette in the stereo. The measured cadence of a classic symphony filled the air. Cicely rummaged behind the seats and found a long untouched teak box. Opening it, she glanced at the row of cassette tapes and selected one that she had not played in months. With a swift motion, she withdrew the Brahms cassette and replaced it with a mix tape of rock favorites. Soon the sound of snare drums, sax and electric guitars poured from the speakers and a rich and full male voice promised to take her where she wanted to be. She drove away into the night, her eyes sparkling.

3

The United jet touched down at the Dallas-Fort Worth airport at 10:32 am. Cicely freshened up at a rest room in the terminal, located a row of pay telephones, and made two calls. She bought a canvas bag at an airport convenience store. Then she walked to the passenger loading zone and hailed a cab.

The wind blew wispy white clouds along the blue sky as they drove east past tree covered shallow hills on Irving Boulevard. It took twenty minutes to get to the Bank of America branch office in Irving that Charles and July had visited two years earlier. Cicely asked the driver to wait and went inside the building.

The lobby had not changed. An armed guard stood idly by the door. Cicely walked past a line of tellers to the vault. Right before it was a desk marked SAFE DEPOSIT BOXES. A platinum blonde in a navy blue business dress watched Cicely as she approached her desk.

"I'd like to get to my box," Cicely said. She felt a tenseness in her stomach.

"The number, please," the platinum blonde said. A sign gave her name as Valerie Black.

"Thirteen fifty-eight."

Ms. Black punched the number in her desk computer and adjusted her glasses. A moment later she read the information displayed on the screen. "Are you Mrs. Ray?"

"Yes, Christina Helen Ray," Cicely said.

Ms. Black placed a card on a clipboard on the desk. "Please sign here."

There were only two entries, the first made by July the day she had rented the box, the second made by Charles a week later. Cicely took a good look at the signature and, holding her breath, did her best at duplicating July's handbook-perfect penmanship.

Ms. Black glanced at the signature. "Do you have the key?"

"Yes." Cicely held out the steel-gray key that Charles had slipped into her purse at Stonehenge.

Ms. Black took a key from a drawer on her desk and led Cicely past thick metal doors into the vault. They entered a room with walls lined with safety deposit boxes. Ms. Black searched for a moment before walking to the right corner and stopping before number 1358. She inserted her own key and Cicely inserted hers. Ms. Black turned both keys and removed the bank key, leaving the box door open.

"You can use one of those," she said, pointing to a row of cubicles. "Put the box back in its slot when you are done and push the lockbox door shut."

"Thank you," Cicely said.

Ms. Black left the room. The only other person in the vault, a gray-haired man in a suede leather jacket and silver-tipped boots, sat in one of the cubicles examining documents.

Cicely slid the metal box from its slot. The box was over a foot long, but not heavy. She opened the hinged top and took out a 9x12 padded envelope, a small black notebook, and a letter. The letter was addressed to Charles' mother in Atlanta. The flap on the 9x12 mailer was intact, held closed by a bit of tape. She did not need to open it to know what was inside: the blaster Charles had taken from the Supracetor's car. She hastily wrote a note on a bank notepad and added it to the envelope's content before firmly sealing the mailer.

Cicely put the letter, the notebook, and the mailer in her canvas bag, replaced the box in the lockbox, and left the room.

She walked into the brightness outside, her coat collar held closed against the blustery wind. The taxi was waiting. She had the driver take her to the nearest Post Office. Cicely purchased a 6x9 envelope and addressed it to Carlos Drake in Houston. The notebook she put inside contained Charles' handwritten record of his experiences at Site One, and detailed descriptions of many Dramtes artifacts.

She went back to the taxi after mailing the notebook and Charles' letter and asked to be taken to an address in Euless. They drove west on the arrow-straight Airport Freeway, past clumps of trees and rows of warehouses, while Cicely wrote on the padded mailer. Fifteen minutes later they reached a small red brick building housing the Fastrack Delivery Service.

Cicely arranged for the mailer to be delivered immediately to the charge d'affaires at the British consulate in Dallas. It was marked URGENT SENSITIVE and was addressed to Commander John Sifford at the Thames House offices of the Security Service in London.

4

Sifford's hand went to the telephone on his desk, to make an appointment with the Director-General's deputy, but before he could grasp the receiver, it started to ring.

It was Amy King, calling from Dr. McClellan's office. In an agitated voice she said, "I think you should come here right away, Commander."

Sifford glanced uneasily at the padded mailer a special courier had just delivered before locking it up. There was a gleaming, elaborately curved object inside. "I am on my way," he said on the phone.

Dr. McClellan had first suspected that something was wrong when Miss King buzzed him on the intercom, halfway through his session with Mr. Petrie-Davis.

"I'm sorry to disturb you, Doctor, but there is a Lady Angela Carlisle here to see you."

"Make an appointment for her," Dr. McClellan had started to say, irritated at being interrupted.

"She is very insistent, Doctor," Miss King said. This time, Dr. McClellan caught the odd edge of urgency in her voice. "Angela Carlisle," he thought. The name was familiar. Dr. McClellan heard muffled voices through his door.

"She says it's an emergency concerning one of your patients, Cicely Denfeld," Miss King said over the intercom. The reference to Cicely jiggled Dr. McClellan's memory. "Lady Torrington's niece," he thought.

Dr. McClellan cast an appraising glance at Henry Petrie-Davis. The man was 86 and suffered from senile dementia brought about by a stroke. He had responded surprisingly well to therapy. "Tell her I'll see her in ten minutes," Dr. McClellan said into the intercom.

Dr. McClellan apologized to Mr. Petrie-Davis and hurried through the session, explaining that an emergency had come up and that he would only be charged half the usual fee this time.

A few minutes later Dr. McClellan came face-to-face with a very upset Angela Carlisle. The girl barely waited for Mr. Petrie-Davis to clear the door before bursting into Dr. McClellan's office, brandishing a letter, the sharp planes of her angular face a study in resentment and bewilderment. She wore a simple dress of dark green and a pearl choker. Miss King came to the door behind her, concern showing on her narrow face.

"What's happened to Cicely, Doctor?" Angie demanded without preamble. "This letter came in the morning post. I have been trying to reach her since then. She's not at school; she doesn't answer her home phone." She spoke very rapidly, her words tripping over each other.

"Please have a seat, Lady Angela," Dr. McClellan said, motioning for his secretary to close the door.

"Cicely says that you will explain," Angie cried. She paced the room impatiently.

"I am sorry, I do not understand," Dr. McClellan said.

Angie waved the letter furiously, "She sent you a recording."

"Did we get a parcel in the post, Amy?" Dr. McClellan asked over the intercom.

"Yes, Doctor."

"Please bring it here now."

"I'm afraid for her," Angie said. "Her letter sounds so final. Where can she be?"

Miss King came back into the room, holding a small brown parcel in her hand. "It is from Miss Denfeld," she said.

Commander Sifford suddenly appeared in the doorway behind her, visibly out of breath. "I shall explain later, Burton," he said, exchanging a concerned glance with Amy King and pressing into the room, "but I need to know what's happened to Cicely Denfeld."

Angie's dark brows arched. Her eyes swept quickly over Sifford. "Who is this man?" she demanded. "What does he have to do with Cicely?"

Dr. McClellan stood up and introduced the two, noting in passing the nervous glances exchanged between Miss King and John Sifford. "Commander Sifford is acquainted with Cicely," Dr. McClellan said. "He has assisted in her case."

"Matters of national security have come up," Sifford said, uncertainly, provoking a disapproving glance from Dr. McClellan.

"Security?" Angie cried, eyeing Sifford suspiciously. "Cicely has never hurt anything in her life." She looked from Sifford to Dr. McClellan, "What have you done to her?" Angie slammed the heel of her hand on Dr. McClellan's desk, barely containing tears of rage. Finally, she sat down in the tall chair.

Sifford glanced at the letter clutched in Angie's hand. "May I see that?" he asked her.

She gave him a glowering look, "Certainly not!"

Dr. McClellan cleared his throat and then took the small parcel from Amy, who stood awkwardly at the door. He tore it open and extracted an audio cassette. Walking back to his desk, he took out from a drawer the cassette player that he kept to hear the cassettes Cicely insisted in using.

"Let's listen to the recording," Dr. McClellan said.

The midnight-blue Aston Martin coupe negotiated the corner briskly and came to a screeching halt in the middle of the wet street. Angie bolted from the car, leaving it double-parked, and raced through the light rain toward Cicely's apartment. Moments later, Dr. McClellan, Commander Sifford and Amy King emerged from a cab and, huddling under Dr. McClellan's umbrella, followed in Angie's footsteps.

They found Angie in the hallway arguing with an elderly woman, the landlady. Commander Sifford produced his Security Service identity card, and the woman grudgingly led the group to Cicely's door and let them in.

The four rushed inside, searched every room. They found no one. Cicely's apartment appeared undisturbed.

Angie recognized Cicely's clothes, still hanging in the bedroom closet. She began to cry, and Dr. McClellan and Amy came to her side and spoke to her consolingly, while, in the living room, Commander Sifford used his mobile phone to call M.I.5 headquarters.

5

Los Angeles was cold, foggy and crowded with cars full of hurried people, but Cicely's room at the Airport Marriott provided a warm and comfortable resting place.

Cicely set out early in the morning, taking the San Diego Freeway north through the Santa Monica Mountains and the San Fernando Valley. She stopped for a bacon and eggs breakfast at Newhall and then took a winding State Highway 14 through the mountain passes to Antelope Valley and Palmdale. It was the same route Charles and Vivian had followed. Increasingly, she felt they now were a valued part of her.

She drove the rented Chevrolet Suburban north through the flat desert to Lancaster. The road was unremittingly straight, lined with Joshua trees, scrubby bushes and whispering sand. Reaching Rosamond, she stopped to take on gas and then veered west, toward Willow Springs. A crisp, gusty wind sent uprooted bushes tumbling across the road. Above the far horizon, the azure sky was cloudless and bright.

Cicely looked at the brown foothills of the Tehachapis ahead, lit by the bright sunlight. She felt intensely alive. A smile formed on her lips, as she anticipated the impending reunion. Charles and Vivian were so much of her...and yet they were not. Life, she thought, may soon become risky, perhaps it would be short, but it would not be dull.

She thought of Charles as she had seen him that one time at Stonehenge. Her life had been so different then, so simple. Charles was the stranger who had helped by using her 35 mm camera to take a photograph of her with the class by the great stones. She remembered that moment well. Later she had left the site through the underground passage and had been walking with the children. Black and white cows grazed contentedly on a field ahead. Charles had joined her then. Dark-haired, tall, she had thought him handsome when he nodded at her. What had been his words? "It's an imposing sight." Something like that. He wore good-quality clothes, a brown hat, and sunglasses. The children had gone ahead to play and they had walked together for a while on the grass field in front of the concession stand. It had been so peaceful.

She had not noticed the incredible stress he was under, the danger he faced. He had been very attentive and offered to bring refreshments from the concession stand. She remembered gazing at him as he walked away and joined the queue. The children were singing. A new group of tourists had emerged from the underground passage and sauntered about. One of them had seemed exceedingly interested in her companion. A young woman in a mackintosh, wearing sunglasses, with dark hair and the facile stride of an athlete…

Cicely slammed on the brakes. A blast from the powerful horn of the truck behind her warned her just in time and she veered to the side of the road, missing being rear-ended by mere inches. Not heeding the truck driver's curses and gesticulations, Cicely struggled with the Suburban's wheel and brought it to a roaring stop on the sandy shoulder. Her hands clutched the steering wheel like iron vises. Her entire body shook. Vivian! She had been there!

Cicely sat quietly, letting the engine run to keep the air conditioning running. Vivian being at Stonehenge changed everything. The memory was not in the limnen because Charles had not seen Vivian before he poured its contents into her drink. But the two must have seen each other later, after Charles walked away. Perhaps, somehow, Vivian had contrived to trick the Bithians into letting her come along. It must have been her purpose to escape with Charles, and if they were successful they would not have been taken back to the Tehachapi site.

They would have followed Charles' intention to expose the Dramtes mission, and would have figured out how best to do that. In a moment of clear insight, Cicely knew what they would have done. Before she left the side of the road and turned around on her way back to Los Angeles, she began to form a new plan.

CHAPTER 28
REUNION

1

The men sat around an isolated table in the lounge of Fallan's Club, near where the portrait of Sir Edward Fallan hung above the stone fireplace. Months had passed since their last meeting. Dr. McClellan, Commander Sifford, and Carlos Drake had finished an excellent meal. Now they turned their attention to goblets of fine port and the few treasured books that each had brought to show and possibly trade with the others.

Sifford was the first to show one of his finds to the others. "*Observations on the Effect of the Manufacturing System*," he said. "Second edition, from 1815, by Robert Owen. Bought it at a bookshop in Chelsea."

"What bookshop?" Asked Drake.

"George Allen's."

Dr. McClellan was next to show one of his books, a first edition of John Aubrey's *Brief Lives* as edited by Andrew Clark in 1898. Drake proudly exhibited a copy of *Micrographia*, by Robert Hooke. The cover and back were somewhat shopworn, but the internal plates were in good condition.

For a time the three friends lost themselves in examination and discussion of their newly-acquired antique books. Then, after the waiter served a plate of Stilton cheese, Sifford told the others, "There has been a new development in the Denfeld case."

"You heard back from your superiors?" Asked Drake. "I was half expecting by now to see something on the news about the information Miss Denfeld provided us."

"Not much new on that front. The Home Secretary has been informed. The papers we provided have been sealed under the Official Secrets Act until further notice."

"What then; she is found?" Asked Dr. McClellan.

"Not exactly," said Sifford. "We believe she placed a telephone call two days ago to her friend Angela Carlisle. The call originated from a mobile phone near Durrington, a village in Wiltshire County."

Drake frowned. "You have tapped Lady Angela's phone?"

"Not wiretapped. We use a different technology," said Sifford. "The mobile phone was unregistered, but the caller's voice was Cicely's."

"I don't understand," said Drake. "I thought Miss Denfeld was in the United States. That's where the material she sent me was mailed, from Dallas. Now you say she's back in England."

"We know she flew to America, and that she was there for a time," said Sifford. "We don't yet know how she got back, but she is here now. We are trying to find out exactly where she is."

"I am surprised that she has not reached out to me," said Dr. McClellan. He looked attentively at Sifford. Years of friendship and his professional training alerted him to something preying on Sifford's mind. "Is something bothering you, John?" he asked his friend.

Sifford pursed his lips. It took him a moment to decide how to respond. He ate a portion of the excellent cheese and took a sip of his drink. Finally, he told the others, "What I am going to say to you must not be repeated or written down." He waited for the others to nod in assent before continuing.

"I have received…something…that proves that the substance of Miss Denfeld's narrative is…factual."

The three men were silent for a moment, each considering the implications of what had been said.

Drake looked around. There were no guests or waiters in close proximity. He spoke first. "Do you mean everything? Including the underground—"

"Yes, everything, including the...visitors from far away," said Sifford.

Dr. McClellan shook his head, his mind racing. "My null hypothesis," he blurted out. "My God, John."

"Your information is consistent with the notebook I shared with you earlier," said Drake. "It seemed real, such detail, but there was always the possibility it was a clever and imaginative forgery."

"No, the notebook is probably genuine," asserted Sifford.

"What about the time discrepancy. The current age of the girl, Gisela," argued Drake.

"I have not thought that through," said Dr. McClellan. "I'll have to look through my records, but I think there may not be a time discrepancy; just a matter of working out an actual sequence of events, because some dreams were out of order. The total time elapsed in her narratives could be years." He looked at the others, wide-eyed. "I have been treating Cicely for some time, and the events of her earliest dreams, real or not, must logically have taken place before she first came to me."

"Yes," said Drake, "if we assume all the story is true, it could account for Gisela being older now."

Their waiter appeared and Dr. McClellan ordered more of the port for all.

Conversation returned to their rare books until the waiter returned with their after dinner digestifs.

"We still don't know how Miss Denfeld came by all this knowledge," said Drake. "but if the technology of the—"

Sifford interrupted. "Not here, Carlos."

"Fine, I'll just quote Arthur Clarke: Any sufficiently advanced technology is indistinguishable from magic."

"I wish we knew what Cicely is up to now. I am afraid for her," said Dr. McClellan. "Afraid for all of us."

"We have a wide net on the lookout for Miss Denfeld, and I will follow through on the call intercepts," said Sifford. "I will be questioning Angela Carlisle in my official capacity."

2

Sifford drove past a wrought iron gate and down a twisting tree-lined road. He felt slightly uncomfortable when approaching the very rich, particularly one as willful as Lady Angela. He stopped in front of the imposing mass of Aylesbend Manor and walked to the tall entry door.

A butler let him in, took his coat and cap, and led him to a square hall. Soon Angie came to meet him.

"Good morning, Commander," she said in greeting. "You look good in uniform," she added, leading him to a well-appointed drawing room.

Seated on comfortable chairs, they talked about the weather for a minute.

"I am here about Cicely," Sifford said.

"I expected that." Angie's angular face showed little emotion.

"Have you heard from her lately?" Sifford asked.

"I also expect you already know that. Don't you?" Her eyes regarded Sifford under ironic black brows. She had never met a naval Commander before, or a spook.

Sifford looked back at her in silence.

"Yes, I have heard from her. Do you realize that she's my best friend?"

"I am not surprised. I only met Cicely briefly, but she struck me as a very pleasant person, the kind that would make good friends. You have known her for quite a while?"

"Since we were kids." Angie crossed her long legs. "Cicely anticipated that you or someone like you would come asking questions."

Sifford knew that anticipation of his visit had not been part of the telephone conversation between the two. "Have you seen her recently?"

"Yes. She and her friends dropped in for a chat yesterday," she said casually.

"Her friends?"

"So you don't know everything, after all."

"Lady Angela, it is very important—"

"There were two of them with Cicely. A couple in their late twenties, I'd say. Very agreeable. They spoke with American accents—Charles and Vivian, from Cicely's dreams."

Sifford stared at her.

"Do you like my outfit, Commander?" she teased. "The dress is by Dolce and Gabbana."

Angie caught Sifford still intently looking at her and smiled. She spoke in the tone of a fashion show announcer, "The belt is by Gucci, a bright red—vermillion."

"You…look delightful, Lady Angela. I did not know those two were… here."

"I thought it was pretty gutsy of them to show up. With you people looking for them and all. But they felt it was necessary. They want you to know they are in England. Cicely cannot understand why you have not made public the information she provided."

"It has been passed on. It is not being ignored."

"There is little more that I can tell you about the Americans. They have put together a small group." Angie stood up.

"A group?" Sifford rose from his chair, admiring the way she looked in her white V-neck sheath dress.

"Please help them. Cicely left a video recording for you." Angie took a flash memory drive from a pocket in her skirt and handed it over to Sifford. "It will explain everything."

As Sifford pocketed the memory drive, Angie began to turn away from him. "Wait here," she told him. "I have something to show you."

She left Sifford alone, and he remained standing, letting his eyes drift over a few framed photographs on a wall, one of them of a teen-aged Angie and three other girls, one of which was likely Cicely. Another wall held paintings: pop art women by Andy Warhol, fantasy art by Ken Kelly, and romantic realism by Jack Vettriano.

"You like?" Angie said, returning. She held a metal case in her hand.

"It's a beautiful room, Lady Angela. The paintings are magnificent...I have only seen prints of some of them before." He pointed to the photograph of the teen-age girls. "Is that Cicely with you?"

"Yes, we formed a clique at school. Best friends forever. Cicely was the nicest of us, the most beloved."

She approached Sifford, moving closer until her face almost touched his. She wore no makeup on her perfectly smooth skin. "There is something we must do together," she said. He could sense a trace of beguiling perfume.

Angie gestured for him to follow her. They left the room together, walking toward the rear of the great house and then leaving it to move to a field at the edge of a country park. She dismissed a manservant standing there.

"You must do exactly as I instruct you," she said, in a voice that was at once airy and commanding. "It is a simple-enough task, but there is some danger to it, and I have been asked to keep you from being harmed."

She stopped at the fringes of the park, where the lawn began to be interspersed with scattered trees, and set down the grey case she had been carrying on a card table.

"Pick it up," she told Sifford.

"Is this the dangerous part?"

"Not yet. Press the white area firmly and the cover will slide away."

Sifford turned the case over and examined it closely. It was seamless, about two feet long, eight inches wide, and three inches deep. There was a white oval area near the edge of what he took to be the top side. He had seen Angie carry the case by a handle, but could see no trace of it now on its dimpled surface.

"What did I tell you?"

"You said to pick it up and open it, but—

"Do it!"

Sifford reached for the case and a thick cushioned handle popped out of its side, as if anticipating him.

He lifted the case warily. It was lighter than he had expected. When he pressed the white oval the entire top side disappeared, leaving visible a shallow box with three objects attached inside.

"Good," said Angie. "I will demonstrate how to do the next part, which is dangerous, to keep you from killing yourself or blowing up my uncle's house."

She grabbed the largest object and lifted it out easily with her left hand. It was about a foot and a half long, with a complex shape that curved from a narrow tubular end to a thicker flat form at the opposite end. "This is the main component of what Cicely called a ranged weapon. Her friend Mr. Ryder said that it is six hundred centuries old and that its Uncial Galamic name is *stratopiu*." As she spoke, Angie placed the device on her right forearm, her right hand holding it near the narrow end. The weapon's thicker opposite end subtly altered its shape to fit snuggly at the crook of her arm.

Sifford began to say something, but Angie stopped him. "Just pay attention for now." She went on to describe the stratopiu's controls, had Sifford identify and call out the various functions, and then returned the unit to its case.

Angie then pointed out and described the two other components in the case: an egg-shaped energy storage device which she called a charger, and an elongated box that provided fault diagnostic functions and contained maintenance tools.

"Now watch this," said Angie. She pressed the end of a flush golden band located about mid-length on the stratopiu. It rapidly popped out and assumed a semi-circular shape.

"Now clear your mind of any thoughts and put the circlet on," she said. "Like you would wear a headband. Place the ruby-colored part up front on the middle of your forehead."

Sifford did as he was told. He felt the circlet press lightly on his brow and temples. Angie approached him and gently adjusted the position of the head unit. Then she told him to pick up the main component of the stratopiu and hold it in his arm as she had done earlier.

Sifford picked up the weapon. It weighed about three or four pounds. When he placed it on his forearm he felt it change its shape to gently attach itself.

Angie pointed at a spot in the sparsely wooded grounds ahead of them. "Do you see that boulder near the small ash tree? It's about a hundred yards away."

It took Sifford a moment to find the particular boulder and tree. "Yes, I see it."

"Now this is the really dangerous part." Angie shifted her position to stand to the right and slightly behind Sifford. "I have preset the power level and effective range. Keep your mind clear and be prepared for the sighting images that the circlet will superimpose on your field of view. Now point the stratopiu at the boulder and press the activation sensor. Tell me what you see."

Sifford moved his right arm as instructed and with his left hand pressed the white activation area on the side of the stratopiu. Instantly, the center of his field of view was enhanced in contrast and definition, and a referencing pattern was superimposed. He told Angie what he saw.

"Very good, Commander. Look directly at your target, so that it appears at the center of the reference lines. It is not necessary to further adjust the orientation of the arm unit. The weapon will release a bolus of bound energy that will home in on the target. The circlet provides the fire control. When you are ready, will the stratopiu to fire, then clear your mind again."

Sifford kept his arm steady and concentrated on the distant boulder. The circlet provided a zoom effect that further enhanced the target image. When he willed the stratopiu to fire the reference grid pulsed brighter and a faint yellow flash emanated from the muzzle.

The boulder disintegrated with a swoosh.

<h1 style="text-align:center">3</h1>

Amy King led Dr. McClellan and Carlos Drake into Sifford's office in Thames House. It was the two men's first visit to M.I.5 headquarters. They greeted Sifford, who sat behind his desk looking attentively at a computer screen.

"Thank you for coming," Sifford said at once. "Do not bother to sit down. We'll be leaving immediately. There have been crucial developments in the Denfeld case."

"Transport is ready, sir," Amy said to Sifford. She ignored the accusatory look Dr. McClellan gave her.

They hurried to an elevator that took them to the roof and quickly boarded a waiting helicopter.

The helicopter flew west swiftly, leaving central London and following the M3.

"We are going to Amesbury. It's seventy-five miles away as the crow flies. We'll be there in a few minutes," Sifford said.

"It is confirmed, what we learned from Cicely is true. The dreams, the visions, everything," Sifford said. "I've been to see Lady Angela. I learned more from her and from a recording and something else that Cicely left with her," Sifford said.

"Something else?" Asked Drake.

"Physical evidence," said Sifford.

"Amesbury. Is that where Cicely is?" Asked McClellan.

"She is nearby, we think," Sifford said. "Let me fill you in. My people have also been busy. We have found a lot about what's going on."

"Amesbury is near Stonehenge," McClellan observed.

"Yes," Sifford said. "It turns out Vivian was at Stonehenge, initially unseen by Charles, the day he and Cicely met, years ago. Vivian had made a deal with the aliens after he escaped their facility. Vivian would find Charles and lead Scahn's men to him. In exchange, Scahn promised there would be no violence. She agreed to make a recording luring Charles into the hands of the aliens and to make no direct contact with him. But that was partly a deception, she co-opted the CIA agent, Chadwick, who came along supposedly to keep her in check."

"Are you sure about this, John?" Drake asked.

"It's told in Cicely's video message. She says she only found out about this recently, after she returned to England and connected with the others. But even before they all got together she knew they would be somewhere near Stonehenge."

"How did she know?" McClellan asked.

"Because she finally recalled enough of the memories of Charles and Vivian to figure out their story, up to the time she met Charles at Stonehenge. Because that's where the site is," said Sifford.

"Chadwick and the aliens—myrmidons—found July, but Chadwick did not hold her captive. She was all the time working to help Charles. Vivian only joined Charles after he had spiked Cicely's drink with the contents of a limnen—the eventual source of Cicely's dreams. Vivian got Charles to start their escape at once."

"How did they manage that, John?" Asked Dr. McClellan.

"It helped them that Chadwick had hired some locals to create a distraction. Amid the confusion, Charles, Vivian, and July were able to slip away from the Stonehenge grounds and the myrmidons. July was their getaway driver. Later they met Chadwick and an attendant he had brought along at a bed and breakfast in Amesbury."

The helicopter flew over Basingstoke and banked to pick up the track of a broad road.

"We are now approaching Andover," said Amy, looking at the map being displayed on her tablet computer.

"My men," went on Sifford, "have found that Ryder sold patents to an insulating material that improves internal combustion engine efficiency. The deal made him a sizeable fortune. He and Vivian bought a farm near Amesbury about a year ago, using the names Joseph and Natali Wright. There seem to be seven of them. They generally keep to themselves, but we are pretty sure they are Cicely, Charles, Vivian, July, and three others. Chadwick and his attendant may be two of them. They are conducting an archeological dig with help from some of the locals."

"A dig?" Drake asked.

"In the message I received from Angela, Cicely says their small group found the site of the original Galam landing on Earth, hundreds of centuries ago. The video shows images of an underground tunnel leading to an artificial metallic object with a cavernous interior. According to Cicely, the buried assault ship incorporates Galam warfighting technologies much more advanced than anything the aliens now have. It would be virtually impregnable and able to vaporize whole cities."

They landed in a field on the skirts of Amesbury. The three men and Amy hurried into a waiting M.I.5 SUV. They followed an unmarked Police car on winding roads to a farm nearby.

The property was near a river, on a shallow rise a hundred yards from the main road. A narrow dirt road led to a small farmhouse. The columns and lintels of Stonehenge could be seen in the distance.

The dirt road went on to a level area with a large tent and a wooden shed. A farm tractor with a backhoe attachment stood untended nearby. Beyond were mounds of earth and small stones.

"That must be the dig," Drake said.

They left the car and joined the Police and two Security Service men in a search of the house. It was empty, but there were signs of recent occupancy.

"Should we go on to the dig, sir?" one of the Policemen asked.

"Wait a moment," Sifford told him.

He placed a call to Cicely's mobile phone. "Hello," she answered after a few rings.

"This is John Sifford, Miss Denfeld. I have seen Lady Angela. I am at the farmhouse, near the dig. Are you nearby? I would like to talk to you and your friends. Dr. McClellan and Mr. Drake are with me."

"You are just in time, Commander," she said. "I regret that I cannot talk to you now, but we are very busy."

"I must insist," Sifford said.

"It is too late to talk further. You must leave. Evacuate the area between Stonehenge and Woodhenge. Right away. But don't go too far. You are about to be amazed."

"She ended the call," Sifford told the others. He turned to the lead Policeman. "The Stonehenge and Woodhenge sites must be evacuated at once. This entire area is in danger."

"I will message headquarters," said Amy.

4

In the Galam assault ship, deep under the Wiltshire farmland, the crew made final preparations. They had worked hard to understand the Galam ship's instruments and gain operational control of the ancient but intact combat vessel.

Charles' knowledge of Uncial Galamic had helped to find and open the door that let them inside. Once an initial survey was completed, they had activated the long-dormant master control intelligence and the many systems that it supervised.

They soon found that the ship provided excellent tutorials on its operation. Their small group faced many problems. Units of measurement were different from any used by the Bithians or by anyone on Earth. Vivian and Cicely had to buy laptop computers so that they could use spreadsheet programs to convert navigational units like degrees and kilometers to Galam equivalents. Eventually they were able to convert world map coordinates to the Galam system.

They took positions in a control room bathed in indirect blue light. There were no windows—virtual display panels would show an outside view. They all wore blue jumpsuits and gray flight jackets Cicely and Chadwick had purchased at a sports store.

Charles sat on a central command chair. Vivian sat to his left in an instrumented pilot's seat and July to his right in the navigator's station. Chadwick sat further to the right at the weapons control position and Cicely perched at a communications post against the starboard wall. Kanuner had a chair along the port wall at the systems control station. John Brewer, a local electrician they had recruited after initially hiring him to help with the dig, sat besides Kanuner, in control of the sensor suite.

Charles called for readiness status. Cicely, Kanuner, and John Brewer answered "Ready." Chadwick gave a thumbs-up sign and Vivian blew Charles a kiss. July said "Course is set, sir."

"We will face the enemy," said Charles, "in its lair, on our terms, and we will try not merely to survive, but to prevail. We will meet them in confidence and strength, for triumph will be ours."

The eyes of the others were on him.

"Let's do this," said Charles.

"Lifting off," announced Vivian. She pressed an icon on the virtual display ahead of her and moved a control stick on the armrest of her chair.

The sound of throbbing engines filled the cabin air and the warship shook.

John Brewer activated the sensor suite. "May God help us," he said in a low voice.

Displays throughout the command center labored to show changing conditions.

From a vantage point near Stonehenge, Sifford and the others, joined by local Police, watched as stragglers were led away. Drake theorized that Charles and the others intended to challenge the Dramtes installation in California and force negotiations with the United States and other Earth nations.

There was a rumbling sound, rapidly increasing in volume. The ground shook and the three friends watched as a squat truncated-pyramid shape rose menacingly from under the earth. The massive hulk of the Galam assault ship hovered over the farmland, clumps of soil and vegetation streaming from its sloping sides. The warship gradually gained altitude, casting its shadow over the field, and then turned unsteadily, as if finding its way, its flat bottom gleaming.

The small crowd nearby heard a high-pitched sound emanating from the gray ship. A shimmering glow grew out from the flat planes of the vehicle and in a moment took on the shape of an enveloping disk. Some people placed calls on their cell phones, excitedly describing the astonishing event. Others took pictures or made videos of the awesome spectacle. The enormous vehicle kept rising and accelerated rapidly away, vanishing over the horizon to the west.

GLOSSARY

Aldui A handheld projected-energy weapon. A blaster.

Aliemt An ancient interplanetary transport guild. Its founding is told in the story of the lovers Aliese and Emtor. The guild later merged with the Indane organization. See *Indane-Aliemt*.

Android A synthetic semi-biological humanoid. Usually employed as assistants to high-ranking Bithian officials, they also serve in various capacities in Indane-Aliemt organizations. Nesdelsen regulations prohibit the use and creation of self-conscious artificial intelligences, but they tolerate their use by others. Command-grade androids are extremely able, and possess intellectual capacities that may match those of their makers.

Athjev The class K star Eta Cassiopeiae B. See *Caten*.

Berenz A Bithian or Nesdelsen official of rank below Vadycrel and above Eberenze, equivalent to the Indane-Aliemt rank of Obiredes.

Bithia One of the three governing bodies forming the Dramtes (the other two are Indane-Aliemt and Nesdelsen). Ruled by the Bithian Prenike and subject only to the preeminent Dramtes ruler, the Exaege.

Caten The Dramtes name for Eta Cassiopeiae A, a class G star 19.4 light-years from Earth. One of the Dramtes-controlled star systems. Caten is part of a binary system. Its companion, Athjev, does not have habitable planets.

Cirsegas An Indane-Aliemt official of rank below Intuger and above Obiredes, equivalent to the Bithian rank of Vadycrel. Ordinarily a lead medical officer.

COSPENC A Secret U.S. National Security Decision Directive: Commercial Space Program and Extraterrestrial/National Cooperation Initiative. This 1953 document supposedly outlines a formal agreement between Dramtes and United States representatives granting the Dramtes rights to construct and operate a facility on American territory. The U.S. Government has never acknowledged its existence.

Cycle A Dramtes unit of time measurement, approximately equal to a solar day. Each Dramtes cycle has 1,000 milicycles.

Desopret From the Uncial Galamic *Daespret*, a planetary commander. A Dramtes official of rank below Prenike and above Supracetor.

Dione A heavily-cratered airless moon of Saturn, bright and icy. Its diameter and orbital period are 1120 kilometers and 65.7 hours, respectively. The site of an ancient and extremely powerful Galamic military installation. See *Keeper*.

Dramtes The Trinity or Triad, the governing body comprising Bithia, Indane-Aliemt and Nesdelsen. Ruled by the Exaege and the Prenikes of Bithia, Indane-Aliemt and Nesdelsen. This alliance is several centuries old.

Eberenze 1. A Bithian or Nesdelsen official of rank below Berenz and above Kneth, equivalent to the Indane-Aliemt rank of Nollecion. 2. *Archaic*, a counselor.

Emkenud A self-propelled hovering device incorporating remote vision, hearing, smell and temperature sensors. It communicates directly with the user's brain, providing remote sensing abilities. Also incorporates a voice projection capability.

Ertugral The Dramtes name for Lalande 21258, a class M star 19.2 light-years from Earth. One of the Dramtes-controlled star systems.

Exaege The rank of the supreme leader of the Dramtes, elected in rotation from among the Prenikes of Bithia, Indane-Aliemt and Nesdelsen.

Galam The ancient empire from which the Dramtes are thought to have evolved. At the height of its power, the Galamic Empire controlled hundreds of star systems.

Gilgamesh The code name for a covert U.S. Air Force laboratory and medical research facility providing technical support to the Dramtes underground installation in California. The COSPENC directive outlines its role in fostering scientific interchanges between the U.S. and the Dramtes. It is located in Houston, Texas.

Hripitur A handheld instrument, about the size and shape of a thin book, used primarily to record, playback, process and analyze sensor data.

Ilaemdu A voice activated self-adjusting, collapsible seat.

Inverat *Uncial Galamic*, empire.

Imdermi A handheld mining tool shaped like a baton. It incorporates a light source and sensors for distance measurement and mineral analysis. The tool can be extended to act as a staff. Its power source can be caused to release its energy suddenly, in an explosive manner.

Indane See *Indane-Aliemt*.

Indane-Aliemt One of the three governing bodies forming the Dramtes. Ruled by the Indane-Aliemt Prenike. Formed through the merger of the Aliemt guild and the Indane, a paramilitary mercantile organization.

Intuger An Indane-Aliemt official of rank below Supracetor and above Cirsegas, equivalent to the Bithian and Nesdelsen rank of Resseps.

Keeper A machine intelligence controlling the ancient Galam fortress in Dione. Deserted for 600 centuries, the stronghold was staffed by a detachment of 350 Imperial troopers during the Yor-Hoerri.

Kernite A hydrated sodium borate, rarely found in Dramtes-controlled worlds but occurring in quantity on Earth in the Death Valley region. See *Picariel crystals*.

Kliettaes From the Uncial Galamic *Lestae*, a shopkeeper. A Dramtes official holding the rank next below Kneth and above Pagres. An assistant to a Kneth.

Kneth 1. A Dramtes official of rank below Eberenze and above Kliettaes. 2. *Uncial Galamic, archaic*, the leader of a small combat unit.

Limnen A device, about the size and shape of a bean, used primarily as a source of pre-packaged knowledge. When inserted in the ear canal it serves as a synthetic extended memory.

Loerde fivuresci A Dramtes farewell. Standard Galamic for (may) chance favor (you).

Major Cycle A Dramtes unit of time measurement. Each major cycle equals 350 Dramtes cycles.

Milicycle A Dramtes unit of time measurement, one thousandth of a Dramtes cycle. Approximately equal to 1.44 minutes.

Monitor An audiovisual console capable of speech, with powerful analytical and computational capabilities. A very intelligent computer and data bank.

Myrmidon A synthetic humanoid of biological origin, usually assigned paramilitary duties.

Nesdelsen One of the three governing bodies forming the Dramtes. Ruled by the Nesdelsen Prenike. There is a small Nesdelsen contingent on Earth. A Nesdelsen crew of 200 is primarily responsible for the operation and maintenance of the starship Xartek.

Nollecion An Indane-Aliemt official of rank below Obiredes and above Kneth, equivalent to the Bithian and Nesdelsen rank of Eberenze.

Obiredes From the Uncial Galamic *Bireset*, the master of a spacecraft. An Indane-Aliemt official of rank below Cirsegas and above Nollecion, equivalent to the Bithian and Nesdelsen rank of Berenz.

Omver The Dramtes name for Epsilon Eridani, a class K star 10.8 light-years from Earth. The Bithian home system.

Pagres A Dramtes official of the lowest rank. An assistant to a Kliettaes.

Picariel Crystals Large perfect crystals of cubic boron nitride used in Dramtes starship propulsion systems. Boron, a metalloid element, is extracted from kernite. In the Dramtes drives the crystals absorb gravity waves, reducing ship inertia and focusing energy on ionized particles that are emitted explosively. The resulting reaction force acts on the ship's reduced effective mass and accelerates it to relativistic speeds.

Prenike A Dramtes official of rank immediately below Exaege and above Desopret. The rank of the supreme leaders of Bithia, Indane-Aliemt and Nesdelsen.

Resseps A Bithian or Nesdelsen official of rank below Supracetor and above Vadycrel, equivalent to the Indane-Aliemt rank of Intuger.

Risper The Dramtes name for HR 8832, a class K star 21.4 light-years from Earth. One of the Dramtes-controlled star systems.

Standard Galamic The language of the Dramtes, derived from Uncial Galamic.

Stratopiu *Uncial Galamic*, a Galam arm-held ranged weapon. The primary component is about 18 inches long and emits bound-charge disintegrators. An ancillary component in the form of a circlet provides sighting and fire control functions.

Supracetor From the Uncial Galamic *Aeprestor*, the leader of an army. A Dramtes official of rank below Desopret and above Resseps and Intuger.

Ucilaum mudipe A Dramtes greeting. Standard Galamic for (this is a) remarkable event.

Uncial Galamic The archaic language of the Galams.

Vadycrel 1. A Bithian or Nesdelsen official of rank below Resseps and above Berenz, equivalent to the Indane-Aliemt rank of Cirsegas. An assistant to a Resseps. 2. *Archaic*, a lead financial officer.

Xartek An interstellar Dramtes ship, stationed in orbit around Neptune. Shaped like a very elongated, thick-tailed teardrop, it is more than a kilometer long. The Xartek is capable of relativistic speeds.

Yor-Hoerri *Uncial Galamic*, the massive conflict which took place 600 centuries ago between the Galamic Empire and the Yorj. See *Yorj*.

Yorj *Uncial Galamic*, a non-humanoid race that fought against the Galamic Empire and was instrumental in its downfall.

Carlos Valrand is an author and engineer living in Texas. He is a contributor to the website Internet Looks (internetlooks.com).

Valrand has participated as an engineer and manager in NASA and Department of Defense projects such as the International Space Station, the Space Shuttle, the Strategic Defense Initiative, the MIM-104 Patriot missile system, and the USAF C-5A and C-130 aircraft.

He has authored various aerospace system functional requirements documents and technical papers, and has developed and taught courses in HTML, dynamic simulations, aerodynamics, and space vehicle guidance, navigation, and control.

The Site is his psychological science fiction adventure that twists and tunnels through the strange dreams and seemingly normal life of young schoolteacher Cicely Denfeld. The narrative tracks the strangely related adventures of Charles Ryder and his partner Vivian Venables as they follow a trail of hidden knowledge that could impact the entire world.